THE FINAL DAYS

THE FINAL DAYS

ALEX CHANCE

WILLIAM HEINEMANN: LONDON

Published by William Heinemann, 2008

2 4 6 8 10 9 7 5 3 1

This is a work of fiction. Names and characters are the product of the author's imagination and any resemblance to actual persons, living or dead, is entirely coincidental.

First published in Great Britain in 2008 by
William Heinemann
Random House, 20 Vauxhall Bridge Road,
London SW1V 2SA

www.rbooks.co.uk

Addresses for companies within The Random House Group Limited can be found at:
www.randomhouse.co.uk/offices.htm

The Random House Group Limited Reg. No. 954009

A CIP catalogue record for this book
is available from the British Library

ISBN: 9780434017751 (hardback)
ISBN: 9780434017768 (trade paperback)

The Random House Group Limited supports the Forest Stewardship Council (FSC), the leading international forest certification organisation. All our titles that are printed on Greenpeace approved FSC certified paper carry the FSC logo. Our paper procurement policy can be found at www.rbooks.co.uk/environment

Typeset by SX Composing DTP, Rayleigh, Essex
Printed and bound in Great Britain by
Clays Ltd, St Ives PLC

For Lesley

One

A telephone directory, particularly when viewed through the eyes of a lunatic, can be a fascinating thing. Hundreds of thousands of names, voices that can be reached simply by pressing the appropriate combinations of plastic buttons. Names, but no identities. How do we know that one Mr. M. Peterson is any different from another Mr. M. Peterson? There are addresses of course, and unfortunately we'll have to get to that in a moment, but just see the names for now, the two Petersons, in a book so big it goes *whump* when you drop it onto a coffee table or kitchen surface.

Of course, despite an identical entry in the phone book, chances are the two Petersons *are* different, either by increments or by vast chasms of personality, and probably the latter. One Mr. Peterson could spend his summers as a park ranger, striding through the wilds of Montana, pissing discreetly behind trees, marveling at sunsets, and shaking his head at discarded food wrap. The other Mr. Peterson could, right now, be performing a fuck position he saw in a movie with his secretary in a Motel 6 whilst worrying about his tax return. They could both be Freemasons, Catholics or Jews, have ingrown toenails, abusive families, courtroom appearances. They could love their wives, their children, shoot guns at inanimate things in their spare time. Or they could have absolutely nothing in common beyond a name, probably don't (asides from liking the Red Sox because their fathers did).

Truth is, they *do* have two things in common, because we're dealing in certainty here. Firstly, a sound that for some reason has ended up *meaning who they are* has been translated by someone clever and dead into printed lines, arcs and dots, and arranged in a fashion so unified you could lose them in the blink of an eye on the same page of a book big enough to be a weapon (*whump*). The second thing is that it would be very surprising if both Mr. M. Peterson and Mr. M. Peterson didn't have ugly, *ugly* secrets hidden somewhere.

The paper in the phone book is whispery thin. One page back from the M. Petersons and the N. Petersons and the two O's (Oswald and Orin Peterson, brothers actually, both insurance salesmen) are new columns of names, impossible to read them all at once. If you hold it up to the light, you can see other names there too, written backward like mirror writing and foggy as ghosts.

Scan the directory, don't read, as we have no real business in a book full of strangers.

Jon Peterson was the best advertisement for unlisted numbers that ever existed. When he held the phone book in his two hands, Jon could feel like the god of his childhood imagination, the god who could hold the green and blue earth like a soccer ball and put his thumb down at random, killing millions of people and hearing thousands of tiny fire-engine sirens as they battled with futility to put out tiny fires. There'd probably be looting too, amongst those that remained, not to mention the millions crushed under the thumb itself, so meaningless to Jon's god that he could put the digit in his mouth and taste nothing but a memory of what he'd prepared for breakfast that morning, this despite the numberless bodies that must have stuck in the channels and furrows of his thumbprint like so much squashed insect.

Jon was looking at his own name in the phone book for the thousandth time, J. Peterson, and marveling at how much he looked like everyone else when categorized there, the lines and letters of his name. It was a fantastic disguise, and it took no effort. There he was, nestled with the other J. Petersons, who had accepted him, without thought, as one of their own, part of the herd.

Jon was fascinated with phone books (along with other, less harmless things). There were perhaps hundreds of them in his house, tomes from as far away as China and Japan, England and France. But he was not a collector, if there are collectors of such things. He was searching for a name, and the more books, the more names, and the more names, the greater the choice.

Unfortunately, the process was not entirely indiscriminate, much as the perfectionist in him would have liked it to be. The foreign directories were simply for his own entertainment, to give him a greater feeling of power. For practicality, the name he ultimately chose would be that of someone located in America. A feeling of power came from imagining the rest of the tiny soccer-ball world breathing a sigh of relief upon learning this knowledge, and it made him smile in a way that would shoo animals.

Also, the name would be located in a city, because you could walk unnoticed in a city.

It would be a woman. It had to be, that was a foregone conclusion, but Jon still prided himself on being an equal-opportunity kind of person. This was also why the ethnic names were never dismissed, although Jon would be the first to admit he never spent much time among the Ahmeds and the Wongs.

But practicality was so boring, those rules wrote themselves, that stuff about choosing a city, one in America. Jon had spent far longer on the philosophical impositions. Primarily, he had considered how some people thought that there was nothing in a name, they thought it was just a sound, or collection of sounds, and it was your personality that counted etcetera and Jon dismissed this as the worst kind of nonsense. He saw his name in his own handwriting almost every time he bought anything significant, and as everyone knows, transacting business is one of the most important things a person can do. How can *that* not have an impact? J. Peterson struck him as solid and ordinary, as American as peanut butter and golf courses, despite, or maybe because of, its European origins. He imagined a slave adopting it after emancipation. He saw it inscribed in brass plaques on office doors, and printed on greasy badges pinned on drive-through monkeys. Above all, he loved its accuracy, its sweet accuracy, because it was *his name*.

Jon wanted his endeavor to lead him to a person with capability, because it would make the later exercises more fun. He had spent an earlier part of his evening looking at the Clevers in this book, i.e. people called Clever (of which there were three), but after an hour's hard deliberation, he dismissed them. He was concerned that they might not be beautiful, something that had indirectly become important in his criteria. This had led him back to the Prettys, not out of any sense of conviction, but because it amused him.

The search was not frustrating, even though the process had gone on for months, because soon enough an individual would spring to life in front of him, shine through their cipher like Christ on the cross. Jon could wait, knowing there would be an epiphany of some kind, and it spurred him on, staring and staring at the names until they scorched into his brain.

Three in the morning now, and he had to be up early. Jon rubbed the bridge of his nose with his forefinger and civilization-squashing thumb and considered the hard work still to do. The big book in his lap was closed quietly and slid onto a pile of similar directories that were painstakingly arranged in some kind of madman's priority.

Even if you lived in a North American city and knew what he was doing, you could at least feel relatively safe in the imposed randomness, that protection of the herd, those millions of millions of closely printed names and their identities hidden behind the corresponding numbers and addresses. If your name was L. M. Victim and you'd taken out a big eye-catching ad, you'd probably be one of the safer ones. The maniac has worked hard to keep it arbitrary, and that is both our fear and our salvation. He is close to making a decision.

The phone book tonight was Philadelphia, PA.

Tomorrow it will probably be somewhere else.

Two

San Francisco.

"The best part is just after where the streets cross over."

"It'd be like Magic Mountain if it went faster, huh sweets?"

"Yeah, Dad, Magic Mountain." But she was pleased, despite herself. They'd already ridden the cable car to the usual sights, and were now exhausting the California Street line for the sheer joy of it. There were far fewer tourists so late in the day, and there was plenty of room to sit down now, although he couldn't persuade her to do so.

"Should we go round again?" Jen's voice, like a co-conspirator.

"We can do that."

Truth was, Dave Wiley wasn't keen on the idea, fantastic as their half-day together had been. For one thing, it was getting time to return Jen to her mother, and following an ugly Christmas (their second apart) he knew it would not do to miss a Karen deadline. There was another reason as well: a strange man had been lounging on a bench at the Plaza turnaround the first time. Dave suspected he'd still be there, and the Financial District was emptying and growing shadows.

"Don't you ever get sick of this thing?"

"Daaad . . ." Dave couldn't see her eyes, though he knew they were rolling upwards in her head, in imitation of Mommy. The decision was in his daughter's hands, no question. Bench hobo temporarily forgotten, it was more that he had thought the aquarium would be his trump card for their afternoon together. Surely it was supposed to be boys that liked trains, cars, things that moved, and her boredom scared him more than anything.

Little Jen smiled over her shoulder to melt his heart and turned her face back into the sweet, cold bay breeze, long loose curls of red hair billowing behind, posing for him like the figurehead on the prow of a mythical ship.

Dave missed the point, it was the views she loved: San Francisco's great dipping canyons of civilization, fleeting glimpses of the Bay Bridge between buildings, the lights on the struts just starting to blink on through the half-fog of an early September evening. Most of her life in the Bay Area, four years downtown, and she'd only ridden the cable car three times before, each time unable to extricate herself much from her mom's protective grasp. The things moved only a little faster than running speed anyway, despite the crazy tilts. Last summer she had watched with envy as some teenage-boy tourists, too young to be trusted with cameras, hung on to rails with only a few inches of board to stand on. One of them was blond, with soft skin and long-lashed dark eyes, and the breezes parted his hair for him. He had caught her watching his profile, and had stuck out a pink tongue, leaving her itching with self-consciousness, for some reason hating the sticky candy bar that Mom had brought along for the trip.

This time, she got to stand at the front of the car where nothing obstructed the views, was loving it, over Taylor now, the biggest drops coming soon, a ring of the bell, a few theatrically bellowed instructions to keep arms in.

Earlier, she had seen the brakeman and her father sharing a smile and then sharing it right back with her, caught out at their paternal indulgence like naughty boys with firecrackers. Feeling a delightful adult electricity shoot from head to toe, she knew instinctively then that the brakeman had a daughter, or wanted one, and settled back into committing to memory the way the stone rumble of the cars set her teeth on edge.

At that very moment, Jen was the eleven-year-old princess of her city.

It would take a person with a dark heart to deny her it.

The last day of the psychoanalysts' conference was tomorrow, and Karen Wiley had decided in the car on her way home that she was going to miss it. Three days of watching old-school therapists lost in mutual back-slapping had been enough. That was the good thing about her first conference after passing her exams being held so close to home—it was just a skip across the bridge to her own private space. She wouldn't do San Diego at Thanksgiving; the organizers always arranged vacation-deserted dorm rooms, and there were usually beds she wouldn't impose on a monastic order.

Dave would be returning Jen soon, and the night would be theirs.

The corridor on the third floor of her Russian Hill condo was deserted, and Karen blessed her good fortune for the thousandth time at having elderly neighbor-landlords that would do anything for a single mother, and passed out around eight after two cups of malted milk. Balancing a light coat, a newish black briefcase and a set of keys, it was left to her toe to nudge the base of the sticky door, but finally it opened. In, lights on, and because of Jen, the chain left off. Then the boots, the final struggle of the day, one hand against the wall for balance, and then the ultimate sensory pleasure of home, thick carpet under stockinged feet.

Wine now, and music.

Another flick of a switch, and the kitchenette was lit like a stage. Delilah, the twice-a-week cleaner and trusted babysitter, had brought the mail up from the box downstairs and put it on the kitchen counter. There were three items, and Karen carried them over to the fridge, sorting through for any priorities. A bill, something about AT&T, and her typed name and address on an anonymous envelope. The postmark was Canaan, Utah, one with an unusually elaborate design.

Completely unfamiliar mail was relatively rare for Karen. If it wasn't recognizably junk, or a bill, or a letter from a distant relative (no one she knew was from Utah), then it could well be correspondence from someone moving to the coast, maybe expressing interest in becoming a new client. Karen needed clients. Two years after the divorce, eighteen months away from quitting her job as a producer on the morning news for the Fox affiliate, and her therapy business had not progressed anywhere near as fast as it should have.

The wine glass came out of the cabinet and was filled with ice-cold Zinfandel, and the smell of wild strawberries. Having stopped biting her nails when Dave left, she was able to slit the envelope open with ease.

She could tell before straightening it out that this wasn't a typical letter. There was no address, no signature. If anything, it looked like a blank piece of paper until it was held in the middle, thumb restricting the bottom third from folding back on itself. Then two lines of spiky, penciled handwriting were revealed in the exact center of the paper, small enough to merit a squint.

This is what it read, from beginning to end:

Help me o god help me hes going to hurt me if you dont do what he says jentle jesus meek and mild look upon a little child save me jesus save me

Just like that, meaning all running together in a flood of concentrated panic.

Karen Wiley, resourceful from an early age, remained calm. She acknowledged the message as she would a distress signal accidentally tuned into by an atmospheric anomaly, like a police channel interrupting the weather report on the car stereo.

Was that all?

No, because entirely against her will, there seemed to be adrenalin moving through her system. She thought of the blue dye that gets injected into some X-ray patients, electric-looking, working its way out to fingers and toes.

The wine went carefully down onto the marble work surface, the glass slippery with a condensation that clung to her fingertips and left a pale stain on the note as she turned it around in her hand, scanned it once more, then picked up the envelope, verified that it really *was* her name and address typed out on the front. She put down the envelope and reread the message, more carefully this time.

o god help me hes going to hurt me

She realized that she had frozen, as if being watched, as if something else was supposed to happen, a bogeyman jumping out of the icebox maybe.

Don't be silly.

The clock on the kitchen wall ticked once, loudly.

What did it mean? If a child was in danger, had written this, then surely someone else had transcribed it. She couldn't know it for sure, but there was something that was childish about the hard lines of handwriting, the pencil marks in deliberate capitals pushed hard into the paper. Karen took a deep breath. Thinking now, she rubbed a spot near her heart with two fingers.

Shortly after she'd left Dave, made him move out of the apartment that she paid for (why did everyone, including supposedly enlightened women, immediately assume that *he* had left *her*?), Karen Wiley had received a series of obscene phone calls. Obscene would be the name for them, but they weren't really; it had started one night with a wrong number, and the man on the other end seemed to have taken it personally. He rang back every night for a week, humming out-of-key show tunes, until one Saturday, when she'd had too much wine. On that occasion, she told him the police had traced his number (she hadn't called the police) and were on the way to his shitty house *right now* and you'd better grab your motherfucking balls and run, asshole . . . He'd hung up like his handset was on fire and never called back.

This was a story that she'd dined out on with her female friends for a little while, how she showed some random pervert that a newly single woman couldn't be messed with, but having got some mileage reporting it to her pragmatic media buddies, she spun it to Dana, a friend from Scotland. Dana, in her measured, ancient accent told Karen a story in turn about how when living in a squat in Glasgow, she had received genuinely horrific phone calls from a man who kept saying he wanted to close up her throat with his hands while he raped her and made her little student bitch eyes water and roll. The local police, seemingly unsympathetic to Dana's punky hair and attitude, were unwilling or unable to stop him. Eventually the calls ended of their own accord and Dana moved on, but still.

From this point on the whole humming caller thing became a lot less funny, and Karen had done her best to evacuate the experience from her consciousness.

Karen looked at the note again.

jesus meek and mild save me save me

Her own beautiful daughter. In the hands of . . . who? No, not possible. Jen was with Dave today, their every other Saturday together relegated to school-runs and Monday afternoons because of his work commitments. She couldn't have written this, let alone been kidnapped, clearly hadn't, wouldn't present like this anyway, all run together in handwriting so stabby and alien. Besides, don't kidnap notes demand something? This was a prank, a fucking *prank*. Karen had waved her daughter into Dad's car from the window that very morning.

But was it really Dave in the car? Had it been an impostor?

Of course not, how ridiculous. For one thing, the letter came from Utah.

Realizing the turn her mind had taken, Karen was able to distance herself from the mounting panic. Come on—had her ex-husband been replaced by an impostor? And had driven Dave's Volvo to her house to abduct her daughter? It was stupid for so many reasons. The note and envelope, along with the viral spores of fear that had floated up when it was opened, were finally set to one side. She took a breathy gulp of wine, both to steady herself and show the empty room that all was well.

She didn't even jump when the phone rang.

Dave Wiley, not thirty seconds into his room, pulled his curtains on the stars, and contemplated the minibar, a wry look on his face.

He was feeling pretty good after his afternoon with Jen. The tourist hotel on Geary that he'd checked himself into was nowhere near as bad as he had expected; the breakfast was adequate, and they had parked his car for him somewhere without too much extortion. This was only his fourth or fifth visit to his daughter in the city; because of the nature of his work, Karen was good enough to drive Jen out to him (that and she had the money, trips to the city could add up) but all in all Dave had to admit that he'd done quite well from the divorce—half the amassed worldly goods of a senior TV staffer was a very fine deal indeed when your life's work consisted of supervising the fresh-off-the-boats handling microchips into cellphone shells. The courts would never have sided with him, they hated the men, but Karen made sure it never got so far. She felt so bad she'd have given him anything just to go, just go, *I'll* pack your bags, and don't upset Jen right now, I think she might be getting bullied at school.

Dave had been pretty lacking in chivalry at first, turning up at inopportune times demanding to see Jen, but really it was Karen he'd come to see. He still loved her, loved her very much, and the extra booze he was prescribing himself only seemed to be making matters worse. One time eighteen months or so ago, he turned up at the house around midnight, sat in the car under the streetlamp all night and then pounced on his wife and daughter as they were leaving for school through the mist. Jen looked scared, a little white mask, but to him, Karen looked more beautiful than ever, as fresh from sleep and a shower as something elemental, her hair a reddish chestnut torrent, the spicy perfume she wore strong enough to catch in his throat. Karen was angry then, and he cried off for a while. But she relented eventually, said Jen wanted to see him, and he complied, pleased. Since then, he'd barely spoken to his ex-wife, and had to be content watching his daughter grow into a miniature version of her.

Dave imagined that his time with Jen was making him a better man, made him want to produce information about his own life for their meetings, let his little girl know that Daddy could compete with the world too. He learned never to ask about Mom but just to enjoy their time together for what it was. He resisted the urge to get Jen to manufacture meetings with Karen like the old days. And gradually, gradually, it became better. He got a new girlfriend, a receptionist at the plant; someone at least ten years younger than Karen, with brown eyes, bronzed skin and discreet but overgenerous breast implants that drew concentrated glances from the boys at the beach. He drank less, or at least stopped drinking alone. He shaved his beard, looked (he thought) ten years younger himself. Now a promotion was beckoning, maybe an eight-grand bump. The message seemed loud and clear: Dave Wiley was finally taking responsibility, kind of. Karen was the ambitious one in the marriage, he had been the steady supporting act, the high-school football player who married above his station. But there was relevance for him now in his own right, and a big part of it seemed due to working towards the time with his daughter.

Dave had to go out into the corridor to make the call he had promised to make, the signal in his art-deco room without a view was atrocious. Karen answered on the fifth ring. He wondered if she had caller ID, if she even recognized his number anymore. Either way, she sounded hostile.

"Yes?"

Hostile *and* apprehensive. Dave knew that tone of brittleness, she was under pressure.

"Karen, it's Dave."

"*Dave.*" She hadn't said his name in a tone of voice like that for a while. It came out heavy, like she'd been holding her breath.

"Yeah, you said ring when Jen's on her way up."

"Well, thank God." Genuine-sounding relief.

Dave was somewhat offended. They'd unconsciously accepted a sort of artificial casualness into their exchanges, nothing so inhuman as the forced civility that less reasonable couples sometimes maintained on separation. Even so, it led Dave and Karen to sound like two actors in the early stages of rehearsing a play. This was very different, this "thank God". What did she think that he'd done with their daughter?

"I don't see you," said Karen. She must have moved over to the living-room window.

"No, I'm back in the hotel. Well, the corridor, because of the signal."

A pause. He strained a little to hear her breathe.

"Then . . . what?" Now she sounded controlled, very controlled. Ah, maybe he'd caught her in some intimate moment, that was the reason for the pissyness. It made Dave more confident.

"No, I put her in a cab," he said. "From the Financial District. We were having milkshakes and there was one just there outside the window; miracle really, you know what this town's like."

Silence.

"And I know you hate us to be late, I know that. Thing is, Kar, we had such a great day. We got a cab, there was one right there. Lost track of the time a little, it was the fastest way to get her home. Did you know, she'd hardly ever ridden the streetcar before?" He was conscious of babbling; this was the longest continuous thing he'd said to Karen in a while. Now he needed her to take a turn, to play the game.

But he was made to wait again, his last question dying in the silence.

"You put her in a cab . . . on her own?" Karen's voice echoed with judgment and he felt the skin on his arms creep slightly.

"Now, *no*—Jen rides in cabs on her own all the time. She did . . . she has for a while. I'd have thought she was a little young yet, but if *you* think . . ."

"Dave, she does not. She does *not* ride on her own."

"But she said you said it was okay. That you let her before . . ."

"Like one time, with Christy. There were four of them, and Christy is what, sixteen now?" Dave had never heard of Christy. He felt guilty and stupid, sent back to square one.

"She never said that."

"Jesus, Dave, when are you going to take some responsibility? A cab from the Financial District to here? Where are you staying?"

"Union Square."

"And you got back already? You not think she'd be here by now?" He hadn't heard Karen this upset for a long while. He wasn't going to rise, but it was important to get the information to her as quickly as possible, extinguish this fire.

"No, listen, *listen*—we got the cab *here* first. To the hotel, the two of us. Then I sent it on with her in the back seat, the driver knew your address. I called you the second I got in, if she'd grown goddamn wings and flown she wouldn't be with you yet. Calm down." Dave was trying to demonstrate to Karen that they were on the same team, that her concern was shared.

"Dave, I'm calling the police."

This was becoming a nightmare, one of his worst.

"No, twenty minutes, give it at least . . ."

"*Dave* . . ."

". . . there's no way she could have got to you since . . ."

"Dave, it's impossible for this to be related, but I got a *note*."

"What did you say your name was, little one?"

"Jennifer." She hadn't.

"Home to Momma now, huh? She been missing you?"

"Uh-huh." There was little traffic. The driver made a right, straightened up, scratched absentmindedly at a tattoo on his big brown arm, bare in a sleeveless shirt.

Jen took the opportunity to turn her attention from the back of the driver's large, closely shaven head to the streaky cab window, watched the dark city pass by with tired eyes. She suddenly felt exhausted and that the journey home seemed to be taking an unusually long while. Eighty percent of the time it was hard work pleasing her father, good as his intentions seemed to be these days. Only occasionally did she not feel like she was playing at small talk with him in some way, sanitizing her school relationships, editing the recent history of Mom's life story, working hard to show Dad that yes, she really *was* having a good time with him, thank you *so* much. To make polite conversation with a cab driver now, even one that seemed as nice as this, felt a lot like more hard work.

But she'd step up to the plate if she had to. Jen was her mother's daughter.

"Your daddy, he sure seem like a nice guy."

"He's okay."

"My daddy, I never knew him."

"What happened?"

"Like I say, I never knew him. Always out partying, causing trouble. Mama said the cops beat him out of town, but I just think he ran off someplace. It had to been tough for him though, my mother—*ooochass*. What did your daddy do wrong?"

"What?"

"He got kicked out though, huh?" It was weird, talking so familiarly like this. When Dad was there with her on the way to his hotel it had been football stats and the California governorship, and communication with this stranger had seemed second nature. Compulsory somehow, yes; but in a good way. Dad gone, the dynamic was off, somehow inappropriate: *wrong*.

"Oh, he didn't do anything," said Jen. "I don't know."

"You got a tough momma?"

"Oh yeah. She's cool though."

"I bet she is. And you gonna be just like her."

"No way. I'm gonna be a vet."

Jen watched his dark eyes crinkle with delight in the rear-view mirror, considered that he might have spun it around at some point to get a good look at her. She also wondered if she was having her leg pulled; Dad always pulled her leg.

A silence, then:

"You like music, little one?"

"I suppose."

"You like Jessica Simpson?"

"Not so much."

"And Christina whosis? She's Spanish, you know."

"Um."

"Well, we're here." She hadn't even noticed the car stop, and the window had fogged up. She rubbed the glass, took a look, as if to verify. She'd been clutching a banknote that Dave had given her for the fare.

"How much, mister?" She craned to see a meter, couldn't.

"That's okay. I don't want your money."

"No?" Jen was suspicious, something in his tone.

"Spend it on something you like, little one. I'll see you in."

"That's okay."

"No, I mean I'll watch till you get in. You don't know who's about."

"Thanks then."

"My pleasure, little one, and . . ."

She scrambled off the tatty, fibrous seat and down onto the road, the end of his sentence cut off by the car door. It was cold now, the street deserted and silent, the cab behind her a warm oasis. Jen sensed traffic noise in the distance, a police siren, the solitary bark of a dog.

She pulled her coat tightly around herself. Looking up, she saw welcoming yellowy light on the third floor. Jen trotted across the road, suddenly feeling hungry.

The sky had closed in since earlier, and there were no stars to be seen. Stepping out of the pool of neon cast by the streetlamp, she became aware of rapid darkness. Jen felt an exhilarating urge to run, to cast off the grown-up events of the day and frolic and buck like some newborn creature. She aimed for the neon pool on the other side of the road and galloped, enjoying the feel of her limbs, a naughty part of her hoping the driver was still watching.

She was barely under the streetlamp when a figure stepped out of nowhere, grabbed her, spun her round and squeezed her and squeezed her. Jen buried her face in her mom's hair, lost herself in the smell of shampoo and hugged back just as hard, dimly aware of hot tears on her neck and hysterically murmured messages of love.

"Jennifer, thank God . . ."

It only lasted a second, not long enough for her to respond even, and then she was being pulled briskly by the hand towards the door of their building, the dim porch bulb blinking welcome.

The cab driver, touched, readjusted his rear-view mirror and drove off into the night.

Three

Responding to gentle suggestions from his therapist, Jon Peterson took four days off work, loaded up the jeep, and headed out into the desert.

He was hunting demons. He had no real expectation of finding any, but he had to admit that either he was a genius or his therapist was, because the progress he was making was remarkable, though his therapist appeared to reserve judgment.

Jon's thinking on the big project that he had set himself had become somewhat stale. Parts of the puzzle were falling into place, but no real action had been taken. Back home, all of the mirrors in the house had to be carefully wrapped in plastic to stop the accusing eyes staring back, asking why was it taking so long, why don't we move today, put the fucking ball in play, you useless *gimp*. The house itself, always spotlessly clean, had developed a severely bad smell; he was having to change the sheets on the bed after every night's sleep, and was resorting to buying a cheap new plate every time he ate off an old one. The final straw had come when the mailman managed to burst a sample of aqua fabric softener while forcing it through his spring-loaded box. Once on the mat, it oozed through the bright cardboard packaging like someone had sent alien semen to him. The smell, some chemical freshness or other, might well have been of maggoty rabbit brains to Jon Peterson, so hugely inappropriate it was in his carefully controlled space.

But a short drive from the house, and there was wide blue sky. Nature had set out her stage in front of him with a beauty so vast as to be immune to fabric softener and television commercials, road rage and credit cards. Jon loved the desert, the freedom, the heat, the grit, the not-quite silence, and he loved the variation in the landscapes. To cast his eyes gradually over the incremental changes of light and color as the distances stretched out allowed his mind to expand into the space, and eventually the purple and yellow horizons of morning became as familiar and owned as the area back home between his lounger and the living room wall. His eyes fizzed in his head with a new sense of possibility.

Jon was standing at the top of a lookout point in a National Park, more than five hundred miles of designated desolation in the state of Utah, some two hundred or more miles to the south and west of the state capital. He was watching the sun as it rose over great red fins of sandstone.

Jon had come up here to begin his day because it was nice to get a vision of the whole landscape before he dug his 4x4 into the dust and set off into the wilderness proper. After all, this was a map of sorts, splayed out beneath his feet in 1:1 relief, one that could reveal far more to him than any ranger issue fold-up. He relied predominantly on instinct to guide him towards the demons, but Jon also knew that no amount of respect for the harsh realities of the desert would ever pay sufficient homage if he found his little truck stranded in one of those waterless canyons. As a result, these little spiritual rituals, the sunrise meditations, had become as crucial to him as the cooler full of Gatorade and ice in the back of the jeep.

Jon heard something in the background. He moved out of his meditation carefully, like a diver adjusting to the bends, or a contortionist unfolding at the end of a show. Entirely returned to the physical world, he tilted his head slightly, as if to better catch the sound.

There were always noises in Jon Peterson's head, all real to him, and they had been there since childhood. He rarely heard voices as such, although occasionally there seemed to be words formed that could be made out, breathy whispers from across the void, though he admitted he had to engage his imagination to ascribe specific meaning in any language we know. Instead, he heard one unending tone, as comforting and familiar as a mother humming to a baby, which had occasional variations that seemed to arise from the original noise in what could be best described as living with the ebb and swell of an invisible, limitless sea. On occasion, the noise could damn him to his knees, other times he could reach into it and gain guidance, still other times it seemed to exist all for itself, independently and outside of him, like he was a bystander at a miracle.

The noises were happy now, and they allowed him to feel every single cell in his body, every electrical impulse, every atom of breath. Jon blinked a tear of salty sweat into his eye but forced the lid to stay open, relishing the stinging pain of it, loving how the world became liquid, color swirling like the painter dropped his palette. He was very familiar with this part of Utah, but these pinnacles and towers were phenomenal enough to surprise him each and every time, like the terrain was somehow trying to claw its way back up to God.

Jon wiped his eyes, adjusted his hat and got back into the jeep, the only car in the rudimentary lot. There were sunglasses on the passenger seat but he could hold off a bit longer, it was early in the day. He wanted to grasp the colors to himself for another hour or two before filtering them through his Ray-Bans.

Jon touched the low range shift for comfort, enjoying the idea that he'd be using it over alien terrain in the hours to come, and slipped the jeep into reverse, pulling out rapidly. Then he set off, without haste, back down the long trail to the base of the plateau.

Near the bottom, just before he turned off the road and into the wilderness, Jon Peterson passed a car ferrying the first family of tourists up to the top, a flash of a father behind the wheel concentrating through sunglasses of his own, knuckles whitening at the sudden and unexpected appearance of another car. Then they passed each other. Jon smiled his startlingly frightening smile into the rear-view mirror, knowing that by the time the man got his family to the top, the quality of the light on the elemental plain would have altered beyond comparison. They would never see what he had seen up there, it was just for him.

The shiver of this knowledge triggered the impulse he had been waiting for. Jon swung the car off the road, thick tires budduh-bumping over a heaped earth shoulder, and then he was away through the uneven desert scrubland towards the canyons and pinnacles, communing with the exposed bones of America, and the demons he hoped would be there waiting.

Eleven hours later, and the pink light of evening that flooded the chasms was threatening to turn blood red.

"Damn, but if the fella wasn't right in front of us all along," Don said.

"Nuh."

"Are you with me, sleeping beauty?"

Milt was dozing on the back seat of the recovery truck, had been stinking drunk since noon. Now he belched wetly, as if in response.

"I said wake the fuck up, bro. This guy looks like a straight arrow."

"What, let him report us. Dead-end shift anyway." Don wondered if Milt was properly conscious, but after a moment he heard movement in the back, he was coming around. Smiling grimly, Don pulled swiftly past the stranger by the broken-down jeep and onto the dirt shoulder, a little too close for comfort, curious to see if the tall man in the mud-splattered clothes would step back from the road any.

He did not.

The call had come in a little over three hours ago, and they should have been there in one, but there was an afternoon card game in Betsy's. Frankly, thought Don, some forty bucks worse off than he'd been that morning, the kind of idiots who wanted to drive these deserted highways without joining triple-A got what they deserved. Besides, it wasn't Don's recovery business. And this guy here, he clearly wasn't local. Probably some city jerk-off with more money than sense, off-roading like this all on his damn own. Should be grateful he got back on the blacktop before he threw the rod or whatever the inane fault would be.

"You, ah . . . want me to deal with this one?" Milt was fumbling with the door handle, clearly not capable of dealing with anything. Don, with unusual foresight, had locked the doors so his errant middle-aged brother-in-law wouldn't fall out in transit.

"Rest up, buddy. Probably a good citizen with a tail-light out. You'll be back with Mand and the kids before you know it."

"That f–f–fuckin' *bitch*."

"Whatever you say."

Don, feeling hard done by, climbed out of the cab and into the eerie desert silence. He couldn't see the stranger from here, the truck was between them, so they were face to face before Don had time to screw on his seen-it-all puss. He was a little surprised to discover the stranger had walked over, they usually stayed by their car.

"Been waiting long?" asked Don, knowing full well. He looked forward to being disinterested in a city-boy complaint.

"No, no time at all." The voice was rich and measured, like someone on the radio. The man was smiling a half-smile as though Don had offered to buy him a drink. It made hairs move on the back of Don's neck, not in a good way.

"My dispatcher said three hours."

"So you didn't need to ask." Still the smile, but no hint of irritation.

"Three hours out here," said Don. "No one passed by, offered to help?"

"Not the world we grew up in."

"Yeah. You should, ah, put your hood up, folks round these parts, they usually stop."

"My mistake."

Don pressed on. "I mean, I know this ain't the park proper, but no rangers? Or the state police, they come by. No benefit in losing someone out here, sake of tourism."

"Just unlucky, I guess." The man shrugged his shoulders as if to emphasize the point, but he didn't look unlucky.

Don thought about the forty bucks he no longer had to spend on Coors that night. He decided he was beaten, found himself needing to give a little. The guy looked too resourceful to have a problem that could be fixed roadside, and it might pay to find some common ground, especially if he needed towing. Hours together back to Canaan with Milt in the cab, and Milt's stomach probably wasn't at its strongest after the all-day sour mash diet.

"Look," said Don, "there was an emergency. Some prick drove an RV full of kids into the back of God's nowhere, went down a slope he couldn't get up again. That was the delay."

So an apology of sorts, but this time the stranger said nothing, as if he could see through the lie, and the silence between them grew weight under the fading desert sun. Don fought an urge to stare at the ground. Instead, he mustered up some thick fluid in his mouth, spat. When he looked up again, he noticed that the stranger had fixed his eyes on a bush clinging to one of the nearby red rock outcrops, like a doctor averting his eyes for the benefit of an incontinent patient.

". . . also, you wasn't where I was told you were."

"I wasn't?" said the man, with genuine interest.

"No. Been going up and down for some time." This was true. In fact, Don could have sworn he'd driven this same stretch of road at least once that night and seen no cars by the side, but all roads through Utah start looking the same when you're arguing with your drunken beer-buddy about your own flesh and blood.

"Like I said, not my day. Maybe not yours either."

Something then made Don dare to look harder at the stranger, only for a second. He caught bright green eyes under a fringe of dark hair. Physically, the guy looked like a tough customer. Very tall, light tan, muscles under an anonymous blue shirt. Cultured yes, but this man knew what he was doing in the desert, or probably anywhere. Don found himself wondering again why he was out here with no proper breakdown cover.

"So. What seems to be the problem with the jeep?"

"Why don't we go over, take a look?"

Jon Peterson, bouncing slightly with the rhythm of the recovery truck, felt phenomenal. It was all he could do not to close his eyes and enjoy the symphony of sound the demons were playing for him. And the color, the color when he closed his eyes, reds and blues and brilliant, brilliant whites, threatened to escape his head and overwhelm them all.

"Good of you," said a voice across the void. It was the one called Don, who'd become friendly. "I mean about Milt. He's going through a tough time at home." The one called Milt was face down in his own drool at Jon's feet across the rear seat wells. The pomade in the redneck's hair smelled like someone had thrown a burning tire into a beehive. Jon expanded his nostrils, filed the scent alongside his other current sensations. Blinking luxuriously, he saw dark orange, watched it swirl behind his eyes like toffee through ice cream.

"I know what that's like," said Jon, who had insisted on riding in the back. "Troubles at home."

"Well, I look after him. He rides out with me sometimes when he gets too drunk to go anyplace else. Doesn't happen that often, but around the holidays, you know families . . ."

"Your other clients, they don't mind?"

"Clients?"

"Customers. The folks you tow." Jon was quietly passing an opaque green plastic chip between his fingers, the shape of a tiny letter T with a very wide down stroke. It was the same chip he had removed from his jeep some two hours ago that would make his vehicle lose all power steering, speedometer, headlight and turn signal functions. He had reasoned correctly that a local mechanic might be able to repair a fan-belt but probably wouldn't know enough about electrics to fix it roadside.

"Oh, they're cool. I usually just tow locals," said Don. "Out-of-staters have the cover which goes to the rival business, and of course the rentals."

Jon himself had cover, was a lifetime member, but the demons had flashed instruction to him. Now he was waiting for further inspiration. He had become a lightning conductor in a storm, anticipating electrical brilliance.

In the darkness at his feet, Milt grunted, shifted slightly. Jon heard something that might have been a yawn, might have been a dry heave, said casually, "I just never renewed mine."

"They're not always great value," said Don. "Take the local firms, you get the personal touch."

"Um."

"We're nearly there. Like I said, appreciate this, dropping Milton off home."

"It's not far out the way, right?"

"No."

So Jon should do them now, before they reached Milt's residence. A burst of static in his brain said to wait. The demons must be cooking up something really good. He looked out of the window into a sea of darkness. A close-to-full moon was obscured by cloud, and they hadn't passed another car in twenty minutes. The CB radio crackled, and Don looked at it. Sal must have closed up the garage, gone to bed.

There was a silence in the cab now, and it was comfortable.

Don's hands were rocking on a large steering wheel that almost touched his beer belly. He had surprised himself by being pleased to have someone to talk to, even if this guy Peterson was a little strange; he seemed shell-shocked somehow, the way he considered everything he heard for so long before replying. Don thought of an uncle who had been at Lan Doc, was never the same again.

Behind, the jeep up on the ramp rattled and squeaked. Peterson had said his hotel was right by the yard, must mean the E-Z Motel, so it wouldn't be too hard to tell him that there was no way his vehicle was going to get looked at that night. It was approaching midnight, and Don was looking forward to his lounger and a baseball game on tape.

Milt was shifting, clearing phlegm loudly and repulsively from the backs of his nostrils.

"That off-roading, that's good sport," said Don to Peterson, by way of apology.

"Oh yeah. I get out here whenever I can."

"What is it you do, mister? For a living?"

"I organize beauty pageants. In Vegas."

"Beauty pageants?" It was Milt, he'd sat up. "You some kind of *fag*?"

Jon, taken aback by this beauty-pageant revelation himself, wondered what the demons were playing at. The words, cooked in some part of his brain he had no influence over, came out slow to him, treacly. "Far from it," he said. "Tiresome work sometimes though, that's why I off-road, clears my mind."

"Beauty pageants ain't work."

"No? You see those things on television, who do you think puts them together?"

"Fag work. I don't see what's so tiring."

"You don't? I'll tell you. The girls."

"Sissy show-offs, fighting over make-up."

In the front, Don tried to put Milt back to sleep with the power of his mind. The stranger didn't seem bothered, though. Don watched the mirror with curiosity.

"No, no," continued Jon, blithely. "My main problem is the aesthetics. Girls with the right look are hard to come by. Take next week, we're doing the ten to fourteen-year-olds. Not an honest face amongst them. Beauty, yes—but they're all groomed to perfection, nothing natural. *Inner* beauty, that's what matters."

"I got a little girl," said Milt, his voice suddenly choking up. "She's a beauty, better than any of those assholes."

"You do?" Jon sounded fascinated. Polite, to include him: "What about you, Donald?"

"Me?" Don chuckled. "Nah, Jeanette, she's barren. Little shit-monsters anyway."

"Yeah, that's what you'd fuckin' say." Milt sounded wounded, teary. "My eldest, Katy, she'd go ten rounds in one of your competitions."

"See, and that's snobs for you," said Peterson. "That's the kind of thing that I'm trying to change. Someone should give her a proper chance."

"Yeah! You wanna meet her?"

"Meet Katy?"

"You wanna?"

"I'd like that. I'm always interested in new potential. Give me your last name, Milt. I'll send some of my people out to meet her."

"Really?"

"Sure. People like you, special little Katy—you're my bread and butter."

"No shit."

"The name, Milt. The last name."

"Trueblood."

"Katy," said Jon. "Katy Trueblood. That's absolutely excellent." He turned to face the bad breath wafting towards him from the adjacent seat and smiled.

"Say," he whispered, out of earshot of Don. "Care for something to help you relax?"

A car passed in the other direction, the first in an age, and light flooded the cabin. Milt caught a glimpse of a floating mask of evil, a cartoon grin. The teeth seemed long and sharp. He blinked uncertainly at the vision sitting next to him, a vision holding a small plastic bottle, and then the light ran away from the face and it was back in the shadows.

Back at home in his trailer, safe and well, and with a blood alcohol level of .32 and his nervous system further compromised by a good dose of Gamma-Hydroxybutyric acid, Milt would remember nothing about either this conversation or the ride home, but his dreams would be vivid, Technicolor nightmares.

Don would not get off so lightly.

One half-hour later.

The recovery truck pulled slowly into the entrance of the auto-yard with its lights off, two dark figures in the front seat, a mud-streaked jeep pinioned to the back at an angle of almost forty five degrees. The engine was cut before the truck even rolled to a stop, carried over the dip of the gutter by its own weight.

It was one in the morning, the clouds had scattered, and the moon now blazed.

Adventure tourism had taken off in the small city of Canaan with some gusto, leading to a rapid population increase, but the place remained true to its humble Mormon roots by being tucked up safely in bed by eleven-thirty. This meant that no one was around to witness the tall man emerge from the driver's side of the truck, stride around the back and begin the preliminary maneuvers necessary to release the jeep back down. If there had been a witness out and about on this dark and lonely side street, they might wonder why the second figure, the one in the passenger seat, did not attempt to help the tall man in his endeavors, but this would have been made apparent in due course.

The jeep was grounded with a gentle bounce of the wheels in their arches. The man reached in and reapplied the handbrake before fiddling with something in the steering column for a short while, unhurried in his actions. Then he emerged again, moved around the passenger side of the recovery truck towards the other figure, and opened the door with one swift movement. The motionless humanoid shape slumped outwards and downwards and it was all the tall man could do to stop it from crashing four feet to the ground, head first.

Given his condition, an onlooker might have thought that the other man was dead, but anyone reaching for a phone would have been checked when the tumbler, a fat squat fellow, was helped to his feet by the tall man and assisted from the truck over to the open jeep door with one limp arm draped across a broad shoulder. Ensconced in the passenger side, the door was closed on the fat man who then slumped against the glass.

At this point, the tall man did a strange thing. He climbed back into the cab of the recovery truck and spent almost five full minutes up there, now in the front, now in the back. Although Jon Peterson had been careful not to touch very much during his journey, he needed to completely eradicate evidence of his presence in that truck. This meant going over the black grooved steering wheel and the rusty door handles, and anything else he might wish to wipe down of his fingerprints. A good cop might still tie it to him of course, but it was a risk he was glad to take.

Task completed, Jon Peterson closed the doors of the recovery truck and dropped the keys down the grate of the gutter on the way back to his 4x4. It started with the first pressure on the ignition, reversed expansively onto the wide street, and set off the way it had come in, lights on so as not to attract unwanted police attention.

Peterson need not have been so cautious when returning with the truck. Sal, who owned the yard, lived in a completely different part of town, one that his wife was hoping would become a fashionable place to live someday. Besides, he trusted his employee to get back with his property sometime, if not as swiftly as he might have liked.

It only took a few minutes and two stoplights to get out of Canaan and back on the long road towards where Jon Peterson had spent most of his day, out in the middle of scarred nowhere, searching for an appropriate tributary of the mighty Colorado river, one that had all but dried up, but not quite. It had to be a damp canyon that flooded sometimes, and one he could access with his jeep, not easy to find by anyone's standards. Thankfully, the demons had taken his hand, and expertly guided his vehicle across some impossible terrain.

He was off the paved road and onto the dirt tracks that striped the desert landscape before the fat mechanic groaned again, stirred and dry-heaved. Peterson had another syringe of methohexital available to him if necessary, but it shouldn't be. If Don came around enough, Jon could simply explain to him that he was now out in the middle of the desert, no one knew where they were, and civilization and fresh water were about a billion miles away in every direction. Besides, Jon could hear himself saying, if you would just sit quiet, all this'll be over in no time and you'll soon be somewhere safe and warm.

Here it came now finally, a tree-rock combination that would have been indistinguishable from the rest of the landscape to anyone else, but for Jon Peterson it was a tableau that had been etched into his brain for him earlier that day, when he had seen it in the blaze of sunlight. Jon felt the familiar tingling and the leather-clad wheel in his hands turned to dust and electricity. Half in a trance, he slipped into low gear, swung left towards an uneven ridge, the engine squealing its dissatisfaction, truck shaking like a ship in a storm, and then they were over and cascading down, Jon barely even touching the brakes, letting the engine moderate for him. The demons were reading the terrain like a musical score.

It took a further half-hour to cover the three miles to the deep hole that the demons had made Jon Peterson dig in the soft canyon floor, a foot or so above the small stream that should have dried up by this time of year. The sides of the canyon were steep, like a skateboard pipe, and the moon flooded the place with light, turning the rocks blue and pale yellow. Peterson killed the engine and the headlights, the jeep parked lopsidedly with the passenger side a foot below the driver's. He looked across at his slumbering passenger and smiled, just two fellas nearing the end of a long journey.

The noises in his head were all-consuming now, one steady gargantuan pulse of red and black criss-crossed with a spider's web of lightning. He'd used a lot of strength earlier today digging that hole, manipulating his podgy victim, and he'd be physically destroyed tomorrow, lying in his unremarkable motel, his empty, dust-smeared face staring sightlessly at a faulty ceiling fan. But that would come later. At this moment the pulse was driving him in monstrous jerks and spasms, muscles tensed, striding around the other side of the jeep where he reached in and pulled Don the mechanic out onto the rocks with enough force to chip a splinter out of the fat man's pelvis. Don must have come to for a moment, for he screamed like an animal, the sound echoing through the canyon long enough for him to wonder who else was screaming.

Then, mercifully, he passed out again.

When Don next opened his eyes, he was sitting at the edge of a meticulously dug hole, deep enough to accommodate a man. His posture resembled that of a fat teddy bear resting against the headboard of a bed, legs splayed out in front of him. The demons had ripped his shirt up the front to expose his stomach, which resembled a large white egg resting over his lap, coarse dark hair running down the front like a zipper.

Don looked unwittingly up at the man in front of him, the stranger from earlier, who was holding what looked like a short curved sword in his hand. It glittered in the moonlight, a streak of liquid silver. Don stared with wonder from the sword to the face of Jon Peterson, and some primitive part of him understood. Then he looked down sadly at his egg-belly as it was sliced open crossways and lengthways and many purple things came out and slicked the rocks between his legs.

Then Don was no longer sitting, but tumbling once more, and it was a shame that the mechanic ended face downwards with his front teeth biting into the dirt and not face upwards towards the sky, because then his dying eyes could have witnessed how beautiful the sky was that night, the stars rolled out in their celestial symphony of light.

Peterson, panting, stood still for just long enough to recognize that the wall of sound in his head was beginning to fade, a quiet roar in his ears like the memory of the sea. Then he nudged the remains of Don's warm guts into the hole with the side of his boot.

Standing there, brow shiny with sweat, it occurred to Jon that he knew now why the demons had given Milt a pass. After a further moment's thought, he climbed down into the shallow grave.

Jon was going to need a small souvenir from the body. Not for any further perversion, but because it would be of use.

The colors of night were beginning their slow turn, dawn was only a few hours away. Jon felt his first wave of fatigue, fought it, and strode back towards the jeep, to the filthy shovel that was in the back there, his mind both on the pile of earth he was now going to have to move, and on Katy Trueblood, the unfortunate daughter of his victim's brother-in-law, who might just be beautiful enough to enter a pageant.

After all, he reasoned, he was going to need a real little girl if he was going to torture that psychologist bitch to death.

Four

"What is it, Mom?"

"It's nothing, baby." It wasn't nothing. It was another letter, the second. Karen bit at her bottom lip. "Eat your loops."

"I told you, I'm not hungry."

"Okay." Karen's hand was shaking a little, the flapping paper making a noise. It took a conscious effort to stop herself.

"Mom?"

"Yeah." Distracted.

"I'm not well, I should stay off school."

"Okay."

"Okay?" Jen seemed surprised, stopped pushing soggy cereal around the bowl.

"You can stay off today. But I want you back in bed. And read your book, I don't want to hear the TV."

"Mom?" Karen looked up from the letter. Her daughter was using a different tone now, removed from the wheedling eleven-year-old with a math test to avoid. "Are you okay?"

Karen put on a tough voice. "Don't push it, kid. Go on, I'll bring your milk in." Then she smiled a little to show that it was all right.

Jen stared across the counter for a second with a quizzical dubiousness any grown-up lawyer would have been proud of. She opened up her mouth to say more, decided that she was on to a good thing, and instead climbed carefully off the stool. Overacting somewhat, Jen limped towards her bedroom, the kinked bathrobe cord trailing behind her.

"If that kid's sick, I'm a monkey's uncle." Lilly was on her fourth coffee, dabbed toast crumbs from the surface and rubbed them between her fingertips. She was Karen's best pal from her time at the TV station, but breakfast meetings seemed to be the only time they could schedule to see each other. Lilly was a workaholic, a journalist who rarely slept and rose at five whether she needed to or not.

"Jen's never off, she can miss today."

"Jesus, I wish my mom had made me go to school."

"You turned out all right."

"You think?" A strand of black hair had fallen across Lilly's forehead. She tossed it back in an exaggerated comic mannerism. Karen didn't even break a smile. "What's wrong hon? You're white as a sheet."

"This." Karen held up the note, and Lilly saw thick black lines of penciled handwriting.

"So let me see."

Okay listen he knows where you are now I had to give it to him
and im so sorry so sorry but id be dead if I didnt and now hes
coming hes coming for you now and I cant stop him
If he knows I told you id be dead so dont show anyone this note
just dont trust me

Lilly whistled softly. "Jesus."

"I know."

"What do you think it means?"

"I think someone needs my help. This looks like a cry for help."

"You're kidding."

"Look at the words. And last time, there was a prayer."

"Last time? You've had letters like this before?"

"One. Yesterday." It was now Tuesday. Despite Karen's best efforts to forget that letter and enjoy her night with Jen, things had been a little strained. For one thing, it wasn't easy explaining her behavior when she'd practically swept the little one off her feet. Karen wasn't prone to crying, except possibly in anger, and Jen was an incisive child, particularly when it came to the emotions of others. But there was no way her daughter was getting the truth about the letter, not even an approximation. This was not the inherent ugliness of having to explain Mr. Snickers the goldfish being found floating in his tank one birthday morning, nor was it the unfortunate breaking up of their family; this was the kind of sickly madness that invited itself into a person's life only very rarely and often vanished just as rapidly and as randomly as it had appeared.

Besides, not all of Karen's business had to be Jen's, and this thing had definitely made itself Karen's business. It was her full name and address on the envelope.

"What was in the other letter?" said Lilly.

"Huh?"

"The other letter. The last one. What did it say?"

"It said '*save me.*'"

Lilly looked into the mirror that took up most of the wall and bared her small white teeth into it, wondering whether there was anyone back there watching them.

Not that there was anything to see at the moment. Karen was sitting at the desk on a folding chair the sergeant had helpfully brought in, clutching the disgusting letter like it had become a good thing; her justification for being at the station, wasting the time of busy people with bodies to identify and murderers to convict. Lilly observed Karen in the mirror, next to no make-up, looking just like Jen in that oversized sweater. She loved Karen, but the girl obviously still had a lot to learn. A cry for help? This was a letter from a nut, a stalker with a hard-on for freckles and tight stonewashed jeans. And Karen a psychotherapist as well, how perfect. She was even in the goddamn book.

Detective Gardner came in with a cardboard tray, three coffees. He looked at Lilly, raised an eyebrow. "To what do I owe the unmitigated pleasure?"

"John, good to see you."

"I like a woman with a good firm handshake."

"Me too. Wanna arrest me again?"

"Maybe later."

Karen watched the act between the two friends. Lilly Hersh and Detective John Gardner were unlikely acquaintances, she knew; the former activist was dwarfed by the big black policeman—he looked as though he was smuggling a cartoon barbell under his tweed jacket, so developed were the muscles across his shoulders. They'd met back when Lilly was officially an anarchist. He'd busted her for possession of weed during some march or other, and there'd been Christmas cards between them ever since.

"John Gardner, at your service," he said to Karen. "Sorry we're doing it in this space, the conference room is full." He had his hand out and she took it, a warm dry paw. Veteran of sensitive situations, he exerted no pressure; given the machine-like potential of his fingers, it was just as well.

"Karen Wiley."

Gardner sat down, the chair creaked. "Ladies, we only have a few minutes, the morning briefing." He thumbed towards the growing thunder of male voices in the corridor outside. "Lillian, you know better than to call my cellphone."

"Embarrassed by the ringtone? One of those kids of yours can probably change it for you."

"I have an extension here, reachable in office hours."

"I'm extremely grateful you'd talk to us like this, don't make me admit it. Karen has something worrying, a note. I didn't want her waiting hours or days for a dick to get out to her because no one got chopped up yet."

"Chopped up? Sit down, will you? You're making me nervous."

Lilly complied, and the big head and shoulders turned slowly to face Karen across the table; Gardner's head didn't move at the neck, he swiveled at the waist, like a child's action figure. "Someone threatening you, miss?"

"I don't know about that." A pause. They all looked at the note in her hands.

She slid the solitary piece of paper to Gardner face down, the move feeling dramatic. The cop put her at ease by flipping the note and reading it with his huge bald head in his hands like a child studying a difficult homework assignment.

"What do you think?" It was Lilly. Karen got the fleeting impression her friend was enjoying this.

"Well . . ." he was still reading. "Letters like this get taken seriously. Got the envelope?"

Karen had. He turned it around a couple of times.

"Postmark is Utah."

"Yeah."

"This is unusual," he said. "I'll ask the obvious. Anyone you know been kidnapped?"

"Not that I'm aware."

"Disappeared? Reported missing?"

"No."

"Can you be certain?"

"No . . ." but Karen had spent much of the previous night on the phone, calling people she cared about, pretending to herself that she was just saying hello. These conversations had cut into time that was supposed to have been with Jen, and that had led to a strange atmosphere. Hard to get to talk to everyone of course, and many—her parents for one—had probably been out to dinner, and . . .

"Panic over, I don't mean to spook you. If there was a real

kidnapping we'd move very quickly. This is likely a harassment case."

"This is a cry for help." Karen surprised herself with her own voice. Gardner looked at her again, sipped his coffee. The movement was passive, but the red-rimmed eyes were keen.

"Miss . . ."

"Karen."

"Karen, the single biggest mistake we can make in the face of this is to get dramatic. I'll be the last person to underestimate the gravity of a situation, but look at what we have here. This note is creative for a loony, enough to send shivers down my spine even, but that's what it is, creative—perhaps too much so. Kidnap notes are rare—despite what the movies tell you—and they demand a ransom of some kind. There's none of that here."

"Loony?"

Gardner glanced at Lilly. Lilly shrugged. "Karen's a therapist," she said.

"Like a doctor?"

"No," said Karen. "I'm a counselor, just recently qualified."

"And what do *you* think, Karen?"

"This is from a victim, not a kidnapper."

"You think so."

"Like you said, this is too creative."

"I did say that, and the minute anything is *too* anything, then I'd make it a policy to think twice."

"I don't follow."

"Say this is a victim, okay?" he glanced swiftly at Lilly, back to Karen. "The kidnapper would have let it out themselves, they don't usually allow the people they kidnap access to cry for help via the federal mail. Besides, there'd be a ransom. Also, shit, excuse my French, are you rich?"

"I . . ."

Lilly interrupted. "Not for this town."

Gardner didn't even look at her this time, kept his eyes on Karen.

"Reason two," he said. "Why, if there was a request for a ransom, would you cough up money you don't have for someone you don't even know?"

"Lieutenant . . ."

"Just Detective, although some say that's enough. I'm a simple guy, but I've seen some things. What do people want? Money, political influence, some perverse sexual kick, it does happen. I'm sorry, Karen. Any kidnapping I've personally experienced has to do with estranged parents. The Lindbergh baby is once a century at most, and even if your daddy was the President of the United States, no one is missing here." He sat back in his chair.

"Do you think Dave could have anything to do with this?" Lilly asked Karen.

"Impossible." The conviction in Karen's voice was powerful, and Lilly wondered if she'd say some more on the subject. When Karen didn't, Lilly said to Gardner to end the impasse, "Impossible, you heard."

"The husband?" said Gardner.

"Ex-husband," said Karen.

"Impossible yes, but I'd look into it anyway." He leant forward again, said: "It's a cliché, but go to the obvious first. You can waste your life trying to uncover motive."

Karen said nothing, but Lilly could see that she understood.

"You should also know," said Lilly, by way of closing the subject, "this is the second of two notes."

"It is?" Gardner became the efficient cop again. "Did you bring the first?"

"I tore it to pieces and it went this morning with the trash. I have a daughter." Karen suddenly felt tired, thought about Jen. Gardner nodded sympathetically, understood. Understood, it had seemed to Karen, everything—the ugly divorce, the obsessive, emotionally weak husband; the stumbling psychotherapy business, the sensitive daughter, now these ridiculous letters. She sipped her coffee to hide her embarrassment. It tasted warm, and pretty bad.

When she looked up again, Gardner's eyes were soft, big dark pools. There was no smile in his face, but there was warmth there. She thought about his big hands, felt tiny in the world.

"It's fine," she said, for no reason.

"Okay," said Gardner. "You're a therapist, you know that a lot of people out there need help. I called this harassment because that's what this is, being bothered in your home, but that doesn't mean that there isn't someone here who really needs your help."

There was a knock at the door, a mop of fair hair and a uniform. The cop roar from the corridor suddenly went stereo.

"Detective?"

"Sure, Len," said Gardner, and the younger cop closed the door. "Time's up, ladies, I hope it hasn't been in vain." His chair scraped the floor.

"You're not going to do anything?" said Lilly.

"If there's a crime here, it's not my jurisdiction. I'm not palming you off." He looked at Karen. "I'm glad you called me."

"That sounds *just* like what you're doing." Lilly sounded ready for a fight.

"Cool it, toots," his tone was playful. "Don't live up to that stereotype you're always fighting against."

"Toots? Don't you live up to *yours*, flatfoot." And then they laughed a little, Karen too.

"I'm glad you called me, Lilly, Karen, seriously. My advice? This is harassment of a sort, whatever the motive of the sender. Any more of these letters, keep them unopened in a safe place. Contact the Postal Inspection Service, let them open them, let them deal with it, I'll get you a number to call right now. I'd call them myself but they'll feel better if you get them direct, no inter-agency shit. If the letters become obscene it's a federal job anyway."

"Right." Karen nodded.

"I got no jurisdiction in Utah, or much with the postal service for that matter."

"So you *are* palming us off, John," Lilly said wryly.

"Yeah, how'd I do?"

Mary Huntingdon had scarcely glanced at the letter that Karen placed into her hands, and now she held it between thumb and forefinger like it was a soiled Kleenex waiting for a convenient trashcan. The way the envelope with its tainted contents continually signaled its presence against the older woman's elegant stockinged knee made Karen want to snatch it back from the therapist, stuff it once more into her purse. The only reason the thing wasn't in the garbage was because Detective Gardner had told her she should probably hold on to it for now, and she needed something to show the feds if they ever responded.

A silence had developed between the two women. It was not an uncomfortable one, nor an angry one, nor even a friendly approachable one: it was a neutral space made softer by the quiet hum of the tape recorder Mary sometimes used, a breathing room for feelings and ideas that occurs rarely outside of therapy. It was a freshly washed white canvas of a silence, a blank page that Karen knew she'd soon scribble all over with ugly, sprawling ink, maybe make a little mud pie in the middle. Then, hopefully, the entire mess could remain in this office to dissolve quietly into nothingness, a fate she would very much have liked for the hateful letter.

Behind Mary, through the window of the office, was a central courtyard. Karen could see leaves on an evergreen being moved by a light breeze. She'd never been lucky enough to know a relationship in which a silence like this could exist before, and she relished it now.

Karen had been in therapy for a long time, had had various therapists in her life. Sometimes she prepared, knowing there was a specific knot to untangle, wanting to make the most of the hour.

Other times she surprised herself with unexpected and artless revelations about herself that couldn't have come out of any kind of conscious preparation. In this instance, with the upset of the letters, she had decided to wing it, see what she came out with. She'd already surprised herself by thrusting the creased envelope into her therapist's hands before they'd even got into the office. It was a statement of intent on her part—we're going to *deal* with this, dammit.

Karen smiled a tight smile into Mary's almond-shaped eyes. Finally, a sufficiently appropriate period of time had elapsed. Even so, there was no wading straight in. So she asked, "Have *you* ever spoken to the FBI?"

Mary shook her head but remained silent, a supportive look lodged in her long, angular face. Karen knew she wouldn't get a real answer from her therapist even if Mary had responded, not that she'd been looking for one.

"You know, I don't think it is the *FBI*, FBI," said Karen. "There's a branch called the Postal Inspection Service. They're a separate office, San Francisco has one. They usually deal with, like, the anthrax threat and obscene materials. I mean, I knew it existed, had to exist, but . . . I've never had any reason to speak to anyone in that line of work."

"Of course."

"I'm saying speak, I haven't spoken to anyone but a switchboard. They're emailing me a form to fill in, assess the threat, I guess."

"You feel threatened?"

"I do." A pause. "Will you read the letter?"

"You're asking me to?"

"Please."

"You sure?"

"Read the note, Mary."

Mary breathed out through her nostrils, and her fingers extracted the paper from the roughly slit envelope. She made use of stylishly expensive half-moon eyeglasses on a chain that hung down into the folds of her white blouse.

Karen studied the therapist as she read the letter, hoping to spot a reaction, maybe some surprise, Mary was always so maddeningly contained. Karen noticed yet again how Mary's slim but sturdy six-foot frame should have made her at least slightly awkward, but she always managed to do everything with such exaggerated composure, like an old-fashioned movie star. Mary was only ten or twelve years older than Karen, but the difference seemed so much greater, and it wasn't just the height; she had a knack of approaching Karen's feelings as a surgeon would, those long alabaster fingers deftly but smoothly pulling apart wounds and exposing hidden pain before the patient had time to flinch.

This was why Karen had chosen to work with Mary Huntingdon; the therapist possessed a clinical coolness that contrasted so fittingly with her own inner heat.

"Well." Mary had stopped reading, observed Karen over her glasses.

"Yeah?"

"How does it make you feel?"

"How do you think it makes me feel?" said Karen. "It says someone's coming for me. I feel disturbed, I feel scared. Do I believe what's written here? No."

"Why?"

"Because it's preposterous. I'm being hunted? I'm not feeling threatened, I mean, I'm really not. The person writing this is seriously disturbed, the threat doesn't even come from them, it comes from an unspecified third party. The policeman I spoke to gave me a shopping list of reasons why this is abnormal from typical harassment cases, he didn't seem too perturbed."

"Have you considered the possibility that this is a prank?"

"I have, yes. I'm a new therapist, only six months ago I printed out new business cards, left them in offices, community notice boards, the church, stuck them up around the campus at Berkeley. I'm out there, sure it could be a prank. But what does it say at the bottom of the letter?"

"It says 'trust me.'"

"It does."

"And what does that mean to you?"

"I don't know."

"Do you trust this person when they ask you to?"

"I don't know. I can't trust anyone who approaches another person with a scare tactic like this. Maybe they're so emotionally scarred they're unable to identify the impact this would have had. After the first letter I lost my appetite, last night was pretty sleepless. But I trust the sentiment spilled all over the page: someone needs help."

"You showed *me* the note."

"It was faster than reading it out, faster than describing it. Besides, I wanted your opinion. Why?"

"Who else has seen this?"

"Not Jen, thank God. Lilly was there when it came with the mail this morning, the officer at the station, you, and then I'm going to send it along with the postal complaint form or whatever the thing is called, let the proper authorities look into it."

"The note says not to show anyone."

"Christ, not you as well."

"Your friend said that to you?"

"No, no. I just never thought not to show anyone. What, I'm supposed to play the game as dictated to me by this message? I mean 'not you as well,' because of the drama of the damn thing. I'll say again: the meaning behind this note is not what's written in it, it's what's in the head of the unfortunate sending it."

"Okay."

"Okay."

Mary's eyeglasses had returned to the folds of her white blouse.

She re-crossed her legs, tugged at her skirt. "Karen, you talked about the embarrassment of asking for help. In our profession, you and I recognize that there's no shame in asking for help, and we do our best to convince others that there's no shame in it. In telling you not to tell anyone, we can identify a rationality in this author, it seems important to them. Have you considered the possibility that this might be someone you know?"

"Go on," said Karen, interested.

"The author must be able to see that they're not going to be, what, rescued by you, going to the police based on information handed to you here. All right, devils advocate, law-enforcement might somehow trace the letter, I don't know. But really, why make such a big thing about trying to stop you telling anyone unless you have a mutual acquaintance somewhere?"

Karen looked down. "The detective said to talk to Dave."

Mary sat quiet, waited for more. Karen eventually said, "That's not a conversation I want to have."

"Why not?"

"Because. Just *because*. Because he's not going to take kindly to me accusing him of . . . *harassment*. I already kicked him out, I restrict his access to his daughter. And, yeah, I'm discounting myself with that statement, I know, he can see Jen whenever he wants, but a line has been drawn under that marriage. We got out easy, considering."

"Easy."

Karen was dismissive. "Yeah, I'm discounting myself. I moved myself on, moved us both on. It wasn't *easy*, change never is. What I mean is we never threw anything at each other. And our baby is, well, she's doing great."

"You don't believe Dave could be responsible for this letter?"

"Of course not. The imagination for one thing. For another, it sounds like he's getting his act together elsewhere. I don't care, it's not Dave."

"Not so long ago, we talked about when he used to turn up outside the house. And he'd cry on the phone to you?"

"A long time ago," Karen corrected. "Anyway, I *am* talking to him about this because it's the right thing to do, I left a message on his machine saying to get in touch. Whether he does or not is up to him. Frankly, it'd be nice to let the man get on with his life." Then she had to stop herself staring at the ceiling.

This isn't how the session was supposed to go, Karen thought, Mary leading me back into these grounds of fertile misery.

"Of course," said Karen, "I haven't told Jen."

"No?"

"It'd scare her stupid. She's a sensitive girl, despite appearances. This is my business, not hers."

A pause. Karen watched the leaves stir on the tree outside, more rapidly this time, as though someone unseen was shaking the branch.

"I sometimes wish that my parents had been more sparing with the truth," said Karen. "Children are not adults, and just because a kid can wield a vocabulary and do long division does not make them ready for something like this."

"Can you think of an example?"

"Of my parents with the truth?"

"Yeah."

"When Sammie died, I guess. They could have handled that better."

"The loss of a sister would have been traumatic for anyone, let alone a person as young as you were. Should they have behaved differently?"

"Yes. No. I don't know. When she drowned, I . . ." Karen stopped to articulate the feeling, and as she did so, she noticed Mary's fingers, the therapist had tented them. The artificiality of the gesture encroached upon their former intimacy. Karen shoveled the complex feelings back into the furnace, flashed her green eyes towards the shelves, taking in the random shit in front of the books on Eric Berne and Jung; North African memorabilia, mostly. Karen said quietly, "We've wasted enough breath on this subject as well."

"Have we?" said Mary.

Knock, knock, knock.

"What is it?"

"You tacklin' that homework, angel-pie?"

"Yeah, yeah."

"Your momma, she thinks that you sneaking on that computer most nights."

"Delilah," said Jennifer Wilcy to her closed bedroom door, adopting a tone of wearied patience, "I *have* to use the computer. Mrs. Reyes, she said no one writes with pens anymore, and that I'm the best typer in class."

"That's good, hon, then you keep that up. But your mom said 'bout the computer."

"If Mom cared so bad, she'd be here to stop me."

"Aw, don't you talk like that," the lyrical voice outside the door sounded genuinely moved. "Your momma, she's got a hard road right now."

"She means the *Internet*, Del. She means I shouldn't be *online*." Jen, who knew she was capable of confusing the kindly maid with the most limited of technospeak, felt a twinge of guilt.

Twice-a-week maid Delilah had been roped in as babysitter while Karen was out at her combined therapy/supervision. What she didn't know about PCs, iPods and programming VCRs to catch *Colombo* reruns belied an instinctive wisdom achieved through a lifetime's experience of hardships and kindnesses.

"And you not using the Internet, then?" Delilah stuck her head around the door.

"No way. I'm revising a test."

Delilah took in the small tidy room, the tightly closed curtains, the music posters on the walls that had only appeared in the last couple of years. Then she watched Jen at the computer screen; squinted at the way the little girl had her legs tucked in under her chair, her face prematurely aged by shadows cast from the synthetic light of the LCD.

"It don't do a little girl no good to sit in the dark," she said.

"Aw Del, stop fussing."

"Just saying. Come help me cook, you can bat out the chicken with the mallet."

"In a minute. I'm nearly finished here."

"Okay. But you stay off the web, Mommy said. Delilah's not such a dumb crow as you think."

"All right then." Jen tapped at the delete key a few times, busy.

"Cause I know if you on there, the phone line gets tied up. Karen says I can take a call from the islands here tonight, my great-nephew's getting wed."

"I said, all right then."

"Come help me cook, huh?" But this time it wasn't really a request. Delilah closed the door softly and padded back towards the kitchen, wondering how much of the garlic and parsley spiked butter she could cram into the French sticks she had picked up from the market.

What poor Delilah didn't know was that broadband had been installed for years now. She could talk to her distant relatives in Antigua, secure in the knowledge that her quarry was working hard, or listening to her music, while all the while, Jen was really doing . . . what?

Chatting with Andrea, her schoolfriend, online.

It was after seven-thirty, time to see if Andrea was there, she said she might be going out for dessert with her family.

She closed down the article on Native Americans she was working on, blipped on the bar at the base of the screen that read *RantJunkie21*. Her screensaver, an idyllic tropical island, flashed for a second and then the chatsite was up. The modem light blinked reassuringly.

Traffic on *RantJunkie21* was usually slow, just one of the millions of random Internet chatrooms with no particular subject. It had become almost exclusively gossip central for Jen and her friends, and she could see that the last message had been posted at 19:22. But it wasn't Andrea or Deb or Amber, the new girl who'd recently moved from Cleveland who they were still trying out; this was a message from someone called Chilllerkid, and from the screen she read:

CHILLLERKID RANTED//: Is any1 there?

Jen could see the new person had sent the exact same message at five to seven and twenty minutes before that. On a whim, she refreshed the page. The screen shifted and slid upwards with a small jerk. It was them again.

CHILLLERKID RANTED//: Is any1 there?

Jen blinked. From the kitchen, she could hear Delilah cooking, heavy-handed with a metal tray going into the stove. She leaned forward into the light, responded. A second later, her words appeared in the dialogue box:

SWEETTHANG RANTED//: whats up?

The reply was very rapid.

CHILLLERKID RANTED//: ☹
SWEETTHANG RANTED//: ?????
CHILLLERKID RANTED//: Grounded
SWEETTHANG RANTED//: me2, lifesux. WTF did YOU do?

CHILLLERKID RANTED//: dad caught me with boyfriend
SWEETTHANG RANTED//: that sux
CHILLLERKID RANTED//: tellme about it

Jen reached out her hand, picked up a plastic cup with a cartoon character on it that she'd obtained from a recent trip to the cinema, slurped a little grape juice. It tasted warm and stale.

SWEETTHANG RANTED//: do I know U?
CHILLLERKID RANTED//: do u know Port Huron Michigan? Truman High?

A high-schooler then. Jen became more interested, as she always was in her elders.

SWEETTHANG RANTED//: negative buddy
CHILLLERKID RANTED//: guess not then. Why r u grounded?

Jen fought for a suitable reason that wouldn't sound juvenile to her new friend.

SWEETTHANG RANTED//: smoking
CHILLLERKID RANTED//: oh man. Thissummer really blew.

A voice from the kitchen: "Jenny Lou, come lay the table!" Jen, lost in thought, didn't even turn her head toward it. Her fingers dusted over the keyboard:

SWEETTHANG RANTED//: grounded just for seeing a boy?
CHILLLERKID RANTED//: well it was more than that LOL.

Daddy caught me with his fat cock in my hand

Jen's eyes narrowed at the bad words. She wrote:

SWEETTHANG RANTED//: ewwww!
CHILLLERKID RANTED//: it was my first time. doU have a boyfriend?
SWEETTHANG RANTED//: of course
CHILLLERKID RANTED//: whats he look like?

Jen had a scanner and a collection of her mom's *Vanity Fair* magazines. She hopped over to the small pile in the corner, flipped through the most recent edition, found a photoset of a movie star looking vacuous and moody against the backdrop of an alley. Then she frowned at the picture. Thinking again, she wrote:

SWEETTHANG RANTED//: beautiful to me. Whats yours look like?
CHILLLERKID RANTED//: do you wanna see a picture? do you wanna see a picture?

"Child, you get out here right *now*, lay the table." The voice was closer. Del had come to the kitchen door, which meant she'd stopped whatever she was doing. Jen knew that this was the tone that had to be obeyed, that note of finality that suggested all favors had been used up. Jen would tease old Delilah, misbehave sometimes, plenty, but she knew when and where her boundaries lay. After all, she was a good kid.

Her knees were already out from under the desk when she wrote:

SWEETTHANG RANTED//: G2G. TTYL

Jen was officially hooked, some bizarro older girl from another part of the country talking so openly to her, an eleven-year-old, about boyfriends and being grounded, and God help us all, *cocks*.

Somewhere out in America, a person calling themselves Chilllerkid wrote:

count onit

And by the time it appeared on her screen, Jen was up, soft slippers moving quickly over the carpet, pulling the bedroom door open and closing it solidly behind her. As she did so, the warm hallway light swept over dead-eyed stuffed toys like the long slow blink of a lighthouse.

Five

Jon Peterson watched the desert sun rise over the sand-whipped aluminum trailer with the acute patience of a trapdoor spider.

He had a perverse love for these frontier towns, developed through his years as a silent, wide-eyed transient. In those mute hobo days, he had been an invisible but ever-present figure in the landscape of towns such as this, hidden from view in his costume of rags and a week-old growth of beard. Time had allowed him to absorb the quality of the light, the character of the people, entire community personalities. He was not so insane as to believe he could control the actions of so-called individuals through his meditations, any more than he could create sweet summer rain on the dry plateau just by clicking his fingers. But when something happened, be it a discovered dime in the crack of a sidewalk or an overcooked diner cheesesteak slapped down by an indifferent waitress, he could see that it was meant to be, it was an event appropriate for its place and time, and he would feel it in the cool chamber of his brain as fate or fortune or destiny.

The screen door banged once, and Jon heard the back end of a string of curses. A man was standing there, scowling under a tatty Lakers cap into the sun and wavy heat. After a second he was moving, lanky, loping strides that whirled yellow dust about his feet in miniature tornadoes.

Milton Trueblood looked small, thin and yogurt-pale, his long black hair curling greasily under his chin. He looked mean too, and very hungover; tiny slate-blue eyes screwed far back in his head, bony shoulders bent forward with the weight of sin. He was pulling on a clean, neatly ironed blue shirt, incongruous over the tank top and oil-stained jeans, and Jon felt a pang of sympathy for the wife that must have prepared it for their trip to the big city, a sympathy that was swept aside when he laid eyes on her.

Mandy Trueblood emerged carefully from the trailer, face shiny from excessive scrubbing, clothes wet from perspiration. She was grossly fat and ruined farther by small clusters of vicious acne. Had irascible Milt waited for her, she would have dwarfed him on the porch, could have so easily mobilized one of her muttony arms and swatted the evil-looking bully like a frog specimen thrown against a classroom wall.

The porch creaked as she descended the two steps to the dry earth, lumbering bulk rolling with careful deliberation. Everything about Mandy Trueblood screamed excess and escape, from the tree-trunk legs in pink pants to the white Palm Springs T-shirt, a faded cartoon flamingo stretched over wide, flat breasts. But it wasn't all bad. She had big dark eyes and took pretty good care of her brown hair, which flicked outward at the ends.

So at least one of the daughters had a fighting chance of being beautiful.

By now, Milton Trueblood was behind the wheel of the orange Camaro, waiting with ill-disguised impatience. He'd gunned the ignition to activate the AC and occupied himself with wringing a spark out of a cigarette lighter. Jon Peterson watched the wife reach the car, studied the velour-clad whale-meat ass with an expression he usually saved for unpalatable television. Milt reached across, popped the lock, then she was in, the suspension rocking, and he revved the engine to excess with a *Smokey and the Bandit* reflex as instinctive to him as a polecat peeing up a tree. Then the rear wheels spat dust towards the washing on the line, a right-turn onto the blacktop without hesitation or signal, the low-slung car disappearing behind other trailers, the sound of the exhaust hanging in the still air. It was a little ballet they played out here almost every month without fail; the big trip to the outlet malls in Vegas.

They were leaving Thursday this time, because Milt had taken the Thursday and Friday off work; in an hour or so, the younger kid would get herself to school and the older one would stay home and watch the baby. Jon knew all this because he'd wrung it out of close relative Don, back when the two of them were still friends.

All was quiet. A skinny cat emerged from beneath the trailer and stretched in the heat. It turned its head and Jon Peterson felt it stare at him in his shady vantage point, primitive and wise. He stared back at the animal through the tinted windshield of his car, not the jeep, an anonymous Chrysler with Idaho plates that he'd rented under a false name. As was his skill, he and his vehicle had dissolved into the background almost immediately after his arrival before dawn, the dusty, road-weary car just one of six or seven in the makeshift lot (but one of the few not up on bricks). Then Jon blinked one of his slow, camera-shutter blinks, and the cat yawned wide enough to swallow a small egg before ducking through a break in the chicken wire fence towards its unknown destination, a final weary straggler clearing the stage for the main event.

It was time.

Jon could have started up the car, scooted through the trees and over to the trailer with the gentlest pressure on the accelerator, but the engine would have alerted any small persons left in there of his presence, as quiet as this edge of the trailer park was. Much better to walk over, get some breaths of boiling desert air into your lungs, acclimatize so to speak, after all, that's what your tireless Bible salesman would have been breathing all day, yeah, give yourself that extra air of realism that consistently makes your work better than excellent, and frankly, better than could ever be necessary because there could only be three helpless children in there, one of them a baby for the love of God.

Out of the car, moving.

Jon Peterson at six feet four or so was no freakish giant, but he was made bigger by a conviction in his movement and the muscular shoulders thrust back in a posture of readiness. He was strolling, casual almost, in a gray suit and white shirt, a pair of glasses high on his nose completing the disguise. Being tall, he was used to having to duck under things, but he walked through the cascading branches of a dry weeping willow tree without so much as a blink, the fabric of the thousands of leaves caressing his face, his ears, running endless tapering fingers through his recently cropped hair.

As he emerged through the other side of this rustling waterfall, Jon Peterson's face seemed keener somehow, and he picked up his pace. There were no real sounds in his head as there were during the inspirational murder of the mechanic, just a steely clarity and intent of purpose that burned like a pilot light.

Exactly in the middle of the haphazard clearing in front of the trailer where Milt's Camaro had been parked, some twenty feet from the door and twenty feet from the cover of the willow tree, he stopped. Then he placed the slightly battered briefcase he had in his left hand down on the ground, bending at the knees as someone in a state of profound animal readiness might. The briefcase was part of his cover for when he knocked on the trailer door, saving the time and effort of having to break the thing down by pretending to sell something for long enough to get one of the children to detach the noise-making inconvenience of a chain.

Something told him that it wouldn't now be necessary.

From the dinginess of the trailer interior, two young girls were kneeling up on the rectangular arc of the rear seat, staring through the window at him. They were not moving, merely staring, and their faces were pale.

Strange white-trash children, to not be engrossed in Barney or Teletubbies or whatever the fuck on TV. Did they know I was coming?

The answer was simple, they couldn't possibly. Even if the news of Don's disappearance had got to Milt and Mandy then neither adult had suspected anything, else they wouldn't have run off to Vegas.

Jon had his hand up in greeting before he had time to think. Then he dropped it slowly, feeling the electricity build in the air. Something made him check his peripheral vision without unlocking his eyes from the girls in the window. This wasn't how it was supposed to go, his expectations had been defied, he'd been clocked somehow, and he was thrilled and elated. Could the girls smell his evil, like animals could? Normally, he placed no stock in that kind of thinking, but since killing and dissecting (sometimes the other way around) a dozen or so stray dogs in his teenage years, most canines would now have nothing to do with him, often as far as growling and raising hackles in his presence.

Carefully now, like a cat stalking a bird, one move, one step too many and . . . what? Empty trailers to the left, empty ruined cars and the road to the right. No one around. Then Peterson smiled, big, he couldn't help it, a wide face-splitter. He was the fox, here were the little white chickens in their coop, watching. Jesus, it was game over already, no "is your daddy home, little ladies" or "I'm from the water company."

The pale masks in the window whitened further. Then the taller of the two figures melted away into the gloom of the trailer, but the other one remained to stare, a wintery, prophetic statue.

The situation felt carefully balanced, and Jon suspected that any move he made would be met with a bigger move. So he made a big move himself. He strode forward.

He had halved the distance to the trailer when the ridged

aluminum door surged open, and banged hard enough against the siding to leave a dent. A figure shot out like a rabbit from a warren, bare feet barely touching the porch.

This then was Katy Trueblood, this was the girl he wanted, and fate hadn't cursed her with her momma's love of Twinkies and pizza, by God she *was* beautiful, and she was slim, and she could *move*. She didn't glance at Jon, but charged around the back of the trailer, legs pumping. Jon felt his heart leap and then he was running too, arms moving with flat-bladed hands, a fast sprint, shoes biting the dry earth. His stride was longer, his speed far greater, but the child could turn and move, turn and move, and soon they were around the back of the trailer, behind another one, her white feet a blur over dry weeds. She gained some distance in the narrow spaces between the empty trailers, but then they were in the open and he nearly caught her as they crossed the road. Perhaps he was having a good time, perhaps he let her get away that once, just for fun, but whatever it was, she was through the chain-mesh gate and into the wrecker's yard like a slippery thing. Jon didn't pause either and then they were blasting through rows of dead cars piled three or four high, Katy using every sharp corner she could to keep herself ahead.

It ended rapidly and without drama. One turn, one twist too many; in trying to save milliseconds she took a corner too close, her ribs and faded cream dress snagging on some crushed, protruding car part, a sharp metal beak, flaking brown paint. She fell hard and fast, the material of her clothes not cut by the collision, but her lower chest dug and bruised, and Katy's legs scraped along the ground with the momentum of her tumble, the dress pulled up over her waist and obscuring her face.

Jon saw her collide, and so when he rounded the corner himself, he was at walking pace. His face was soaked with sweat but he was pleased to discover that his breath was smooth.

He took in the fallen figure, the long slim legs, tiny fissures of blood beginning to well from the scrape along the ground, a nebulous red cloud gaining shape against her skin, the modest underwear of a child adorned with a tiny pattern of balloons.

Throughout the whole thing, neither man nor girl had made a sound.

A nod to the blue, blue sky and he was moving again, checking his fallen prey like a methodical hunter. Her pulse was even, her lungs hitching but steady, the grazes on her legs minor, the internal damage from the hefty collision with the side of the car uncertain but hardly likely to be life-threatening. She was unconscious for some reason, or faking it, but that was fine.

When he returned to the clearing in front of the trailer, he was struck by how surreal his briefcase looked there, carefully placed like a stage prop and surrounded by silence save for the whisperings of the tree. He was carrying Katy Trueblood in his arms as a rescuer might, head cradled by his big shoulder, grazed and bruised lower legs dangling from his hand at the back of her knee. There was a reason for this method of transportation beyond convenient portage; if someone should see him he wanted to be able to claim that she'd been hit by a car and he'd found her, and only the most suspicious of minds would fail to believe, at least in that moment of discovery. Of course, there had been no one; the western edge of the trailer park was an empty graveyard filled with corrugated aluminum tombs.

He didn't pause long enough to see if the other girl had remained in the window, but glanced at the trailer door, which remained darkly open, as he swept over to the trunk of his car. The girl moaned slightly at the spidery touch of the willow tree, tried to shift, but her fever was slight, and Jon could manipulate the trunk open with one hand, the girl only so much bunched fabric over his shoulder.

The trunk was a sheepskin-lined coffin that he had prepared earlier with knock-down furnishings from a closing Kmart, plenty wide but not quite long enough. He lowered Katy in with care. She moaned again, and turned her face into the softness of the rugs as though to find comfort from a bad dream. Jon reached gently in, lifted her eyelids, checked her pulse once more. There was a syringe in his breast pocket, wrapped in cotton and primed with a cloudy solution. He slipped it out, identified a strong violet vein in a soft, brown arm, and delivered a mindful dose. Then the syringe disappeared back into the pocket, magician-quick.

A cockerel crowed somewhere on the other side of the park, late for the time of day.

Jon closed up the trunk of the car, locked it. There was no issue with suffocation, nor with the possibility that Katy might manipulate the lock from the inside in the unlikely event that she should wake up; he had made tiny modifications to the car that the rental company wouldn't notice until far later, if at all.

This time, all business, he *did* duck under the branches of the willow tree.

The inside of Milt and Mandy's trailer was shrine-cool, the battered air-conditioner clinging to one of the meshed trailer windows like a tenacious parasite. Entering, it took Jon's eyes a moment to adjust to the gloom. Then he removed a pair of clean surgical gloves from his pocket and snapped them on.

He didn't see the other little girl at first, off to the side and so not silhouetted by the single large light source, the broad, bug-stained window that they had initially spotted him through. She was barefoot, maybe six or seven years old, and dressed in a smaller version of what looked like Katy's dress, and Jon recognized a hand-me-down. He wondered briefly why she hadn't run as her sister had, or screamed even, and again a shadow crossed his face as he speculated about how they had seemed to know he was coming in the first place. Then he realized that it didn't much matter.

Jon moved forward slowly, his gray-suited body big in the space. The girl, much younger than she appeared in the window, was looking down at a bassinet, where a baby slept. Jon followed her gaze down to a tiny, wrinkled face, clean fluffy blankets pulled up to a puckered pink chin.

"He was keening earlier, but I quieted him now." She spoke through quiet tears, her words carefully chosen, her voice barely hitching. Then the girl looked up, met his eyes.

Jon Peterson punched her in the face as though she were a grown man.

The hand that gripped Ella's arm was solid and sure, and she could feel his dry animal warmth through the billowing white material, papery synthetic through repeated wettings. Alone in the women's changing area, she'd balked at putting it on, both because it was shapeless and strange and because tiny black bugs had been disturbed when she lifted it off the peg, crawling out of the puffy cream-cake arms and dancing in confused whirls against the hardboard. After an uncharacteristic moment of doubt, she'd been reassured stepping out and seeing ward member Jeake over by the baptismal pool. The pharmacist had been transformed by his costume from a dour dispenser of medicine to an overstuffed Michelin Man; two of him could have fit into one garment, and she had to stifle a laugh, much to his disapproval. There had been a choice of costumes for her in the dressing room, but the overriding similarity seemed to be that these garments were washed rarely, if ever.

"Having been commissioned of Jesus Christ, I baptize you in the name of the Father, and of the Son, and of the Holy Ghost . . ." Jeake's voice was reedy, and it wavered with the drama. He had told her by way of conversation earlier that most baptismal pools have the short prayer written on a plaque, just in case the priesthood holder forgets. He'd done it hundreds of times before though, and his eyes barely flicked that way.

Then she was going down, by God she was, backwards, towards the corner of the pool as they'd been advised to do, in order to give her body the best chance to be fully submerged. There'd been a baptism last month in which some silly teenage girl had tied her hair in a long pigtail that fell halfway down her back, and it floated up when she'd been dunked, you had to go right under. Ella was more worried about her voluminous shirtsleeve not breaking the surface, not that it was the end of the world, they could just go again, but how many goes should you really need at this?

The hand at her back was like an iron bar, and she held her nose anyway, no fear of hitting the side, the pool was jacuzzi small but deeper than she'd thought, and Ella, while broad across the hips and shoulders, was hardly a tall woman anyway.

Total immersion emptied her head of all worries, from her self-conscious feeling about the baptism to her work to her personal life to everything and by God but *was* there a moment of revelation down there amongst the water and the bubbles of her own breath? A sense of rebirth? Anything?

If there was a feeling other than exhilaration and relief when she came up, then she hadn't yet the spiritual compassion to recognize it. However, those sensitive enough in the congregation could see a smile on her face that surely wasn't there when she went down.

She was changed and out before the priesthood holder, rejoining the service with wet hair hanging limp in thick clumps over her ears. She was only half-listening to another member bear his testimony to fill in time, when a thick voice whispered in her ear. Ella was miles away, turned her head to catch the repeated words. A young policeman bent down and spoke in an uneasy stage whisper that was loud enough for all to hear.

Ella gave an apologetic glance around the seats as she stood and followed Officer Kyle, her eyes cast down to Kyle's loaded belt as it rocked with his stride. They'd all just have to understand. Highly irregular, there'd need to be explanations, but what was left for her to do in there anyway? Welcomes, hymns, a closing prayer, photographs on the lawn. But it had all been for Ella and just one other candidate, *her* moment with God, dammit. She was upset, but the feelings were forcibly slammed into a drawer at the back of her mind. Ella would receive the gift of the Holy Ghost on Sunday.

Once they were outside, Kyle turned to her, blinked in the brightness. Beyond the full parking lot a semi rattled down the highway, maybe too fast. His plump face was apologetic, but he got a good dose of the hard-done-by in there too.

"Jeez, Chief, I'm sorry. I called your cell a half-hour ago."

"What's up?"

His notebook was ready. "Attempted homicide, likely homicide given condition of victim, a little girl. Milton Trueblood's place, Mountain Pastures Mobile Home Park."

"Damn, but I shouldn't know that name. You have him?"

"Yeah, but it ain't Trueblood, we don't think. Um, you coming?"

"Well, I'm not walking back in there now." She thumbed over her shoulder at the white chapel, impossibly brilliant in the afternoon sun. A couple of smartly dressed people had appeared in the shadow of the porch, watching. Ella pretended not to notice.

Kyle was looking down at his shoes, pretty well polished.

Ella McCullers swallowed. She said what she'd been telling herself since she stood up. "We were about done in there anyway."

There were more moments of awkwardness, but Officer Kyle took it like a man.

"You want a ride, Chief?" he said.

"Nah, I got my personal, I'll follow you. Try not to drive like your grandmother."

Ella parked on the road by the trailer park, and was pleased to see that the two patrol cars had done the same. Deputy Johnson was alongside her the minute she emerged from her Accord. As ever, his uniform seemed a little small on him.

"Go," she said, walking.

"Okay. A little after eight thirty a.m., a Gladys L. Walson passes by, sees blood seeping from under the trailer door, goes to investigate."

"Neighbor?"

"Uh-huh. Elderly lady."

"Brave woman. Who passes by here?"

"Huh?"

"What, we have the scrapyard to the left, four empty trailers to the right. The road, but there's no vision from there. What was she doing?"

"Ah, looking for her cat. Cat never came back this morning. Gladys started on her side of the park, worked her way around. Here kitty, she shakes a box of food."

"Did she find it, the cat?"

"I don't know. She's in her trailer, her daughter is with her."

"Then what happened?"

"She opens the door, goes into the Trueblood trailer. She don't know what happened after that, she thinks she fainted. Lot dust on her clothing would confirm that she took a fall straight after opening the door, never actually went in. Pretty hardcore in there, Chief."

"But she wakes up?"

"She wakes up, returns to her own place, makes the call at nine oh one, the dispatcher has it."

Ella stopped, her eyes scanning the dry earth of the makeshift clearing. Not too much hope there. The wind spat up a little grit, and they narrowed their eyes.

"First responder, you?"

"CAU, me and Walt, ten minutes later. Time now ten a.m. We'd have got you sooner, but you had your, you know, at *church* . . ."

"Good. Who else is here?"

"Me, Walt, Kyle just got you, Jerry Unwin. Ennis and the rookie are giving a drug talk at Liberty Community Center. They'll stay available for skunk patrol."

Johnson wasn't kidding. Canaan City Police had a staff of

fourteen, including eleven officers and three civil service employees, but the biggest headache of recent months had been unsecured pets and an unprecedented outbreak of skunks. Still, leadership of the force required a steady and clear mind; the natural beauty of the surrounding area was of increasing interest to tourists, and Canaan's population could double or even triple on any given day without notice.

"Okay," said Ella. "So show me."

They approached the makeshift porch, the trailer door half open. Officer Walter Maar was busy unraveling crime-scene tape. He nodded, pausing to allow his colleagues through, the Chief a curious presence in her Sunday best.

From the chill through her wet hair, Ella could feel that the AC had evidently been going strong for some while, but it wasn't improving the reek of baby mess, sweaty socks and rotting fast-food. From the porch, she could see a great tide of blood seeping into the threadbare carpet like a shadow cast by something impossible, a fly or two already beginning to march over the proteins. Deputy Johnson was hovering behind, partially blocking the light. She didn't say anything, and he moved once he noticed.

"It's all right," Ella said at last, turning back to the light. "I'm not gonna poke around in there until Matt gets here with the forensics from Red River, probably enough trampling done getting the little ones out. When did the ambulance leave?"

"Half-hour ago, Gladys called the medics before us."

"Good. Mercy Hospital?"

"Yeah."

"What did the paras say?"

"Not much, they never do. Holly, seven, that's the middle child, probable skull fracture, probable hemorrhage, she was bleeding from the head, that's the blood you're looking at."

"Lots of blood."

"Yeah, it doesn't look good, it doesn't look good at all. That she's alive is a miracle. They got her breathing again, but I'm sure time is short. Looks like she was beaten with a tire iron or something. When I walked in there I was sure she was dead. Killer probably thought so too."

"The medics were here first?"

"Only just. Did I not say that?"

"It's okay. How long between the attack and the discovery, you think?"

"Hard to tell. Can't be that long, she'd never have lived."

"Was she tampered with in any other way, or don't we know?"

"We don't know."

"What about the others?"

"A twelve-year-old, Katherine, and a baby. Katherine, Katy, the eldest child, is nowhere to be found, though we're searching the trailer park and the scrapyard. Could be her blood too because there's so much of it, 'cept we don't think so because . . ."

"Because there's none outside the trailer."

"Right."

"Always a possibility she might come back."

"Right."

Ella's heart was in her mouth. "The baby?"

"The baby is fine, seems unhurt. Thirsty I think, the parents left him all day."

"Where are the parents?"

"Mandy Trueblood and the baby went with the ambulance. Milton went bugshit when we tried to talk to him and started beating at the side of the trailer. Then he took a hefty swing at Walt. We put him in the backseat of our car while he cools off."

"Do you know where they were when all this happened?"

"Trip to Vegas, apparently, probably a two-or-three nighter, neither of them have anything to be back here for until Monday. Got as far as the I-70 turnoff, realized Mrs. Trueblood had left her purse. Our man doesn't get trusted with the money, it seems. They arrived about five or ten minutes after we did, early enough to see Holly wrapped in bandages and full of tubes."

"Mm." Ella was thinking, put a bitten thumbnail to her teeth. "They just leave their kids like this?"

Johnson shrugged, a cop shrug. "They probably do it all the time."

Ella looked at the trailer. She'd grown up in a trailer. Johnson was saying, "Do you know this clown? When we cuffed him he was screaming about your head on a plate."

"Yeah," said Ella. "Milton Trueblood, there've been domestics. We were formally introduced when Dewey brought him in a couple months ago, although I heard about him causing trouble in bars before now, hassling the female backpackers. He's a card-carrying asshole."

"Think he could've done this?"

"What'd the wife say?"

"Said Milton was with her in the car to Vegas, and I believe it, lest they're pulling some conspiracy on a grand scale. She was torn up at seeing her baby girl, and this town don't breed the best actors in the world."

"Yeah."

Ella walked over to the willow tree, ran her hand down a branch, careful not to strip the dry leaves. Johnson stayed with her, watched as his boss stared into the middle distance.

"There are disturbances down here all the time," he said, hoping he was narrating her thoughts. "Chief, they should close this park. You see how many empty lots there are? Haven for kids with drink and drugs and that scrap metal yard is always getting busted into. We called the owner, he couldn't care less, us poking around in there. Not even gonna come down, though we told him his padlock was smashed off. And no, I don't think it has anything to do with *this*, damn thing was rusting into the floor. Someone should probably talk to the city."

"Probably."

"What do you want to do?"

"Okay, yeah . . ." She moved out of her reverie, shifted gears. It was important to Ella that she appeared unswerving in front of her deputies; she may have been two years in her post, but as a woman she was always going to be the outsider on some level.

"Keep searching the area," she said. "I want that other little girl found, and there's always the possibility this creep is still around here someplace. Extend the crime scene beyond the trailer to encompass the yard here, and watch where you put your feet in case there's some tracks we haven't all scuffed out. Let County know there might be someone driving around covered in blood, though if they've got the standard-issue thinking hat on you'd assume they'd stop someone like that anyway. Yeah, find a picture of the missing kid, get it out as well. Don't dust, we'll wait for Matt."

"There's a scene in Blanding, it might be dusk."

"We'll wait anyway. For kiddie-killers, we need the biggest guns in our arsenal."

"What are you going to do?"

"I'm gonna have me a little word with Milton Trueblood."

Abrupt now, steeling herself. The dress shoes felt large and square-toed as she walked away, clumpy plastic heels already caked with dust. Ella was always incredibly comfortable in her uniform, and she missed it now. It gave meaning where she held no shape and maintained a questionable posture.

The patrol car containing Trueblood was on the opposite side of the road, the scrap-yard side, and Ella had barely glanced at it approaching the scene. Officer Jerry Unwin hadn't been there last time, and now he was standing by his vehicle with his thumbs in his belt loops, looking up and down the road with his mouth pursed in a silent whistle as if he had nothing better to do. He smiled at Ella as she approached. When she ignored him, Jerry opened the rear door to the smoke-filled car like a teenage boy condescending to his prom date, and then she was inside, the door closed behind her.

Ella could see fine through the cigarette smoke, but her eyes watered anyway; Jerry had cracked the front window a little, presumably so the suspect wouldn't die like a slack-tongued dog. Milt had handcuffs on, but his shirt was ripped up the front, perhaps as a result of the struggle to get him in the car. He had his feet against the grill separating the front from the back.

Milton turned to look at her, the butt balancing in his sneer.

"Oh-ho-ho. Backseat of a car together," he said. "Remind you of anything?"

"That was a long time ago, Milt. Another age."

"Yeah, but you remember, you remember, I was the highlight of your fuckin' schooldays."

"Milton . . ."

"I poked you like a kid pokin' holes in a loaf of bread with his finger. And you loved it. I opened your *hole* . . ."

Ella sat there, tried to dry swallow in a way that he wouldn't notice.

She couldn't deny what had happened, knew from the moment she heard his name that this was probably going to come up again. It was a small town, it was so many years ago, but she felt so much shame, not just drunkenly allowing a teenage Milton to bend her over the counter of her parents' kitchenette over the course of some forgotten seventies summer, but so much shame about *everything she had done in her life*, half of it, as a recovering alcoholic, that she could barely even remember. But Ella McCullers had turned it around and then some. She was a part of God's family now, and she had a job to do, Chief of Police. It was a real privilege for a woman to hold such a place in the community, let alone one with a past like hers, reasonably well concealed, but still.

Milton was looking her up and down like a drunk rodeo clown might size up a bull. Ella wondered if she would gain some strength from God now, or whether she'd just have to rely on the same old finite reserves.

"What's with the get-up?" he asked, finally. "We gettin' married? We goin' to *cheeurch*? I'm sorry angel-pie, I'm betrothed to another, a much younger woman, but if you want one last ride . . ."

"Slide your skinny ass any farther over, and I'll shoot you in the face."

Milt kept his distance. The conviction in her eyes forced him to smile; Milton's teeth were blackened, but none were missing. Then he casually stabbed out the cigarette on the backseat; a pointless gesture, there was barely an untarnished surface to ruin.

"The past is the past," she said, by way of reopening negotiation. "I found God, I could help you do the same."

A beat.

"Smoke?" His voice had become quiet.

"That shit'll kill you."

"I would've rolled the window down, but."

"Milt, for the love of God, your *kids*."

"Ah." He fired another, expelled a little more blue haze.

"I have to ask; did *you* do this?"

"Of course I fuckin' did. This is my getaway."

"I'm sorry, for what it's worth, but . . ."

"You ain't sorry 'bout fuck all. Cop whore, lock me in here."

"What, you wanna go to jail?"

"I didn't do nothin', did I kill my fuckin' kids? Fuck you."

"Milton, I need to know, there might be no time." She glanced him up and down, his eyes seemed to be losing focus. "Is there anywhere that little Katy goes? Someplace she might have run to?"

"Huh." He snorted out smoke.

"What's that?"

"Aw, I don't know, no one round here 'cept a few old spade trailers that I hope you're pullin' apart right now. Could've moved us all to The Heights if Mand's lousy brother would've pulled his thumb out his ass then cut me in on the business. What the fuck'd he know about cars before I came along, showed him?"

"Okay."

"Yeah, okay. Let me the fuck out." Even with the unpredictable nightmare chain-smoking next to her, Ella was able to manufacture a small mental oasis in which to think.

"I said *let me the fuck out*." He kicked at the grill.

"Nothing's your fault," she muttered. "Nothing's your responsibility." Ella was working the thumbnail, not really arguing, not even looking at him.

"LET ME . . . the FUCK OUT."

"I don't think so, Milton. Swinging at a cop, leaving your babies to some monster. You have priors, your time is borrowed."

"Not monster, *boogeyman*."

"Huh?"

"Boogeyman. Don't you even read?" He was animated again, leaning forward, educating the cop bitch. "I'm a father, my kids never play up. Mandy's idea, though. Babysitter costs money, can't trust family, so we started telling stories." Milt made a face. "There's a boogeyman out in the trailer park, see? Eats little girls, strips their flesh, red and bloody."

"You say that to your children?"

He sniffed. "When we gotta go away someplace. Started with bedtimes, proof effective. I gotta vivid imagination, just another thing to be proud of." He swung his hips up, bucked a little air. "*I* was left by my pa from age of eight anyway, my eldest one's practically grown by comparisons. A little boogeyman story caps it off when we're on an overnighter. Mand leaves milk and cookies, and the rugrats get too shit-scared to step off of the front porch."

"Vivid imagination, huh? How long were you gonna be away?"

"Don't take that tone with me, I love those kids, everyone knows. They're never in trouble at school, Katy, she spells things, big words like you never heard. Holly . . ." tears were welling now. "Holly's gonna be the best damn painter you ever seen, those pictures she brings home."

"Boogeyman, Milton. Did you tell them the story *this* time?"

Behind her, there was a hard knock at the window, someone with a phone, gesturing to Ella. It broke the spell of civility in him.

"LET ME . . . GO!" This time Milt swiped hard at the grill, like a frantic animal, but he made no attempt to escape when Unwin opened the door to let her out. Instead, he just kept rattling. "LET ME . . ."

Ella was into the sunlight again, slammed the door on the din. The confrontation with Milt had blasted away much of the nerve she had brought to the scene.

"What've you got?"

"Ennis just called," said Unwin. "Finished his whatever downtown, thinks there's something you should know."

"Yeah?"

"Ever heard of a guy named Don Keynes?"

"No."

"He's disappeared, his wife called us up yesterday morning. Ennis took it, wouldn't be worth mentioning probably, 'cept Keynes is the elder brother of Mandy Trueblood."

"Oh?"

"Think the two incidents might be related somehow?"

Ella sighed, big. "Okay. Get Walt over here, tell him I said to drive this unit to Mercy. Get the cuffs off Trueblood and let him see his kids if he wants, might be the last time. But make sure he knows we're gonna need to talk some more."

"Yes Ma'am."

"Now gimme the phone."

Ella walked away towards the boundary of the scrap yard, presumably, Unwin thought, so she could make the call in private. Instead, she bent over sideways and spread her feet apart in such a way as to drum-tighten her floral skirt between her ankles. Before he could blink, Ella was banging the flat of her hand against the side of her head, violently almost. It was a mannish performance, and bizarre to look at in these waterless badlands on the edge of civilization, but the gesture was recognizable enough; following the baptism there had been water trapped in Ella McCullers' ears, it was uncomfortable, and she needed to get it out.

Over the course of the following day, the shadows moved across the floor of the hospital room with the slow smooth swing of many different Daliesque clock hands, sometimes growing shorter, sometimes growing longer to the point when they would probe the dark wells beneath the furniture and slide out into the corridor.

Holly Trueblood was resting on the precipice of an eternal sleep. Doctors and surgeons and specialists had done what they could, and now the girl was left in the arms of an irregularly piled bank of machines that appeared to do little more than blink and pulse, but were somehow charged with the biblical power to breathe life into tiny, battered bodies. No one gave Holly much of a chance, that she was certain to die was a mantra repeated in minds from the moment of her discovery by the somewhat green ambulancemen, to the cops who had seen her, to the tired-eyed Johns Hopkins-educated genius who had found a way to repair the gaping flesh-and-bone window that allowed access to the gray matter of her brain. Her parents, relocated temporarily to a nearby motel, held bitter conversations at a volume that caused guests in nearby rooms to complain to the management. They screamed words like *vegetable* at each other and cuddled and wept while their baby boy slept next to them in a motel cot.

But Holly did not die on that day. Neither did she die on the next.

On the third day, her heart stopped twice. It was enticed to beat once more by a quick-thinking Pakistani nurse who had made herself Holly's best friend.

On the fourth day, Milton Trueblood, who had not yet received the court order keeping him away from his children, was an almost constant presence by the side of his second child. This was because he had had a dream the night before, a foggy vision that made his balls creep up into his belly and sent him puking Jack and coke into the john like greasy black paint. Uncharacteristically, it was only the first time he'd been drunk since the events of the past few days, and the first day since Canaan Chief of Police and one-time fuckbuddy Ella McCullers had signed the release of the trailer back to its owner. Unfortunately for the police investigation, the content of the dream was forgotten rapidly in the light of the perceived waste of premium liquor, a half-full bottle given to him as consolation prize for his shitty luck by a sympathetic barman.

In the dream, he had been out in the Canyonlands, backlit by a sickly, bloated rind of a moon. He was walking with Don, his brother-in-law who had also disappeared in the real world. Both of them carried picks and shovels. Milt was ready to open his mouth and bitch, the digging equipment was heavy, he wanted to complain about the tiring pain of this pointless journey, to ask why won't you pull your fucking finger out and start that recovery business you're always yapping about and cut me the fuck in and stop working for the goddamn Dago.

But Don had stopped walking and was pointing at a canyon they were standing dangerously close to the edge of, and the canyon was full of blood. It shone black in the moonlight, and it lapped at the rocky sides like the ebb of the sea, but it most certainly *was* blood, it left a smudgy tide mark and it stank of copper and of hot feverish disease.

The canyon was a giant vein in a body that was dead, or dying.

Milt turned quizzically towards Don, who somehow should know what this vision meant, and Don was opening his mouth to explain it to him, but Don's mouth somehow kept opening, stretching out into an impossible cartoon scream.

Don made no noise. Instead what came out of his mouth was caked earth and dirt, and it wouldn't stop, just kept on coming out of his mouth, running down the sides of his chin, so much worm-ridden grave filth like someone had opened a sluice gate in him. In the dream, Don was dead, consumed, and he rotted in fleshy strips, quickly, like speeded-up film.

Then the colors changed, as a picture on an old television set is wont to do when the tube becomes swollen. The sky went green. The earth went purple. The blood in the canyon remained black. Milton had no one left to whine at, so he picked up the shovel and began to dig, meaning to plant his companion in the psychedelic earth.

The first contact between metal and ground produced a small geyser of blood. Milton blinked at it, then bent down and stuck his finger in the hole, like a storybook character attempting to stem the first destructive signs of a dam about to burst. As he did so, another geyser sprung up, and another, and another. Knowing no better, Milton put his mouth over the largest of the holes and drank deeply, the stinking liquid hotter than his throat, and then he wasn't drinking blood anymore he was kissing someone's boiling, churning mouth, and by God he needed this person in some inhuman organic way, more than love, more than passion, like his whole body would explode if he didn't get a good squirmy fuck right then and there.

Then, cutting across his conscience, a smooth, cultured, recognizable male voice.

"Wake up," the voice said. "Wake up, you ignorant infant of a man, so you can witness the destruction I will cause."

Milton did as he was told, and found himself awake, maybe more awake than he'd ever been in his life. He was panting and stiff-dicked, staring mindlessly at the roof of his trailer, the waxing Utah moon projecting quivery net-curtain patterns onto the wall.

It was then that the gassy vomit began to rise in his chest.

The dream had been so vivid that Milton remained by Holly's hospital bed throughout the fifth day as well, only leaving her side to smoke out where the ambulances parked.

It finally happened on the morning of the sixth day. The Daliesque shadow clocks were pointing fivewards.

Milton would have been with her, but he was on the payphone at the bottom of the stairwell, hearing how if he wasn't back operating the picker machine that afternoon then he could punch out for good. Mandy was there though, occupying a wide plastic chair in the corner, working at needlepoint as her momma had; it was a hobby she never cared for, but it was giving her a familial comfort now. Her fat face was pale and moist; news was constantly filtering through about the continuing police investigation, and there was some very disturbing news to digest.

"Khaaa . . ." said the small body in the bed. It was an expulsion of breath, little more than a whisper, but it sounded loud in the room. Mandy dropped the needlepoint, struggled out of the chair, crossed the floor. Her movement alerted the nice nurse, who was passing in the corridor.

Together, they looked down at Holly. She had been motionless for six days.

"Khaaa . . ." she said.

Her eyes were open.

"Is she . . . *dead*?"

The nice nurse barely had to glance at the life-giving machines. She shook her head. "She's alive, Mandy. Your baby girl is alive."

"Where are you going?"

"To get Doctor Warwick. Talk to the child, squeeze her hand."

Mandy did so, breathing heavily. Holly tried to speak again and couldn't, but she *was* alive. Unfortunately, the poor glassy eyes that had witnessed the unimaginable things on the borders of the other side could not yet so much as register movement back in our world.

And so it was that little Holly lived through that day as well, and the day after, and for many weeks and months and years to come, although it would take an awfully long while before she could go to a normal school and play sports or have a boyfriend, but maybe she never really wanted those things much anyway.

There were tears of joy, and everyone, especially the reformed Milton, was grateful to a merciful God and the surgeons and machines through which He had performed His miracle. Given the situation however, it seemed fairly safe to say that on this occasion, God's love had manifested with a real sting in its tail, although that might simply be what therapist Karen Wiley in San Francisco would call *contaminated thinking*.

Either way, Holly Trueblood, the one person at that point capable of positively identifying Jon Peterson, would not say another word for eight long months.

Six

Karen Wiley is sleeping.

There may be no glassy-eyed toys or shiny boy-posters to stand sentry for her, but when the diffused light catches the curves and hollows of Karen's face, she could be more than simply mistaken for her beautiful daughter, she could actually *be* her. When asleep, Karen's personality, her ironic inquiry, her suspicion, her humor, and even the disquieting past that is the fuel in the furnace of her soul are all quieted, doused, relegated to surfacing in the night-shrugs and moans familiar to anyone who has watched their partner sleep for a length of time. She was also capable of a cute frown that no wakeful boyfriend has ever been perceptive enough to recognize as probably her most adorable feature; combine this with the unconscious pout she makes when dreaming about only just missing one of the city's unpredictable buses, and you have a sulky sleeping vision, a naked innocent wrapped in Egyptian cotton.

Karen leaves her bedroom door open with some reluctance. As a girl, Karen always relished the enclosed safety of four walls she could call her own, and has spent her life building cardboard castles ever since. As a teenager it felt satisfyingly indulgent to be able to seal off the world in this way, but because she has never quite managed to achieve psychological security, it proved to be necessary in adult life also.

That had to change with the birth of her child.

Coincidentally, Jennifer has recently started closing her own bedroom door while she sleeps.

It is darker out in the corridor, and there is no natural light until the space opens up into the living room and kitchen. Jen's room is down a short passage, her bathroom next to it. The bay fog has lifted from the small rectangular window like a curtain from a stage; a slice of moon shining through the pane next to her door. Beneath the window is an aspidistra, an unexpectedly grown-up gift from Dave, given shortly before he was made to leave. Jen tends it with adult jealousy.

Through this door the daughter is sleeping also, and her thoughts are less troubled than those of her mom. Jennifer Wiley is popular at school, doing well. And she has somehow made a fascinating new friend through the Internet, a high-school girl whom she isn't quite ready to share with her school friends. In fact, Jen was mightily pleased when the girl going by the username of Chilllerkid suggested that they find a site uniquely for themselves, a sort of private place to exchange secrets. Chilllerkid's communiqués push strange quivery buttons in Jen, though sometimes the more intimate disclosures repulse her.

If Karen looks a lot like her daughter when relaxed in sleep, then Jennifer looks like an angel that somehow got left behind. Jen always goes to sleep on her back, even though it sometimes colors her dreams. The curtains are pulled tightly closed and the room is scented, womb-warm and pitch black.

There is one more person in this family, a person never seen and rarely mentioned.

In the gloomy hallway outside Karen's room, not so very far from the front door, hangs a photograph. This is a picture—one of many—that has been locked in the dark until very recently.

Sammie, Karen's sister.

Karen is only just beginning to unpick the nightmare of her sister's death, and Mary Huntingdon has an uncanny knack of asking the hardest questions in a sensitive way. Karen hopes that this is the beginning of a real, *adult* healing.

Jen knows a bit about Sammie, and so only asked about the unfamiliar new picture once, to confirm who the sunny girl in the straw hat was. After that, Karen's daughter didn't seem too interested in the ghostly child-aunt who looked just like her, somehow having the sixth sense to know that certain recondite changes were being made—*had* to be made—following the recent bad times and the divorce. As for Karen herself, she was changing, growing, she hoped. Progression, emotional maturity, closure. Reassuring words for a credulous, therapy-conscious public.

The hallway photograph is not the most striking portrait of Sammie that she could have had framed; the Polaroid seems tiny and insignificant next to a large but tasteful Monet print that serves to remind Karen of the serenity of Brittany's Belle-Île every time she enters her home. By contrast, the frame around Sammie's small picture is big and chunky; in protruding slightly from the wall it draws the viewer towards the image like a child's viewfinder into the past. There are mountains in the background of the picture, a lake as well, big and glassy under boundless skies. In the foreground Sammie is holding something that might be a bunch of hand-picked flowers. The features of the girl-figure are unclear, there are only the contours of a formless sundress.

Shadows here contrive to obscure the face.

The corridor outside Karen's apartment is cold, gloomy, all burnished wood and dark green paint, like the walls of an old-fashioned gentlemen's club, only cracked and peeling in parts. As the only tenant in this building Karen could complain about the slight deterioration of the public spaces, but she feels a little sorry for her well-meaning and doddery old landlords, the Durants. The scruffy door across the hall leads to their apartment; they've owned the building for ten years, although Karen has the larger accommodation. Mr. and Mrs. Durant don't need so much space in their old age and there is more money this way. Besides, the side of the building that they occupy has better views.

A slight breeze moves the net curtain covering the huge third-floor window at the end of the corridor. It looks on to the fire-escape, but would be utterly impractical to get in from outside even if an intruder could reach the rusting ladder that rattles down to allow escape; they'd need some kind of super-strength to stop it clattering with enough ruckus to wake the dead.

Beyond the curtain is a half-view of the deserted, neon-lit street. Wet road reaches for the crest of a small hill. Dark, unobtrusive cars line the sidewalk, their engines long cool. Residents mostly, from surrounding buildings. One of these vehicles is a new Jeep Wrangler; muddy, but well maintained.

Left of the window, away from the view of the silent street, the corridor opens up. Minutely concave stairs covered in thick green lino spiral down around a wrought-iron art-deco elevator shaft. The elevator itself has been stuck in the basement since the quake of '89.

On the ground floor, sizeable blocks of moonlight fail to chase away shadows as impassive and stone-ground as the structure itself. Like oil down a plughole, most of the blackness here pulls towards the basement stairs, a merciless yaw to the great tomb beneath, all hot clanking pipes and giant cobwebs spun by unseen, red-eyed predators.

No need to go down there. Not yet.

There is nothing else of note in the entrance hallway, only a featureless locked door to the third apartment, currently vacant and not likely to be occupied in the near future. This is almost unheard of in this part of town, and somewhat irresponsible in a city with so many homeless, but Mr. and Mrs. Durant, with their questionable health, would rather keep it this way for the time being. Shame really; Mr. Durant was a capable handyman with big retirement dreams for the place.

Karen Wiley and her daughter were solitary tenants in this brownstone mansion, and the size is gratuitous for their needs; echoing, empty. Of course, Mr. and Mrs. Durant would have preferred that ex-husband Dave had not been pushed out, and continue to privately assume that he left her for another woman. Good people in the traditional sense of the word, their sympathy can be infuriating.

The front door is more modern than the rest of the building by some thirty years, and is loaded with wire-reinforced glass and two deadbolt locks. It certainly could be penetrated with a pick and a tension wrench, the internal pins popping up one by one so they rest on the shear line as the cam is twisted, but anyone attempting it would have to be pretty good, probably a locksmith to have spent so much time practicing. They'd also have to give this enterprise the kind of intense concentration that would be better employed watching for patrol cars and insomniac neighbors with twitchy telephone fingers. No, the security on this front door is fallible, but is at least sufficient to satisfy the most exacting of insurance companies. Ordinary criminals are far, far more inclined to hurl bricks and smash glass, to seek out or (more likely) happen upon obvious opportunities to commit their despicable little crimes; the vacationing family, the badly secured bicycle, the phone on the car seat, the frail and the elderly.

The security expert who installed this particular door had suggested to Mrs. Durant that her building is an unlikely first target based on the safety features and location, as overlooked as it is by other buildings, although he did mention at the time that the possibility of attempted forced entry could never be ruled out. There are plenty of irrational, stupid, drug-addled criminals to defy the statistics, he said.

And one or two *different* kinds of criminals to defy statistical evidence also.

Outside, the porch light has been smashed. This afternoon, someone paid a fifteen-year-old brat twenty bucks to throw stones at it. The bulb was put out in one giggly underarm shot, the purchaser of this antisocial activity already streets away, and the only witness, a shopping-laden passer-by, worked hard to ignore it.

More can be seen than just the pool of neon in the foreground and the haloed orbs of streetlamps across the road.

Nothing. Still deserted.

Of course, this is how it should be for the hour; the guts of a light mist exposed by neon, the otherworldly night howl of an occasional siren neighborhoods away, distanced by geography and class. No sudden flash of lightning here, no Frankenstein's monster.

but back in the basement

Jen is terrified of the darkness in the spaces under the building. Even at her age, she fears going down to the basement alone. Shame for Jen that this is where the washer/dryer is kept, and that today Karen made Jen launder her own sports kit after the September rain made the mud cling. Shame for them both that Jen, hurrying in her irrational child-fear, never noticed that the surround in one of the narrow rectangular skylights was dangerously loose and rotting out of the frame

he was going to pick the lock, that's why he smashed the light, now there is no need

Away from the door, down the stairs, down, down, down.

the basement

A small maze of rooms, veiled in darkness.

Shapes. Household debris in storage, transformed into crude, lurking hunchbacks. A stench of steam. Beneath this floor, where no one ever goes, blind things scurry.

A gray rectangle towards the ceiling of the largest basement room indicates that natural light can, sometimes, penetrate this space. The window is dilapidated, the frame unimproved since shortly after foundations were laid.

The frame falls inwards, seemingly of its own accord. Despite the considerable incongruity of this action in the quiet building, the disturbance to the status quo seems natural somehow, inevitable, like a leaf falling from a tree; an impression enhanced by the soft, silent landing of the pane on to a pile of freshly laundered towels, which absorb the shock like a big spring. The imperceptible nocturnal noises become closer, as though the night itself is seeping in.

Nothing else moves for quite a while.

The arm that eventually reaches through the window is like a shadow with a mind, and it is followed, further down the gray rectangle, by a black-clad leg. The way the joints bend independently of one another, and the fact that the torso is not yet visible, give the impression that it is not the figure of a man entering, but a fat black mutant spider, folding itself deliberately through a space in that way they sometimes do, cautious but predatory with hateful arachnid concentration. Finally, a thick body follows the two limbs, then another leg, the motion fluid as it swings in. Then the shadow figure is inside, clinging to the window frame with black gloved hands. It drops with a soft thud, careful to avoid the displaced glass.

Once more, all is silent, nothing moves.

The figure raises itself to full height, a shade amongst shades.

Jon Peterson is standing in Karen Wiley's basement, and the demons have him.

Heat, light, color, euphoria.

The brightness in his head is so strong, he is almost afraid to open his eyes for fear of melting any object he looks at. Peterson has taken pills in his ever more extreme quest to intensify his life, experimented with substances that have sent him vomiting into gutters and guzzling water until the veins in his forehead grew so fat they threatened to jump out of his skin. He has injected things and watched faces of gas station attendants morph into animals from beyond the pit. He has seen dead people try to pull themselves out from under the sidewalk and he's smoked bad shit that made him goofy and scared and sent him twittering to bed like an infant bird.

Nothing compares to this.

He's early, you see. He shouldn't be here. Not yet. This is a preview.

And as a result, Jon Peterson has no idea what is going to happen here tonight.

Preparation has been done however, though this time there are no shallow graves arranged anywhere. He always does his homework while the demons are off chasing rabbits across the back country of his mind. He's seen the building schematic, for example, and he knows from reconnaissance exactly which locks are on which exterior doors and how to pick them, painstaking hours of stone-cold sober practice in his basement, dusty drawers filled with different greasy lock models that feel cold when you pick them up then smell of hot copper after long periods in your hands. He's driven past the building a dozen times since he selected Karen because he knows he needs to see it on a practical level before the demons can do their stuff, has to be aware of the size, the shape, the amount of human traffic at different times of day, but never on those occasions with the intention of going in.

From here on though, every experience is unique, different, new. He can read a blueprint, but it can't prepare him for the actual sensation of sharing Karen's space with her, the feel of the raised ridges on the wallpaper through his skin-thin plastic gloves as he walks past, the cool wood smell in the stairwell as he climbs up, the way the moonlight catches things just so, particularly the way the brilliance bounces off the sword he has secured in a home-made scabbard across his back, so scrupulously sharpened you could bleed out if it so much as dusted over those fleshy tubes in your wrist. He might as well be the first visitor on another planet, each new sensation magnified and expanded in the liquid visions of a brain that has embraced madness on its own terms.

Peterson glances around the entrance hall, glances towards the door and the porch light he had put out as he strides slowly up from the darkness. His eyes fall upon a tidy bundle of letters sticking out of the apartment mailbox assigned to the Wiley family, unlocked and open; such concerns about privacy are lessened in a building with only one tenant. It remains uncollected from that morning, Karen having had her hands full with groceries, and it being Delilah's day off.

It would be exciting to peek, to steal, to learn, so he helps himself to a souvenir, a little treat for later—two letters to Karen and something for Jen. Then he turns his senses inwards, back towards the sensation; the greatest prize is upstairs.

As he emerged from the darkness, so he ascends into it.

upstairs

It is on the landing that he perhaps looks most terrifying, here in this space where Jen has skipped and jumped and Karen, weary from work, had anticipated the safety of her home. Jon Peterson is conscious of his proximity to them, never has he been closer, his quarry perhaps only one thickness of wall away. If either he or Karen were to make a sound now, then he might hear her or she him, and the demons respond to this realization by jumping in delight, flooding his mind and heart with images of beautiful destruction, of a willowy white torso sliced from asshole to mouth, and of the multicolored rainbows that emerge from within. More than anything else, he decides now, he wants to damage Karen so long and so hard that her spirit will give up before her body does, will escape with a death sigh so slow and weary that he can catch it in his mind for eternity.

He pauses midway down the corridor, outside the Durants' door. He knows there is life within there also, he has watched the old woman scurrying in and out of the building on one errand or other. He knows the man is sick, his mind rotting in its fleshy prison, and he has no real interest in hastening their end. But he is also aware that they might have a part to play if he enters Karen's apartment and the screaming starts. If Mrs. Durant interferes, he won't hesitate to drag her in front of her ailing husband and turn her inside out.

Farther down the corridor, a floorboard creaks under the ball of his foot. He freezes, feels the sensation with his whole body, at the base of his throat, over the skin of his scrotum. Did Karen hear that? Is she sleeping? If so, has the unfamiliar noise made her roll over, has it changed the course of her dreams? She must be disquieted generally because of the letters, her sixth sense must be in overdrive. Gingerly, tenderly, he raises his foot back up. The floor creaks again. No, it was far too quiet for anyone to have heard.

He smiles fit to bust his ghastly face.

Karen Wiley's door. He traces over it with his hands, wishing he could remove the gloves, feel the smooth wood under his palms. His nostrils flare, fill with a subtle smell of pine. It is the scent of the polish that she must use on the door, which the demons are showing him in kaleidoscope tinctures of forest green.

This lock is also familiar, and he reaches into the jacket of his tracksuit for his small pick and wrench. Because it suits them to do so, the demons flood the corridor with a thick, invisible fluid while he works on the lock patiently. This sensation of being in an underwater world is to help him, to force him to go slow, to regulate his breathing, to negate his worry about being heard, to make his muscles feel weightless as they complete their sensitive task.

It takes five minutes.

Then he stands, reaches over his shoulder, slides the sword from its sheath. He fills his left hand with Karen's door handle, feels it channel golden electricity up into his brain.

The door sticks a little, leading to a tense moment, but eventually he can allow it to swing open on a gentle push. Dangerous not to be holding it steady, but he likes the way it looks as though someone is inviting him in.

Her house, her daughter, her scent, her body, soft and willing, being opened like a flower.

He closes his eyes, the corner of his mouth ticking unconsciously. The sword nearly slips from his hand.

symphony

He takes one step backwards, opens his eyes again. It is all becoming too much.

The door to Karen's apartment might as well be the portal to another world. He can see the corridor to the kitchen, the plant that belongs to the daughter beneath the window at the end, the jumble of items nearest to him in the hallway, the telephone, the painting he cannot quite make out, a photograph. There are so many secrets in there, so much to explore, and it cannot end tonight, it cannot be over now, there are things he has planned for Karen that might allow him to feel these euphoric feelings forever.

but

Not if you do it right now, not if you kill her before the plan comes to completion, you'll slaughter the golden goose, you fucking idiot, all your work in vain . . .

And somewhere, deep in his soul, like the plangent sounding of a bell, he feels something else, something he almost never feels.

fear

Fear, Peterson feels fear.

He closes his eyes once more, trying to control this sensory overload, trying to manage the potential that he knows exists within him. The demons whirl and sing in hellish, jubilant pandemonium, effervescence radiating from his every pore.

Stop

now

When Jon Peterson opens his eyes again, he is alone.

He is alone in a cold, dark corridor.

He swallows once, hard.

Then he sheaths the sword, carefully, so as not to cut himself, a precaution that would never have occurred to him in the last few minutes. Now he reaches forward, closes Karen Wiley's front door. He takes extreme care, not daring to look in there anymore.

Jon smiles wryly as he does this, understanding. He is the child who wants to open his Christmas presents early. Understandable but inexcusable.

There are better things yet to come. Be patient, Jon Peterson. Be patient and be rewarded by your patience.

He reaches into his tracksuit jacket, retrieves the next letter. Two and a half weeks have passed since Peterson kidnapped Katy Trueblood, and in his eagerness he is now delivering the sixth. But this one is special, not just because it is the first he has delivered by hand; this is the one that will kick the game to a higher level. There is a pen in his hand, but his arm shakes with uncontrollable tension as he tries to write on the envelope. Perhaps fearing overload, the demons are chasing the hard-won, hard-found name of his victim from the conduits of his mind. He settles for only marking Karen's address; not ideal, but at least the words come quickly to him.

After the briefest of pauses he slides it under the front door with a haste that borders on the panicky, far enough so he couldn't retrieve it if he wanted to without opening the door again, this action now an unthinkable prospect.

Jon sincerely hopes that Karen Wiley is enjoying the correspondence, and that her sleep is not being disturbed *too* much.

Seven

The following morning. The rain was holding off, but only just.

". . . and precisely what is it you're accusing me of exactly?"

"Aw Dave, will you just . . . not?"

"No, I think I have a right. Now I'm doing stuff wrong when I'm not even doing stuff."

"It's not that. And it's not that you're being accused. In taking this to you, I'm following advice that sounded intelligent, at least when I heard it."

"From what, who, the cops?"

"And what's with that tone? Dave, you're not a suspect." Playfulness was not her strong suit, but Karen attempted a wry smile anyway. "Was there something else you needed to tell me?"

"Oh, so I'm *not* a suspect."

The smile slid, her face went vague, uncertain. "No one is, doesn't seem to be. They haven't, you know . . ." She turned towards the salty bite of the wind and wrinkled her nose in a squint, a sharp sense of the ridiculous digging deep. Together, they watched a damp Stars and Stripes wrap and unwrap itself in complex flapping knots around the bendy flagpole at the back of the boat.

When he spoke again, his tone was soft, although there was no chance of another tourist hearing them, not over the heavy throb of the twin diesels.

"So why the personal attack, Kar, here, now? The ink is long dry on that scrap of paper, you don't get to randomly, you know, attack me anymore."

"Dave, see it from my point of view."

"Inappropriate is what it is. This is a turning point for me, I thought for us, first trip out together with Jen since, since when?"

"I always took trips with Jen. You weren't interested. You had beer and basketball and Internet porn and friends you couldn't grow out of."

"Well, that doesn't sound like me now. I swear to God, Karen, this is a highlight for me, these Jen trips. And now you suddenly here? After all this time? Jeez."

Karen softened. "No, I know. And you're right about the other thing. Truth is, I didn't think there ever was a good time to ask."

"Guess not," said Dave, and he leaned forward like the kid during recess who never saw the note that got passed around. "So, what'd they say?"

"The police?"

"The letters."

"Aw, those goddamn *letters*." This a bit loud. A nearby Englishwoman who was insisting on leaning over the bow and photographing the propeller spume made a little face like the gamekeeper just farted in her rose garden. The youngish couple with the colorful history saw this and smiled at one another, almost teenagers again.

Karen shook it off first.

"Well?" said Dave, once he had lost eye contact with her.

"Well nothing, Dave. I have an appointment with an office-bound fed late this afternoon and I'm dropping them off, unopened."

"Wait, wait. *Unopened*?"

"Five letters, three unopened, first one in the garbage, best place for them all, probably. I had to wait until there was enough to constitute what they call sustained harassment. You know, they've been arriving less frequently as this thing has gone on. Probably phasing out now."

Karen looked away, not even really believing this herself. In fact, she was only following well-meaning and reasonable-sounding instruction, given to her first by a sympathetic but overworked officer of the Postal Inspection Service. No, she had been told by that distinctly uncertain-sounding representative, you keep the letters if any more arrive, the ones that imply pain and torture, you keep them, unopened, until there is a sufficient number to make a case—after all, there is no specific threat contained in the statement I'm seeing here, you're probably dealing with a crank. No, I agree, there is no reason why an upstanding citizen should have to be exposed to such ugliness, abuse of the US mail is a federal crime, you're quite right about that, Ms. Wiley, so I suggest you simply do this: You don't need to see the content if you can recognize which mail is—ah—*bad* from the writing on the envelope. When you see this font right here, just hang on to the letters, don't even think of opening the damn things, you don't need that. Let their number get to five, six or so, and then forward them straight on to us. If it has become ugly then you'll never need to know. We'll get all over it, launch a full investigation.

But what constitutes ugly? Karen had asked.

We'll see. Here's my card with the address of this office, the number of my personal cell and please don't hesitate to call if there are any other questions or developments. Now, is there a safe place you can store these letters, if any more of them arrive?

Sadly, Agent Corbin from the Postal Inspection Service was something of an idiot, but, sitting rigidly across from his desk in a bright fourth-floor downtown office, half-listening to the familiar buzz of people shuffling documents and using telephones and photocopiers, Karen reasoned that the man in the big glass skyscraper *must* be right, even if he didn't seem to be taking her theatrical-sounding story all that seriously in his grave post 9/11 world. Surely there could be no upside to her opening the mail with the black typescript on the envelopes that was turning her lobby mailbox into a dead drop for horror. And yes, if the phone started ringing or some stalker appeared, of course she'd contact law-enforcement again.

So Karen vowed then that she would keep the letters, pass them on to the proper authorities. That *must* be the right course of action.

"Wait, wait," said Dave, jolting her back to the present. "You have an appointment—today? You mean they're here? You brought them on this trip? Five letters?"

"Four, first one in the garbage." She blinked at him through the fine spray. "Crazy notion, but it made more sense than going home to come out again. And you know, there was always the possibility that you could have, I don't know, shed some light on the issue."

"You are kidding."

"I was told to talk to the obvious suspect. I know that's not you, but statistically the husband . . ."

"Can I read them?"

"Not so fast, mister. What the hell good would that do?"

"Don't say you're not interested yourself. After the chewing out I got for putting Jen in that cab? You're all coy now, this was serious as shit at one time."

"What did I just say, Dave? There was some bad timing, I get that note the one damn moment she's not with someone we know and trust. These are all garbage fodder, believe me when I say it."

"Ah, yeah, but you don't believe it, do you? I mean, *some* people might believe that, people are pessimists, no good can come of this and so on."

"I do keep hearing that."

"Give me some credit for knowing you. Someone here you think you can help, maybe?"

"Oh, back off, Dave. Don't you think I would have opened them if that was the case? I unload them to the Postal Inspector now, in six to eight weeks I call agent whosis up and he tells me they got nothing for me, the letters are random threats from the sad guy in the newspaper underwear who lives at the bus station, and by the way there's a militant strain of anthrax or a new wafer-thin mail bomb being developed and would I only bother contacting them again if the material gets overtly pornographic, whatever. They were hardly encouraging on the phone."

"You've been talking to Lilly about this."

"It's another perspective. I tell you, she got far more interested in it than me."

"Well, it *is* interesting. Lilly probably smells a story."

"Smells of something."

"So why not open them?"

"Fascinated, aren't you? You think my life is lacking drama?"

"What is this now, your brave face?"

"This is my *cold* face. I made my peace with the letters, just because it comes through my door doesn't make it my problem."

"Kind of like me, huh."

"Huh?"

"Kind of like when *I* came through your door."

She glanced at him, took a fresh mental photo. Dave was looking sad in the gray light of morning, his eyes cast down, knuckles wet from spray and white from grasping what must have been a very cold metal rail. Small flakes of paint-rust stuck to his hands as he moved away from her. He rubbed them off absently, palms pushing down the sides of his jacket.

She knew that he sometimes had a way of slipping into the dramatic like this, the pained *unlucky me*, and whether he had a point or not, he always seemed to do it in an overtly self-conscious way, as though the real feelings were getting filtered through a performance that he assumed she would better relate to.

But no, not so fast, this was the longest conversation they had

had together in a while, and at least they were relating like adults. Dave seemed to be finally moving on, and quite nicely it seemed. Karen was inwardly pleased for him, without a hint of condescension.

"We can get into that stuff if you like," she said, at last.

"Probably not a good idea."

She smiled, he smiled and laughed, but when she reached out to touch his hand it felt colder than the rail. It was the first exchange of mutual approval between them in over a year, their fragile wisps of breath whipping south across the rippling, freezing bay towards San Francisco's second most beautiful bridge, industrially huge and fallible as man, solid steel shoulders working thanklessly to unite a peninsula.

"Where's Jen?" he said, trying to prolong the moment.

"She's round the front, can't wait to get locked in that tiny cell they have over there." Karen shrugged, turned again, appraised her diminishing hill-clung city, twin tracks of white water cleaving out behind them.

"Yep," said Dave, watching her leave him all over again. "Can't believe we never took her here before." Karen's face was as wide open to him now as it sometimes was in the old days, clear and eager in her yellow parka hood.

It was time to tell her.

"Listen, Kar, you need to know something."

"Okay."

"I don't really know how to say it, so I'll just say it."

"Okay."

"I'm going away. I mean. I'm leaving."

"The city?"

"Well, yeah the city. Ashley and I. We're, we got serious, I don't know when it happened. Ashley's dad has some land, this land has been in the family forever, they thought it'd be useless for cultivation, they've recently been told otherwise."

"Okay."

"He wants to turn it into a concern and he wants me, us, to run it, manage it. I mean, there's not much money there, not much, less than we make now, but we'll build a house and I think I need this. I want to settle down again."

"I thought your job was going so well."

"It is, but, this is a chance for a new start."

"Which one was Ashley?"

"I hope you're joking. Six months going on seven."

"Six months, Dave." Karen held some cold air in her lungs. "Where?"

"Hawaii."

"*Hawaii?*"

"You know I love it there, you remember."

"As a destination for vacations. We sat on a crowded beach, fell off an inflatable banana. Now you want to live there?"

"*We* want to live there. Ashley's half-Hawaiian."

"And you're going to what, grow things?"

"Hearts of palm, we're going to try. Hey, misty mornings, cups of the best coffee you've ever tasted, barefoot for dinner. I want out of that tech plant I'm wasting my life in and I want a country with some rainbows in it."

"Yeah, I can see the brochure."

"No, there's more. I finally figured it out."

"Okay," she said, readying herself for another speech, hoping he wouldn't get emotional.

"With the best will in the world, I was never happy when we broke up. Well obviously, not just *when* we broke up. After, long after. For far too long."

Dave swallowed. Karen watched the little hairs on his Adam's apple bob up and down.

"I couldn't work out why," he said. "But I was always trying to live my old life, Karen. The same one as I lived with you, except you weren't in it anymore. And my career? That's not everything, the last leaf I'm taking from your book."

"What leaf? What book?"

He seemed to make up his mind.

"What book? You know. Quitting the money job for the job you want to do, even if there's a really big possibility it isn't going to work out."

"I'm protected. I have savings, the ones I didn't give to you. And I'm not going to Hawaii."

"I don't mean the money. I mean looking for what makes you happy even if it means disrupting your life, the life of those around you, the life of your child . . ."

"I'm *right* for my job."

"Oh? Where are we, Wednesday? Shouldn't you be with someone?"

"Don't be an asshole. People schedule therapy for evenings, mornings."

"They do, do they?"

"Don't get sidetracked, *the life of my child*? *Our* child! My God, Dave. Am I getting accused of irresponsibility here? Who's running away to grow vegetables in paradise? Who *always* seems to be running away?"

"You never gave me any choice."

"And *you* never learned that your choices could always have been your own."

The ensuing silence stung them both.

As if to close the matter, Jennifer came running up, threading between the hips of tourists. She was twittering about something, really too old to have dangly mittens attached by a string that looped through her fleecy jacket, but it was a worthy, appropriate interruption, and Karen needed to think. Dave was such a big part of Jen's life. She was his *daughter* of course, but Karen had to admit to herself that Dave still felt like a considerable part of her own life as well, especially now there was this threat of him going. Always a phone call away, she'd never previously doubted that he'd return to her if she asked him to. Absurd though that thought always was to her, it did occur from time to time, particularly now, with the advent of these kidnap letters.

A little arrogant, Karen?

Probably, but at one point David John Wiley was the only man she thought she'd ever love, at the wedding she had even taken his last name, against all her better instincts. But sexual politics aside, exactly what kind of serious commitment starts with the woman buying her own engagement ring?

Jen completely ignored Karen.

"Dad, there's a spooky man at the front of the boat."

"Did he talk to you?"

"No, but he looked at me."

"He probably looks at all bad little monkeys who run away from their parents."

She wormed her way into his jacket, snaked a hand around his waist.

Karen fought a baffling urge to pull a sourball face at this display. Jen was acting like such a damn baby today. It was play acting, play acting for Daddy. Karen wondered if Jen was always like this around him.

"Will you go and have a look, Dave?" said Karen. "I'd feel happier if you had a look."

"Aw Kar, Scrappy Doo here sees spooky people everywhere she goes."

"Dave?"

"I'm on it," he said, moving. "Although I don't know what I'm supposed to do. If I'm not back in five, get them to turn this crate around and fling out lifebelts."

Jen giggled, and he gave a little wave once he was out of earshot. They both waved back, all smiles.

Jen turned her attention to the view of the city, listened for a moment to the chug of the diesels. Child-play or not, Karen was going to speak to her daughter as near to an equal as she deserved.

"Nearly there, babe. Alcatraz. You always wanted to go."

"I can see, Mom."

Karen held her child lightly by the shoulders. "Listen, Mommy needs to tell you something."

"Sure."

"Will you look at me?"

Jen sniffed, face dutiful, mittens waggling in the breeze.

"You love Daddy," Karen said. "And I do too, at least, you know I want him to be happy."

"Okay."

"Well, he's got something he needs to tell us, and he's telling us today. It might be a little upsetting I think, but we want him to be happy and he's made his mind up. Good for him, yeah?"

"Yeah."

"Good girl. It's okay to feel bad if you do, changes are always weird, right?"

"Right." Moisture had stuck some of Jen's hair to her cheek. Karen moved it with a forefinger, smiled into her daughter's face.

"Mom?"

"Uh."

"Is this because he's going off to live in Hawaii?"

"I . . ."

"With Ashley?"

"You already knew?"

"Of course, I'm not *stupid*. What did you think? Ashley's letting me pick out the colors for my room."

"*Your* room?"

"Jeez, I live here, Mom, in the city, this is my home. Wow, don't be so needy. But I'm going to visit of course, and Ashley's cool. I was practically a baby last time we were on the Big Island, it'll be great this time."

"How long . . . how long have you known?"

"I don't know, for like, weeks?" said Jen, as though pressing home a personal victory. "I thought it'd be better if he told you personally. It's not like this was any big secret or anything."

Karen blinked, somewhat stunned, hands still on Jen's shoulders. Instead of the expected mutual consolations, she found herself staring at a spot on Jen's fleece.

Jen fidgeted under the gaze. "Mom?" she said. "*Mom?*"

Karen dropped her hands, feeling very alone. "What is it, honey?"

"Am I old enough to fly on my own? Dad said to ask you if it would be okay. Christy flies to Seattle to see her dad."

"We'll have to see about that."

"Flying is safer than anything else for young people to do. The airlines have special staff."

"I told you, we'll have to see."

And then it began to rain properly, great sheets of gray tears that seemed to plummet in lashes of differing strengths and rapped on Karen's hood strongly enough to echo there. Mother and daughter quickly followed the rest of the tourists who had been braving the elements into the covered cabin, where the windows steamed and Dave could not be found immediately. While Jen ran off and searched for him, Karen sat on a crowded bench and tried to take her mind off the things that were troubling her by tuning in to the chatter of nearby tourists; unfortunately, they were speaking in a language that she could not understand.

Lilly, knowing that Karen had the double whammy day of giving up Jen to Dave for the weekend in the morning and a potentially sticky meeting with a representative of the Postal Inspection Service in the late afternoon, scheduled a rare lunchtime appearance. Her venue of choice was Madame Chan's Seafood House and Raw Bar, a busting upscale clam shack with an unpromising green awning and winsome sea charts on the wall depicting ancient countries terrorized by poorly rendered monsters with donut-looped vertebrae.

Madame Chan's also benefited from having a series of high-backed booths along the rear wall, perhaps a touch too close to the flavorsome clouds of vermouth and court bouillon pluming out from the galley-like kitchen, but far enough from other well-heeled diners who might have struggled not to stare when Karen punctuated the animated recapping of her morning's events by slopping Anchor Steam all over the table and partly into her own lap. While Lilly worked to attract an unoccupied waiter, Karen, unconcerned, ran a finger up the side of the glass to catch the bitter foam.

The beer was a compromise. Lilly had found herself talking them both down from Absolut martinis.

"Thank you for this, for actually wanting to have lunch with me," said Karen, once the waiter had replaced everything but the table. "God knows I'm exhausted talking about him, so God knows how exhausted you must be listening."

"No problem."

"I often think this about Dave: If it was me being the bad guy throwing all the punches, why am I the one so close to K.O.?"

"You underestimate your internal resources."

"I hope so."

Lilly tore off a breadstick paper with her teeth, and Karen watched the elfin face, always alight with conspiracy and mischief, dark lashes above eyes as impenetrable as oatmeal stout. Breadstick annihilated, Lilly reached across and pressed her hand to Karen's. The small, strong fingers felt smooth and cool.

"What you have to realize is all this, what's happening to you, is a good thing. It might not seem it now, but it sometimes takes two people to end a relationship with roots as complex as yours. Don't get down when he starts thinking for himself, never mind the crackpot nature of the scheme. Be pleased for him if you can."

"I think I probably am pleased. You know, deep down."

"Then do you think we could visit him in Hawaii? I like rainbows and good coffee too, though I don't tan at all."

"That's it, I'm too controlling. I controlled it up to now, I probably still want to. And Jen, I think about Jen as well. If she knew he was leaving, why not tell me?"

"Okay then," said Lilly. "That's a different thing. I don't really know kids, thank God, but it sounds like boundaries with her. She's learning about independence with her stupid little secrets here, and you'd better get used to it. There'll be plenty more in the next ten years."

"I suppose it was an adult response to a situation where I thought she'd play the child and get upset on my behalf, something *I* could never rightfully do, having kicked him out in the first place."

"So all that therapy training wasn't in vain. Don't take away her sweet glory of getting to be smarter than you for once. Didn't we love that, getting smarter than our parents?"

"I suppose."

"Smart kids learn fast that information is the real currency. Whatever her real feelings were, she evidently internalized them. Wonder where she learned to do that, Karen Wiley."

"Jen used to be open about her feelings," said Karen. "Especially when Dave first left."

Lilly shrugged. "She's getting older."

"I don't think that's it. I think . . . maybe she's talking to someone else."

"Well, that's okay, as long as she's talking."

"I suppose."

"To what, like a friend from school?" Lilly was hungry. She plucked a napkin out of the wineglass it had been stuffed into.

"I don't know. I don't think so. But someone. On the Internet? Or maybe not, I don't know."

"They grow up so fast."

"What's *that* supposed to mean?"

"Isn't it something you hear? Now watch while I fold my lips together and shake my head slowly in a 'things ain't what they used to be' kind of way. Try it, you'll feel better. And order more beer, the waiter likes you better." This for the benefit of the Korean maître d', who had appeared behind Karen with two steaming oval platters.

The food was good, and plates came and went. They were both getting tipsy. Lilly delighted in watching Karen relax and unwind, it was so unusual these days.

In fact, this was just as Lilly wanted her.

Karen was feeling so in her element that her eyes barely narrowed when her friend reached into a handbag and pulled out an envelope. It was small, brown and unmarked.

"What's that?" asked Karen, spooning up the last of the ice cream.

"Information. Don't be mad."

"Don't make me mad."

"I talked to someone."

Karen stayed silent.

"Christ, I felt bad for you," said Lilly, flashing the envelope between her fingers like a street magician. "We got nothing from Gardner, I even put the bastard on speed-dial, my *ass* to serve and protect."

"I—"

"They told you to keep them unopened? Palmed you off to the feds?"

"The Postal Inspector. Gardner was following protocol."

"They make up their own protocol."

"This is what the ancient Greeks would call your tragic flaw. Stay out of it, Lilly."

"Look at you. You're *fascinated*, we all are. Let's stop being the victims here. Aren't you tired of being the victim?"

"Those letters are probably nothing. A crank."

"Listen to yourself, you've said it so often that sentence doesn't even mean anything anymore. It's got to being that even if this thing *is* nothing, it has to be something."

"What have you got there?"

"Let's put it to bed, you and me, once and for all."

"What information? Who did you talk to?"

"Open yours, I'll open mine. I know you brought them, you have a meeting at five."

"Don't be ridiculous."

"Aw, Karen. I'm not Dave, I'm not rubbernecking here. I can bring something to this."

"Why should I want what you have to bring?"

"Because, believe me, you really, really do."

Karen looked deep into the eyes of her friend, searched for the truth behind this mysterious performance. Lilly was craning forward, her face above the coffee cup so earnest it practically beamed with righteous evangelism. But if there was anything other than honest desire for the facts to be detected there, Karen couldn't see it.

Years ago, there had been plenty of talk around the TV station about how Lilly could use people, how she could discard those who became uninteresting to her, how she could be a mean little flirt with business at the root of every relationship she struck. Karen, then the senior executive, was pleased that she had reserved judgment. Lilly had helped her through some difficult times, and had manifested no ulterior motives whatsoever. And she did possess a genuine knack for uncovering the truth about people and their situations, or rather the bullshit behind the lies. It was an easy trait to like.

"Okay," said Karen. "Imagine I want what you have to bring."

"I met with a guy."

"What guy?"

Lilly swallowed, looked down and stroked the ridge of her napkin. "This guy, we used him before, when I worked on the *Chronicle*. He's a friend. I mean, he's a bit erratic, but this is no ordinary dirt-digger. He's ex-cop, ex-fed. He's good. Really good. I think we should go see him."

"A private investigator?"

"Among other things. He submits articles to the underground press, he plays a mean jazz piano and I'm fairly certain that he appears on no computer records anywhere in these United States, although I could be being dramatic on that point."

"Okay, Mrs. Spillane. I'm getting the check."

"We should go and see him."

"Forget it. I hand on the letters to the authorities this very afternoon, as per."

"We should go and see him right now. Karen, we have time."

"Fascinating, but not a good idea. You think he's going to get me to open the letters. I've made my peace with the responsibility."

"Just listen to this one more thing."

Without shifting her gaze from Karen's, Lilly opened her unsealed envelope, unfolded a sheet of raggedy notebook paper.

Lilly knew the hastily scribbled information on there was the clincher. She talked fast, only glancing down for occasional confirmation.

"The postmark on your letters, Canaan Utah. Fact: There were no kidnappings in that town in the last six months, but there were, count them, *two* in the state of Utah of note, although there may be more; classifications are fuzzy; kidnap, disappearance, etcetera. Two serious 'happenings,' let's say. The first was open and closed, a junkie hairdresser out of Ogden sprung her child from care, took her across state lines. They found them two days later in Reno, dead in a motel bathtub. The junkie slashed the kid, then herself."

"Awful. How do you know all this?"

"My guy. He knows, I asked him to find out. This stuff is a breeze to get. Managed it all without leaving his house, as far as I know."

"And you what, you just sat on this piece of paper? Throughout our entire lunch?"

"I didn't know if you'd be keen. I wanted you amenable. He is expecting us."

"You exploitative little so-and-so."

"The second kidnapping, well, the second kidnapping is a little more interesting."

"Interesting how?"

"Admit you want to know. You don't have to say I did the right thing."

"*Fuck*. Okay, so I want to know."

"Fact: Katy Trueblood, eldest child of three, was taken from her trailer just outside the municipality of Canaan, Utah. Same jurisdiction: out there, population centers are few and far between. It was ugly, her sister was very badly damaged. Local press made considerable hay, but that girl is *gone*."

"I have no connection with these people. I've never even been to Utah."

"So how's about it," said Lilly, ignoring this. "Are you coming with me?"

"I'm not sure. I am sick of Gardner's radio silence."

"And your reservation has been duly noted. One meeting won't kill either of us, and I'll claim any fees on expenses. At least, that's what I've been doing until now." For Lilly, the subject was closed. She looked around the restaurant as though she'd just woken up. "Man, you raised your hand like, ten minutes ago. What are they, *brewing* the check?"

Karen had been mentally rehearsing scenes in a drab office with dusty blinds and a reek of Scotch, and so was pleasantly surprised when the cab passed through Japantown and Richmond and finally pulled into a short and tidy driveway that led up to a two-story detached residence with large bay windows and a wraparound balcony, better suited to a young family than to Mike Hammer or Sam Spade. The lawn out front was immaculate, and Lilly had to chide the driver for almost flattening what looked like freshly planted cyclamen as he made the turn.

"Pays well, the sleuthing business?" asked Karen, once the cab was a cloud of dust. They were blinking in the reflected sunlight of the whitewashed house. In the street, a couple of well-dressed kids on rollerblades resumed their hockey game.

"I told you, he's a lot of other things," said Lilly, careful with her heels on the cobbled brick path up to the porch. "But yeah, false insurance claims, companies will pay lots of money to get admissible evidence from a reliable source." She shrugged. "He's had this place as long as I've known him. Do you wanna ring the bell up there?"

The door was answered by a small, clear-skinned girl of around five years old with very wide brown eyes. The child held Karen's gaze through the screen door for a long, silent moment, and Karen felt as though her soul was being bored into by an exceptionally cute drill.

A large hand appeared above the child's shoulder. It seemed rough and aged, but was pale next to the girl's tan complexion, and the lightness of touch gave it the impression of capability.

"Her name is Kaya," said a voice so throaty it was almost a whisper. "It means wise child."

"I thought you named her after the Bob Marley album," said Lilly.

"I didn't name her."

The girl did not move, but the screen door swung outwards, pressed open on its spring by a tightly muscled forearm. The sun chased light onto pale gray eyes in a spare, craggy face that would catch fascinating shadows in its lines and hollows.

"I'm Egan Blake. Please, come in."

The little girl suddenly turned and ran back into the house, feet trampling over polished floorboards. Lilly entered first, then Karen. The man addressed Karen with a smile into her eyes as she passed, and she decided her first impression was that she would like Egan Blake, recognized his measured stillness as a hard-won attribute.

The uncluttered reception room was a good size, if lacking the natural light that they could see through the doorframes to the living room and kitchen, and it smelled faintly of well-polished wood. There were canvas prints on the wall and dark-skinned elders staring sternly from sepia photographs that climbed the staircase in measured installments. There was singing from somewhere else in the house, the voice of a young adult woman.

"That's Tadita," said Blake, gesturing towards the kitchen. "We're entertaining friends tonight. Only person I met who doesn't cry when she chops onions."

"It's beautiful," said Karen, listening. "What is it?"

"Tadita and Kaya are Chumash," said Blake. "She's singing about creation, about the rains."

"What are the words?"

"You could ask but I doubt she'd remember. It seems the Chumash had a separate language for singing, and the meanings were lost. Shame." He smiled again. The unusual lines that ravaged his face made Blake's age difficult to identify, but he was probably well through his fifties or early sixties, maybe more.

He took their coats and then held a small door open that Karen assumed led to a cupboard under the stairs. "You two watch your heads on the exposed light. The space opens up once you get down there. Lilly, you know the drill."

"What, her first visit and Karen gets access to the sanctuary?" Lilly pouted. "Egan, you're getting slouchy in your old age. She could be working for the CIA."

Blake nodded. "Karen, it's an ugly storeroom with a big computer in it. Feel privileged."

He wasn't kidding. In stark contrast to upstairs, the space under the house was large but extremely cluttered. What looked like surveillance equipment was stacked in disorderly piles between the wooden and stone foundations of the house, some of it clearly as old as Watergate. The single light source was an exposed bulb that hummed quietly. There were old computer shells and music systems that had been gutted for their parts, as well as full-length Yamaha and Sony piano keyboards, propped up on their ends one behind the other like the medieval dead.

"Excuse the mess," said Blake, following them carefully down to the exposed concrete floor. "Nothing gathers dust as well as old musical instruments. Wonder why that should be?"

"It's because you don't let your wife down here to clean," said Lilly.

"She's not my wife."

"Excuse me, your partner."

"She's not my partner."

"Well, whoever's responsible for the upkeep on that palace upstairs. Don't tell me she's your maid."

"Tadita does as she pleases." The light danced in his eyes. "As, I think, do you."

Karen smiled to herself, suspecting that Blake would get considerable mileage out of winding up someone like Lilly. Here was a man who probably played at being enigmatic to hide the fact that he really *was* enigmatic, had a darkly interesting spiritual core to guard.

"And what exactly do you sit on around here?" said Lilly, in mock exasperation.

"Of course." He had barely removed his level gaze from Karen, but he looked away for long enough to throw a tie-dyed sheet off one La-Z-Boy and move a pile of books off another. Karen identified an FBI organization and functions manual and binders filled with forensics information. Blake sat with his back to the one live piece of gadgetry, a top-of-the-range PC with all surrounding mod cons; it looked like the terminal on a spacecraft.

Blake had an unusual habit of stopping whatever he was doing and staring wide-eyed into the middle distance as though he was suddenly thinking of something he might have missed. He did this now, before reaching across and switching on his green shaded desk lamp. The immediate area to his left was flooded with light, but the overall impression was still that they were conversing down an extremely cozy manhole, the smell of warm, dusty electronics and fresh laundry contriving to put Karen at ease. She allowed herself to sink back a little into her chair.

Lilly sneezed twice, mouse-like, the sound not getting past the top of her nose.

"I suppose the question is," said Blake, addressing Karen, "where does responsibility begin and end? Here you receive this correspondence from a what, I'm told, a child in need? Someone you apparently have no personal connection to or investment in? You can say, 'well, let's make it the job of the authorities to sort this out,' say you hand on the responsibility, but this person never reached out to the authorities, they reached out to *you*. What if you really are the only person who can help? Do you know what I'm trying to say, Karen?"

"I think so. Responsibility isn't always something you ask for. But what if the police *are* better qualified to deal with it? Makes more sense that they would be."

"You're a psychologist, right?"

"I'm a psychotherapist. I recently qualified."

"Because this person, they didn't write to a street sweeper or a longshoreman. You think there's a reason for that?"

"Detective Gardner said that as a therapist Karen was a more likely recipient of bothersome correspondence," said Lilly.

"Lilly told me that you've kept the letters without opening them. Why did you do that?"

"To pass them on to the Postal Inspector."

"Later today?"

"Yes." Blake's gray eyes were on her, unblinking. Karen felt it needed more. "Look," she said, "if a person gets a single obscene phone call, no one gets all over *that*. You have to get probably half a dozen before you got a response from the cops, and even then I know a person who never got taken seriously. This isn't so different."

"All the more reason to open the letters yourself, surely."

"Damn mister, you and everyone else. I have responsibilities already, the ones I sought out for myself. I'm responsible for my child, for my family, for my clients, for paying the rent every month and for putting food on the table. I don't indulge the uninvited weirdness, I can't afford to, and Agent Corbin said I didn't have to."

"You sound good with responsibility, Karen. And by that I don't mean to condescend." He averted his eyes, looked at his hands. "But responsibility usually seeks people out, not the other way around."

"I don't understand."

"You said that you *actively sought* responsibility. May I ask why?"

"My parents were progressive with my upbringing. I had to set my own boundaries."

"So you're far from being what, a passive person."

Karen shrugged. "I'd say so."

"Yet you don't open letters that allege to be from a kidnapped child."

"I let Lilly bully me into coming here, didn't I?"

"I'm guessing that no one bullies you into doing anything, Karen. I think you might feel too close to something with this, maybe something personal that strikes a nerve."

"I don't think—"

"Is this why you don't open them? Do you feel connected in some way to the language? Or to their author?"

"Okay, this psychobabble then. Is it in with the fee, or—"

His voice became so deep it was barely audible.

"Forgive me. I'm really not suggesting a literal connection. I'm just impulsive in my theorizing, take my word for it. What I'm saying by that is I'd have done something different, I'd have torn them open right there on the mat. But if I implied you were shunning a moral responsibility then you have my apologies. It *is* an unwelcome dilemma, and I empathize with your wanting to sidestep it. Let me put it like this: I don't give to charity as much as I should, someone else's uninvited need right there; *that* comes under the umbrella of responsibility to a similar extent. Probably more so, as at least the motives of charitable organizations are overt. Bottom line, human nature is always to try to ascribe meaning where there is the appearance of none, and I've made a career out of almost precisely that."

"I'm not sure that I follow you."

"I'm saying that no matter how preachy I just sounded, my motives aren't all about responsibility either. If they were, I'd be donating more than five bucks a month to give a child sight. Okay, I'll admit it. I'm plain old intrigued. Your problem is a fascinating one, I'm a sucker for these things. Beats creeping around taking photos of burnt-up warehouses or lecturing the new intake at Quantico."

"I thought you were struck off that particular circuit," said Lilly.

"Oh, and by the way," he said, "there's no fee today, Karen. This is just an initial consultation. You have a similar process in your line of work?"

"Depends on the therapist. Though *I* don't usually talk as much."

Egan Blake gave the impression of being a man who did not laugh often, but he laughed a little then, and bent his head down as he did so. He looked up quickly as though to make sure that Karen was laughing also. She allowed him a smile that was brief, though completely genuine.

"*Kee-riste*," said Lilly, watching them together. "Can we get to the point now? Open that bag up, missy."

Karen had the letters in a clear plastic wallet inside the small backpack. Blake's eyes were on her and not the wallet as she passed it to him, requiring her to find his hand with it. When this was done, she sat back. The chair, worn enough to have been climbed on by generations of children, felt comfortable as a warm embrace.

As his attention was now focused elsewhere, Karen allowed herself to stare. It felt good to see the wallet being turned over in his capable-seeming hands, although she was slightly disturbed when he reached into a desk drawer and pulled out surgical gloves.

"Fingerprints?" said Lilly.

"Yes," said Blake, applying the gloves without any of the dramatic snap so beloved of television pathologists. "Although I'm not so much worried about obliterating the prints of others, there'll be a trillion partial marks on here anyway."

"You're worried that they might be dusting later and your prints would be recognized." It was Karen who said it, quite happy to join in and encourage his air of mystique. After all, this unusual man was now working for her. He smiled crookedly, understanding that she could indulge him without mockery.

"Doesn't hurt to leave Egan Blake off the evidence," he said. "But do tell the police that you talked to me, by all means. Don't ever hold anything back if you're asked a direct question, I have nothing to hide. Well, nothing more than anyone else."

"Yeah right," said Lilly. But Blake was busy, putting on eyeglasses that made him seem positively timeworn. He still hadn't taken the letters out, but had turned the clear plastic wallet around in the light like a scientific specimen. He unfastened the clasp and removed them carefully, like ancient documents.

The empty wallet went on the desk, and he held the envelopes like cards in a poker hand, thumb fanning them out so the postal marks were visible, side by side.

His glasses flashed. "The first letter. You discarded that?"

"Yes," said Karen, unwilling to justify an action that made perfect sense at the time. Blake resumed his study.

"You got the first letter September thirteen," said Blake.

"That's right, lucky thirteen." Lilly had told Karen in the cab how much she'd let Blake know in advance.

"Do you remember the content of that first letter?" asked Blake. "What it said? I only know the gist of the second."

"Yes."

"Do you remember exactly?"

"Probably not *exactly*. It came at a bad time and I thought Jen was compromised. She was supposed to be with her dad, she was not."

"Is there anyone that could have known this that might have wanted to exploit your fear at that time?"

"No."

"Jen's father?"

"Dave, and no. That letter sat in the mailbox downstairs and then later on my sideboard. No one could have known what time I was getting home and Jen was out of contact for only ten minutes in a cab home. It was bad luck, extremely bad timing."

"Did you see the cab driver?"

"No."

"Did Jen say anything about him?"

"No. She seemed more concerned about me. I was distressed."

"Okay. Tell me what you remember of the content of the first letter."

"It was short," said Karen. "Shorter than the second letter."

"What did it say?"

Karen swallowed, suddenly feeling very self-conscious. "There was a prayer. 'Gentle Jesus meek and mild.' But gentle wasn't spelled right. It was spelt with a J. J for Jentle. 'He's going to *hurt me* if you don't do what he says.'"

"Is that all?"

"I think so."

"Does any of that mean anything to you?" said Blake.

"The prayer, sure, I've heard it before. My dad used to say it with me, a long, long time ago. What does it mean to you?"

"Well, off the top of my head, I can say that it's a well-known old Christian hymn, now better known as a child's prayer. But in this context it's most interesting to me as possibly the most unthreatening and feminized portrait of Christ that I've ever heard."

"You think that's relevant?"

"Despite its use by William Blake and its recurrence in the carol 'Once in Royal David's City' there is positively no mention of the word '*mild*' anywhere in the Bible. Regardless of what he might mean to people around the world, according to historical records Christ wasn't mild by anyone's standard. In the sixteenth century the Protestants threw out the Papist pantheon and the Virgin Mary and got back to the principle of one vengeful God and his Son Jesus Christ. Calvinist artists had Christ looking distinctly sissified. Probably because there were no other girls in the story anymore, you understand. Since when do grubby Aramaic Jews have baby blue eyes?"

Karen and Lilly looked at one another. Blake wasn't smiling this time.

"I have a whole other problem with the word 'meek' in the present understanding of the word," said Blake, "but I won't bore you with that. The point is that when Marx wrote that religion was the opium of the people, this is probably the kind of thing he had in mind."

"So this is a Christ supposed to inspire sympathy," said Karen.

"And in the most cloyingly obvious and westernized kind of way," said Lilly.

"Perhaps. This is a doe-eyed Bambi of a prayer," said Blake. "Juxtapose it with some random 'he' who is going to 'hurt me' in your letter, change the G in gentle for a J like a helpless kid who can't spell yet, and we have some mighty dramatic attempt at spooking going on. This is especially so given that many people will have encountered these words in their childhood at some point. Childhood is the key here."

"I believe that," said Karen.

"This is manipulation, and not in an especially sophisticated way. Unless there's a level of irony at work."

"Irony?" said Karen. Blake removed his glasses, put them on the desk.

"You'll have to forgive me, Karen. Lilly knows this about me already, but I'm no Sherlock Holmes, Angela Lansbury, whoever the heck. If I have the answer to anything then I say it out loud immediately at the moment of realization, and when I speculate wildly I tend to say that out loud too. Frankly I'm not in the game of holding back answers until there's a complete and incontrovertible picture that I can astound the guests in the drawing room with."

"It also means he'll happily talk the hind legs off several donkeys," said Lilly.

"May I look at the second letter now?" said Blake. "The opened one?"

"Of course."

Blake returned the glasses to his nose and read the second letter slowly, the light off the lenses eclipsing his eyes. After a long moment he placed the letter on top of the envelope and put the small pile down, seemingly dissatisfied.

"This letter came on the fourteenth," he said.

"Yes."

"The day after the first letter."

"Yes. I opened it in the morning."

"The third letter came two days after that."

"Yes."

"There was another two-day gap before the next, the eighteenth."

"I think that's right."

"Just establishing a timeline. Then the next letter, the fifth and final to date came a whole four days later, the twenty-second. Today is the twenty-fourth."

"Okay."

"Does Jen know about the letters?"

"No," said Karen, surprised. "At least, I don't think so."

"Have you thought about telling her?" he said.

"Now what the hell good would that do?"

"*Two* bodies live at the address these are mailed to, Karen. Might she know something?"

"She knows a lot of things, is probably sensitive to even more. But not about this."

"Because you haven't opened the letters."

"Right."

"Could Jen have picked up any mail herself, maybe didn't show it to you?"

"She doesn't pick up the mail, she never does."

"Never?"

"*I* pick up the mail. And if she had, she'd tell me. We're extremely close," said Karen, knowing this last statement wasn't as true as it used to be.

"You should ask her."

"Leave it alone, Egan," said Lilly.

"No, it's fine," said Karen, unable to control the color rising in her cheeks. "Mr. Blake has proved his enthusiasm, and by that, *I* don't mean to condescend. Lilly mentioned a kidnapping in Utah, which is where the postal stamp on these letters is from."

"Will you ask your daughter just this once?" said Blake. "About the mail?"

Karen didn't want a stand-off, didn't want a fight, above all didn't want to allow her daughter anywhere near this sorry mess of intrigue. "I'll talk to her tonight," said Karen, meaning that maybe she'd ask Dave if Jen had said anything to him. "But may I ask you a question in turn?"

"Of course."

"Everyone I've spoken to about this has acted interested but never worried. Even the cops, once they established that no one I knew had been kidnapped. Keep the letters and so on, we'll look at them later. Probably a hoax, a prankster, some sicko with nothing better to do, they said. Why this sudden urgency to call my daughter? Do you believe that we're in danger?"

"I'll hold nothing back, I promise you. But yes, I am perturbed. I'm bothered by the patience of your harasser. I belittled the attempt to spook you with the language earlier but there's something badly inconsistent and I don't know what it is. I won't mention your daughter again. Anyone would be disturbed by a threat to their child, real or imagined."

"I appreciate that," said Karen, thinking of the little Native American girl upstairs, and of sturdy bare feet on hardwood floors.

"Do you know what graphology is?" said Blake.

"The interpretation of handwriting."

"Of course you do, you're a therapist." He passed the second letter back to her. Karen looked carefully at the words, Lilly craning over also.

"Now, it's not a science I'm comfortable with, and I consider it to be different to what's called handwriting analysis. I don't like making state-of-mind decisions based on whether or not a person puts a smiley in the dot above the lower-case i," he said.

"More complicated than that," said Karen.

"No, I know. You'd probably be better at this kind of thing than me, so I'd like to call on your intuition if I may. What do you see here?"

"Well, I'm no expert, but I see slow, deliberate writing," said Karen, carefully. "In pencil. It was put down with some force."

"Slow and deliberate. What do you conclude from that?"

"I don't know. I'd have thought that might mean that someone was trying to disguise their writing. The lines waver a couple of times, could that also be indicative?"

"Maybe," said Blake. "The graphite breaks in one place here. What might that mean?"

"Undue force with the pencil. Stress, nervousness, anger?"

"Who else," said Blake, "writes slowly and deliberately?"

"I don't know."

"Could this be the writing of someone who was only learning to write?"

"Yes," said Karen, seeing it.

"Who learns to write?"

"Someone uneducated, someone backward?"

"Who else?"

"No," said Karen. "A child?"

Blake said nothing.

"But the language, you said— "

"This is not a child's language, despite the 'Jentle Jesus' attempt to make it appear that way."

"Then . . ."

"I would posit that this could be a child under duress, being *made* to write a letter. Why, as a kidnapper, disguise your handwriting when you can make your victim do the writing? And look at the envelopes: Times New Roman. If you're writing letters by hand, you usually write envelopes by hand. A child wrote this, then maybe the kidnapper typed the address."

"You know this for a fact?"

"Okay, I can't know it for sure. But I believe it. What do *you* think?"

Karen looked at the words until the letters swam before her eyes. Eventually, she was able to separate the markings from the meaning they signified. It was like identifying the picture in a Magic Eye poster.

"Possible," she said.

"Look at the way the loops curl in the d and a of 'dead'," he said. "I see someone's forced hand, I see pain, but I also see . . ."

"A *girl*." They said it together.

"Listen," he said. "The NCIC is a nationwide computerized information system which serves all levels of the criminal justice community: federal, state and local. It's a resource that I am able to exploit from time to time. Karen, I'm going to show you a short series of forensic photographs that were uploaded to that database recently. They've been significantly abridged. I can't tell you how I obtained them and you can't take them with you. I'm doing this because you need to know that I'm a serious man with useful capabilities who would like to help you if you'll let me. I've made my peace, and so no, I don't need to see the content of those letters you've left unopened, you've made your decision. But hear me now. This will not end here. You'll want to come back to me, and when you do, I want you to believe that there's someone in your corner in whose abilities you feel secure."

"What do you have?" said Lilly.

Blake was looking at Karen as tenderly now, she thought, as his gaunt face would allow. Karen thought briefly of her own father before taking a fleeting, subconscious dash past brightly spotlighted portraits of all the serious-seeming men who had let her down in the past.

"Show me the pictures," said Karen. "Then I have to go."

They were still in Blake's printer tray. "I'm assuming Lilly told you the *details* of the kidnapping that took place in Canaan, Utah on the ninth of this month," he said, passing the documents across.

Karen nodded, occupying herself with the sheets of paper, five of them in total. Not wanting Lilly to look over her shoulder, Karen passed them to her once she had finished.

The paper was standard copy upon which photographs had been printed in black and white. The quality was not good, and Karen realized that Blake was showing her copies of copies; he hadn't been sent the originals. There were two Polaroid photographs per page, one above the other, and they weren't parallel either with each other or with the edges of the paper. It looked like a hasty job, like someone had photocopied two smeary beer coasters. Serial numbers and what could have been the address of a return email had been struck out with thick black magic marker before the pages had been through the printer, possibly in an office far away.

The subjects were just discernible. Page one was the exterior of a silver Airstream trailer, the backdrop of a mobile home park behind. It looked like a relic from the fifties, a ramshackle porch added sometime later. Karen's gaze moved downwards to the second photo, a close-up of the trailer door, swung open on its hinges.

She thumbed the page.

If there was ever any question of the documents becoming a photo story then it was dashed by the pictures on pages two and three, which were close-ups of tire tracks and exterior ground markings, the copies on page three so blurry as to be useless in their current format. A hand was visible in one picture, placing a scale in inches next to something indistinguishable, probably a footprint.

On page four the photographer had moved inside the trailer. In the best-quality copy, the picture at the top showed a wide shot of the interior, a humble home. Because of the limited space and the need to show the whole room it had been taken with a different lens, 20 or 30 mm.

Karen had little experience of trailer living, but in her idle, affluent way she thought she could imagine the type; trinkets in place of ornaments, commemorative Elvis plates on the wall, a car or a bike up on blocks out back, a woman overwhelmed by the clutter and indifference of at least one other occupant. Karen's gaze was eventually directed to a great black irregular shadow across the floor, and she swallowed, her throat tight.

Blood.

The picture below the shot of the interior was the close-up of a baby's cot; empty, sheets ruffled, a discarded pacifier. Karen turned the page.

It is the forensic photographer's duty to document everything, no matter how trivial it may seem. The final page had two close-ups of objects on the walls of the house. The top one was a portrait photograph, two young girls next to one another, hair wetly brushed, looking smart and old-fashioned in school uniforms. The daughters, then.

Karen spent no time with their faces. She was looking at the picture below.

Someone in the home apparently liked needlepoint. One particular effort had been displayed on the wall in a small, jaunty frame like the crosshatch key on a telephone, the borders spilling over one another. Letters in thread spelled out a child's prayer, a love heart and a crucifix stitched carefully in either corner. The clumsy platitudes of a loving mother.

Gentle Jesus, meek and mild.

Eight

Once more, the quiet hum of the tape recorder.

". . . he hit the nail on the head, you know? After about two minutes in his stupid basement. In all the time you've known me, when did I not step up to the plate?"

Mary Huntingdon remained silent. She had sat outside the light source for this evening session, her angular face only just catching the flicker of the several candles that she used to make her consulting room feel more ambient. It was a nice enough place to work during the day and she'd personalized the rented space as much as possible with books and some modest sculpture, but it could still seem like a hospital waiting room once the lighting panels in the ceiling were on.

"Those letters," said Karen, her hands gesturing more than usual. "I knew there was *something* stopping me from opening them. I confront, I don't step back. Never. And he saw that. I didn't realize it at the time. I think because I don't ever like to be told, you know? I'm never good in that child place, that place of feeling controlled."

"Controlled?"

The hands moved again, a gesture of dismissal. "Aw, I have a ridiculous notion: if you know me, you control me. He only had that one insight. But I think it was his sense of certainty. Very persuasive attribute, certainty."

"Did you show them to him?"

"The letters? No."

Karen's busy eyes searched bookshelves that looked positively Dickensian in the bobbing candlelight. She wasn't reading the titles, she was reliving her earlier meeting with Egan Blake.

"Would you have done?"

Karen blinked. "Would I have done . . . what?"

"Shown him the letters," said Mary. "Had you known at the time that there was some kind of subconscious mechanism stopping you."

"No. I don't know." Her eyes went back to the books.

Karen had manifested disappointment at the question. She didn't know the answer herself, and she didn't much care. She'd unloaded the letters to a secretary in the Postal Inspection offices a little over an hour ago and as a result was feeling good for the first time in ages, feeling like a free woman. She'd even managed to forget her concern that Jen was with Dave for the coming weekend, that there wouldn't be anyone waiting for her at home.

The meeting that Karen had been anticipating for so long had completely defied her expectations. There was no grave ceremony with men in dark suits, no passing of the tainted torch, just a single secretary who tucked gum into the corner of her mouth when Karen emerged from the elevator and who looked as though she must have seen it all in the space of one long weekday. Karen announced who she was, and gave the name of the agent who had received her the first time. Then one moment she was holding the envelopes, the next she was not. It all happened so fast.

Karen had spent the two minutes as she left the building feeling disappointed at the disinterested abruptness of this exchange, and the next hundred and twenty feeling pretty damn good that things were at last getting back to normal, and that the sun would rise the following morning on a brand-new day.

Karen looked at Mary, the therapist's eyes dark behind her glasses.

"I was just impressed with his insight," said Karen, finally. "Anyone can sound profound. But Egan seemed to see something in me." She shifted, fidgeted, in the high-backed chair. Mary had come to realize that Karen did this when she was close to her child place; she fidgeted.

Mary's face expressed nothing. "What did you say his name was?"

"Egan Blake." Karen's eyes shone as she said it.

"In what way did you like him?"

"No, no, God, not like *that*." Karen squirmed, almost tucked her feet up on to the chair. "He's old enough to be my . . ."

She trailed off.

"To be your . . ."

Karen laughed, delighted. "To be my father, I almost said. Can you believe that?"

Mary smiled. It was time for the million-dollar question.

"You said earlier that the letters made you think of Sammie. Can you tell me in what way?"

"They didn't at the time. They're not doing now, the letters are gone *now*." Even her tone was child-like. Emotionally, Karen was wide open.

"But they gave you that sense at the time," said Mary. "Not a literal connection, of course. Like a feeling of misplaced responsibility?"

"Yes. If I didn't open them I wouldn't have to confront the reality."

"What *is* the reality, Karen?"

Karen swallowed. "Sammie is dead."

"Then you've known the reality a long time, we've discussed it here."

"But that feeling of responsibility. Like *I'm* the reason my sister died. Like it could be my fault if something happens to this child in Utah."

"That's not true," said Mary, very softly. It was hard to know to which event she was referring. If Karen heard, she didn't recognize that she had.

"There was a smell in that guy's basement today," said Karen. "Like an old vinyl smell. Kind of like how you imagine static would smell if it had a smell, warm and crackly and mellow, yet kind of modern too. Or maybe it's the sleeves of the records I'm thinking of, like that smell of old books, that dry tobacco musk. Whatever, I smelled it today, and I smelled it in the basement under the cabin my parents used to rent for vacations when I was nine and Sammie must have been eight, or nearly eight. I'm probably thinking of the smell of pot too, God knows the grown-ups were doing plenty of *that*, but never in the basement with the tinned food and the old records, least as far as I know."

"What were you doing in the basement?"

"I don't remember. I could have been daring Sammie to do something, I was always doing that. The basement was spooky, like all basements are if it's dark and you're on your own, but Sammie was fearless, you know? I had this hateful trick I used to pull sometimes where I'd turn the light out with her somewhere in the room, and I'd shout something inane about cooties coming to get her, but she never panicked, she always got to the switch. I mean, I was never a bully, but the things I *did* do, those nasty, random big-sister things, I don't think she once tattled to Mom."

"Big Sur was where you vacationed as a family?"

"Always, I told you before, right?"

"I thought you said you vacationed in France as a child."

"Yeah, I probably said that to avoid talking about Sammie. It was after she died that Dad started taking us to France, to a friend's house. But those were the memories afterwards, a whole new chapter. All I know is this: following the . . . *incident* we never went to the cabin in the woods again."

"Hardly surprising."

"It never even came up. We just always went to Provence or to

Brittany, no questions asked. But I would have screamed and yelled had they tried to take me back to the cabin. And I'm not a screamer or a yeller, but I was so scared."

"Scared?"

"I mean grief-stricken, we all were. But I convinced myself one time that I'd seen Sammie's ghost." Karen shifted again in the chair, seemed to make herself smaller. "I saw her two days after the incident on the drive home through a blur of tears, and again in my bedroom a couple of weeks after we got back to Marin County."

"You never told me that," said Mary.

"No. I woke up in the middle of the night, just sat bolt upright straight from sleep, and there she was in the doorway, still in the same dress. It took a long time before I could sleep with the door open after that."

"Why do you think you saw her at that particular moment?"

"I didn't see her. I saw a shadow cast by something else on the landing, like an object. But I was convinced that she was coming to get me. Coming to take me to where she was. Because it should have been me."

"It should have been you?"

"No, it shouldn't have been *anyone*," said Karen, and she stared, hard.

Mary could see that somewhere during this last exchange Karen had left her child ego state behind, lost it in the build-up to the story she was about to tell. Mary was a little disappointed at this, would have to find out if and where she had gone off target with her interventions when she played back the recording. She had been inwardly hoping that Karen would remain excitable and child-like, because usually Karen proved so guarded and careful about what she chose to reveal. Now Karen would talk as though she were pressing certainties home that she herself needed convincing of. This was unusual for the recollection of a vivid memory, unless there were about to be omissions or discrepancies.

The kind an adult might feel the need to factor in for some reason.

"Those mornings in Big Sur were beautiful, truly beautiful," said Karen. "They were cold though, even in summer sometimes. Sammie and I shared a bed when we were on vacation, a big cozy bed with lots of home-made knitted covers piled on top of us. But even so, I remember waking up cold in the cabin and I'd make us both cocoa on the stove, the proper stuff, and Sammie and I would go out onto the porch in our dressing gowns, this ramshackle wooden porch, and we'd watch the mist glide down through the trees like an army of chilled-out spirits. I remember sitting there in a silence that practically shivered, hot mugs in our cold hands, except an ancient forest is never really silent; those big trees would whisper and move if you stayed still among them for long enough. And there'd be a cute little deer or two, their coats steaming in the morning sun, they looked almost biblical when the light got behind them. Every single day they'd be there, so tame you could practically touch them."

"You made the cocoa?"

"I liked to. It was a job I liked to do. Normally Mom made it, there would be less chocolate slurry in the bottom of the mug when she did it."

"But not that morning."

"You have to remember, we're talking about the late seventies here," said Karen. "My parents were still chasing this, this sixties life-style, they still do to some extent, though my dad is such an advert for success in commerce, it's ironic. I don't know if they ever did achieve nirvana, those hippies, but the way they talk, I could believe that they came close to it in Big Sur in the sixties. It's such an elemental place, you know? Brooding mountains and thunderous surf, ancient redwoods and river valleys. But things had changed a bit by the time we were there. Big RVs; that Highway 1 got mighty busy, especially in season. I mean, it was never all *that* bad, but I think that by the late seventies they were all chasing a dream that had moved on."

"A dream that had moved on?"

"I could just be being cynical, I guess. When your parents don't give you anything to rebel against then you have to find something to complain about. I had to move away from home before I realized my folks were actually pretty cool. Up until then I was this uptight little miss with her eye on the prize, academic, sports, whatever. The opposite of them, kind of. Why go into network television unless you've got that ambition, that desire to thrive in corporate structures? It's only been in the last few years that I figured out it was time to stop running away from *their* lifestyle and start doing something that I really wanted to do. And I'd have done it far, far sooner, but I was good at what I did before, at least financially, which some would argue is the only proof that counts. Lot of people are like that, I think. Dream one thing and do another. Why might that be?"

"You were saying, that morning."

"Yeah. Here's the thing: the hippy boat may have sailed, but there was still this vibe they'd all create in the evenings, this group of them. They'd tell stories, they'd dance, they'd sing, they'd splash naked in the river. There was a poet who was always there, I forget his name, but he's published. He was like the leader of this motley crowd, and his wife was *always* naked; floppy breasts in the moonlight. We used to hide in the bushes and laugh at them. The fun they got up to was harmless, but there'd be at least one sundown in the two weeks when, as a group, they'd get hugely, and I'm talking *galactically*, fucked up. This is another thing where that sixties vibe got a little skewed during the seventies, got a little more sinister. See, there may have been chemicals by that point, I don't know for certain."

"How do you feel about that?"

"Well, I thought they were irresponsible then, but I only do now because of what happened."

"And what was that?"

"It was the morning after one of these big party nights, and our folks hadn't come back to our cabin. I knew they'd be on the floor of someone else's cabin, or maybe they'd be sleeping propped up against one of those redwood trees, dew hanging off their noses and glistening in their hair. I distinctly remember that I wasn't worried. It happened sometimes, and the cabins were all close together, little clusters of them. I knew they'd probably be asleep in one of those, and if not, I could easily find some friendly people without going far. There's this thing, I don't know if they do it today, but you couldn't lock the doors of the cabins. People just trusted each other.

"I don't know who had the idea first, me or Sammie. I imagine it was probably me, because that's how I was. I was the leader, I instigated stuff. Part of it came from that I was the big sister, but another part of it was that I think Sammie always wanted to please me, you know? She always just went along."

"What was the idea?"

"The previous day we were all supposed to go for a picnic at a place called Pfeiffer Beach, have you heard of it?"

Mary nodded.

"But when we got there in the car—me, Mom, Dad, Sammie—the rangers or the state police had shut it for some reason so we never even got to see the sea, only smell it, and me and my sister ended up wolfing down peanut butter and jelly sandwiches by the side of the road. The thing was, we were like hugely disappointed, we'd gone to bed disappointed the previous evening, and we were probably both a little pissed at our parents, because *their* day wasn't spoiled by the beach being closed, they still had their party to go to later that evening. I don't think we'd ever been to this beach before, although I'd be surprised if that's true, it was such an attraction.

"Did you ever run away as a kid? Did you ever want to? I think that running away is probably something that passes through the mind of every child at some point as a way of testing the boundaries, not that they know that's what they're doing. Few ever go so far as to actually do it, and God help the ones that do, but this wasn't even like that. This felt like assuming responsibility. The idea was that *I* was going to take Sammie down to the beach, just her and me. We'd swim, we'd play, we'd build sandcastles, we'd come right on back. I even remember packing food, like food had been the point of the exercise; go down there and eat.

"There was some distance to walk between the cabins and the beach, probably two or three miles, but most of it was downhill. We packed a backpack with food and drink and I was probably all bossy and officious because I made Sammie brush her teeth before we left. Later, that was one of the bits that always set off the tears, she died with clean teeth.

"No one saw us as we walked through the cabins and no one saw us as we passed through the local picnic area that marked the edge of the settlement. I remember Sammie's little footfalls behind me on the bark of the forest floor, I remember the light from the sun like a kaleidoscope through the green of the canopy and warming my cold bones when we passed through a clearing, I remember those cute little wooden nature plaques every so often, marking distance along the trail. I don't remember if we even spoke to one another during that time, though I suppose we must have done.

"After ten minutes we crossed the stream on the road bridge that doubled as the camp entrance, and then there was a stretch of the walk that must have been half a mile or more along the shoulder of the highway. By then the mist had probably burned off, it was going to be a beautiful day, and I sometimes think: if only there had been a car passing by, maybe they'd have stopped, asked us what the hell we thought we were doing, and we'd have headed right on back.

"Then, when it came time for the turn down the canyon towards the beach we ducked into the trees, we could keep the single-track road to the left for a bearing. Not once did we get lost, not once were we in fear of getting lost. The reason for the detour was that we wanted to avoid the booth, the rangers kept a booth at the entrance to the parking area. I didn't know if they had it manned all the time, but it made sense to avoid that if we could. Again, it was never a sense that we were doing anything wrong, just a practical approach to the job at hand. We hadn't come so far to get put in a pickup and driven back up the hill.

"This meant that when we at last arrived at the beach, we just kind of broke from the cover of the pines all of a sudden, there was no defined path like the tourists would have taken. We heard the sea before we saw it, smelled it too, that scent of seaweed and clear ozone. It must have been near on a full hour after we left the cabin by now, a lifetime's walking for two little girls. But there it was—cold yellow sand running down to dark blue sea, gray boulders as big as houses, and it was all for us; not another soul in sight.

"We took off our sneakers and scrambled down the dune and walked towards the water, the beach so vast that the sea didn't feel like it was getting closer at first. But then the texture of the sand began to change, get more clumpy, that great sandcastle texture, so we set up camp, roughly equidistant between the edges of the bay where the coastline curved around. This is a three- or four-mile stretch remember, and we were the only people on it, so we must have looked like tiny dots in this great panorama of nature, dwarfed by the rocks to either side of us and those massive swaying pines somewhere behind, an agoraphobic's nightmare.

"Thinking back, I believe there was definitely this subconscious hum in my ear by that point, not guilt exactly, just the idea that a boundary was out of whack somewhere, something wasn't quite right. I mean, the idea to go out on our own wasn't unheard of, it was just that we'd always be stopped or given someone to go along with. Now that we were finally sitting still it was occurring to me that no one even had any idea where we were. Again, I wasn't worried precisely, except maybe about catching hell when we got back, probably because that bullish side of me was still thinking screw you, folks—if you can leave us to wake up on our own then you can leave us to take trips on our own. Sad thing is, at that very moment my folks were up and worrying, going from cabin to cabin to see if we were among their friends. They told me later they'd actually cried off the party early the night before, were asleep in our cabin all along. They just hadn't woken up with us because it was so damn early in the morning.

"Then Sammie said she was going to look for rock pools, that girl was a nut for wildlife. I told her in my sternest parental voice to come back soon young lady, or at least to call me if she found something. Then I just sat and chewed the sandwich I'd brought along, watched my sister get tinier and tinier as she wandered over towards the rocks and the sea, towards a portion of the boulders that were being swallowed up by the incoming tide. They were like a kind of natural promontory, a way of walking out over the crash of the surf without getting wet.

"Sammie walked off with a real stride, she never had that strange aimlessness that some kids have. Boulders that looked big from a distance looked even bigger with Sammie stood in front—the top of the nearest one came almost to her head. She walked around the side, I assumed she was looking for a way to climb up. Obviously she did climb up, but that was the last time I saw her alive. She should have clambered up the back, come out front and waved, at least waved goodbye. But I wasn't her mother and she'd have never thought to show off to me like she would to Mom. I just sat there like an idiot, a pathetic little actress munching a bagel that I didn't really want and secretly wishing I didn't have all this grown-up responsibility, which, of course, I didn't.

"I want to think that I heard a scream then, but I couldn't possibly have. She was too far away and the wind was too strong. I don't know whether it was because I got so spooked on my own, or because I knew intuitively that something was wrong, but suddenly I was running towards the rocks, running hard, looking for her, my parent persona smashed like bone china.

"I always sprint with my head down, and I remember looking at her footprints on the sand as I ran. They were the only markings on the pristine beach, and I recall seeing how much larger my strides were than hers and thinking of course they are, because I'm running. Strange how the brain will single out the weird snapshot bits, those funny moments of daydream are so often the things that stay with you. I'm pretty sure I'm trying to formulate something profound about the passage of time, how her footprints could be so close together and mine so far apart, and yet it was still her that got there first, met her fate. But of course, the race was long over.

"The rock turned out to be roughly the size of a single-story house, maybe not quite so tall. It was easy to see where Sammie had scrambled up, the footprints led right to the edge of the sand and the rock sort of sloped away around the back, a natural staircase. The sea was very loud at this point, the sound of the surf magnified in echoes, though I couldn't see the sea anymore. Then the stone leveled out at the top, like a big cratered tabletop that must have been fifty feet in diameter, an irregular fifty feet. It looked like the surface of another planet, and you could see down to where other rocks were in similar formations like giant steps down, rubbed smooth by salt water. You could probably jump between them but you'd break your neck if you fell. Sammie's rock pools were up there too, big, deep ones with seaweed trailing out of them, like if you pulled hard enough something evil might be on the other end. And it smelled bad. The sea was so close, so loud, and the wind howled.

"Sammie should have been visible from up there; everything else was, even my dumb-ass backpack all the way away on the beach where I'd been sitting. The only thing I could pray was that she'd climbed off the rock and was around the side somewhere, or was hiding from me. That happened sometimes, but I think we both knew that this wasn't a day for fun and games. Besides, I knew those rock pools would have kept her fascinated for hours, especially the one with the seaweed coming out of it.

"Why did I do it? Why did I get down on my hands and knees and even bother to look? Did I have to confirm that she'd slipped off the wet rock and into the sea, that she was *dead*? I don't know, but God help me, that's what I did, my clothes getting messed up as I edged forward, stained with that dark gray stuff that wasn't quite sand, and I could feel the spray of seawater thrown up by the waves. Because the edge wasn't sheer, it kind of curled under, I had to pull myself over more than was safe to get a vision of the water. With those big waves and irregular blasts of wind I was lucky not to get thrown down myself."

Karen paused, her mind in the past, but her eyes focused on Mary. The therapist didn't need to glance at the clock to know that the allotted time was well up.

"What did you see?" said Mary.

"Sammie's pink backpack. It was floating in the heavy current, but it wasn't what you would call floating, it was heaving massively up and down with a kind of lurching motion like it was caught in a powerful machine. Of course, it was just the power of the swell. And the water was slapping at the side of the rock beneath me with that disgusting noise like those massive sumo wrestlers make with their hands on their bellies, but so damn hard it sounded like thunderclaps.

"Then the current, this vicious current, it turned the backpack over, and it *was* Sammie, her arms through the loops. She was still wearing the backpack, and she was looking at me with totally white eyes, I swear to God; I could see a fat line of pink beneath the whites of eye like her whole fucking *head* was flooded. Then the sea, it just picked her body up and threw it at the rock below me, threw her like a person might throw a rag doll, but it didn't stop there, it pulled back and threw her again with the same godforsaken strength. I expected to see stuffing come out of her or something, but it never did, she just kept getting thrown, again and again, her head bent at one unnatural angle then another in this unholy dance. The way the sea made her move it was as if she was still alive, but there was this one time, this one throw when her head got bent right back under her body. She was flung full force onto her *neck*, there was this cracking sound in my head, and I knew that was it, as if I needed confirmation. There was never any blood, just black seaweed and this briny, sickly stink.

"I was screaming, I must have been, the sound probably tiny and pathetic among the crashing and the banging and the howling, and I remember thinking later that she was *already dead*, why was this still going on, why did this need to keep happening, this poor dolly that had been my sister just kept getting thrown and thrown. A harmless creature whose only crime was curiosity and who could never have stood a fucking chance in that cauldron. But still I kept watching."

Karen checked herself, blinked, raised a finger to her eye to wipe away a non-existent tear.The hum of the tape recorder sounded very loud in the space between them.

So that was it.

Or was it?

Mary waited, aware that her every move was being watched. She wouldn't tent her fingers or set her mouth, knew from experience that any movement might break the spell of Karen's memory.

"Time's up," said Karen, eventually. During the last parts of her story it was beginning to look like a stand-off, like she was daring Mary to contradict her or intervene. Now she slumped, her energy discharged. Mary couldn't hear the sigh, but she saw it, her client's chest heaved as if testing the weight that had been brought to bear.

Karen raised her eyes.

The small, sad smile that played around her lips suggested a woman who had scored a tiny victory but had been through the mill to get it. It was also a hopeful smile, but not a hope that comes from the pure of heart. A hope that the listener is understanding and believing.

Mary remained as still as possible, trying to process this new knowledge as rapidly as she could. These revelations were so sudden, so graphic, somehow so unlike Karen. But how? How were they unlike Karen? There was a lot of trauma trapped in there, that much was certain, and this story had undoubtedly been primed to come out for some time.

No, it was the drama. The level of drama was strange.

The detail in her story was characteristic, to be sure; Karen had proved in the past that her visual memory was remarkable. But the delivery: dramatic. Yes, it had been a performance, wrought from Karen's own self-awareness and her knowledge of the impact she could create.

Mary's sinewy figure bobbed in and out of the light as she considered, shadows chasing shadows across her lean, pale face. When the light caught her glasses, it threw lines of silhouette up onto her forehead. To Karen, it turned the therapist's face into an angry, judgmental mask.

"Perhaps we should pick this over next time," said Karen, into the damnable silence.

"Okay," said Mary, quietly, conclusively, and this time she did tent her fingers.

Something stopped the therapist from asking the questions that she might have done at the end of a session, simple questions about the journey home, plans for the weekend; inquiries designed to bring the client back to the present. Mary's instinct told her that Karen's consciousness was already well integrated into the present, had been there throughout the telling of her tale.

And so Karen, the last client of the day, raised out of the armchair and was shown sympathetically towards the door.

CHILLLERKID RANTED//: r u there yet, Jen???

Dave Wiley's old Dell began to blink, dutifully.

Swamped by a fluffy old Tweetie Pie robe that belonged to Ashley and smelled like skin lotion, Jen padded back over to the computer.

The unfinished floorboards felt harsh on her bare soles and she had to tread carefully so as not to catch a toe on an errant tack. The carpet in the loft room was being sold at a weekend flea market that following morning; they needed to save all the pennies they could, Dave had said, as between them they wrestled the cylinder of rubber and fur down the stairs and into the garage.

Jen, having never really known in her life what it was like to *want*, smiled beatifically.

Just before this, Dave and Ashley had also told her that Hawaii would be an expensive place to live, at least in the short term, so although you'll be very welcome, it'd perhaps be best if you don't come out for the first couple of months, baby. Can you understand that? Jen had mollified them with gifts of hugs and promises and reassurances, correctly believing that Dad and Ash would receive her any time she wanted to visit. Dad, so confident in front of Mom, had seemed to turn inexplicably worried and gray once she'd exited stage left.

She wondered if Mom was, right now, pondering over Dad's imminent departure. This was information that Mom really should have figured out for herself before today, and Jen couldn't blame Dad for not wanting to mention it until the last minute. Mom certainly had been distracted recently.

But despite Dave's now obvious reservations, he and Ashley really *were* going to move on schedule, that much was certain; the monitor had become the only source of light in a stripped room. Jen hadn't really believed it up until she arrived and saw the way the house had been packed back to a series of faceless chambers. Not that Dave and Ashley's pad in West Oakland had ever felt much like a home to Jen, but it *was* disquieting to see a place she knew so familiarly reduced to an empty, soulless shell. It reminded her of Grandma Wiley's house after she died, the furniture distributed between the family and the weeds claiming the lawn out back.

Jen shrugs when she needs to lighten her thoughts. Of all her unconscious imitations of Mommy, this is the gesture she mirrors most accurately of all.

She was away from the screen because she had been opening the door a crack to let in the light of the corridor while she surfed. Jen liked to use the computer in the dark, but knew from experience that an alternate light source would stave off the headaches if she was going online for long. Besides, it was spooky up here on her own with the room so cold and bare. She glanced over at the mangy sleeping bag in the corner that would be her bed for the night, the loose cushions from the couch downstairs hidden beneath it, one of the few items not yet in storage for shipping. Jen found herself missing her snug, secure bed back in the big city, a place to sleep that wouldn't separate into three soft islands in a sea of potential splinters when she turned over. Then this cynical thought was shoved to the back of her mind, treasonous as it seemed towards her stressed-out father.

CHILLLERKID RANTED//: r u there yet, Jen???

Twice the message had come up in the last minute. Jen felt the familiar thrill that she always felt when Chilllerkid was online.

Tonight, of course, Jen had been expecting her.

SWEETTHANG RANTED//: loud n clear
CHILLLERKID RANTED//: did u get my letter this morning?
SWEETTHANG RANTED//: as per!
CHILLLERKID RANTED//: did u open it?
SWEETTHANG RANTED//: u said not 2?!
CHILLLERKID RANTED//: u have it now?
SWEETTHANG RANTED//: yup
CHILLLERKID RANTED//: close ur eyes and count to 10

Jen reached into a downy pocket of her robe and pulled out an envelope with her own address on the front.

She closed her eyes and began to count, slowly.

That morning, obeying Chilllerkid's instruction, Jen was up bright and early before Karen in order to intercept the mail. It had been breathlessly established during their most recent shared effort in the chatroom that Chilllerkid had a secret to share with Jen, a really important one, something to do with the child's horoscope. It had been gradually and convincingly revealed over the course of many heart-felt online conversations that Chilllerkid, or Eloise from Michigan as she had identified herself, was not only a high school cheerleader with a very healthy grade point average, she also managed to make extra allowance doing some kind of astral readings out of the annexe attached to her house. Naturally, Eloise's mom knew about this, and actively encouraged it. Eloise was the seventh child of the youngest of seven, she had explained, which made her special. She also suspected that Jen was special too, although in what way neither of them knew at that stage.

But Eloise seemed to have figured it out now.

Information, a secret, hidden in Jen's stars. This wasn't information that can be properly imparted in a chatroom, or even in an email. But it could be sent in a letter, for some reason.

Jen was a bright child and had always maintained a healthy skepticism about people that she met online. But Eloise was very credible. Demanding, too. Jen was expected to be online at the same time every night. Earlier chats about boyfriends that could end in graphic discussions of the relative merits of various sexual positions, short gushy seminars on Johnny Depp that could lead to what proper grown-up movies could teach you, and (worst of all) the innocent Q and A's about tampons that could turn unbearably, cringeworthily intimate without warning have given way to mutual personal confessions of a kind that Jen has never found with her mother, or at school with her too-cool friends.

You can sympathize. Eloise certainly could.

CHILLLERKID RANTED//: Did u do it? Did u count?
SWEETTHANG RANTED//: Is counting part of it?
CHILLLERKID RANTED//: its all part of it

The fact that Jen's "star chart" was there on the mat within the apartment rather than down on the mat inside the front door to the building did not strike Jen as strange; before the Durants became sickly, they used to bring up the mail sometimes and slide it under the door.

SWEETTHANG RANTED//: should I open it now?
CHILLLERKID RANTED//: wait one moment for me

It never occurred to Jen not to pick it up, that this might *not* have been the message for her. It was the only correspondence on the mat, so therefore the only mail of the day, she thought. Jen was excited, and when children are excited they are even more inclined to see themselves as the center of the world. Besides, the amount of mail through the door had been getting gradually less and less. Mom's new business was hardly setting the world on fire.

SWEETTHANG RANTED//: is this a moment now?

What Jen has *not* noticed is that though her address (but no name) is on the front, the mail bears no stamp or postal print. This means that it could only have been delivered by hand.

CHILLLERKID RANTED//: Jen, I need u 2 do sumthing. That place we talked about.
SWEETTHANG RANTED//: ????
CHILLLERKID RANTED//: I want u to touch yourself there.

Horror.

Although something similar has happened before.

SWEETTHANG RANTED//: don't be a PIG

The other time it ended with the connector being pulled out of the bedroom wall and her own angry, disgusted tears. It was several days before Jen would visit the chatroom again. This enforced absence was the point at which Eloise stopped the sexual entreaties and became an agony aunt.

CHILLLERKID RANTED//: not like u think, babe—I promise.
SWEETTHANG RANTED//: Then like ???, El? R U being gross again?
CHILLLERKID RANTED//: I only want u 2 center yourself. To KNOW U r the center of your universe . . . Please touch yourself

Jen felt her face flood red with shame. But still she writes.

SWEETTHANG RANTED//: not on ur life
CHILLLERKID RANTED//: I promise that the stars point to u.
SWEETTHANG RANTED//: no
CHILLLERKID RANTED//: lets do it together. Im touching myself

Now Jen looks down at the sealed envelope in her lap, looks past it to her bare knee, white in the harsh light thrown in from the landing. Her nightgown has fallen open. The T-shirt she wears to bed is really far too short for her; Jen has grown out of it, there is a big expanse of thigh.

SWEETTHANG RANTED//: fuck you, monster
CHILLLERKID RANTED//: fuck me

The edge of the reinforced packet of secrets digs into her skin as she moves it slowly towards her. It leaves a sky trail in the flesh that is even paler than her skin.

SWEETTHANG RANTED//: fuck you MONSTERR

Then the light of the world rushes in.

Fuck you monsterr . . .

Jen flipped the robe back over her legs in a way that suggested she was cold.

"Not good for you to sit in the dark," said a friendly, surfer-girl voice from behind her.

"No," said Jen.

"I brought . . . *Jesus Christ*. Who the hell writes like *this*?"

Jen turned around, not bothering to try and hide the words on the screen. She suddenly felt very sad. "How long were you standing there before you flipped the light, Ash?"

"I just brought, I brought you some . . . *Jesus Christ* . . ."

Jen, looking every bit her age, stared up at Ashley as she read over the conversation. Her dad's lover was wearing an identical robe and had removed her make-up with something that smelled a bit like honey and milk.

Ash was a slow reader. Eventually she allowed a giant chocolate cookie to fall off the plate she was holding; it fractured into crumbs, all over the bare wooden floor.

It had been a long day, but it was not quite over.

"Karen, when you come in at night, you must put the chain-latch on the door."

Mrs. Durant had been waiting for her. As Karen was padding

down the corridor to her apartment, the old woman had appeared out of her room like an inadequate jack-in-the-box.

"I just did, Mrs. Durant," said Karen, obediently.

"Not tonight. *Last* night. When I came down this morning to get the mail the chain was off. I know it's a little thing, but it's our last line of defense in here, you know?"

"The chain was off the door?"

"I'm aware that I'm busybodying, but about things like this I make no apology. First the chain gets forgotten, then the bolts, then we might as well invite in, well, anybody."

Mrs. Durant folded her arms and the bony, up-thrust chin demanded a response.

Karen blinked, searched her memory. She hadn't left the chain off, she knew she hadn't. In fact, she wasn't entirely convinced that she hadn't gotten in *before* Mrs. Durant last night. But Karen was feeling magnanimous. Bone-weary after the events of the day, sure, but magnanimous all the same. The responsibility of the letters really had gone to someone else, and tomorrow was another day; a little matronly chastening about building security from Mrs. Durant represented a happy return to normality.

"I agree with you, Lenore, about locking everything properly on the door. It won't happen again."

"Are you going to bed now? Did you want fresh milk for cocoa?"

Karen smiled, and the beam of unfamiliar affection nearly rocked Mrs. Durant on her heels. "No thank you, Lenore. And I am sorry about not locking the door properly."

"That's fine," said Mrs. Durant.

The old woman watched with something approaching suspicion as her sole tenant let herself into the apartment and closed the door. That girl badly needed to get herself another man while her looks still held. There were worry lines, pain lines around the long-lashed eyes that hadn't been there when she first moved in. Also, it was not good, never good, for a little daughter to be growing up without a man about the house, no matter how temperamental that man might prove to be. Mrs. Durant thought of Mr. Durant, propped up in bed; irascible and unpleasant when lucid, needy and pathetic when not. Men up until this point in Lenore's life had always represented boundaries, focus, structure. A woman without a man was almost certain to find folly, she thought, either through hysteria or misadventure. Thank God that Armand's health had held long enough to see their twin girls grow up and move on. The fact that neither Debette nor Charlie really called anymore wasn't bothering her, much.

Mrs. Durant pulled her knitted shawl a little more tightly around her shoulders, frowned in a way that scrutinized the entire empty corridor. This building was getting impossible to heat.

Perhaps a breeze was getting in from somewhere.

The apartment was black but the machine was blinking.

Twelve messages in bright electronic numerals. Fat red light from the single angry eye, intermittently tracing up the near wallpaper.

On off, on off.

Karen, who had imagined herself standing with her hand on the wall, taking her shoes off in the light of the doorway, scrapped that plan. Twelve voicemail messages was a number unheard of since her days in TV.

A strange new drone of fear in her head, she reached for the play button before she even turned on the hallway light.

The phone rang while her finger was on the switch, making her jump. It took a moment to answer it.

"Yes?"

"Karen?"

"Dave, is that you?" For some reason she had been expecting to hear an unfamiliar voice.

"Christ, Kar, I've been trying to reach you all night."

"No, my cell is off. I had therapy."

"Did you get my messages?"

"I just got in. Is that you, twelve messages? Are you all right?"

"I don't know. I mean, we're fine. Jen is here, and Ashley. Jen got a letter."

"A letter?"

"One of your letters. *Jen* got one."

"Jen got a . . ."

"She'd opened it, *we* opened it. I don't know if that's what we should have done, but . . ."

Karen felt the blood drain from her face. Her hand was on the wall now, though the shoes weren't coming off.

"Karen?"

She listened to her breath coming fast and ragged.

"Karen, are you there?"

As though all the oxygen in the room was pulling away from her.

"*Karen?*"

Dave's voice, urgent, yet somehow tinny and pathetic. She realized she was holding the phone at a distance. Composure now. Composure: "Dave, I'm here."

"I'm sorry if we shouldn't have, didn't mean to, we didn't *know* . . ."

"Doesn't matter now."

"No."

"What does it say?"

"Ah, it's a demand."

"A *demand*?"

"You know, instruction, like a proper ransom note would have."

At last, thought Karen, a demand. Like a *proper* ransom note would have. There came a strong urge to giggle herself away from sanity. She fought it, fought it adequately.

The lights still off, she carried the phone through into the living room, watched a steely starless sky silhouette a cut-out cardboard city.

But somebody now wanted something. Finally, blessedly, somebody now wanted something.

"Karen?" Dave was sounding upset, lost.

So let's give it to them. Let's just fucking give it to them.

"What does it say?" Cool as a cucumber.

"Do you think I should come over there? Or you to us? Jen was in a chatroom before, there might be a situation here." Karen heard an anxious female voice speaking in the background; maybe Jen, probably Ashley. She ignored it.

"Dave, what does the letter say?"

"It's confused, it doesn't make a lot of sense. I mean, there's a lot of things we don't . . ."

"Dave, for fuck's sake. The demand. *What does it say?*"

"It says: 'Go to church.'"

Nine

Two weeks after the kidnapping of Katy Trueblood and the bloodying of her little sister and the trailers were being dismantled or taken away. It happened with a speed that was remarkable; for a short while it had seemed to eighty-year-old Gladys Walson that the light of the entire world was shining into Mountain Pastures Mobile Home Park.

The news about Katy and Holly only broke locally, but it broke pretty big. Vans from Channel 6 and Channel 11 double parked alongside the wrecking yard within only a few hours of the incident, and an earnest young woman who smelled of hairspray talked to Gladys like she was an idiot.

Despite the lights and the noise and her fainting momentarily at the scene, that first night the old woman was unwilling to leave her trailer in case Edgar came back. She eventually did so on her daughter's teary-eyed insistence, and ended up watching the news in Carol's bakery-warm kitchen. Gladys had felt like a celebrity for most of the day, and both mother and daughter were mildly disappointed to see that her interview was not featured.

Edgar, of course, is the name of the cat.

There was much coming and going all that day and all the next, a blur of uniforms searching through the trailer park, junkyard and surrounding area for poor Katy. Gladys told the same story to people she didn't know more than a dozen times; faces and events began to run together and ultimately she had to cry off to rest. She was furious with herself for not being more capable of helping, understanding that she had discovered the crime scene, but remembering very little before she fainted.

The conversation that really stood out to Gladys was with the wide-hipped Chief of Police, who came by later. She introduced herself as Ella and refused tea and asked the same sorts of questions as the others with the same sort of attitude, but at the end when Gladys suggested that they might pray together for the girls, Ella agreed, and readily. *"I'm hoping to come back and see you,"* she had said afterwards, but she hadn't yet. Probably busy, her hands full with all the evil in the world. That woman had walked a difficult path, you could see it written across her flat sturdy face, but there *was* something remarkable about her, some strange intensity of understanding, or maybe doubt.

Gladys wondered if, like herself, Ella McCullers had recently seen the devil walking the streets of Canaan, Utah.

The following day, the *Canaan Daily News* ran with a school picture of the girls on the front page, Katy's hand posed on Holly's shoulder. "WHAT KIND OF FIEND?" demanded reporter Earl Michelson in his headline. Gladys knew Earl well. In the sixties she'd taught him how to read properly at the now derelict Hope Elementary. In his article, Earl failed to ask worthwhile questions about how the two little girls had come to be left alone, instead played up the horror of the incident with as much relish that small-town journalistic propriety allowed. Later in the piece there were some wise remarks from Ella the policewoman, advice to locals to keep calm, not to panic, to please send your children to school as normal.

The town was horrified by the events and then it gossiped. There were juicy rumors, the most persistent of which involved a local mechanic and his wife, Don and Jeanie Keynes. Don was the brother-in-law of Milton, the worthless father whom Gladys heard cursing out his poor family night after night through the thin walls of her doublewide. Neither Don nor Jeanie had been seen since the kidnapping, though retired custodian Ted Humboldt told Gladys in the ice-cream aisle of the mini-mart that Jeanie was hiding out in her house on Walnut Lane, was calling in sick from her job at the nursing home. Gladys also knew the nursing home, played bridge there some days. She'd never met Jeanette Keynes though. She could ask around.

Just like Katy, Don had vanished off the face of the earth.

He managed to make it on to the front page of the paper the following day, though—a small black and white photo. The police wanted Don Keynes for questioning, Earl reported, ominously.

Edgar, meanwhile, was still nowhere to be found. Gladys even ventured past the diminishing police circus and out through the broken chain-link fence into the junkyard with some of his favorite fish-biscuit treats, a place she usually didn't like to go because of the bad kids and their bikes. No luck. She tried to enlist one of the many cops who were still standing around to help, but Gladys had plenty marbles left to know when she was being humored.

On the evening of September 11, Channel 6 news, lacking any further information but conscious of the continued appetite for the story, found a different angle. They flashed up the picture of Don Keynes, had graphics mount the words MISSING: WANTED FOR QUESTIONING below it in big letters, and then focused exclusively on the "problem" of Mountain Pastures Mobile Home Park. It seemed that some local citizens were expressing concern about an area on the outskirts of their small and law-abiding city that was becoming a haven for the problematic. Those in the know said that this incident had been on the cards for some time; not the attack on the poor little girls, no one could have predicted that, but there were certainly *drug deals* going on around there, and in the adjacent wrecker's yard too.

It'd been common knowledge for a while. Where there are drug dealers there are gangbangers, and where there are gangbangers, well, you don't need *me* to tell you what happens next, said talking head Gary Hudson Green of Gary's Outdoor Activities. Channel 6 got some more footage of townsfolk, including a harassed-looking Mayor Mancina as he bustled through the dusty portico of Canaan's pint-sized City Hall. He'd certainly take a look at any petition requesting the closure of Mountain Pastures, he said. The concerns of the townsfolk were the mayor's concerns, just like they'd been the concerns of his father before him.

Gladys watched this new twist of the story with growing concern. There were squatters in a nearby trailer, she knew—a dirt-poor but exceptionally polite family with a child who would wash her windows for a couple of quarters. There was another trailer with a busted lock, but the older high-schoolers who came up there to make out kept it pretty clean, with the exception of cigarette butts and discarded prophylactic packets around the entrance. Beer cans sometimes. Graffiti on the empty trailers was getting pretty bad also, but what could you do? Younger kids mostly caused that, fifteen- and sixteen-year-olds who'd give attitude but still say "yes ma'am" when you raised your voice. It was unfortunate that the junkyard made such a great track for their buzzing little dirt bikes. Drugs? Gladys didn't know anything about drugs.

The 6 report closed with footage of the trailer park shot at dusk, and Gladys was surprised to find that she'd made it on to the news after all, in a swift montage that included the slow gumball flash of the Trueblood crime scene interspersed with punk-kids pulling wheelies for the camera. There she was, outside in her slippers and robe, not the good ones, still looking for Edgar and clearly unaware she was being filmed. Edited into the footage of rude youth and police cars and graffiti like that, Gladys realized that she had been made to look like a stumbling and confused old biddy, community trash that needed sweeping up. They were making her little trailer park look like *Detroit* or somewhere. Gladys, who always kept her home and appearance immaculate, found herself blinking back angry tears and hunting for a pen to write a letter of complaint.

In a twist that surprised very few commentators, it was revealed the following morning that Don Keynes, brother-in-law to the victim's father, was now the only suspect in the investigation. Earl Michelson managed to find a photograph of a family barbecue, and the *Daily News* blew it up for their front page, Don looking fat and happy with a cheeseburger in each hand. Milton and Mandy, relocated to community housing, were too traumatized to comment, but in an uncharacteristically in-depth piece of investigative journalism, Earl had discovered that the reason for this development was that the Trueblood trailer was not only covered, but positively *blanketed* in Don's fingerprints. Earl admitted that this might not sound too strange in itself, but the markings were remarkable for their freshness and their presence in the bedroom and on the baby's cot, places where Don had never been much known to go. In some areas, squealed Earl, they had even been put down *over* the blood. The police said the investigation was ongoing and would not confirm or deny Earl's article, but Gladys knew that Earl's older sister Abigail had been answering the 911 calls there since the Ford administration; anyone with half a brain could guess where the story had leaked.

From then on, the investigative side of the story was as good as dying, if not quite dead. Everyone breathed a collective sigh of relief when it was reported on the news that Holly Trueblood had awoken from her coma on the lunchtime of the fourteenth, but once it became public understanding that Katy's was a kidnapping within the family—well, folks still gossiped, but the blowhards began to lose interest. This was a random boogeyman no more, he had a face and a name, and he looked like a white-trash mechanic who liked cheeseburgers; their own children could be considered safe again. Sad fact of the matter is that thousands of children go missing, each with a right to public outcry, but if the abuse happens within the family then it lacks the random fear angle that makes it play so well.

That and there's just so many of them, thought Gladys, as she got down on her knees that night to pray to Jesus for the safe return of Katy and her cat. Faces on milk cartons, sure, but our interest can only tolerate so many news stories on missing children.

The police rope around the Trueblood trailer remained in place for two more nights, but on the second night the sole officer remaining on the scene fell asleep in his patrol car and some of the ever-present kids played dare and snuck under. Gladys saw and called 911, but no one much cared. By lunchtime the following day all signs of the cops were gone, the only legacy a stray flutter of yellow tape.

Meanwhile, support was growing for the closure of Mountain Pastures. A petition was circulated demanding regeneration. Earl Michelson, having exhausted the Trueblood angle and not afraid of being late to the party, camped out in his car behind the willow tree with a photographer and ate Slim Jims for an hour and, sure enough, got a shot of two winsome teenagers emerging from a busted trailer, her in a bra, him buttoning his fly. "UNDERAGE SEX ON YOUR DOORSTEP!" screamed the *Daily News*. "What is the mayor going to do?" Then city ordinance enforcement came in for a severe tongue-lashing for allowing so many trailers to lie derelict. "How are we supposed to maintain the tourist boom when such havens for impropriety are allowed to fester like fungus upon the face of our town?"

Mayor Samuel Mancina, fresh from a stern-looking photo-op by Holly Trueblood's bedside with a bewildered Milt, called a meeting which he didn't attend, and a zoning officer was promptly sent out. The woman, Suzanne Zelman, immediately condemned eight of the nine units, most of which had been red-tagged by the gas company. When it came to her turn, Gladys apologized profusely to Ms. Zelman for the rotting cat food that was sitting out on her doorstep. She was sure Edgar was coming back, it was *so* unlike him to vanish for this long. Suzanne was sympathetic; Gladys's trailer, ironically the oldest one in the park, was the only one to pass inspection.

It took several days for Suzanne to track down a man named Derrick, the owner of the land. He said he lived in Nevada and had placed responsibility of the site in the hands of an equally slippery operation called the Austen Family Revocable Trust. They said that Mountain Pastures was supposed to be managed by one Terence Jacoby, a Monticello realtor, who couldn't be reached. In the end, being as he was in violation of about a dozen articles of rule R392-402 in the state administrative code, Mr. Derrick's voicemail was given an ultimatum: redevelop the site or see it dissolved altogether. The *Daily News* was satisfied, the mayor dodged a bullet, and the people felt suitably avenged for the recent brutality.

Trucks came within a week.

It turned out that the mobile homes were not particularly mobile. It took much cursing, sweating and a special tractor to move the five salvageable units, and a whole lot more cursing and sweating to dismantle the three that weren't worth saving for recyclable parts. Gladys, watching, had no comprehension whether the workmen were from Derrick or from the city, and she didn't much care. Her home had been built before 1976 and as per state law could not be moved from the site provided her trailer was sufficiently maintained. The rent was fixed, so no one could squeeze her out. All this had been neatly documented for Gladys by her daughter Carol, a paralegal secretary who loved her mother very much but didn't want her living with them quite yet. Not that Carol was particularly keen that her Jesus-loving mom was going to be alone on what was to become a piece of wasteland next to a junkyard, but the truth was that Gladys didn't even want to move. She had been there since Pappy Walson died of leukemia in the eighties and had seen that home through vandalism and storms and once a contaminated water supply that threatened to put every single resident in the hospital. Besides, reasoned Carol, her mother was surely in a better position now that the rest of those rotting rat-havens were being towed away.

Once the light of the world had shined its beacon away from Mountain Pastures Mobile Home Park, it looked very much like the place where a disreputable funfair had once been: a featureless wasteland of crusty tire tracks and dancing litter; the junkyard across the road looming like a fortress, with new and reinforced security features. Only the willow tree remained from before, battered, bruised, but very much alive, leaves turning with the season. The kids and the squatters had moved on, and Gladys was left in her trailer on the edge of a void, a huge hot muddy car park for a driveway, the ancient and solitary guardian of the past.

Then, on Tuesday, September 21, the cat came back.

Gladys, up and dressed early that morning, felt a minimum of nostalgia on what was supposed to be the last day's labor for the contractors, in this case electrical engineers from the city. She'd come to yearn for quieter days, empty as they'd be of dust and engines and cuss-words and the stench of diesel. The memory of the Trueblood kidnapping was finally fading and she hadn't seen that family but once when they came with a U-Haul to collect their belongings, Milt thinking that no one was watching him as he took a baseball bat to his air conditioner like the mindless thug he always was. On the positive side, volunteers from a community church were coming out to see her sometimes, and that could be nice, but they ate all her cake and were inclined to talk too much. No, it was time to rest. Good honest rest, she'd earned it.

No sooner had Gladys put her feet up to watch TV than the peace was disturbed by voices from outside.

"You be careful, Dutch. I don't think you'd get comp if we don't use the bucket truck."

"Nuts to that. Do we wait all day?" Dutch had a great body,

worked on it tirelessly. It'd be fun to climb the pole with his hands and feet, show this sissy kid who insisted on wearing his hard hat in the van.

"You need your tools?"

"Gimme." Dutch's toolbox was handmade, had apertures on the side where he could loop a stitched belt, throw the whole caboodle over his shoulder. It wouldn't be so much fun to climb with that bouncing against his ass, but there was no disconnecting the redundant drum without it.

The utility pole was barely taller than the remaining trailer, and Dutch had scaled it in seconds, gloves biting into rusty grips. His head was at the service box when for some reason he felt the need to crank his neck and turn around.

"What the hell . . ." he muttered.

"What are you doing?" called sissy-boy from below.

Dutch pretended not to hear. He grabbed the handle of his toolbox, slid it onto the top of the creaky mobile home. He followed with his feet, careful to stand near the edges where the walls reinforced the roof. These things weren't built to be walked on.

"Dutch!"

Gladys, irritated by the raised voices and intrusive banging from above, snapped off *Days of our Lives* and stepped outside. She took in the electricity van, the willow tree, and the skinny freckly kid in the hard hat and oversized fluorescent jacket. He was gazing intently up at the top of her trailer, one hand protecting his eyes from the brightness of a rich September sun. He ignored her as she walked down to him and followed his gaze.

There was a huge man on top of her trailer, another engineer, and he looked sweaty and pale, sun shining through the tight blond curls on his head. He wasn't looking down at them, he was staring at something by his feet.

"Dutch!" squeaked freckles.

"Dammit boy, what is he doing on top of my house?" Gladys was past being surprised by pig-ignorant workmen, they'd been a staple of her existence for days.

"Dutch!"

Dutch seemed to make up his mind.

Scarcely glancing at his onlookers, he pulled back a huge boot and, with a disgusted gesture between a kick and a slide, shoved an item off the roof. It was a movement designed to put his foot in as little contact as possible with the object in question, but there was still enough force there to propel what looked like a bloated and putrefying pillowcase some distance through the air and onto the ground directly in front of Gladys. After a short roll and an awfully long pause, the matted sack split wetly and slowly and silently along a man-made seam like the flowering of an obscene plant. Gladys screamed as the cat's head and legs belched out of the widening gash and onto the dust in a small pile at her feet, having been carelessly amputated and sown up inside his gas-fattened belly, many days before.

It turned out that Edgar had not gone so very far after all.

Before there were colors there were shapes, and before there were shapes there was nothing, and that nothing was intolerable, thought Ella, as she paced in circles around the empty waiting room of the Reagan Family Mental Health Clinic. She was waiting for Holly Trueblood to finish her latest talk with Arnold Lau, a specialist psychologist and friend whom she had unofficially engaged to try and speed up Holly's memory of events, if any memory existed. Unfortunately for Ella, *talk* was proving to be the wrong word. The primary witness in a flailing investigation had a hole in her head the size of the Lincoln Tunnel, and hadn't made so much as a peep since she woke up ten days ago.

If Holly Trueblood had any joy in her young life up until her encounter with a madman, then that joy could be found in painting and drawing. Mrs. Martinez from the school had shown Ella picture after picture during the informal police interviews with classmates and teachers, and even Ella could see that Holly had a talent that belied her age. Unusually for a seven-year-old, she didn't paint people, she painted landscapes, broad-stroked and colorful, and always with a big, cheerful yellow sun. "If she pulls through this she'll probably get better still," said Mrs. Martinez, without irony. "She might learn to put in the dark bits."

It was Dr. Lau's idea to bring art materials to their second session, and what Holly had begun to do with those materials had become Ella's only other lead, and it was a tenuous lead at that. At first, Holly just stared into space, said nothing, that big idiot bandage wrapped around her fragile head. Despite this, she was recovering remarkably quickly, was now feeding herself—chocolate mousse appeared to be her favorite—and sometimes she blinked knowingly at Taslima, the friendly nurse. Taslima was in there with them now, would shortly put a stop to the session and drive Holly back to the hospital. Holly liked being taken out, although she showed no desire to return home or even much interest in seeing her parents, to Mandy Trueblood's great distress.

It was the office-presentation sized pads that did it. Lau brought them in and fastened one upright on a stand. Holly had never known a space as big and grown-up looking as that to draw on, and it was all for her to do with what she liked, said Dr. Lau, gesturing at the paints and brushes that he'd picked up from the store. Even so, she hesitated, uncertain, but then Dr. Lau took a magic marker and drew a big cartoon picture of his own face to prove that it was OK, and even Ella had to smile when she saw it, a me-so-solly Chinese caricature complete with chopsticks and pigtail hat.

The following days pleased Taslima and the psychologist, but they were maddening for Ella, who could see Katy's chances fading with every hour. Holly's first attempt at anything was a baffling series of rectangles in black paint. She would spend seconds painting the shapes, rapid and irregular, then spend the rest of the hour painstakingly filling them in with more black, extremely careful never to transgress the borders, ignoring any attempt to talk to her. At first, her breath would get quite labored during this process, but when the time was up she would readily take Taslima's hand and allow herself to be walked out to the car.

Lau didn't offer any insight into what the rectangles might mean, he just provided more paper. "Let's establish a nice daily routine for her here," he said. "Routine is useful in times like these."

Ella was unable to be at every session, and once she realized that she wasn't building a special relationship with Holly like Lau and Taslima, she stayed away, marshaled her detectives to pursue the few useless leads, to not lose hope. Most of those assigned to the case assumed that Don and Katy were across state lines together somewhere. There was a bulletin out for a man and a girl, but nothing was coming in. It was during one of these dog-day afternoons when Lau called, as excited as she'd ever known him.

"Color," he said. "There was color today."

The color turned out to be yellow, but the rectangles stayed the same. The following day there were greens and blues, and one session was spent doing nothing but mixing paints. Holly had started tugging at sleeves when she wanted something, and Lau took a risk and filled in a rectangle himself, and so did Taslima. They were careful to stay in the boundaries that Holly had drawn, and Holly seemed satisfied.

Lau told Ella that he was pleased with Holly's application with the rectangles. He saw a persistence there, a willingness to set herself and complete time-consuming goals that, in his opinion, demonstrated an eagerness to identify with being alive. Conversely, he was concerned that she should remain so totally inward-looking. Holly didn't seem to recognize family members and as yet had failed to shed a single tear.

The following day found Lau still trying to inspire new ways to play. He suggested that Holly might like to draw a circle. Holly didn't seem to listen, just carried on mixing paint. Lau took a paintbrush and drew a circle himself. When Holly noticed what he had done, she stood up and walked over to the inexpert shape, inspecting it as though a foreign object had materialized. Lau wondered if she might fill it in, saw it more as a trust-building exercise, but Holly tore it down.

"Holly!" said Taslima.

"It's okay," said Lau. "Did you not like the circle, Holly?"

Holly wasn't angry. She handed Lau his circle and started work on the piece of paper beneath, her small hand clutching Lau's paintbrush like a fine penman.

After two minutes she sat down again, mixed some more paint.

She had painted a picture of Jon Peterson.

To be charitable, it didn't look much like Jon Peterson. Frankly, it couldn't possibly have, but for a seven-year-old with only two minutes to spare in her broken mind it was about as near perfect a rendering as anyone could hope for. The body was long and lean, an elongated triangle for a torso. The hands were huge, like fat wriggly worms. She didn't spend so long on the face as she spent on the shoes, which were presumably the last things she saw while face down in her own blood, but she sure as hell remembered to put the grin up there, a large moon-shaped curve filled with pointy triangles like you might see on the face of a cartoon shark. Hair, no ears, and two quick stabs for the nose. Holly didn't much bother with the eyes.

"Who's this, Holly?" said Lau, and then sorely regretted his question.

Holly looked curiously at Lau, and then walked over to Peterson with her freshly mixed black paint, an amalgam of all her other colors. She began to fill in the shapes of the body from the outer edges, just like she had the rectangles, until all the features were obscured.

Lau was aghast. Both he and Taslima tried to convince Holly to stop, but Lau was frightened to take away the paint or impose any kind of physical restraint. At this critical stage, and with Holly's history of trauma, he thought it might ruin their relationship for good.

After Holly and Taslima had left for the day, Lau and Ella stood together in the room and stared at the painting for a long time.

"It's very hard to identify people from their shadows," said Ella, eventually.

"I know," said Lau.

"But there is one thing," said Ella. "Don Keynes is a short, fat man. This shape is of a tall man, and slim."

"Yes," said Lau, and a futile half-hour was spent describing the picture prior to defacement.

Ella McCullers and Dr. Arnold Lau had an unusual friendship, based as it was on a mutual appreciation of the other's ability to conquer addiction, of all things. Both were alcoholics back in the seventies, and they had plenty of time to bond over endless cups of weak tea at a Baton Rouge branch of AA. This was in Louisiana, at a time when Ella was still running away from herself. Lau was a decorated FBI agent who was just about managing to separate work from time with the bottle, and thoroughly despising his mosquito-ridden posting. I drink because I like to, Ella would say, filling her tea with crunchy brown sugar. Lau wasn't quite so self-destructive, but he was coming through problems of his own based on a bad break-up. Ella thought Lau was a bit of a pencil-neck mommy's boy, but he did convince her to stay in town for a while, to not take off in two weeks like usual, and Ella ended up staying four whole months. Sometimes she was sober and sometimes she wasn't, and Lau would have to come over to the squat and hold her hair for her while she puked and wept, but at least one had found another they could trust.

A year or so after Ella left town, Lau decided to retrain. He went to DC and spent a lifetime studying on his parents' inheritance, having realized that by joining the FBI he was neglecting his real desire, which was to help people, children specifically. He never lost touch with the Justice Department though, finally becoming a celebrated psychological profiler, but he was always careful to remain freelance, rejecting decoration and focusing primarily on his Georgetown private practice. Ella and Lau exchanged sporadic letters, but Lau was always enigmatic when it came to talking about the precise nature of his job. Ella sympathized.

Lau got tired of the hustle and bustle of city life and took semi-retirement, moving to Utah about the same time as Ella was taking up her post as Canaan Police Chief. There'd been a dinner or two since, but any relationship that Ella might have liked to rekindle had mostly failed to materialize. She didn't know how much Lau had learned about her checkered past since he'd moved to the area, maybe that had put him off. Or maybe it wasn't just her. Thankfully, he'd jumped at the chance to help Holly. He insisted that it had to be on an unofficial level, independent of the chief medical officer and only cleared with the parents.

"She'll probably draw another boogeyman before long, believe me."

Ella blinked, lost in the past. "What did you say?"

"Another boogeyman," said Lau. "This is a gradual process which I daren't try and expedite."

"Boogeyman, you said."

"Yeah," Lau polished his spectacles. "Well, you never saw the picture before she filled it in. As evil a face as I ever saw a child draw, and smiling as well. A smile or a frown is not something a child misses. Gave me the creeps, and I don't spook easily."

"Mm."

"But by that I'm not inferring it isn't someone she knows. That's one spirited little person, measured, resilient. I'm glad of the opportunity to help."

"We're grateful to have you," said Ella. "Even with health

insurance, it can be hell to find specialists, for children too." She stood, stretched her legs. "I only wish you had longer."

"That's why I wanted to talk to you. You know that in two days I'm supposed to go back, teach a class in our nation's capital. I've been committed to it for months. Sure, this is semi-retirement for me, but it can't all be kayaking and rock-climbing."

Lau chuckled, but Ella was studying her feet. She'd always known this was a favor, that he wouldn't be available for long. Lau sensed her disappointment.

"Look, Ella. Understand that I wouldn't leave if I thought we were going to discover something that would help you catch your man, but in terms of the trauma, Holly's needs can be as equally well catered for by another psychologist. I've taken a liberty and spoken with Kathleen Jackson, her office is on Main Street. She's young but good, and grateful for day clients. I made some calls, the city says they'll pay. Frankly, I wouldn't be putting all my chips on the prospect of what Holly can remember anyhow."

"I'm not, it's just . . ."

"I know, you're frustrated. You told me, there's little else. But when it comes to children and resilience, we know little about the timing. This process could take days, it could take months. In adults, a return to a pre-traumatic level of functioning can take up to a year, perhaps a little more, but with children all bets are off. Resilience is a unique experience based on the child, and taking as a reading the foundation that Holly had to start with, that sad proto-redneck family life, well, the prognosis probably isn't great. I'm not gonna force her."

"I agree," said Ella, but this time she was scowling out of the window.

"I've been talking to Holly every day for a week," he said. "When we started, one of the conditions of my helping you out was that you loaned me copies of forensic documentation. I said it was to help me get a handle on what Holly had been through. That was a partial lie."

The face tightened further. "What are you talking about?"

"There's a profiler in San Francisco. You don't know the guy, but I work with him sometimes in Washington and Virginia. We go back a while, I trust him absolutely."

"I gave you those photographs in confidence."

"It hasn't been betrayed. Listen. The day you called me, he called me too, quite the coincidence. I can't tell you the nature of our telephone conversation, I'll let him do that, but he checks the police wires and he's very interested in your case, and in Holly too. Now that I'm leaving for DC, well, I want you to let him help you."

"You'll have to do better than that."

"I have a number you can call at Justice. Like me, he's not officially in law enforcement anymore, but he'll check out. You deserve more help. Everyone's buying this Don Keynes kidnap thing except you and me."

Ella bristled. Lau she knew, respected. A complete stranger was too much.

"Forget it," she said. "I'm not indulging random frat buddies, I have a department to run. If this really mattered to you, you'd stay here." But Lau was busy, scribbling on the back of one of his business cards. His fountain pen was expensive, decorated with a tortoiseshell pattern. Ella ground her teeth.

"Let's just say he's very persistent," Lau said, and he was looking right at her, had the card held out. Ella allowed herself a glance down, saw a series of phone numbers and an email address.

"Dammit, Lau. You think *I'm* not persistent?"

"I know you are, Ella. More than anyone. Just take the card, think about it later."

"Screw you," she said, but she took the card. None of the numbers looked like the Justice Department.

Arnold Lau nodded, made for the exit, paused long enough to pick up his briefcase.

"Lau?" Ella was waving the card like she was clearing a bad smell. "His name?"

"Blake," said Lau. "Egan Blake."

Ella's mood was not improved any when she marched out of the clinic and into the blinding sunlight of a white-hot morning. Lau's Beemer was already dust in the shimmer, and she was treated instead to the sight of Milton Trueblood, lounging against the side of her blue-and-white and dressed for whatever the occasion was about to become by pulling on a dusty suit complete with bootlace tie. It was the first time Ella had seen him without his baseball cap, and he'd plastered his hair down in an uncompromising parting with what could well have been hog wax, if they make such a product. Despite this get-up he'd forgotten to shave, and if it wasn't for the pristine sneakers, Milton would have borne an uncanny resemblance to a frontier mortician.

He detached his meatless rear from the car once he saw Ella striding across the deserted lot, but she chose to ignore him and made for the driver's side. Officer Jerry Unwin, her wheelman for the day, was pretending to fill in a crossword puzzle. She knuckle-tapped until the window descended and refrigerated air plumed up into her face.

"What's *he* doing here?" she said, leaning down.

"Asked if he could speak to you."

"Did he pester Holly when she came out?"

"Na, he stayed fifty yards like he's supposed to. He waved from across the road but the kid didn't wave back. You want me to arrest him again?"

Unwin was being sarcastic. People were sympathizing with Milt and Mandy now.

"That'll do. Wind up the glass, officer. I wouldn't want you breaking a sweat."

Ella stood, found Milton keeping a respectful distance.

She walked around the car, then deliberately walked past him, so rapidly that he had to trot to keep up, not stopping until they were at the edge of the lot. Across the road from the junction, a slow McDonald's served breakfast.

She turned, heel on the curb, stared at him through her damp hair.

"What could you possibly want?"

"I'm here to apologize."

Ella frowned. He didn't look apologetic. He was rotating a toothpick between his lips in a way that threatened to impale his brain.

"For which part, Milton? For abandoning your children? For badmouthing me all over town? Or is it for boasting to everyone about being the lousiest lay of my young life?"

Milton removed the toothpick and stood with the sun in his eyes, sweat gleaming on his forehead.

"I miss my kids," he said. "I know you don't believe that, but I'd do anything to get things back the way they was. I want you to help me."

"And for this you apologize? Get out my way, I have a job to do."

"*No*," he said, and the conviction almost made Ella step back.

She instantly surged forward, got in his face despite being a foot or more shorter.

"No *what*, asshole?"

"No, I'm not apologizing to get you to help me. I'm apologizing because I'm sorry."

Ella stared into the watery eyes, tried to read his face.

"That's right, and I *am*," he said. "I have fuckin' feelings. You talked to me about finding God before, you thought I wasn't listening. Well, let me tell you, Katy gone, Holly beaten half to death, I *was* listening to you. Yeah, I believe in God. I mean, I never went to church, but I believe. I envy you with all your fuckin' certainty about things, your little ceremonies. You never had the childhood I had."

"Whining really suits you, Milt."

"Fuck you."

"Yeah, fuck me. We also talked about responsibility that day, I remember."

"No, I'm here because I want to know. Where's God *now*, we're sat around here doin' all this believing?"

"Oh, but God's listening, Milton. The question is, what've you got left to say?"

"I already said it."

"You said nothing."

"I said I'm *sorry*." He wiped his nose with his hand. "I'm sorry for the things I did to you and I'm really sorry for all this. You . . . you'll find my girl?"

Ella looked him up and down, took in this surprising new Milton, the different clothes, the modified attitude. The court had him beginning an educational course for negligent parents, she knew; this repentance might be a requirement of that program. There was little compassion to be read there, but at least he was stone-cold sober. Was it temporary? Was it an act?

When she saw him begin to rotate his idiot toothpick, she got up close to him again, like a fierce lover.

"Do *better*," she hissed, and walked away.

"Ella," he called out, and she hated hearing her name from his mouth. "Ella, I have nightmares."

Ella kept walking.

"I have nightmares where I see the devil."

Ella stopped, against her better judgment.

"That's right," he said, crying. "I see the devil, least that's who I think it is. Every night now, I see him in my dreams. He takes my Katy from me every night and he laughs and he laughs."

"Milt . . ."

"I *know* that you don't think Donny took my girl. I know you think it was someone else. I know you think it was some*thing* else. Please, Ella. I want you to teach me how to pray."

Ella chewed her bottom lip, mind working ten to the dozen. Across the lot, Unwin had gotten out of the car and was waving the radio mic.

"Milton, if I find out that this is a set-up of any kind . . ."

"It isn't. Jesus, ask Mandy, she knows how I've been . . ."

Unwin, still waving. There was an urgent call for her, or a message.

"Wait here," she said, and reluctantly jogged towards the patrol car.

"Johnson," said Unwin, once she was within earshot. Ella took the receiver, sat behind the wheel.

"Slim, what's the good word?"

"Mrs. Walson at Mountain Pastures," said Johnson, voice thick with static. "I don't know what you know, but she lost her cat the day the Trueblood thing went down."

Ella looked at Unwin, who shrugged. "Copy, Slim."

"Well . . . it turned up yesterday evening. Mutilated or something."

"Why wasn't I told, over?"

"Kyle responded, thought a dead cat was a Code-1, at least as far as bothering the Chief at night. I wouldn't mention it now, but it looked so unusual I put it in a garbage bag and got the vet to take a look. You'll wanna get back here, hear about what some sicko did."

"Wait. This cat. They find it within the Trueblood perimeter?"

"Ten-four, boss."

"*Shit,*" said Ella, not into the radio. She looked up at Unwin, shook her head in disbelief. "We completely tossed that, right? We were never more careful." He shrugged again.

"En route, Slim," she said to Johnson.

Ella stood and handed the radio to Unwin, who took her seat and gunned the engine.

She didn't walk around to the passenger side straight away. Instead, she looked across the heat-hazy lot at Milton, who was scuffing his sneakers in the dust, lost in a world of his own. Then she thought of God, and the devil; found herself wondering where the old-fashioned bad guys had gone.

Ten

It was different from the other letters, though the handwriting was the same.

It was shorter this time. There was none of the personality, no agonized plea, no threat of violence, real or imagined.

Go to church
Daddy says Go to the church of the final days
2pm Tuesday

It was a coldly beautiful morning.

"I come up here to think sometimes," Agent Rice was saying. "On a clear day you can see forever, as the movie says."

"I don't care for heights," said Karen, squinting in the brightness. "Views I like, not heights." She watched him close the fire door, carefully so it rested on the latch. She was concerned that there didn't seem to be a handle on the outside.

"Interesting city you choose to live in. Me, I love it up here when the sun shines, but I'll stand in the rain and cloud if there's something tricky to chew over. Back in Iowa, my family equates this whole state with sand and palm trees, with brown hardbodies and loose morality. I guess they only got it partly right."

"We should be grateful that *Baywatch* so thoroughly penetrated the heartlands."

Rice chuckled, his tan face creasing. The FBI issue white shirt was brilliant in the sunlight, the FBI issue tie a dark noose. "C'mon," he said. "I'll show you the edge."

"No, really."

"Hey, no pressure, these walls are at least four feet high." He was already traversing the broad, flat roof, scuffing loose gravel as he passed the box-tops of ventilation shafts. Karen found herself following him, irritated by this unexpected turn of events and trying not to look like she was walking a tightrope.

She caught up around the corner of the stairwell. His back was to her, elbows on a brownstone wall. Agent Rice wasn't a particularly fat man, but his flesh bulged where the shirt tucked in. Karen arranged herself a little further down, doing her best to ignore the sixteen-story drop; hardly ant-person stuff, but enough to be mortal.

"Gum?"

"I'm good."

"Are you?" Rice had a crooked smile beneath level blue green eyes. He folded in his stick.

"Am I what, Agent Rice?"

He shrugged and turned away, studied the city away out north. Leaves were beginning to turn beneath them, in shady wells between low-rise structures and up and down steep boulevards.

"Am I *what*, Agent Rice?"

"Are you good?" he said. "Your upset, your trauma. Are you coping?"

"I . . . I don't know," said Karen. "As well as could be expected, I suppose."

"Mm," he said, and she saw him pursue the gum around his cheek. "Do you know why you're talking to me?"

"Pardon?"

"I said, do you know why you're talking to me?"

Karen blinked, not understanding. He looked back, his face encouraging, seeming to want an honest response. She gave it her best.

"I presume—where should I start? It was revealed to me two days ago that my daughter is being stalked over the Internet—*groomed* I've been told this is called. I'm a good mother, despite the looks you people keep giving me, but I'm told by my daughter, who otherwise won't speak to me about this, that it could have been going on for as long as two weeks."

Rice nodded.

"Ah, no, wait," said Karen. "Cops invaded my ex-husband's house about a week before he's due to emigrate and confiscated all of his computer hardware. His fiancée, who turns out to be very nice by the way, probably now thinks I'm a paranoid harpy. And in the middle of all of this, there are these letters that keep arriving."

"Right, the letters. They did tell me about the letters."

"Good, because Jen picked up the last one because she was *told* to pick it up, which suggests that the letters and the cyber-stalker are connected."

Rice nodded again.

"I'm sorry, Agent Rice," said Karen. "Just how much of this do you already know?"

"Did you tell it all to Agent Menzies?" he said.

"Of course."

"All of it?"

"I've told about eight people, I've had half that number hours of sleep these past nights. I'm called back here on a Sunday morning to see Agent Menzies, on the phone he said there was an update. Now I meet you, get pulled out onto the roof. Yes, Agent Rice, you're lucky to have such a great view from the top of your office. I suppose I'm just a little anxious for you to get to the point."

"That's right," said Rice as though he'd just thought of it. "Agent Menzies can't be here this morning. I thought you'd been told."

"He's not coming?"

"Nah."

"But I only spoke to him yesterday."

"Well, you got me instead."

"Thanks then," said Karen. "I think I'll take that gum now."

Rice tapped a stick out of the packet, handed it over.

"Menzies, he'll be hard at work now, scouring the chatrooms," he said. "We know your perp's username, Chilllerkid, with three L's. I mean, he could change that, he probably will, but he has no reason to know that we're on to him. We also know the site, his hunting ground, so to speak." Rice smiled. "Agent Menzies has this knack, he can pass himself off as an eleven-year-old. He goes into these pages and makes with the pillow talk. He's caught about ten perverts like that. Me, I'm no good at it. I think I got one on the hook then I'll go throw in something about the latest baseball trade."

"Easily done," said Karen, studying his face. Rice seemed smarter than Menzies somehow, more acute. On the night when Jen had opened the letter, Agent Menzies had been sympathetic, almost patronizing. Rice spoke as though addressing an equal.

"I mean, there are other ways of approaching this," he was saying. "Sites have cookie jars. Do you know what that means?"

"Websites log their users. You could get an IP address."

"Makes him traceable, with any luck. There's been success like that in the past. We confiscate his hardware, hope for evidence. But this doesn't happen as often as we'd like."

"No?"

"We like the publicity. Put it this way—if every pervert who attempts to groom a child thinks there is a one in two chance they were chatting to a cop or a fed then, well, they'll pretty soon quit. Pedophiles get caught for other reasons, because they input credit card details, sometimes into sites invented by us. That's how you wipe out the virus en masse."

"Isn't that entrapment?"

"Well, there are rules, they have to be soliciting. This needn't concern you now."

"Are you saying you won't catch this guy?"

"I'm saying that individual cases get prosecuted because suspects are either foolish or unlucky. We got a guy once, real wealthy, left his personal trainer alone in the kitchen. This woman turns on the TV, you know, one of those integrated DVD things, she's only looking at two Asian kids doing the unmentionable on a filthy mattress. That guy won't be admiring sunsets anytime soon."

"That's awful."

"Isn't it?" Rice didn't seem to think it was awful; the gum was getting quite a workout. "Maybe that's why I brought you up here, Ms. Wiley. Remind ourselves just how big and strange the world is. Look, you can see the bridge towers."

Karen gripped the sharp corner of the wall, and Rice smiled and chewed, smiled and chewed, the gum in his mouth like a fat white slug.

"All right, Agent Rice. So why *am* I talking to you?"

"You tell me, Ms. Wiley."

"Imagine for a second that I can't imagine."

He moved towards her, careful to keep his clean shirt off the wall.

"Who's Jonny?" he said. He'd lowered his voice.

"Excuse me?"

"Jonny. Who is he?"

"I . . . I don't know. What's this about?"

"He's mentioned in the letters. I'll be brief, you want the bottom line. Agent Menzies got in touch with the Postal Inspection Service following your reporting of the Internet perp. He was following up this unusual poison-pen letter angle, you understand. You had a meeting with the inspectors previously and dropped off some mail as was suggested. At that time you told him you hadn't opened the letters."

"Friday, but no, Mr. Corbin wasn't available, I said that to a secretary. I did precisely what I was told to do: keep them, confirm harassment is taking place."

"Yeah, that was probably a mistake."

"A mistake? You think I should have opened them?"

"There's little protocol for this kind of mail crime. He assumed it was a hoax, an attention seeker, he was probably trying to protect you. You must have felt the same."

"Don't tell me how I felt."

"But a hoax had crossed your mind?"

"Of course."

"Are you a clinical therapist?"

"Where is this going?"

"I mean, those letters that Mr. Corbin received, they didn't look opened. Of course, there are ways of getting into letters then resealing them so they *look* unopened . . ."

"Am I a clinical therapist?"

"I don't know if you've had hoaxers before, Ms. Wiley, but there are certain things that you should not do, regardless of your profession. Did you tell Mr. Corbin that you thought they were cries for help?"

"I might have said something like that."

"Is that why you responded to them?"

"Excuse me?"

"You responded to the letters and you lied to us about that."

"What?"

"You responded, and you said you didn't."

"I most certainly did not."

"That's okay, that's your right, it's a free country. Letters three through five, the ones you claim not to have seen. We know, because there's a dialogue there."

"I don't understand, I *never* opened the letters. No one opened the letters. What kind of dialogue?"

"Did you show them to your daughter?"

"God, no. I mean, she was curious, we all were, but I had them locked away. She never saw them, there was no way."

"I want to believe you. I want to believe that some crazy is just *imagining* responses."

"What did the letters say?"

"Ms. Wiley . . ."

"What did the letters say?"

Rice sighed. "They arrange meetings, Ms. Wiley. Meetings that had to be attended on pain of death for the author."

"My God."

"Precisely, those letters are very convincing to anyone who might be sensitive. It's clear from letter four that you missed the meeting arranged in letter three, letter four arranges another meeting. Letter four has blood on it."

"Blood?"

"Letter five implies that you attended the meeting on that occasion, but in none of them is a location ever specified for such a meeting to have taken place, so I don't know how that happened. Unless you're being communicated with in another way *besides* the letters."

"Or the letters aren't meant for me."

"Excepting the last one, your name and address, neatly printed. You do know the handwriting on the last envelope doesn't match the writing in the letters?"

"What was I supposed to have attended?"

"What do you think?"

"The Church of the Final Days?"

"The Church of the Final Days," repeated Rice. "Possibly, though I don't know, this is the first mention of it. And this is also the first time that the name 'Daddy' has come up. What can you tell me about that?"

"I can't tell you anything. It sounds like madness. Why would I go along with something like this?"

Rice took the gum out of his mouth, screwed it into the wall with his thumb. He moved closer again, moderated his voice. It grated on Karen, who was aware of the tactic.

"I'm not as compassionate as my colleagues, Ms. Wiley. I can't bite my tongue as well. But believe me when I say that I joined law enforcement to help people like you and your daughter, and it makes our jobs a good deal harder when victims withhold information. It would take a heart of stone not to be affected by those letters, I can understand."

"I never opened the letters."

"Because, frankly, you're at risk of turning this whole thing into a burlesque show. This is a low-priority case, a bedtime story, and, unless I'm very much mistaken, it's your responding that could make it into something else, something worse."

"What about the blood?"

"That's the sort of thing I'm talking about. You never go to the movies? You never heard of letters written in blood?"

"It was written in blood?"

He bared his teeth a little. "No, Ms. Wiley, it was *not*. And that's the kind of mental leap that I'm trying to stop you from making. There was blood splashed across the bottom corner, very frightening I'm sure. We're analyzing it, for what it's worth, but don't assume that the letter writer didn't cut themselves for your benefit."

"What about the kidnapping in Canaan, Utah? There's a correlation . . ."

Rice stood up straight again. "Yeah, I read Menzies' report, you told him you'd done some real deep thinking, he hadn't seen the letters at that point. Quite the amateur detective, aren't you? You never read the letters, but you seem to know everything."

"I never said . . ."

"Well, since you're so personally involved, I might as well tell you. Yesterday, I pulled the file. Canaan P.D. have a suspect they're looking for, a warrant out for a relation of the girl, an uncle or something. And I'm no specialist, but it's plain to see that the handwriting in your letters doesn't match either the missing girl's *or* the relation under suspicion. My advice to you? Monitor your daughter's Internet activity. Shred anymore letters that arrive. And what I'd say to anyone: keep yourself safe, lock your doors, take precautions without going to extremes. Don't stop living your life. *Do* stop thinking so much. We'll do what we can."

"Did you tell me to stop thinking?"

He checked his watch. "I have another meeting at ten, a busy weekend. Please don't think we don't appreciate your cooperation, Ms. Wiley, your coming in. Agent Menzies will be in touch, and you have his number."

"What? This isn't over . . ."

"If you'll follow me, I'll escort you to the elevator." Karen received a tight bureaucratic smile. "Unless there's anything else?"

"Yes, Agent Rice, there is. Show me the letters. Three through five. If I've already seen them, it can't do any harm."

"What good would that do?"

"Because I *haven't* seen them, and now I want to know. What else did they say? Who's Jonny? Who is Jon?"

Rice shook his head. It was all Karen could do not to throttle him.

"*Please,*" she said. "If I find out later there was something I could have known . . ."

"Be sensible, Ms. Wiley. You'll stay away if you know what's good for you." Rice began to move. "Would you care to follow me?"

"I've been nothing but sensible, and this is where it gets me. Don't you dare walk away from me."

He came back over, closed in again. It turned out he chewed gum to disguise some moderately bad breath.

"Just don't do anything stupid," he said, quietly. "Please don't think of pursuing this yourself."

With that, Rice had had enough. He gave her his back, strode towards the fire door.

*

Deep in the bowels of the Royal China, a Cantonese waitress had marooned Lilly on a greasy island table amid a deafening sea of customers, rattling, steaming trolleys and impressively hostile service. It didn't matter where Lilly ate Dim Sum in San Francisco; twenty years in the city and it was the one activity that could still make her feel like a tourist.

"Braise duck . . ." yelled the tiny woman who had flung chopsticks at her moments ago. Lilly moved her head slightly and a small square dish came clattering down, thin slices of dark meat in a sauce flecked with pepper and fat.

"Vietnam spring roll . . ."

Detective John Gardner pushed his way two-handed into the huge, basement-like room and found himself at the back of a line of optimistic would-be diners. He was at least a foot taller than anyone else, so he and Lilly saw each other at the same time. She concentrated on maneuvering food into her mouth while his massive torso swerved through the crowd like a rudderless battleship.

"How've you been?" he asked, sitting down moments before colliding with a freight train of empty dishes.

"I'm good," said Lilly. "Thanks for having lunch at such short notice."

"You kidding?" he found his paper napkin. "Diane has me on this diet, this healthy fat, healthy starch thing. She told the office so now I can't even get Doritos out of the machine, they're all finding it hilarious. Lost like five pounds herself, not that I think she needed to."

"Seafood porridge," shouted a voice in a hurry. "Barbecue pork bun . . ."

"Yeah," said Gardner, receiving food, tea and chopsticks all at once. The napkin went into his shirt collar. "What can I do for you?" he said to Lilly. "No one usually pays to watch me eat."

"I was worried about Karen."

"Oh?" He bit into what looked like an errant cloud.

"When she called me the other night for your phone number she said she had problems, also that she didn't have time to talk. Now I can't reach her, no one answers."

"Yeah," said Gardner. "She didn't want to call 911, guess she felt it was too sensitive an issue. I was flattered that she'd trust me after one meeting. I put her in touch with the right guys."

"Police?"

"Feds."

"You did that?"

"Well, they're a bit more sensitive than local cops. I have a contact there, thought this might be more up their alley. The obscene letter bullshit had gone on for long enough."

"So it *was* another letter."

"I remembered the postmark was out-of-state, officially, you know, they can take a look." Gardner sipped some tea, the cup looking like a doll's house accessory in his big black fingers. "Don't know how she'll get on though; G-Men are more about fraud and terrorism than spooky-fruity language."

"Karen's tougher than you'd think."

"Mm-hmm." Gardner was hungry, Lilly knew he only had a short time for lunch. She used a finger to trace a circle on the table.

"So," she said. "Do you know what the letter said?"

"I'm sure Karen'll tell you herself. Damn, did you try the little pink ribs?"

"What did the letter say?"

"No re-heated shit here."

"I mean, John, in all the years I've known you, did I ever use our relationship to further my career, to get a story?"

"Na," he said.

"Were you ever an unnamed source? I'm in features now, for Christ's sake, I don't go near the newsdesk. I care about Karen and I should know what that letter said."

"I'm not kidding, try the ribs."

"It was what was in that letter, wasn't it? That's why she wanted to call you? She called me from Dave's house, Dave the ex. What's he got to do with it?"

"Nothing, I think."

"I told her to open the letters, that this wouldn't go away."

"She never opened the letters?" He licked his fingers.

"She wouldn't. And she wouldn't let me open them either. But you know what the last one said. Fuck. I introduce her to you, I introduce her to Egan Blake, she's thick as thieves with the both of you in no time. Where am I going wrong?"

"Who's Egan Blake?"

"Years it's taken me to get to know Karen Wiley, and I've helped her with this poison-pen thing from the start. Now I want to know: what the hell is happening here?"

Karen Wiley returned home from seeing clients at the downtown office she rented by the hour, parked the car, and then stopped herself from climbing out onto the sidewalk.

There was a man in front of her apartment building.

He was tallish, and wrapped up more warmly than the weather dictated. He had a red baseball cap pulled down over dark features, and in his hands was a clipboard. When a passer-by approached, the man waved a pen, but the hurried pedestrian stepped off the sidewalk, crossed the street. Karen watched this, then climbed out of her car, feeling the man's eyes on her. She took some time extracting her bag from the back, waited for another passer-by.

In the bag was a can of mace.

Presently, two young women came walking down the street, and Karen ran for her front door at the same time. Surely enough, the man called out to the two women, but they ignored him also. Karen tried to use this distraction to slip past, push a key into the lock.

"Save the whales?" said Egan Blake, spinning around.

"Christ, I didn't recognize you."

"Or the rainforest? There's always something to save." Mischief shone in his craggy face. "How about global poverty, drop the debt? C'mon, I can tell you have a social conscience."

"What are you doing out here?"

"We have a meeting, remember?"

"At seven. It's what, five? You were coming for dinner."

"Right, sorry." Blake reached into a cavernous pocket of his huge coat and pulled out a damp-looking bottle of Chablis. "This needed time to get cold again. Besides, I like being around people when they're cooking."

"What are you doing out here?"

"What does it look like?"

"Like you're collecting signatures. How long have . . ."

"Since noon. Look, I got four full pages, back and front." Blake flipped through paper, crinkly with ball-point pen. "You know, people today—I was losing hope, but they really seem to care."

"About whales?"

"Whales, trees, school prayer, reuniting the remaining members of *Monty Python*. Take this young person." Blake pointed the butt of his pen at a floridly dressed man who was approaching rather rapidly. "Would you excuse me a moment?"

"Okay," said Karen.

Blake adjusted his cap, brightened his voice out of his usual tombstone whisper. "Excuse me? Excuse me, sir?" The young man made to ignore him, but Blake took a large step forward. "I'm sorry," said Blake, flapping the clipboard. "Only one moment, I promise."

The young man stopped, took in Blake, took in Karen on her doorstep, assumed she was another of Blake's victims.

"Okay, but I have no time," said the man.

"That's fine," said Blake. "But did you know, at this current moment, homosexuality is still outlawed within the Russian Federation?"

The man blinked behind his bifocals. "It is?"

"My group and I feel it's high time that our government, with its message of tolerance, should place pressure on newly democratic countries to drop dark-age policies. Would you sign?"

"I . . ."

"Would *you* sign, miss?"

"I certainly would," said Karen, taking the pen. Having scratched her name, she gushed at the young man. "Can you imagine the scene in Moscow?"

He shrugged, took the form, and they both watched him print his name in an elegant script.

"I thank you from the heart," said Blake. "And so do our cousins in the former bloc."

The man found the time to wink at Blake before sashaying on up the road.

"You're outrageous," said Karen, once the man had crested the hill. "Is homosexuality really outlawed in Russia?"

"I don't know," said Blake. "Can we go inside now? My feet are killing me."

"Names," said Blake, running a crust of bread around the deep white platter. "That was the point."

"Whose names?" she said.

"Passers-by."

"Are we so short of options? You're reduced to canvassing?"

"On the contrary," he said, giving her the full benefit of his gray eyes. "I think your letter writer is watching you, or he has been, and I think he might be struggling to tear himself away. Okay, he might not have signed his name on the clipboard, more people passed me didn't than did, but maybe if I caught him by surprise, he might have tried to be, you know, *too* normal. Then there's the possibility that he used a fake name, but in your case a handwriting sample could be just as useful. In all honesty, it was mostly about me getting a sense of the field, trying to blend in, spending a little quality time getting to know what might be so appealing about this particular address—and to take a look at the kind of people who pass by it everyday."

"Baby," said Karen to Jen, who had been pushing around cold pasta for fifteen minutes. "I think it's time for you to leave the table now."

"I don't want to," said Jen, and she looked at Blake for endorsement.

"That's right," said Blake. "Jennifer can stay and load the dishwasher."

Jen groaned, started to get down. "I know what's going on," she said to Blake.

"And what you don't know, you figure out," said Blake. "You'd be a pretty good detective."

Jen tugged at a strand of hair. "Did you ever kill a person?"

"Jennifer . . ."

"That's all right," said Blake. "No, I don't kill people. That's not usually productive."

"But some people do deserve to die," said Jen. "Don't you think, Mom?"

"No," said Karen. "No one deserves to die."

"Is there ice cream?"

"I made flan."

Jen rolled her eyes at Blake, meandered towards the living room.

"Do you ever get tired of people telling you how smart she is?" said Blake, once they could hear Krusty's muted shtick.

"The sole consolation," said Karen. "Every conversation at the moment is about her dad and Hawaii. I wonder if I'm driving her away."

"Scary times right now," said Blake. "Confusing."

"Do you think that she knows Chilllerkid? You know, personally?"

Blake shook his head. "I don't know. Instinctively, I don't think so. She's too incisive, and she suspects everyone."

"She talked to you."

"I'm not pleasing."

"How did you know she'd be involved? How come you knew that Jen would get a letter?"

"I didn't."

"Nonsense, you practically predicted this."

"If someone knows you, they know you have a kid. I make a lot of open-ended statements, makes me sound clever when things happen." He swirled the dregs of his wine.

"Did she recognize any of the names on your clipboard?"

"No. But how about you? Do you want to take a look at it?"

"I thought you'd never ask," said Karen, standing. "You want coffee?"

Blake had spent the two hours before dinner with Jen in front of the TV, avoiding talking to Karen about the case, promising there'd be plenty to say after they'd eaten. But Karen knew that they'd been discussing the Internet stalker together, and she found herself wondering how it had come to this, inviting strange men over for dinner to chat about predators and their sexual deviancies with her eleven-year-old daughter.

Karen was in such a strange and dreamlike place, outside herself and otherworldly, yet never more attuned to the energy surrounding her tiny family unit. That energy felt pretty good right now, with Blake here. Things *moved* when Blake was around, answers seemed forthcoming. There was to be no more of the stagnant unknowing that had characterized her relationship with the letters up until now. Of course, relating in this way meant trusting her instinct as opposed to the authorities, giving more power to the feeling part of her brain as opposed to the thinking, and that could be dangerous, made her feel vulnerable again. It also meant sidelining others; Lilly, for one, with her grasping fascination, and Mary, who insisted on exploring troublesome questions from the past.

"Here," said Blake, he'd produced the clipboard from his bag in the hall. "I doubt we'll get anything, but take your time anyway. Look at the handwriting as well."

Karen glanced quickly at the columns, no names jumped out. Then she started to read from the top:

JOSÉ EGLESIAS
CHRISTIAN MANN
ORLAITH MANN
ROGER F. TOMLINSON
SARA JANE MILLS

The people that walk past your house everyday, Karen thought. Maybe you're in, maybe you're out, maybe you're washing the car and you accidentally splash one of them with the hose. What if one of them was to suddenly crack?

CAROL SHUMANN
DAVID SAMPSON SMITH
BURMA CLEMENTS
X. T. BONE
DAVID CAJIGAS

Some of the marks are almost illegible, unreadable. Some are decorated with stars, love-hearts. Some names spill off columns, spill into other names, make them illegible.

JOHN TERVEY
LIBBY MARX
SAMUEL ZAIDI
JACKIE LLOYD-WRIGHT
JONATHON PETERSON

*

Jonathon Peterson.

Jon Peterson.

Peterson signed his name.

Peterson has met Blake.

Though Blake is smart, he's not clairvoyant.

Peterson's vigil outside Karen's apartment is infrequent, random. He still likes to tease himself though, test his own resolve. He can't let himself see her, not yet, but he can walk past occasionally and stare up at the windows where he knows she is. The whole building pulses with the thrill of her energy, with his need for what she can give him. So simple to make a quick detour, to pass by her home just that one more time.

Always the exciting possibility that she might be coming in, you see, or going out. His previous experience breaking in taught him that it was still too early, that he had to wait, but . . .

Today there is a pest with a clipboard, another mindless city insect with an agenda to push. Before Jon has time to cross the road.

Sir . . . sir . . . just one moment . . .

Peterson glances. Paper, pen, a clipboard, a list of names. Peterson walks on.

Sir?

A *list of names*.

Peterson stops. The clipboard-person pounces, is saying something, save the . . .

Peterson swallows, his throat tight. The building beside him is throbbing with Karen Wiley's power, an itchy rash that he needs to scratch, so badly. The heat of this desire is scorching his flesh, like pushing the side of his head into the coiled rings on an electric cooker.

He can't let himself stop for long, the demons will take over.

Sir . . .

The wagging of the pen, up, down. The irritating, persistent nag. Jon glances at the clipboard, knows precisely what this particular insect wants from him.

Jonathon Peterson. As American as peanut butter and batting cages.

Jon takes the pen in a steady hand. The other man's eyes are on him, rude how he stares.

Jonathon Peterson. On brass plaques and pinned to drive-thru monkeys.

JONATHON PETERSON

Carefully printed. Peterson looks at his handiwork, not his signature, but his name. The camera clicks: there I am, nestled amongst the cowering, terrified herd. He wants to smile, despite the power of his other emotions. He can't though, or he runs the risk of being remembered.

Is HERE, he'd like to have written next.

But the building is burning, he's going to burst out of himself, *time to get away*.

Jon will curse himself later for leaving his mark, but he never can resist seeing his own name. It is all he can do not to be the most prolific graffiti artist in the world, and this was a goddamn invitation. Besides, his arrogance intensifies the closer he gets to Karen.

Anyway, he most likely doesn't need to be back here anytime soon. He's achieved so much already, it would be wrong to criticize such a simple mistake.

"No," said Karen to Blake. "I can't say I recognize anyone here, or the handwriting."

"That's okay," said Blake. "Perhaps there'll be some significance later."

"Like I said to you before, Agent Rice mentioned a Jon or a Jonny. I see a few of those, but . . . no, nothing even feels familiar."

"Interesting that the fed said that to you," said Blake. "Did Rice look like he was lying?"

"*He* thought that *I* was lying."

"Could it have been a smokescreen?"

"He didn't seem like he was lying. Why would the FBI lie to me?"

"Because, Karen, if they have a suspect already, perhaps someone wanted for crimes we aren't even aware of, they might need you to maintain your behavioral patterns. We don't know that Rice's comments about letters three through five are true either, he wouldn't show them to you. All we know for sure are the contents of one, two and six. The ones you've seen."

"Letter six. The Church of the Final Days," she said, and shivered. "Haunting."

"Everything has sounded scary up until now, the drama, the language. Difference here is that we finally have a real place, something to go on."

"A real place?"

"Of sorts."

"You found it? How? You found The Church of the Final Days?"

"I don't know for sure," he said. "I think so. And it's a good deal less frightening than you might think."

"So?"

"So guess where it is."

"Utah?"

"More specific."

"Canaan?"

"Close enough," he said.

"Jesus, spill already! You think I haven't waited long enough?"

"Okay," said Blake. "We're talking about somewhere roughly forty or sixty miles to the south-west of Canaan, but it's still quite a coincidence. If I'm honest, there *is* another church with a similar name, somewhere in the Texas panhandle, and there have been two, maybe more, Churches of the End of Days, slightly different I know, one in New Mexico, one in . . ."

"Egan . . . you know this has to be the one."

Blake put his glasses down on the table. "You have no connection with Canaan personally, do you?"

"I'd never heard of it before all this."

"Your family, or . . ."

"Do you not think that I'd have mentioned it before now?"

"Sure," said Blake. He took a sip of coffee. "The Church of the Final Days is the last complete building in a ghost town named Crescent Canyon. I assume that place isn't familiar?"

Karen shook her head.

"I've printed out some photographs that I downloaded." Blake reached into his bag, slid a clear plastic wallet over to Karen. Fascinated, she found herself thumbing through amateur photographs of tumbledown wooden cabins. There was little to distinguish the location, but it looked like midwinter; in one picture a rosy-cheeked middle-aged couple were standing by their car, snow chains on the wheels. There were words too, a brief social history.

"This is a place that sprung up as a copper mining district in the late 1800s," said Blake. "Never managed more than a hundred residents. Not much else to say, 'cept the minerals ran out and the town was returned to the dust by 1920. Typical ghost-town story. Crescent Canyon is hardly on the tourist trails because, well, it's not convenient to get to and there's not much there to see: the old mine, some roofless timber shacks, the usual stinky tunnels and bottomless shafts. That's how I found it; there are people on the Internet who take pride in documenting places like this, try to visit every single one. A retired ranger from San José lost his dog there, he thinks down a tunnel, is warning other aficionados off."

"Why did they call it The Church of the Final Days?"

"The residents didn't, I don't think."

"No?"

"Not while it was a working town. Records have the church there as the First Ward of Crescent Canyon, just a Mormon outpost that had to close due to lack of population. Did you get to the photograph of the church yet?"

Karen hadn't, it was at the back.

"Beautiful," she said, smoothing the page out on the table.

"Yeah, this one I found on a different website. There's a local artist, sells her prints on the net. You can't make out much detail because of the black and white, but see the way the clouds look like they're swirling out of the roof. Reminds me of the wisps you get when you snuff out Episcopal candles."

"Or spirits," said Karen. "Escaping."

"Of course, it's not a big place and the windows are put through. Looks more like a barn with a bell-tower, but they built this structure to last. Incredible location, too. Look at the view from the graveyard."

Karen was reading the inscription that the artist had written beneath the photograph. "'Mrs. Dolores Creighton, *The Church of the Final Days*. Crescent Canyon, 2004. Thirty-five-dollar print, includes packaging and frame.' A snip at twice the price."

"This was the number-one hit that popped up on Google," said Blake. "But, and here's the thing, there's no other reference to this structure being called by this name, at least on the net. Though you've got to remember, information uploaded is never comprehensive. Local historians might not be online yet."

"What are you saying? This artist renamed the church?"

"I don't know."

"So what, if we find the artist, we find the answers?"

"Oh, the artist wasn't hard to find," said Blake. "I got the name, a phone number, even an email. Dolores Creighton takes pictures, she's trying to sell them. She's in business here, she wants to be found."

"So?" Karen leant forward. "What did she say?"

"Nothing," said Blake, carefully. "She hasn't responded to my messages yet."

"God . . ." Karen threw up her hands. "And I thought you might have her out in your car this whole time."

"Remember, this whole line of inquiry could be irrelevant," said Blake. "Much better to pursue what we can verify. I'm still waiting for information that I've requested regarding the postal mark on your earlier letters. We know it was Canaan Utah, but if I can find the precise—"

"Horseshit," said Karen. Her eyes were shining.

"Excuse me?"

"You're going, aren't you?"

"Going?"

"You're *going*, Egan. *Here*." She tapped at the printout. "Tuesday, two p.m., The Church of the Final Days, like the letter says. You think the solution lies here, this meeting."

"I think," said Blake, quietly, "that the request to meet you there fits our growing profile of a disturbed fantasist. I think it's an appropriately gothic extension of delusions that began with the letters. I think a stage is being set."

"You *are* going."

"Yes. You want to come with me?"

"What?"

"You should come with me," said Blake. "To Utah."

"I . . . I can't do that," said Karen. "Tuesday is the day after tomorrow."

"So?"

"I have regular clients. I have Jen. Delilah's a treasure, but she's not paid to . . ."

"Bring Jen with us."

Karen narrowed her eyes. "Did you mention this idea to her already?"

"No, that would be crossing the line."

"Right," said Karen. She got up, took the coffee cups over to the sink.

"You should come with me."

"Look, Egan," said Karen. "I won't deny that I'm scared. But perhaps that was the point of this all along, someone wanting me to be scared. Well, now I'm gonna do the least scary thing. I'm going to stay here, live my life. An abandoned church, a rendezvous with the letter-writer? That's just weird. And dangerous."

"Staying here could be equally dangerous," said Blake. "You and I don't get to decide what's dangerous anymore. I thought you were going to be more proactive."

"Proactive in taking responsibility. Dropping out of my current life and vanishing into the badlands doesn't sound very responsible."

"You still don't get it," said Blake. "He was *here*. He got as far as your corridor and he slid that envelope under your door."

Karen blinked in surprise. Blake lowered his eyes.

"That's right. Probably broke in through the basement. There's a loose window."

"How do you . . ."

"I had a look around earlier today, and I surmise from your landlady that he left the front door open in his escape. When the *thing* here finally happens, there'll be hair and fiber down there and they'll be collecting the kind of evidence that convicts a murderer. Of course, you might not be around to see it."

"Goddamn it, Egan. I don't appreciate being scared. I didn't hire you to try and save me, I hired you to stop the harassment. I can save myself."

"You think that I'm trying to *save* you? I'm not trying to save you."

"No?"

"I'm trying to save Katy Trueblood, and that girl's time is running out."

"Katy . . ."

"Save the child, and your harassment will stop, I guarantee it." It was the first time that Karen had seen him register real anger; he looked like a disgusted grandfather, and it pissed her off.

"It feels like playing the game," said Karen, and she could feel her own fury beginning to rise. "I would help that girl if I could, and you know it. Don't make out that I'm self-serving because *I am not*. I admit, my decisions have not been entirely my own until now, that hurts to recognize. But I will not be scared out of my own home."

Blake seemed taken aback by this blast of sudden heat, as if he hadn't realized she would be capable of it. If Karen didn't suspect otherwise, she could almost imagine that he looked impressed.

"I'm sorry," he said, finally. Then he sighed, rubbed the bridge of his nose with his thumb and forefinger. Gradually, he pushed his fingers back, massaged his eyes, steadily, methodically.

Karen watched. Sometimes it was easy to forget that Blake was an old man, but sometimes it was impossible to ignore. Blake's contrition ended with him reaching for his glasses again.

"Karen, I want to show you one more thing, something that was figured out after the discovery of Jen's Internet stalker. I'm showing it to you because you have a right to know everything I know, and because you should be reaffirmed that the Hardy Boys elements of this case are only gaudy wrapping around genuine horror, the extent of which we don't understand yet."

"You and your preamble, Egan." Karen's voice was light but cautious. She was pleased that he wanted to talk about the case again; things had become too personal for a moment, intimate.

Blake kept a pen in the breast pocket of his denim shirt, another habit that he shared with Karen's father. He clicked it three times with his thumb, turned over the paper so he was facing a blank page. "Watch this," he said, and printed:

Chilllerkid

"Note the three ells in the name," he said to Karen, who was looking over his shoulder. "I assumed the reason was because Chillerkid with two ells was already taken as a username. You know how it is."

"Maybe," said Karen. Beneath he wrote:

kidchiller

"Make a word," said Blake. "It's an anagram."

"Kid," said Karen. "Child, chill."

"Okay," said Blake. He printed:

child

"Make a word with what's left," he said.

Karen took the pen out of his leathery hand, found herself writing:

llerki
Kill killer
CHILD KILLER

"Child killer," said Blake. "Chilllerkid spells child killer. That's why the three ells."

"I . . ."

"And you know what's really disturbing about this?"

Karen said nothing. She was reading over her own handwriting, again and again. Hell was gaping open in the white spaces between the words.

"I missed this," whispered Blake. "I didn't see it, and it took Jennifer to show it to me."

Her first sensation is of lying on a cool bare mattress, head thumping, heart pounding, with nothing but the memory of a formless nightmare, of not being able to run fast enough.

Katy Trueblood is not dead.

She realizes this because, gradually, her body is making her aware of pain, of bruising, of a strange narcotic headache that soon subsides. But initially she thought she was dead, that it was all over. It was not an unreasonable assessment.

She has awoken to an unfathomable darkness.

She has awoken to the total absence of light.

In a timeframe that we can measure, Katy Trueblood was taken by Jon Peterson two weeks and four days ago. To her, this time will stretch the length of several lifetimes, and day will not follow night. This is because Katy has awoken to an unchanging blackness so absolute that she cannot see her own hand in front of her face.

Day one.

After a length of time staring into nothing, Katy tries to move, but her moving breaks the silence, which is also absolute. There is an awful crashing sound, very close.

Katy freezes. She has heard the scrape of chains, like a creature in a creaky horror movie.

She remains still, hears nothing. She moves—again, the clanking. Elbows pressed into her mattress, she stares into the void, but it wouldn't matter if her eyes were open or closed.

Eventually, Katy figures it out, and the answer is no more comforting than the imagined horror. Attached to her ankle is a large, old-fashioned shackle, weighing as much as her bare leg. When Katy reaches down to touch, she brings back the smell of blood-warm rust on her fingers.

Perhaps she faints again after this, the darkness is so absolute.

Later.

Katy is standing, has stepped off her mattress onto a concrete floor, is wary of banging her head on something unseen. The weight of the shackle is pushing into her ankle and bare foot. The only way to walk is to reach down and pick it up, to help her foot to move with the burden. In the blackness she doesn't know what direction to move in, but after five awkward and terrifying bent-double steps towards God-knows-what, her unprotected shoulder bangs into something tall and solid and rigid. Katy is knocked to her ass, and she screams and screams.

Later.

Through more nervous groping, Katy has discovered that the tall-and-rigid something is a trunk-thick support of timber that distributes splinters. She also now knows that the shackle around her ankle is attached to a heavy chain, the other end of which is manacled to the timber. She has reached as far as she can up this vertical strut, but it disappears higher than she can reach.

The darkness has already been so total for so long that Katy is beginning to see stars and shapes and blobs of color.

Day two?

The primitive part of Katy Trueblood's brain has taken over. Her options are limited, so it only takes a short while to exhaust them. She doesn't know words like radius or diameter, but she does know that she can take about eleven blind, labored steps away from the timber that is the center of her new universe before the slack on her chain is used up. She can then hobble in a perfect circle at this distance, because the larger shackle around the beam rotates with her, rather than wrapping up around the pole.

Today is a day for shouting and screaming. She can do nothing about the darkness in the room, but at least she can exercise some control over the silence.

After some hours there has been no response and Katy's throat is in agony. She has learned from her own noise that the room must be really quite large, far larger than her chain will allow her to travel. Saying that, the echo is dull, so perhaps she is underground. The realization of this possibility, combined with the near hysteria that the endless darkness has bred, sets off a fresh bout of screaming.

Later.

Katy has used the temporarily pain-free world of her madness to sit on her mattress and test whether the shackle will come off her foot. It is not blood-pressure tight, but is abrading the bumps of her bony ankle. Despite the irritating amount of give, it will not come off. Blood wells from the scraping, but mostly there is just more bruising. She doesn't want to cripple herself, even in her most manic state.

Later.

Much like in her old life of days ago, the one shared with an erratic and violent father, Katy takes comfort in being systematic. Routine allows her to not have to think, keeps real madness at bay. By crawling to the extent of her chain and crawling back to the pillar, she can survey all of the floor available, inch by inch.

The ground itself seems to be solid concrete on an even level, textured in a way that scrapes her knuckles, with no hint of hollowness. It is harsh on her bare knees but not cold, and she is not especially chilly, despite still being in her summer dress. She would like to smell a close basement odor, anything familiar and graspable, but the room has no scent. Even her mattress-island hardly smells; it is newer and more comfortable than her bed at home.

She must be halfway through her blind investigation of the floor when her hand touches something unfamiliar and she pulls it back in horror. Then she panics because she has lost the whatever-it-was in the darkness, starts groping again.

It takes no time to rediscover. She has found a metal cover, roughly the size of a large kitchen tile. By digging with her fingernails, she can prise it up, not too heavy.

The stench from beneath is disgusting but familiar. She puts her ear to the hole, for this is what it is, but she hears nothing. Then she uses her hand to reach down, finds a broad, circular, moist-walled pipe, but her arm is not long enough to touch the bottom. A sewer. Finally, she is forced to roll away, retching a little from the smell, her chain clanking and pulling. Katy lies still, listening to the sound of her own heartbeat. Then she gets up on bruised knees, feels around for the grate-cover, replaces it carefully over the small, stinking hole.

Later.

Katy has tugged her mattress over to the timber pole, where she prefers to sleep. This is pure animal instinct, based on the intuition that there are fewer directions from which to be attacked with a beam at her back.

Now something wakes her.

Katy is on her knees quickly, peering about in the pitch-black, turning her head one way and then the other so as to best use her increasingly sensitive hearing.

Nothing.

Bunching up the chain, Katy hobbles off the mattress, in a direction chosen seemingly at random. She lets out a short scream when her free foot kicks something small and round and hard, something that bounces away. She drops, ignoring the pain in her knees, scrabbles about. Her hand touches something, knocks it over, she feels wetness on the ground, wetness on her palms. More scrabbling turns up a plastic beaker, now empty of water.

She puts her head in her wet hands and tries not to cry.

Later.

There was something else, the thing she originally kicked. Having covered the immediate area, Katy is now lying flat on her belly at the end of the chain, reaching out with the tips of her fingers.

Nothing, nothing, nothing.

Something.

Round, smooth.

An apple.

It threatens to roll away, but the tiny grooves in the concrete floor are holding it steady. Still, she has to walk it back gradually until she can hold it in her hand.

An apple.

Later.

Katy, sitting, thinking, on her mattress, has an empty beaker and an apple core. She crawls over in a direction she is familiar with, drops the core down her toilet, listens for any kind of splash that might indicate depth. This is not useful. After some deliberation, she goes to the end of her chain and flings the plastic beaker as hard as she can. It pains her to let this one new possession go, but the clatter and roll is edifying. She now knows that the walls of her prison are farther away than she can throw.

Later.

The routine becomes clearer. Katy sleeps, and when she wakes she has an awful headache but there is food and drink. It is placed at random in her circle, usually at a distance from her bed: fruit, ham, once some cold fishsticks, never a plate. She has little sense of direction, and sometimes it can take her an hour or more to find her meals, head throbbing, as she has to be careful not to knock over the water or milk that she is given. She rarely goes hungry, though sometimes, infuriatingly, there is no food at all, and her search is pointless.

Most terrifying of all is the knowledge that the someone or something providing the sustenance is in the room with her, at least temporarily, and perhaps on a permanent basis. This is someone or something who can see without light and who can enter and exit without altering the quality of the darkness or making any noise. At one point, half-awake, half-asleep, she thinks that she hears the sound of her plastic water beaker being placed oh-so-carefully on the floor, but it takes her hours of motionless silence to sum up the courage to investigate.

Next time she'll shout if she hears something like that, say a big HELLO. She already has silent conversations with invisible people, imaginary people. Perhaps these are the ones who leave her the food and protect her from the monster.

Because there is a monster.

Quite a bit later.

Here's a strange thing: there was no water after waking up this time, not particularly strange in itself, but a shame, because Katy is thirsty today, tonight, whenever this is. She opens her mouth to ask the invisible people for a drink, when she realizes that in her exploration she has surely traveled *more* than eleven steps, beyond the distance that the chain allows.

This must be a mistake. The shackle is still around her ankle; irrespective of the mental torture, the chafing on her leg is actually the most physically uncomfortable element of her confinement. Headaches on waking soon pass, but she can never forget the soreness.

Katy turns, chain clanking, retraces her steps. A bit of an expert now, she does this rapidly at first, then slowly with her hands extended once she knows the wooden pillar is nearing. She finds it without incident, turns back, begins to walk, slowly, careful to count.

One, two, three . . .

Fourteen steps.

So.

The chain *is* longer.

It must have happened while she slept.

But how was she not woken? How come she is *never* woken? By *anything*? There is the controlled silence while she is awake, but things happen while she sleeps, she used to be such a light sleeper.

Her food must be drugged.

Still, fourteen steps now, more territory. Encouraged, Katy pulls herself back along her chain like a weary convict, feeling all the way to the pillar. There it is, something different. An extension; a new stretch of chain, an addition. If only there was some light, she'd know for sure.

Later.

As she suspected, the extra foot or so of leash doesn't reveal anything new; a little more floor, more scary groping, more darkness. She still tries shouting a bit once at the extent, as though the extra distance might make her loud enough to be heard by a rescuer. Then she walks this new circumference, making the territory her own, de-scarifying it.

Later.

The circle is widening, bit by bit, little by little, time and again. More chain. More floor. More freedom. Why?

It is frustrating. Sometimes ages seem to pass without the chain growing, sometimes the extensions happen in quick succession, but the increments are always tiny, only a foot or so at the most. Katy thinks that the chain might have been growing days before she even realized. But she never hears anything, is never aware of anything. Where will it end?

Correlations: on the days that she refuses her food, the chain does not seem to grow. She could try starving herself, avoid the tranquilizer she must be ingesting. She could sleep with the chain wrapped around her, see if that wakes her. But she badly *wants* her personal space to grow, it gives her something to live for. Besides, she doesn't want to jeopardize the routine, has a sneaking suspicion that she is being allowed to live because she abides by the rules. Surely if someone was going to kill her, they'd have done so by now?

And Katy Trueblood badly wants to live. She wants to see her sister and baby brother again. She wants to see her friends, her mother, and even in her darkest moments, her father. Milt can cook up a pretty good oil-drum barbecue when he's sober, and Katy has happy memories of her last birthday . . .

Later.

Nowadays, the first thing Katy does upon waking is haul herself up, defying the pain in her head and hobbling to the extent of her leash—pale, blind, filthy, eager. But her senses have not been blunted, they are sharper than ever.

Something is out there today.

She is aware of it before she touches it, something that looms. Not food, not water, something huge. A wall? Instinct informs her of its presence. She approaches on hands and knees, preferring to be small, to not risk being knocked down. Her hand touches something and she squawks in surprise, but does not withdraw. Feels something dry. She runs her hand around, the pads on her fingertips transmitting information.

A rectangle.

Next to it, another rectangle. And another. And above it.

A bookshelf.

Katy stands, reaches up. The bookshelf is taller than she can stretch, extends out on either side farther than the chain will allow her to travel. As far as Katy knows, it could be an infinite wall of books. Climbing is out of the question, the shackle is too heavy.

All the books are near identical in size and shape. Katy maneuvers one out from the bottom shelf, reaches behind, finds roughly finished wood.

There she sits, in complete blackness, a randomly chosen phonebook in her lap, one of perhaps thousands. Katy riffles thin pages, feels scented breeze on her face.

So strange, books in the darkness.

Later.

The chain is so much longer, three times longer than when she first noticed a change. It gives her access to more books, which she pulls out, piles on top of one another, tears pages out of.

Now:

Katy has been asleep for three hours. She wakes slowly, her head throbbing. She doesn't open her eyes anymore, there's no point. Sleeping and waking are so indistinct, it is more like a consciousness that gradually manifests itself behind her eyes.

She wakes rapidly this time, because something is different. Really different.

Katy reaches down to her shackle. Still there, her foot now numb with the pain. After so long, her flesh has been grated to shallow mush, her foot is a sock of dried blood.

But the chain.

The chain has gone.

With the chain gone, she can travel as far as she likes.

This is a scary possibility. Up until now she's had long periods of time to explore tiny increases. She lies for minutes on the mattress, the consciousness behind her eyes considering. She's safe on the mattress, safe with the books. What if this is a trap?

It's all a trap, Katy. Besides, what if the chain *not being here* is a mistake? She suspects she hasn't slept for all that long, maybe the chain has yet to be replaced.

This gets her moving. Not the idea that she doesn't want to be chained up again, but the idea that she might be awake when whoever doing the chaining returns and touches her bare skin with icy hands, ghoulish fingers.

Without the chain dragging behind her, she can reach the bookshelf quickly. Should she try and climb? No, she chooses to travel to the extent of her most recently permitted distance, to travel beyond. The books are familiar, reassuring, she hugs them as she moves farther than her boundary, then farther again. In the pitch blackness with no limits it feels like walking in space. So unusual to think that anything could happen at any time, with no warning; the only confirmation is when you feel it, when all is too late. This must be a newborn's experience, with a newborn's intelligence; but with a hard-wired knowledge of the awful possibility of the universe.

The bookshelf ends. She's three times farther away from her mattress than ever before.

The books weren't against the wall. The shelf was free-standing. To travel beyond is to walk a precipice without a handrail. Should she go around the back of the bookcase? Should she . . .

Is that a noise behind her?

Katy staggers forward as if pushed. Hands out in front like a sleepwalker, she gains speed until she is running through the void, running away, running in any direction until . . .

crash

A wall. Katy was almost ready for it, so her arms and wrists take the brunt, she holds her footing. Her hands are all over it immediately, scrabbling, searching. Her feet aren't her own, they sidestep along, arms frantic, feeling for a door, a doorknob, a . . .

light switch

A light switch.

Her fingers grasp the familiar corners of the plastic square first. She hasn't knocked it on, so now there is a choice. If she pushes it, her attempt at escape might be exposed.

But there will be light.

Again, the noise. Laughing?

There's no debate. Whoever brings her food, whoever is in here now can obviously see in the dark, so she might as well equalize the odds. Even so, something stops her, something not right . . .

Small greasy fingers massage the switch. It takes quite a lot of effort to depress.

Click, strobe, hum.

Strip lights flicker in a high ceiling. Across a huge, windowless room, whiteness rolls out as blinding as the black. Katy closes her eyes but it is still too bright, she can see the veins in her eyelids. She pushes her fists into her sockets, watches red flares, stars.

But she did manage a glimpse in that first moment, enough time to see there is nothing in the room with her. She has to risk another look, to disregard the pain in her eyes.

Nothing. *But something is*

Directly behind her

But something is

the monster.

The monster, right behind her, inches away, smiling.

Eleven

Canyonlands.

Blake, used to watching and waiting for long periods, couldn't help being distracted by the eagle as it hovered without motion in the updraft of a distant rock face. With fingers that were damp from wiping sweat, he adjusted the focus on the 400/f2.8 long lens that had been his eyes for the last four hours and marveled at the living tableau of the magnificent bird quaking in his unsteady sights. Slowly, carefully, he placed his left hand and arm on top of the lens as close to the center of gravity as he could, and pushed with his index finger, trying to minimize vibration.

Snap.

The eagle seemed to be looking in his direction. Fascinated, Blake lowered the apparatus and allowed his glasses to slide from his damp forehead and onto the bridge of his nose. It took a long moment to find the bird with his own eyes; it was suspended in shadow and there were the obscuring waves of a gasoline heat emitting from the earth.

When he raised his lens again, the eagle was gone.

It was Tuesday, and the time was approaching 2 p.m., the instructions specified in Karen's last letter. Blake couldn't be certain that he had the location correct, or even that the letter wasn't referring to some twisted mind-fuck of a different nature, but from the point yesterday morning when he first recced the abandoned church in his rented Land Rover, he felt in his gut that this was the right place; there was something so desolate and apocalyptic about the bombed-looking mausoleum in its waterless vale.

Blake had discovered that The Church of the Final Days was merely a dot on most maps of the area; a dot among many dots and arrows and symbols with the words *Crescent Canyon* or simply *Ghost Town* printed next to it in a small font. He also learned that the Canyonlands were not known for their ghost towns, and suspected that tourists rarely made it this far; if yesterday's exercise had achieved anything it was the discovery that the going was pretty tough once off the black vein that ferried cars between the adventure sports outposts of Canaan and Moab. He figured eight miles as the eagle flies from the main road to The Church of the Final Days, but a good deal farther when factoring in the twists and turns, the weathered sinkholes and worrisome dips.

But then, having made the effort, the church itself couldn't be missed. For a land renowned for vistas so large as to be hard to comprehend, it struck Blake as appearing very suddenly, hidden by the landscape until the last moment and then holding sway in its own basin-like valley at the foot of a ridge. It engendered a strange sense of surprise, this derelict structure standing all alone, looking as though it had dropped from space.

Blake noted how smoke from a forgotten fire had stained the stone above the six gaping window cavities, and he shivered despite the heat.

The dull air roundabouts was heavy with spirits.

Today, however, Blake had started before dawn and come around the back, after a long conversation with a ranger who acted like he would rather this strange old tourist wasn't trying it on his own. They were talking about another road, this time to a lookout point, thirty or so miles farther along Route 192; about halfway along that, Blake had found an unmarked turnoff through cottonwood trees and juniper bushes that eventually vanished southwards over some uncompromising inclines and canyon hollows. The ranger knew it, thought it was tough, would have much preferred that Blake stuck to Copper Ridge or even the Metal Masher trail, something with maintained waypoints. But Blake was adamant. He loaded up his wagon, and for the duration of the morning he had driven well and with care and had luck on his side.

A cautious navigator, it had taken him another two hours on top of his three-hour off-road journey to hike with his equipment and supplies from where he had left the vehicle in a shady clay copse to his current vantage point, roughly a half-mile to the west of the church. This was the place he'd decided upon yesterday that would give him the best view of the surrounding area; no one could approach the building from any direction without him seeing and photographing through his long lens. Prepared to indulge all possibilities, he wasn't ruling out the idea that someone could already be in the church, had been waiting there for longer than the three-and-a-half hours that Blake had been spying, but they'd have to have hiked to the spot or been dropped off by a car; there was no other vehicle around, and they would still have to leave at some point when no one else arrived for the meeting. Blake had also considered that the letter-writer might be hiding in the same way that he was, perhaps wanting to spy on whoever arrived, but he'd thoroughly scanned the surrounding area and was yet to register any tell-tale sign. He partly hoped that he'd see the FBI or a government operative, but he knew that they'd probably have dismissed this as folly, even if they'd bothered to get so far as Utah in their thinking. The idea reminded him that the whole enterprise could be pointless, that wild-goose chases seemed to be more his line of work than anything else.

Blake adjusted his cap with an automatic motion, a cape at the back keeping the sun off his neck. Then he checked his watch: 13.48.

Twelve minutes to go.

Blake shuffled his elbows in the gravel, resisted the urge to let his nerves make him yawn, breathed in the hypnotic, perfumed mist from a scent-roasted barberry bush some thirty feet below. He concentrated instead on refocusing his lens on the forsaken building, on the road that snaked through the only driveable passage to it. For some reason he was nervous for Karen, though he knew from his morning phone call that she was, right now, many miles away in San Francisco; that she wasn't alone, that she was in session with a client in a bright building full of people.

13.50 . . . 51.

Blake turned his head slightly.

Someone was coming.

He heard it before he saw it, a dull crunch of tires that was amplified into a quiet grumble of white noise. Blake moved the scope, but it was dust he saw first, beyond the basin, a plume of brown fog announcing arrival. Whoever it was didn't need the cover of secrecy, then; it looked like someone in a real hurry.

Eventually, a small brown hatchback broke cover, dust streaked and tired. It was completely the wrong vehicle for this kind of exercise; the road from the highway must have been just about passable in it.

Blake was very still now, concentrating, the consummate professional. *Snap*, went his camera. *Snap*, a registration plate, a make and model. The sun flashed across the windshield of the moving car like rapidly winding microfilm, obscured his view of any occupants.

The car slid to a halt in front of the church, kicking up a new cloud of dust. A decision seemed to be being made in there, like the driver hadn't had the expected result upon arriving at the church.

High up from his vantage point, Blake began to will the driver to get out, his mouth moving, praying he would get more than just a useless profile in a dark car.

It seemed like he waited an age, but it was really only seconds.

Blake thought he heard the transmission, the car going into reverse. It suddenly lurched into a wide three-point-turn in the broad clearing before the church, and he was convinced he was going to lose the stranger back through the pass, a day's exertion for a number plate. But the car, obscured by the structure, did not appear on the other side.

It had stopped, right in front of the entrance.

Blake's heart leapt as this was confirmed by the sound of the engine cutting, watched as the dust clouds dissipated, listened as the silence of the canyons was reasserted on the scene.

Another long moment and the sound of a door opening, the muted *thunk* of a door closing. He heard nothing more, pressed his face into the wet eyepiece, hardly daring to breathe.

Long, slow beats while Blake watched and waited, the person evidently now inside the church. It would make some sense if this was the letter-writer, ten minutes early, waiting. Blake considered changing his position, maybe shifting a hundred yards to his left so as not to miss a picture of the face when they departed.

Satisfied with this plan, he was about to raise himself up when a small figure in dark clothes and broad black sunglasses appeared around the side of the church.

Blake cursed under his breath, slid back up to the eyepiece.

It was Lilly.

What was *she* doing here? How did she even know?

Lilly, a lone and tiny figure in the milieu, looked uncertain, like a small animal on unfamiliar ground. She wasn't dressed for the desert, she looked hot and pale. In her hands was a cellphone, she was taking pictures with it, pictures of the church, of her surroundings.

Lilly checked her watch, which prompted Blake, at least half-a-mile away, to do the same: 13.56 . . . 57. Three minutes until zero hour.

Get out of there.

Lilly meandered around the building, inspected some of the haphazardly strewn gravestones, only a handful of which were still upright, a clutch of foul teeth. Blake had done the same during his investigation yesterday and he knew there was nothing there to read; a century of dust had bitten out most of the inscriptions.

Blake considered. He wasn't entertaining the possibility that Lilly was the letter-writer. He knew Lilly was here because Karen must have told her about this, against his advice, and now, characteristically, Lilly's curiosity had gotten the better of her. But what to do now?

If he called down to Lilly, he would reveal himself and might put paid to the meeting that was scheduled to take place. If someone else *did* show, then maybe, if there was time, he could stay in hiding and then scare them off once he'd had a good look, taken his pictures; there was a trusted Glock 17 in his small-of-back holster. But maybe Lilly had already tainted the tryst, fucked it up with her appearance. But then if Karen was *never* going to turn up, maybe Lilly, a woman on her own, might replace . . .

On a whim, Blake pulled his sights off Lilly, pointed the lens up the road towards the pass.

Nothing.

No one else coming. Just the sounds of the land, birds, an insect, whispers of air.

When Blake swung back he was surprised at what he saw.

Lilly was standing stock still in front of a gravestone. He could just about make out her features, and the uncertain curiosity that had defined her character since arrival had been blasted off her face.

She now looked terrified.

The stone she was staring at was facing her, had its back to Blake, perhaps he couldn't see what she could see. But there was no question, the stone was what she was looking at. Something he missed yesterday? With one ear out for any approaching vehicle, he gradually lowered his sight from Lilly's face, down her frozen body, the phone slack in her hand, to the object of her horror.

No.

Blake hadn't seen this stone yesterday because it wasn't *there* yesterday. Of course he would have seen it, it stuck out like a living soldier on a battlefield of massacre.

This is because the stone that Lilly was looking at was freshly minted.

Impossible. So what the . . .

Even as he was digesting this unexpected twist, Lilly had begun to back up, then turned and ran like the devil was on her heels. Blake barely had time to adjust his vision before he was hearing the car door again, the engine, the bite of rubber on grit. Clouds kicked up from behind the church and the car emerged, speeding towards the pass, the engine a tinny roar. Blake's first thought was that Lilly was driving too fast for the trail, she could have an accident, she . . .

But what exactly had she just seen?

For the first time in the exercise, Blake developed the feeling that although the letter-writer probably couldn't have known that he was there or that Lilly would turn up, *everything was still going according to some maniac's plan.*

The sound of Lilly's car faded into the distance, and Blake was left with his thoughts once more. Breathing hard, he picked up the lens, looked back at the church, performed a thorough, fruitless sweep of the area.

Still nothing.

Finally, he went back to the stone that had scared Lilly so badly, the inscription that he wouldn't be able to see unless he went down there. The longer he stared, the more it seemed to challenge and mock, the unturned card of an opponent.

So still, so quiet.

The stage seemed to be inviting him in from the wings.

Blake climbed to his feet on tired legs, ruining any cover he may have had in two seconds flat. Leaving the camera behind but conscious of the gun at his back, he began to half-run, half-scramble down the incline, not the sensible route, but the quick one, dislodging chunks of gravel in a way that threatened to unbalance him and send his old bones rolling down the hill.

Once he reached the bottom of the basin, the church felt even more like a well-lit film set, deserted of extras. Blake wasted no time, but sprinted the final hundred yards of level ground, panting now. There was no question, he could see with his own eyes, the headstone *was* new, brand new. Blake stepped over the chalk and weed outline that indicated the unofficial edge of the burial ground and strode towards the marker. It was an expensive finish, a professional job in dark granite, the early afternoon shadow from the church reaching across its face.

His labored breathing the only noise in the valley, he moved around the front, his footsteps feeling slow and gluey, like in a nightmare.

Blake stood where Lilly had stood, looked where Lilly had looked.

He hadn't smoked a cigarette in thirty or more years, but he damn well wanted one now.

Etched onto the freshly polished stone in an elegant script:

Karen Wiley – R.I.P.

*

Lilly cursed as the rental pitched worryingly over a particularly rock-bound stretch of track. Wrestling the wheel with wet hands, the next ridge dropped her six feet in two seconds, leaving her guts exposed in the immediate past.

Slow the fuck down, girl. Driving like this is going to get you killed, and dead you're no good to anyone; to the police, to Karen, and the story that you've traveled hundreds of miles for will never be told.

Okay. So . . . *slow the fuck down.*

Lilly breathed, got the car under control in time to negotiate a blind corner without the anti-aircraft splatter of stones on bodywork. She was rarely fazed by anything, but the sight of her friend's name on a tombstone in the middle of nowhere was . . . what? Weird? Surreal? Scary? No point denying it, there had been that icy fear, a need to run away, so unfamiliar to her. The oppressive atmosphere, the anticipation of something bad happening, someone coming as the time neared the top of the hour, the creepy feeling that she was being watched, that at any moment . . .

Lilly laughed, a short gasp above the reassuring whistle of the air-con.

Man, The Church of the Final Days. It had felt like such a long shot, bordering on fantasy, like something Egan Blake would indulge, but she had to admit it had really exceeded her expectations. This *was* something to write about, to read about, a cover story for the magazine. Backwater mystery, a committed and committable letter-writing lunatic, an exotic location . . .

But what about Karen?

Lilly wiped sweat off her forehead.

A name on a tombstone meant nothing. Well, it meant *something*, but not necessarily the death of her friend. Karen was back in the city. Lilly hadn't told her she was coming out here, knowing that Karen would have resented her for it, her morbid, self-serving curiosity.

What then, was the meaning of the marker? Someone was mightily fucked in the head. The expense of the thing, surely—and to get it out here, it must have weighed . . .

But is Karen okay?

Lilly was about a third of the way back from the church to the highway, the point where the road straightened and improved before worsening again prior to the junction. Lilly risked a glance over to the cellphone in the adjacent seat, not expecting much.

Little bars of light. Not many, but they were there.

A signal.

She could make the call, a routine howdy, confirm that Karen was fine. Then she could get back to her motel, make some more calls, find a local photographer, get an interview with whoever enforced the law in this stricken wasteland . . .

Lilly slowed down the car a little more. One eye on the bumps in the road, she reached for the phone, licked her lips.

It was closer to one o'clock in San Francisco.

Coming up the stairwell from the laundry room bearing a pile of Mr. Durant's yellowing underclothes, Mrs. Durant had time to observe the Wileys' cleaner bustle out of the building with the mild suspicion she always saved for minorities unfortunate enough to be ethnic. *Karen Wiley's* cleaner, she corrected herself, punctuation always iron-clad in her thought process. There hadn't been a proper family in the upstairs apartment for a long while now.

The front door banged shut and Mrs. Durant's thin mouth twitched a little.

She was rounding the banister in the downstairs hallway and feeling the pain in her tired knees when she became aware of a shadow out of the corner of her eye, a human-shaped shadow to replace the departing cleaner through the long window of the entryway. Mrs. Durant grimaced, before placing her washing at the foot of the stairs and walking over to where a tall man in a deliveryman's uniform had begun to squint at the buzzers outside. When he saw Mrs. Durant watching him, he stood up straight and gave her a polite smile.

Help you? she mouthed at him through the reinforced glass.

The tall man didn't reply. In his hands was a device requiring a digital signature, at his feet a wrapped and labeled box, large enough to deliver a soccer ball in. Mrs. Durant nodded that she understood, reached out to unlock the door.

"Thanks," said the man, tapping his machine once the door was opened. "Jennifer Wiley?"

"Upstairs," said Mrs. Durant. "I'm the landlady. Delivery?"

"Yes," said the man.

"Want me to sign for her?"

"Thanks," said the man.

He seemed to take a long look at Mrs. Durant while she scrawled her signature with the plastic pointer. She was too old and cynical to blush under scrutiny, but he *was* attractive, blond highlights under his cap, remarkable eyes, an accent that was pure Deep South. Mr. Durant had been a good-looking farm-boy too, back in the day.

"Say," said the man, taking back the machine and eyeing the washing that Mrs. Durant had placed in the hallway. "Would you like me to carry this package up the stairs for you?"

"Is it so heavy?" Mrs. Durant was looking over his shoulder, there was a double-parked delivery van. Traffic wardens in San Francisco are impressive in their dedication.

"No, not so heavy," said the man. "But I saw you had washing, and I could save you an extra trip on the Stairmaster there."

Mrs. Durant allowed the tall man one of her rare smiles.

"Sure," she said. "Why not."

The man picked up his package and stepped over the threshold.

"Jen, it's Lilly. Is your mom there?"

"Hey Lilly, what's up?"

There was a whoosh of static. ". . . speak to your *mom* please?"

Jen pouted at the receiver. Lilly usually chatted for a couple of minutes if she got to the phone first, whether Mom was in or not.

"She's not in yet," said Jen. "Did you try her cell?"

"It's *not* . . . do you know . . . she *is*?"

"Work, I guess, she switches it off. Lilly, the reception is terrible."

"Jen, I can't . . . you *hear me*?"

"So I'll tell her you called, yeah?"

". . . something *now* . . ."

There was a noise, and Jen jerked her head around. "Okay, Lilly. I gotta run, there's someone at the door."

"Everything . . . *goddammit* . . . everything *okay*?"

"I gotta get it. Look, call back when you get out of whatever tunnel you're in."

"*Jennifer* . . ."

Jen eased the receiver back into the cradle, walked towards the door. She was too short to see through the spy-hole and too lazy to get a kitchen chair to climb on like Karen had told her to. Distracted by a thousand childish things, Jen pulled the door right open.

Blake wasn't having much luck. The route back up the valley had been a darn sight more challenging than his impromptu journey down, and by the time he'd reached his backpack again his clothes were drenched and he was beginning to feel nauseous. Aware of his physical limitation but conscious of the long hike back through the canyons to his ride, he sat down heavily in the dust and reached for his flask, swirled water and spat; swirled again, drank.

Blake, better prepared than Lilly, had an iridium sat-phone that could all but guarantee a signal. Shielding his eyes from the sun, he flipped open his bag, seized the hi-tech ingot, found Karen's home number, dialed.

Engaged.

Blake dialed again, let it ring, and hung up once more when he got the voicemail, preferring not to leave a message that couldn't possibly make sense, no matter how well articulated. The phone went back into the bag and he rested his arms on his knees, tried to clear his brain.

He wasn't too worried about Karen just yet. Unless there was a team of letter-writers, Blake believed that his quarry would now be away from the city, would probably be out here, wanting to somehow savor the aftermath of this new twist. And there was certainly no one buried beneath that headstone, at least not recently; the ground was hard as poured concrete. So what was it, another message? A death threat? What did it mean?

Blake began to feel optimistic, despite himself. One of the toys in his bag was a basic bi-chromatic fingerprint kit; someone would have had to sweat to get that marker out here, and fingertip secretions stick to polished stone like hairs to a bathtub. And then there was the paper trail such a monument would inevitably leave, to stonemasons, to couriers. For every new move made by the letter-writer, at least twice as many leads could be expected to bubble up, and Blake was convinced this granite cipher might make a sizable splash followed by sizable waves.

His breath back under control, Blake counted ten and stood up, gathered his equipment. He had a strong analytical brain, usually capable of compartmentalizing the worry and solely focusing on the science, on the theory, always on the theories.

But still . . .

Below him, the ancient church, baking silence and blinding light.

After closing the door on both Mrs. Durant and the friendly deliveryman, Jen carries the package into the kitchen and places it on the table.

She doesn't open it straight away. She sits in front of it, rocks back a little on the chair.

Her address, sure. Her *name* though. This package is meant for *her*.

Don't open the box.

Chilllerkid, the last letter, the ensuing panic in the adults, these are not things that have dropped off Jen's radar. Her Internet activity isn't monitored, that would hardly be practical, but there had been lengthy and mutually embarrassing conversations with her mother and a narrow-eyed cop about knowing when a webchat is taking a certain *turn*, you know Jen, a certain *turn*, and Jen would feel sick to her stomach, not least because she wasn't actually supposed to turn off the computer when the bad chats started but instead call on Karen and then they could *both* carry on chatting so that the policeman could . . .

Jen hasn't surfed much since and can't tell her friends why. Chilllerkid is yet to put in a reappearance, is yet to once more slide his big shark's fin above the waterline.

But now.

Something in a box, two or more things probably, judging from her sense-memory of the noise it made when it went down on the table. Two things that are quite well wrapped, and judging from the weight, the box is perhaps slightly larger than necessary for the contents. Not too heavy, not too light. Just the right size for you, Goldilocks.

Tick, goes the clock.

You can't go through your life feeling afraid. Mom goes through her life feeling afraid.

Jen didn't think the first time, with the first letter, the one at her dad's. She had her suspicions about Chilllerkid but never felt in danger, could never have understood the severity. This time she knows, or she believes she does. The content of this box is going to be . . . *bad.*

Should she call for Mrs. Durant? Wait for Mom? Dial 911?

No. She's opening the box. We're in this together, Jen and Mom, Team Wiley.

No bad men gonna push us around.

There is a utility knife in the kitchen drawer. Jen rummages until she finds it, points it away from her stomach with both hands, has to push hard with her thumbs to get a razor-sharp tongue of steel to slip out. She's already behaving in a way that would drive her mom apoplectic.

The package is well wrapped and it takes a while to get into. Job done, Jen carefully retracts the blade of the knife and places it on the table. There are now just four loose flaps between Jen and the *something* addressed to her. The spring of the cardboard encourages, beckons, is already lifting up on one side.

The box, up on the table, is at chest height. Jen almost wishes she'd opened it on the floor, now she has to get close to peer in. She peels back the flaps as though something nasty could jump out, maybe fasten itself to her face.

The reveal is both expected and yet totally unexpected.

Jen stares down at a sea of Styrofoam packing peanuts.

She doesn't want to dip her hand into them. She disturbs the top layer a little with the tips of her fingers. Still nothing jumps out.

Inspiration.

Back in the drawer is a pair of ridged salad tongs. Jen could get a sense of the contents without having to reach in herself. She backs away, turns, finds her weapon of choice among whisks and peelers.

Advancing on the box once more, there is a quiet humming in Jen's head, her subconscious laying the groundwork for the state of shock she's about to be in.

Jen starts in the corner, working the utensil through the packing foam until she feels the cardboard at the bottom. Then she stirs until she finds the thing in the box. The second tong goes in on the other side, and Jen squeals when it doesn't quite hit the base, but presses into something that gives a little. Moving the tong away, Jen is able to grasp the object with her clumsy chopsticks, attempt to unbury it.

Here we go . . .

A twisty tie, a plastic bag, a fairground prize smeared crimson on the inside like badly wrapped meat. The dismembered hand comes up palm first, fingers curled with rigor, the thumb pushed back under with the pressure of Jen's implement. A hand with no arm is all knuckles and gore, and Jen screams and swings it away, catapulting it across the kitchen floor where it stops face down. The fingers point towards her, a science specimen come to life.

fleshy bagged spider

Jen doesn't want to faint but she is. *I'm fainting*, she thinks. *This is what fainting feels like*

and you KNEW, you had at least an IDEA, didn't you

She doesn't want to go to the floor, that's where the hand is. It seems to be *looking at me*

The pattern on the lino rushes up, sickness and bile, sickness and bile.

Jen manages to catch both the box and the table on her passage down, spraying out a fresh fountain of foam. Katy Trueblood's neatly butchered ear is expelled from this froth with such force that it too seems to make an unholy scuttle for freedom.

Lilly, not knowing who else to call, managed a garbled two minutes with Detective John Gardner in San Francisco, but gave up when the signal finally cut out. She focused instead on driving the road as best she could. The quality of the surface had decreased dramatically and her teeth seemed to rattle over every goddamn bump.

Off-roading! What do people see in this hobby?

To make matters worse, the scenery appeared less familiar on the return journey, and once she almost stopped to verify that she hadn't taken a wrong turning. There were so many memorable features, gnarly trees, odd-shaped rocks, they'd all blurred into one big-sky daydream.

Girl, you don't want to get lost out here, in this shifting landscape, don't want to die out here, be a small dry corpse all picked apart by buzzards.

Impossible, there were no other turnings.

Still, she'd slowed right down, was going much more carefully. It was what allowed her to finally pick out the distant highway, a thin belt slicing through the middle distance. The track seemed to improve at the same time, and the sense of returning to civilization was palpable.

Whoopie-fuckin-do, I live to fight another day.

There was a vehicle stopped along the 192, roughly, Lilly imagined, where the turnoff to her dirt track would be, a tow dolly attached to the back. The man standing next to it was wearing a ranger's uniform and hat. *Great, the cavalry has arrived.* No way that Egan Blake would have let Karen's letter lie, that much was to be expected. Truth be told, she was surprised not to see Egan in person, had a whole speech prepared explaining her presence out here, her concern for Karen. But instead of buying the plane ticket, Egan had evidently got the tree-cops to send a uniform.

The ranger bobbed in and out of sight as she worked the car down the dirt track, and he still had his back to her as she drove up; it wasn't until she was on top of his jeep that Lilly realized he had parked it across her turn-off. She imagined he'd hear the crunch of her tires, but the man didn't turn until she gave a couple of cheerful peeps on the horn.

The ranger faced her with what Lilly considered to be extreme slowness.

These unhurried hillbilly types. Probably very well-meaning.

He was a tall man with a tan face, and as he approached he gestured that Lilly should wind her window down. She complied, and heat flowed into the car, though the ranger didn't seem to be sweating.

"Ma'am," the face came down to her level, peered in. "I am sorry."

"Excuse me?" said Lilly.

"I closed this road a half-hour ago, I had no idea anyone was up there. I shoulda checked, but it's unusual for, you know . . ."

Anyone to be up there, leastways a woman on her own, Lilly thought.

"Why is the road closed?" said Lilly, raising her sunglasses.

"I'm afraid I don't know that, the cops just radioed out. Perhaps you could tell me?"

"I have no idea," she lied. "Just me up there, far as I know."

The ranger said nothing, but the eyes that had been searching her became very, very intense, as though he were capable of X-ray vision. *Maybe this one isn't so dumb after all.* Lilly knew she hadn't done anything wrong, but perhaps she should be a bit careful.

He was permitted a moderate smile. "Striking little town they must have had at one time," said Lilly, gesturing back up the track.

"That it was," said Jon Peterson, and he placed his hand on the roof of her car. "You out here on vacation?"

Twelve

"No, this isn't a vacation, sad to say. I'm a journalist, writing an article for *Time Europe* on America's forgotten ghost towns."

The weak and diminishing part of Peterson's brain that ministered social interaction gave a little hiccup, found itself prodding ineffectually into the red lightning fog that had descended over much of his cerebral cortex.

I'm a journalist.

Karen Wiley isn't a journalist.

Peterson blinked. The small woman in the car was beginning to look rather unsettled by his staring, but he was no longer able to recognize the nuances of ordinary communication.

"Sir?" she said, eventually.

"Call me Chip."

"Chip?"

"Ma'am, this is going to sound a little strange, but I'm going to need to see some I.D."

"Why?"

Because Karen, you'll show me it really IS you or I'll snap your neck like a fucking bird.

"You're under no obligation," said Peterson, reasonably. "People are a bit edgy round these parts at the moment, is all. If

I told you a little vandalism was going on . . ."

"Vandalism? I thought you didn't know why the road was closed."

"I'm assuming. The kids, you know? They come out to the park with their schools to raft or bike, but, frankly, the supervision isn't up to much."

"Up there?" said the woman. She had developed a smirk, was telling Peterson in no uncertain terms that she thought he was lying. It didn't matter; Peterson was seconds away from using a fistful of hair to smash her brainpan against the door. But she bought herself some more time by dropping the smug face and unfastening her seatbelt.

"I'd very much like to speak with you, Chip," said the woman, quickly and quietly, in a way that seemed conspiratorial. "About the ghost town and the church. You know, for my article? Let me put it this way, I don't think you've been told to come out here because of the kids."

"Ma'am?"

She rested a hand on the window frame. "My name is Lillian Hersh. I didn't bring my business card, but I'm staying at the White Rock Lodge for a couple days. Do you know it?"

I'd like to speak with you, Chip

Peterson nodded, and this time he looked at her properly, for far longer than could be considered appropriate. A pale, pretty face, a button nose, the hot desert breeze stirring a surround of glossy black hair. And that manner of speaking; refined, urbane, almost challenging.

My name is Lillian Hersh

It seemed to take an age for the knowledge to filter down, to fight through the demonic reverie to the microphone on the main stage, but once it got up there it resounded like a bloody cathedral scream.

This is NOT Karen Wiley. That means you've FAILED.

KILL HER ANYWAY

"Chip? Are you listening?" The woman was registering impatience.

Impatience is good. It means she's not on to you. It means she doesn't suspect, not yet. Better say something, Jonny-boy, you're off the script now.

"I'm sorry, ma'am. Could you excuse me for a moment?" Peterson was shaky, managed to maintain the mask but dropped his cheery Ranger Rick voice. The difference in intonation was subtle, but it was a troubling slip, indicative of his unfamiliarity with disappointment. Unable to think of any reason to be excused, he turned his back and walked towards the open door of his jeep. The woman's voice followed him, elevated to the next level of concern.

"Chip? Mr. Ranger, sir?"

Peterson ignored her.

In the back of his vehicle was his sword, a Japanese World War Two antique that had been obsessively polished with seven grades of stone so it would disjoin flesh in a bloodless whisper. Despite his craftsman's admiration for the grain and the shine of the thing, Peterson was no collector, nor was he an enthusiast, practicing twirls and shouts in a weed-ridden yard; he'd chosen it because he wanted a slicing weapon with which to kill, and it could be (and had been) picked up at a memorabilia convention in an untraceable way. Besides, the killing wasn't really the point, delightful as it felt; he'd begun to feel an affinity for the blade, a connection, and damn if holding it wasn't becoming something like letting his soul blaze free.

It was because of his uncertainty that he looked to it now, lying unsheathed across the dead center of the back seat. The demons gave a colorful roar when they saw, and, overwhelmed, he had to put his hand out for support, dropping his head onto his arm in a way that slid his foolish costume hat over his face.

KILL HER ANYWAY, they were screaming, over and over.

But I can't.

At least he shouldn't. There's no careful escape route planned for this one. It was supposed to be the climax, the endgame, and he should never have needed an escape. If he kills the wrong woman now, all that tightly structured work becomes irrelevant, he's just a murderer, a sap on the news, a hunt for what, a footnote in aging local lore. And Karen Wiley will live on . . .

KILL HER ANYWAY.

He stares at the sword with tired eyes, but finds it gives him the wrong kind of strength. The demons neither care nor understand the subtlety of his mission. They don't work for Jon or for his psychological cause, they merely inspire the action. He's been helped to learn this over time, the *real* role of the demons, but out in these primitive lands of wind and ghosts and anima, where they grow powerful to the point of unmanageability, there can never, *will* never, be any sort of personal perspective.

KILL HER ANYWAY.

Because they're not there while you're painstakingly sharpening your sword, or wasting hours looking through your telephone directories. They're not available in the dark of night when you really need them . . .

all that WORK *so you can spend half-a-minute feeling* ALIVE

they're a MUSE, *that you worked so hard to find and now they're here and* WHAT *are you going to do, with your idiotic tombstone and your child-games in the dark and your fucking ranger uniform and a* JOURNALIST *turns up? To write the story of how* FUCKED UP *you are?*

You FAILED, *didn't you? You truly are* SPECTACULAR.

She never even put in an appearance. KAREN WILEY *sent a pod-person in her place, another pod-person, full of guts and organs and void of any kind of* LIGHT.

She never showed up, but WE'RE *here, Jonny,* WE'RE ALWAYS HERE. *For when you succeed, and for right now, for when you* FAIL

FAIL

For when I . . .

Peterson stands up straight, adjusts his hat.

Cold consciousness floods his skull like iced seltzer.

The demons fall quiet, their concise, one-voice bellow disintegrating into bleary murmurs.

Jon reaches for his CB, pretends to speak into it, one eye on the darkly clad woman in the cheap rental. She seems satisfied with this performance, at least enough to look away from him, to stare patiently at the vista through her dust-smeared windshield.

Jon Peterson has figured out a useful way to let Lillian Hersh live.

Then the fog came, and even the moon and stars were obscured.

"How is she?" said Karen.

Detective Gardner couldn't say for sure. "I'd say much as when you left. Still kind of stunned, that's a given, but I said it before, we got lucky the way Jen blacked out, could've hit her head. You should probably try and make her talk about her experience before she sleeps tonight."

"If she sleeps," said Karen, peering through the fog at the cluster of uniformed figures outside her apartment building, busy amongst the hazy neon swirls of the squad cars. "What's happening up there now?"

"Well, the feds are pretty much in charge," said Gardner. "They got the major evidence out, now they'll be picking up packing peanuts with itsy-bitsy tweezers. Who knows, you might get your apartment back tonight."

"I can't think of anything worse."

"There'll be a, wait . . ." Gardner found his notebook, "an Agent DeMedici in touch in the morning, I think I pronounced that right. He's not here at the scene, but we spoke on the phone. Nice-ish guy."

"Jeez," said Karen. "How many faces can the feds put in front of me?"

Gardner looked her over, decided she was hiding her fear behind a very convincing mask of weariness and irritability.

No, wait, not fear. Terror.

"They're happy for me to liaise as well," he said, kindly. "You wanna hear what else I got while you were away?"

"Sure." Karen rubbed her eyes, deep in their sockets.

"Okay," said Gardner. "I'll be brief, there isn't much. First, we more or less cleared the delivery guy, completely unrelated. His organization will be all over this in the morning, internal investigations, how did human tissue get into the system, etcetera. But someone there has leaked it already, probably a disgruntled employee. It'll make your breakfast bulletins, though you can tell by the lack of press here that they're not taking it seriously or they only got half a story. They'll figure it out. I mean, it can only help in terms of people's awareness, but we'd like to release it our own way. Frankly, just another good reason not to come home immediately. Let your landlady handle the inquiries, she has the kind of sparkling personality might suit that."

"I'm sure."

"Secondly, it's starting to look like we got no fingerprints, 'cept the ones already belonging to the hand, obviously. Point is, someone wore gloves, never took them off, but that ain't the end of the world. There's gonna be DNA, not just on the box, but also on your other letters. They'll probably trace the company that manufactures the packing peanuts, find out if it comes from some special supplier, they'll even be going over the underside of the box with a toothcomb, see if they can find out if it was put down on a surface that they can trace. And there'll be any number of avenues I might have forgotten. I guess your letter harassment case gets the treatment now, but you can't be sure of even that."

"Excuse me?"

Gardner leaned in a little. "Don't believe everything *CSI* tells you. Predominantly, at least in the short term, they're going to focus on *you*. Why Karen Wiley? Why a therapist? Why your building? They're gonna be interested in your clients, they're gonna want names, addresses, telephone numbers of everyone you met on a professional basis, perhaps some personal ones too."

"My career is over, that's gonna take time to get my head around."

"It doesn't have to be that way, you'll rebuild. I'd say you seemed like a capable woman if it helped any, but you'd probably break my balls. Did I mention the press won't mention you by name until the case is closed?"

Karen didn't seem to be listening.

"Karen, agents will probably want to talk to your ex-husband. What's his name?"

"Dave. David."

"He still around?"

"Not for long, he's moving house. Damn, that reminds me."

"What?"

"I was supposed to take Jen to meet Dave tomorrow afternoon, say goodbye. He leaves for Hawaii in, like, two days. I'm worried about Jen, you know, her father leaving while all this . . ."

Gardner didn't want to touch the family stuff.

"Stay strong. Remember, this'll blow over. You have somewhere to stay in the meantime?"

"Yeah, my mom is here, we'll drive to hers. Shit though, if I'd been home half-hour earlier."

"You couldn't predict this."

"No," said Karen.

Her mom had parked a little way up the street. Karen steeled herself to set off through the mist, to leave the reassuring presence of the big detective, but there was something strange about the way he had begun to look anywhere but at her.

Gardner has something else to say, she realized. Karen stayed put, rubbed at the back of her neck, gave him time.

"Can I ask you something?" he said, finally.

"I don't know, John. I don't think I can hear anymore bad news."

"Not the investigation. I was going to say, did you hear from Lilly recently?"

"What?"

"Lilly, did you hear from her?"

"No, why?"

"Probably nothing," said Gardner, stalling. "But I had dinner with her the other day, she was concerned about you."

"About me how, John?"

"About you and the letters. Thing is, she calls me today, literally minutes before I hear from the switchboard about your incident here. This time she's sounding scared like I never heard, scared for you, for where you are. Now, you know what Lilly's like, nothing much ever seems to panic her, but she *is* panicking about something, won't tell me why."

"What are you saying?"

"I don't want to add to your general stress level, but now she's dropped off the radar. I'm not going to worry, she makes contact when she's ready, but I think she'll try and get a hold of you first. Will you tell her to call me if she does?"

"Is she in trouble?"

"No, but I think she knows more than me, maybe even more than you."

"I'm not following."

"For one thing I know she went to Utah or someplace, that much she *did* tell me."

Karen blinked. "Utah?"

"Yeah. Why would she do that, y'think?"

Karen shook her head, was struggling to digest that Lilly might have gone to the rendezvous at the church.

The cops don't know that The Church of the Final Days is a real rendezvous. But neither, for that matter, do I. Only Blake knows if someone showed up there at 2 p.m. today, and he hasn't called yet. If

I start babbling about an abandoned chapel right now, then I'll pretty soon get the loony stamp from law enforcement. Agent Rice already thinks I'm encouraging the psycho. But how did Lilly know about it? I didn't tell her, Blake wouldn't have told her.

Gardner told her.

"John," said Karen. "Did you tell Lilly?"

"Tell her what?" Gardner was wiping his fingertips on a tissue.

"About The Church of the Final Days. Did you tell her about the sixth letter?"

"I told her it was gibberish. I told her to back off. She was concerned about you."

"Concerned about me, but *asking* about the letter."

"Yes."

"And you told her."

"She's never used me as a source, she's godmother to my kids."

"Look me in the face and tell me that you didn't reveal the contents of that letter."

"Damn it," said Gardner, struggling to keep his voice down. "No one understood the extent, we understand now. None of us could have imagined what we were dealing with. Were we worried for you when you got the first letters? Yes, but neither I, nor Lilly, nor the FBI—the *FBI*—could have comprehended the extent. Yes, I told her."

Karen took a step backwards. "There's a child out there had her left hand amputated," she said. "Removed."

Gardner swallowed. "Yes."

"If she's alive, how long has she got?"

"I don't . . . there's time."

"I'm not the victim here, so *no*. You tell me, John. How long has she got?"

"I don't know. It depends on whether or not he wants to keep her alive."

"And I can tell you that he does, should I tell you why? Because this is a very familiar kind of kidnapping scenario, the worst kind, where the kidnapper shows you how badly they want something by demonstrating how far they're willing to go. And the kidnapper here *does* want something, believe me. But there is no money involved, there is no ransom demand, there's never going to be."

"What do you think he wants?"

"What he wants is to cut that little girl up and mail her to me, piece by piece."

Gardner nodded, fought an urge to study his shoes like a big, scolded child. Karen felt some sympathy for the man, chose not to act on it.

In the distance there were more sirens, not even related. She was about to turn away, when he said: "Indefinitely."

"Indefinitely?"

"In answer to your question. That's what the pathologist said, indefinitely with a hemostat, tourniquets. The child has lost a hand and an ear. If the perpetrator planned plenty in advance, he might even have the facility to transfuse blood. She could live indefinitely, pending infection. But the lower arm probably has hours before it'll have to be at least partially amputated. Anoxia? I don't know."

Karen nodded. Together, they listened to the crackle of police radios. "I have to be with my daughter now," she said.

Gardner watched her stride away, curtains of mist closing in her wake.

Normally, Ella liked the graveyard shift in the station. She could have chosen to use her rank to exempt herself from the inhospitable hours, the occasional shouting drunk in the cells, the long stretches of emptiness—but to take her turn with time off the following day to catch up on shut-eye, it really wasn't too bad, and it showed the guys she was still a team player.

But tonight was different. Tonight she felt spooked out of her skin.

Sure, she wasn't alone in the purpose-built single-story building.

If she chose to seek them out, there was Teri on dispatch and Ennis working his way through a Napoleon biography in the staffroom, but Ella wasn't in the mood for socializing. In fact, she'd taken herself into her plainly decorated office with a box of cookies and a pot of coffee, had closed the door and then dropped the blind as well, an almost unheard-of indication that she wasn't to be disturbed.

Reason being, Holly Trueblood had drawn another picture.

The picture itself—which Ella had spread out on her desk, a paperweight or mug on each corner to stop the large sheet of paper rolling up—wasn't so much what was disconcerting, although it *was* fairly horrific, at least on a par with Holly's earlier portrait of Jon Peterson. No, what perturbed Ella was the idea that Holly Trueblood was still mute, was still hauntingly, eerily silent, yet had access to a place in her brain where creatures like this existed and could have life breathed into them with such creative effectiveness.

What does it all mean? Ella's mind ran through the events of the previous days.

Kathleen R. Jackson, the psychologist recommended by Dr. Arnold Lau, had taken over where the senior physician had left off and was encouraging Holly to paint. The problem was that once Lau left for Washington, Holly no longer seemed interested in the art materials, not even producing the ubiquitous rectangles. Lau himself had evidently withdrawn his concern from Ella's investigation; he hadn't checked in at all since his departure. *He's abandoned us*, was Ella's uncharitable line of thinking. It wasn't that Kathleen was incapable, although the young therapist would be the first to admit that she lacked Lau's experience. Still, she had persevered, even when Ella became distracted by other issues at work and stopped telephoning for updates.

However, the physical aspect of Holly's recovery continued to be remarkable; enough so that she was now able to concentrate for long periods at a time. A local church had dedicated the sum of a collection plate to purchase Holly a gift, and Holly's best friends from school, in coordination with dedicated nurse Taslima, had been allowed to choose that gift for her. A hand-held games console was selected, much to the consternation of some of the older members of the congregation, but the decision stood once Dr. Warwick at the hospital decided an electronic game might aid with Holly's recuperating coordination. And never mind whether it's a worthy gift in the eyes of the Lord—let's just try and make her happy.

So Holly's life was brightened; the console was a hit. But it didn't get her talking any, nor did it lead to any revelations in the stagnated case of her missing sister.

The only time that Holly was to be forbidden from playing was during therapy, and today, the imposition of this boundary was what had led to the painting of the new picture. Prior to the console, she would stare blankly at the walls, at her feet, anywhere but at Kathleen. It was worrying; Holly behaved similarly during the court-appointed visits from her mother, and Kath was concerned the fantasy life of the computer game might become a relationship *in succedaneum*. So she said no to the console. Holly could have it back in fifty minutes' time, if she wanted it.

It had been identified previously that Holly didn't care to sit on the comfortable couch reserved for clients; she liked to use a straight-backed wooden chair similar to the one at the Reagan Health Clinic. Seconds after Taslima had prised the furiously bleeping game from her fingers, Holly stood up and pushed this chair over. Not in a violent way, but the protest was clear. Before Ms. Jackson could say anything, Taslima had righted it for her.

Holly knocked the chair over again.

Taslima was in the process of righting it once more, but Holly was over on the other side of the room, to which Lau's large art pad had been relegated. There were no paints available, but there was a selection of magic markers in a plastic pot on the desk, and when Kathleen offered them, Holly didn't hesitate in selecting the black.

So what the hell is it? thought Ella in her darkened office, poring over the picture in the pool of light from her desk lamp.

Ella had been contacted about the picture as soon as the session was over, though neither the therapist nor the nurse could offer insight into what or who it might represent. Holly, of course, was saying nothing. She'd spent far longer creating this than she had the painting of Jon Peterson, and the time spent showed in the detail. Additionally, Holly made no effort to deface this one as she had previously.

It was another figure that filled the canvas, very different from the picture of Peterson. While that effort was distinctly a picture of a person, admittedly disturbing, this one was clearly a monster.

The hair was a series of Medusa-like snakes, the eyes were huge and square and cartoony and seemingly void of life, and the mouth was an irregular rectangle full of broken teeth. Most distressingly of all—and the feature that Holly had spent the most time on, according to those who were present—was what looked like multiple slashes in the face, slashes across the face, but particularly around the eyes and the mouth.

There was no way this could be mistaken for a repeat performance of the previous picture; this was something new.

Ella's fear, and the unspoken fear of both Kath Jackson and Taslima, was that it was a picture of what had been done to Katy prior to her kidnap, and that Holly had witnessed it. Ella couldn't let this idea go, even though she realized later that the theory was somewhat trashed by there being no blood other than Holly's own in the trailer, and given the extent of the cuts in the picture there would *have* to have been blood, but still . . .

A knock on the door made Ella jump. Officer Ennis waited for a response before sticking his head in as though expecting to have something thrown at it.

"Chief, I'm sorry," he said.

"That's fine," said Ella, still distracted by the picture. Holly had drawn big square eyes. Terrified eyes? Slashes across the face, *all across the face . . .*

Ennis cleared his throat. "You not gonna believe this, but there's someone out here wants to see you."

Ella looked up. "A crazy?"

"Don't think so. Says he has an appointment."

She glanced at her chunky wristwatch. "It's well past midnight. We have office hours."

"He says it's about the Trueblood case. He says you'll wanna speak to him."

Ella sighed. "Did you let him through?"

"Yeah, he's out in the . . ."

"Okay then."

Ennis retreated and Ella sighed again, stood up and flipped on the main switch. Strip lights flickered in mesh cages.

There had been any number of public tip-offs regarding Katy Trueblood, none of which had produced useful leads, mostly paranoid neighbors pointing fingers at one another. The number of call-outs had increased also, and there had been one near-fatal shooting in a family home when a husband tried to sneak in after a heavy night and the gun-toting missus was convinced it was demonic Don.

The next tap on her door was light, little more than a dusting. Ella, ready, opened it to reveal a gaunt, gray-haired man in a scruffy jacket. Judging from his dust-streaked face and the way he held his skeletal frame, he was close to the point of exhaustion, but his eyes were alert, and they opened very wide when he saw her, as if filing away her appearance in his mind.

Ella felt disconcerted, as she always did under scrutiny. But then the man extended a long, bony hand.

"You must be Chief McCullers," he said, in a voice barely louder than a whisper. "I'm Egan Blake, and I'm pleased to meet you."

"Egan Blake," she repeated, carefully.

The man gave a small, polite smile.

"I don't recall contacting you," she said.

"I'm sorry for barging in so late. Didn't Arnie Lau tell you I was coming?"

"No sir, he did not," said Ella. "He told me that I should *consider* contacting an Egan Blake, formerly of the FBI, if I needed help. I told Lau he was taking a damned liberty."

"Hmm," said Blake, running his finger over his chin as though they shared a mutually knotty problem. "So, you're saying you *don't* need help?"

Ella glanced down the corridor to where the shadow of Ennis lurked. Irritated, she turned back into her room but left the door open, not quite an invitation. Blake followed anyway.

When she next turned he was beyond the threshold, hands respectfully behind his back. Ella was over by the office's age-old Stars and Stripes, and she suddenly became conscious of Holly's picture, the large childish scrawl the only document on the desk.

"Look," she said to Blake, "I'm going to need to see some kind of ID. You say you have something new on the Trueblood case?"

"Perhaps," said Blake, reaching for his wallet. "Did the Bureau in San Francisco ask you for the fingerprints from the trailer yet?"

"No," said Ella, walking around to inspect. "San Francisco? Are they going to?"

"Damn, but they're slow. Expect a call."

"Did they find Don Keynes?"

"Don Keynes is probably dead."

"How would you know that?"

"I don't. Call it a hunch."

"Then there's not a lot of point in getting them the fingerprints," said Ella, concluding her inspection of his details. "Don't you have cop ID?"

"Retired, ma'am. But there's a DC number you can call. I hoped Lau would pave the way."

"That'll be fine, Mr. Blake. I have good reason to trust Arnold Lau."

"Call me Egan."

"Egan. Listen, we only lifted Keynes and the family from the trailer. His prints were circulated, on all the channels as soon as."

"No, I know," said Blake, "and Keynes will certainly jump to the head of the most wanted lists, but that's not the priority."

"What's the priority?"

"Primarily, they're going to need to ID a child's hand."

"A child's hand?"

"Yes."

"Where is the . . . what about the rest of her?"

Blake shook his head. "Missing."

"Katy . . ." said Ella. She sank into her chair, began to tear at a thumbnail. "How did they make the connection?"

"There's a therapist on the West Coast," said Blake. "May I sit down?"

Ella nodded.

"This therapist, Karen Wiley, has been receiving notes from a kidnapper," he said, "but no one in her circle of acquaintances has been kidnapped. She's unconnected, as far as we know, but this has been going on for the past month—the powers that be assumed it was some kind of prank."

"But not anymore though, huh?"

"We think the kidnapper is trying to arrange a meeting with her, but she's never played ball. The postmark on the letters was always the same: Canaan, Utah. Today, UPS delivered to the psychologist what looks like the hand of a Caucasian female, ten or twelve years old."

Ella swallowed.

"And an ear," said Blake. "Or part of an ear."

"Why wasn't I told about this? About these letters? Katy was taken on the ninth."

"No one made the connection, Chief. No names were ever mentioned. Canaan PD seemed to have an open-and-shut case, and, more importantly, everyone thought the letters were a hoax, or at worst an unrelated stalking. They'll make that connection now."

"*I* could have made the connection. But *I* couldn't have known." Ella was furious, almost brought her fist down on the desk. "The goddamn postmark should have been enough."

"I know," said Blake, gently. "But the next thing is that all this is going to start adding up."

"There any reason why he'd kill an animal?"

"An animal?"

"A cat. We found it on the roof of a trailer, suspect it was done the same day as the kidnap. It was . . . butchered very badly. Had we found it earlier, it might have been significant of something worse than kidnapping. Isn't cruelty to animals a psychological sign?"

"Commonly assumed, but usually in juveniles with tendencies. J. M. McDonald, *The Threat to Kill*. Might be a dated theory, though."

"Unlikely to be a juvenile," said Ella, "given the strength of the attacker. Or are you suggesting it has something to do with the kidnapper's childhood?"

"Did Holly draw this picture?"

"Huh?"

"This picture on your desk. Lau told me about the paintings. Is this one of Holly's?"

"Yeah." Ella was distracted. "Is Katy dead, you think?"

"I don't think so," said Blake.

"How would you know that?"

"I have some theories, I'd like to tell you about them. Did Holly draw it today?"

Ella cleared her throat. "This afternoon."

"And she's still not talking?"

"Right. Lau thinks she might have sublimated the terror she experienced, but it's a slender lead, one of our more desperate attempts."

"Do *you* think the drawings are significant, Chief?"

"Yes. I don't know."

"Can I see the other one she did? The other picture?"

"She painted over it. But I can try and give you a description."

"Can we do it in the car?" said Blake, moving.

"The car?"

"If you'd permit me, Chief McCullers, I'd like to show you something."

The high beams of the Chevy pickup with the light bar and the police markings cleaved through the desert night, speeding southbound on the empty 192. It was the sole beacon in a sea of darkness that stretched across the wasteland of the Canyonlands for tens, maybe hundreds of miles. Chief McCullers had to drive carefully or she'd miss the turning to Crescent Canyon.

Inside the cab, bathed in the glow of the dials, a silence had descended. *I bet Egan Blake is pretty good with his silences*, thought Ella, as the truck ate up the central road markings. *Both the comfortable AND the uncomfortable ones.*

Her irritation at being barged in on in the middle of the night had given way to a kind of respect for the man, but it had then fallen gradually back towards irritation; mostly irritation with herself, because Ella was now finding that she wanted Blake to respect her in turn, and that put her in a kind of arrears. Ella hated being in debt to anyone.

Blake had been silent for some ten minutes and was clearly tired, resting his shoulder against the doorframe. Eventually, he stirred a little, said: "Why do they call it The Church of the Final Days?"

Ella stretched, flexed her hands on the wheel. "I'm sure you've asked around," she said. "And no one much knows, right?"

"Right."

She cleared her throat. "Well, in truth, everyone kind of does know. You ever live in a small town?"

"I lived on a reservation outside of Cloverdale, California until I was twelve."

"What happened then? You rode the rails?"

Blake said nothing.

"But you have some Indian blood in you, huh?"

"Don't we all?"

Ella heard the smile in his voice. She smiled back, glancing across at the craggy face, suffused in the warm light of the dashboard.

"Anyway," she said, "you'll know that those small-town legends die hard, and people are apt to make too big of a thing, perhaps even more of that thing, if, on the surface, the communal face is trying to forget. Do you follow me?"

"I'm not sure. Are you saying Canaan has a dirty secret?"

Ella shrugged. "Nothing anyone who'd lived locally for a while would be proud of. Saying that, I don't think folks generally give it a second thought, 'cept around Halloween when the kids sometimes make sport. Point is, I'm not surprised when you say that you found something strange at The Church of the Final Days. A spooky legend will attract some freaks, not to mention the location, all dramatic and remote. And the name itself. That's bound to scoop up cranks."

"What's the legend, Chief?"

"I say legend, but it *is* reality. I just don't know precisely what that reality is anymore. I doubt many do. I dare say people who would play harum scarum know next to nothing about why the name exists."

"I know it wasn't called that when Crescent Canyon was a working town."

"Right. Shame those miners didn't leave a stronger legacy, we could've promoted the place as an attraction." She gestured through the windshield. "But we got enough natural attractions, you understand."

It took Blake a moment to understand that she was referring to the scenery. Taking her cue, he looked out into the spectral vastness, where the yellow moon in the star-strewn sky was approaching full. In the far distance, dark towers of rock seemed to keep pace with the vehicle, solid shadows in a midnight blue horizon.

"I mean," said Ella, "if Crescent Canyon was a ghost town by the turn of the last century, then by the middle of that century it was a dustbowl. Hardly surprising, poky little place in the middle of nowhere, hanging on to the teeniest thread of metal."

"You got many of the descendants living in Canaan?"

"I don't know about that," she said. "Wait, this is the turning coming up."

Ella had been watching out. She slowed the car right down, pulled in until the gravel crunched, wanting to make sure.

The only marking for Crescent Canyon was a wonky metal pole, the sign lost or stolen. Ella made the hard right, felt the texture of the road change through her hands on the wheel. It had been years since she'd driven up here, and she couldn't even remember the reason; she wasn't enamored with off-roading like some of her deputies, Johnson particularly, who organized rock-crawling events and modified assembly-line stock in his spare time.

"You hear of a man named James Earl LaGrande?" she said to Blake, once the main road had vanished from her rear-view mirror and red tail-light fug.

"James Earl LaGrande," repeated Blake, trying the words out. "I can't say I have."

"He's someone the FBI will probably have had a file on, if you have access to such things. I can't put dates to the events, but his church started up in the late sixties. Not up here, you understand. Initially there was a Church of the Firstborn of the Greatness of Time, back in Canaan. This particular church, which was already pretty extreme, eventually excommunicated LaGrande, the very prophet who pioneered it."

"Why?"

"I don't know, take your pick of the reasons. He was a dissident, he had blasphemous visions, he channeled Moses, he convinced another member to let him take her pre-teen daughters as bed-fellows. The fundamentalists can be problematic because many will recognize individual visions over the preaching of one moderate pastor. And this guy was charismatic, by all accounts. Really charismatic."

"A cult leader?"

"That came next. LaGrande certainly had the makings of it. His father was one of those who left Utah after the LDS outlawed the dual-marriage thing, set up his own sect in Mexico. By the time LaGrande was born, it was one of the largest polygamous churches in the world. So it was in his genes, perhaps, though LaGrande wasn't happy with Baja California. He wanted to reclaim the promised land. Him and his brother."

"What was the brother's name?"

"Don't ask me, an apostle name I think. Anyway, they went their separate ways after LaGrande was rejected by the Greatness of Time. The brother took over the leadership and LaGrande himself disappeared. But he resurfaced, the proverbial bad penny. And this time he had a whole new doctrine."

"The Church of the Final Days."

"He'd been wandering, you understand. He'd been a month or so in the great wilderness, some say forty days, but I think it was a lot longer than that. He'd talked to the devil, he'd talked to the Lord, he very possibly talked to the sasquatch. He alone knew where he'd been, but his clothes were tattered, his feet were bare, and whoever or whatever he'd spoken to had told him the end was coming. Announced himself like that on Main Street, must've held up what little traffic there was back then. Preached on street corners in hundred-degree weather."

"An instant hit, right?"

"A curiosity, but he soon picked up a loyal group of followers. Very loyal. But the atrocities continued, even got worse, came to a head when he impregnated an eleven-year-old the same year he planned to run for mayor, if you can believe that. She miscarried, Lord help her. Moab, the next town over, was already picking up the beginnings of a burgeoning tourist industry. John Ford had filmed that western locally, and the Canaan city fathers needed to compete. They were never likely to be in the race with a barefoot Judgment Day pseudo-Christ overseeing the sanitation. LaGrande had to go."

"And he did?"

"I can't remember what they got him for or what they threatened him with, but he was run out of town by the end of the decade. But he'd made provision. One of his visions for a new church involved the Crescent Canyon ghost town, maybe a place he stumbled on during his wanderings. He didn't find it the way you and I did—*this* road didn't exist back then in its current condition; bad as it seems now, it would barely be discernible from the desert. The bit we're getting to here, the smoother bit? That was cleared for LaGrande by a local contractor, someone loyal. There were any number of others willing to help."

"What happened?"

"Well, at first he must have slept in the old shell of the church, living on donations of food, whatever, but he'd preach to anyone who'd come out to listen. It didn't take long before someone contributed a trailer or two, so some of the flock could stay nearby. Others smartened the place up, put in windows, applied paint."

"And LaGrande continued to preach."

"Right. Everyone in town knew he'd set up again outside of city limits, but those that weren't faithful chose to ignore. People had greater things to be suspicious of than one lone crazy preacher setting up in a derelict church in the middle of nowhere."

"Did *you* ever hear LaGrande preach?"

"Me? No, God knows what I was doing at that time. Flunking math, probably. My old man might have checked out what

LaGrande had to say at one stage, but my old man mostly worshiped Jackie Gleason."

"So," said Blake, "who did LaGrande kill first?"

Ella glanced across. "How do you know he killed people?"

"Where else is this story gonna end?"

Ella nodded, turned back to the road, worked the truck over dips and crevices with the exacting concentration of someone who knew she had the main body of her attention focused elsewhere.

"It started with the sacrifices," she said. "LaGrande would kill girls, rarely boys, and he buried them in the Canyonlands, so deep they couldn't be found. They were sacrifices to a God of Judgment, designed to stave off the end of the world. He knew much of the wilderness like the back of his hand, not surprising, the amount of time he must've spent wandering. Got away with it for near on four months, because the parents were complicit, they always covered for him. They must've been brainwashed."

"That's horrific."

"No one really figured out how many he killed. Some say so few as two or three, families moved away once they'd made their godless contribution. It was probably a whole bunch more; easy to lose bodies out here."

"How did they catch him?"

"What eventually happened was that he ordered the killing of his brother. Actually, he ordered the killing of the leadership of quite a few other rival churches, all local, but that never came to pass, and the attempted slaying of his brother was the one that got him."

"How's that?"

"Yeah, one of LaGrande's brother's wives was a convert to The Final Days. She was supposed to do it, kill her own husband, but it went wrong, something. There was a fire, I think; that accounts for the current appearance of the church. But LaGrande had already fled back to Mexico and the rest of the loyal members had dispersed. But he was caught sooner rather than later. I don't have the details, but I know he died in an El Paso jail, or maybe south of the border. In the end they could only pin two murders and one attempted murder on him. And then there are those that say he *still* tried to order gangland-style executions from his cell."

Ella fell silent, suddenly feeling weary, from telling the tale, from the late night, from the tension of driving a difficult road that was rapidly deteriorating into nothing.

Blake, conversely, was completely revived.

"Incredible," he said.

"What is?" she was irritated again, revved the engine, something in his tone.

"That this . . . I don't know," he said. "That all this happened. And it got covered up. Pretty well, I have to say—I'm thorough with my research."

"Oh, save your awed little voice, I know what you're thinking. Crazy Bible Belt recidivists, multiplicity of religion in dirt-water burgs. We got sixteen churches in our town, we're pretty set for churches. People exercise freedoms, sometimes, very occasionally, things happen. Big price to pay, but what could you change?"

"I understand," said Blake.

"No, you have no idea. Yeah, you can say it, it's not a dirty word. *I'm* a Mormon." Blake had sunk back in his seat, she had to speak to an unreadable silhouette. "But call me extreme, or insane, or even old-fashioned, and I'll punch you in the nose, mister. I earned what perspective I have, so don't judge my town or its people based on anything I just said. It was a long time ago."

Ella dropped her shoulders slightly, as though absorbing an emotional blow.

Why on earth did you just say that?

Why do you have to justify yourself to this man?

Is it SHAME, Ella? Is it shame because you're one of them now? One of the God-botherers? What was it that you said you were going to do when you retired? Go be a missionary, like you told Member Jeake? Spreading what? Your unique brand of self-doubt?

You thought you were confronting the demons of your past by taking that dunk in the water, but all you're doing is burying your dumb old spinster's head in the sand.

Milton Trueblood's voice: *Where's God now, we're sat around here doin' all this believing?*

"I'm sorry," Ella said to Blake. "I don't know what came over me."

Blake had leaned forward again. He seemed to be fascinated by the yucca moths outside, risking life and limb in the brightness of the headlights. When he turned his head to her, wide-eyed with that way he had, he looked like a friendly ghoul.

"People are far too quick to judge," he said. "And I'm meaning me."

"I guess so," said Ella, quickly. "Mostly, we're welcoming folks. Good Christians, and that's how come I can be so honest with you."

"I appreciate that," said Blake, and he was knocked back in his seat as the truck bridged a particularly cavernous pothole. "Watch out, these last turns are real doozies."

The Church of the Final Days appeared suddenly, hidden by a rock until the final moment, and it surprised them both. The yellow-white tunnel of Ella's beams that chased across the south wall did not quite reach to the roof of the structure, and, more than ever, it resembled a bleached, rotting tomb.

Ella braked rapidly, then reversed up a short incline to the right of where the pass broke cover. Her intention was to flood the scene with the twin lights of her truck, but the glow from the moon and stars was pretty good too.

Then the engine was killed, and there was a whole new breed of silence.

"Ready?" she said. Her voice was steady, she refused to feel spooked by this midnight jaunt. Blake was squinting at the church, he didn't look happy about something. Then he turned, gave a quick bob of his head.

Both Ella and Blake had brought along heavy-duty Maglite flashlights, and anyone inside the church at that moment might have mistaken the pair of approaching humans for something from out of space, nocturnal flotsam floating in the rays of four powerful beams. Two of the beams descended the short incline, one a little ahead of the other.

"Over here," said Blake, gesturing with the light. His voice sounded different outside the cab, even deeper maybe. "The grave is on the left-hand side." Without waiting for a response, he stepped over the unmarked threshold to the larger of the two small burial grounds.

Ella followed him, trying to ignore the looming presence of the church, the leering oblongs of window. She couldn't help but be aware of the ancient graves strewn beneath her feet, humble and irregular markers threatening to trip her up.

Who the hell is this man I'm out here with anyway?

What if he just turns around and . . .

"Gone," said Blake's voice.

Ella strode over to where he was standing, joined her beam with his. Together they stared at a clump of dry grass, petrified in the brilliance of the spotlights. She could see where a marker must have been placed; a section of grass was flattened, but it was already springing back. The stone couldn't have been there for long.

"Gone," said Blake again.

"This is where it was? The brand-new tombstone?"

Blake didn't reply. On a whim, he raised his beam, scanned the area where the wilderness met the churchyard, the area that he had run across in broad daylight earlier that day. A couple of jackrabbits turned and bolted as his flashlight passed, eyes gleaming red. The amassed shadows of encircling hills peered in on them all.

"Someone must've been back and taken it," said Ella, after a moment.

"Yes," said Blake. "And they did it in the last eight or nine hours. Since I was here."

"Could've been someone else took it," said Ella.

"Nah, I think he was here. He might have been watching the whole time, I don't know. I got no prints off the stone, it'd been thoroughly wiped. I got no pictures either, and now the thing is gone. Take some effort to move, I'm guessing, someone on their own."

Ella and Blake looked at one another.

Where's God now?

"I'm gonna take a look inside the church," said Ella. "We've come this far. If someone was back here, they might have left something else."

She didn't need his approval, and Blake watched her walk away from him, a squat, middle-aged policewoman with a loaded belt hanging off thick hips.

He waited until she had vanished around the corner and he could see the beam from her flashlight splashing around the interior, lighting the church up like a jack-o'-lantern.

Blake stood there and sighed, ran his fingers up the bridge of his nose, momentarily let his light swing free at arm's length.

Glint.

What was that?

Blake froze.

Something there.

He remained in position, not quite daring to move. Flashlight beam paused in mid-flight, Blake traced it back over the ground, roughly around the area he had been swinging it in before.

Nothing. Nothing . . .

Glint, glint.

Blake moved quickly, something small was hidden in a tuft of weeds. He covered the boneyard in rapid, jerky strides, legs aching from earlier exertions. He placed the flashlight down, moved in with fingers, eyes.

A cellphone.

It was a cellphone.

Small, ultra-modern, familiar. Could this be Lilly's cellphone? She hadn't been responding to his calls.

Blake glanced over to the church. Ella's spotlight had stopped circling.

Hurriedly, Blake reached into the jacket for his own sat-phone, brought up the eerie glow of the holographic contacts screen, found Lilly's number, pushed dial. Would her phone even work out here?

The phone in the grass chirruped, softly.

Blake hung up.

It *was* Lilly's cellphone. Had this been here before? No, he'd gone over the ground earlier that day and it would have been obvious to spot in broad daylight.

This was dropped when the gravestone was removed.

But why? Deliberately? As a message? A cry for help? Had she thrown it out of a car?

Has Lilly been *taken*?

"You find something?" Blake started at the sound of the Chief, she was coming up behind him.

He reached out with one long finger, pushed Lilly's phone further back into the weeds. Then he stood, picked up his flashlight.

"I was tying my shoelace," he lied. "Did you find anything in the church?"

Karen's mom gave her a mug of cocoa, sat her on the pagoda, and Karen watched the bugs dance in the phosphorescent glow of the swimming pool, long into the evening. It was warmer here than it had been in the city, though a portion of the fog had followed them upstate.

Sometime around twelve, Jen's silhouette appeared in the patio doorway, and there was the sound of the door sliding open. Barefoot and wrapped in a quilt, Jen picked her way across the landscaped garden, past expensive-looking outdoor furniture. *Grandma would go ape if she could see you trailing her good linen through damp grass,* thought Karen. *Oh, what the hell. Tonight, surely, all can be forgiven.*

Jen hopped onto the bench. "I can't sleep," she said. "Can I sit here with you?"

"I guess," said Karen, and Jen pressed her body close.

Karen took a breath of midnight air, tinged with the smell of well-maintained grass and sweet chlorine from the pool, and together they listened to the soft noises of the night, the rustle of trees, the chirp of the crickets, innocent and friendly compared to the blare and yell of the city.

"Mommy might need to go away for a while," said Karen. "Like I said before. Can you understand that?"

Jen was usually resistant to anyone speaking to her like a child, eye-rolling and sighing coming as standard whenever Karen talked about either of them in the third person. But this time Jen just stared right back, unblinking, any sassiness blasted off her face by the events of the day.

"I know the timing is as bad as it can be," said Karen, "and I know we should probably stick together. But I don't feel right about going home straight away, do you?"

Jen shook her head, one white cheek rubbing against the downy quilt.

"You remember Egan? The man who ate dinner with us?"

Jen nodded.

"He's trying to solve our problems right now. I'm gonna go help him. I trust him, I think. Do you think we should trust him?"

Jen nodded again, but as if she hadn't really heard. "What about me?" she said. "Where will I go?"

"Well, I want you to think about staying here, with Grandma. She could take you to school, and she and Grandpa never see enough of you. You can swim in the pool, you can have your friends over, she's even gonna take you riding. How about that?"

Jen digested this and there were more long moments while she stared at the halogen-lit water, at wisps of steam drifting shy of the sapphire surface.

"Mom," she said. "What about you?"

"Me?"

"Yeah. Are *you* okay?"

Typical Jen, thinks of others first. Karen knew from long experience that there was no point in lying to her daughter.

She smiled. "Baby, I'm tired, you know? But I feel I can't just sit around. I feel like I sat around for long enough. Do you know what I mean?"

"Can I come with you?"

Karen had been anticipating this. "Yes," she said. "Of course you can."

"Okay," said Jen, and swung her legs a little.

Moments passed. "Do you want to?" said Karen.

"I don't know." Jen frowned. "I could miss a whole bunch of school."

It was Karen's turn to nod. *I'm a manipulative genius*, she thought. *Jen knows precisely what's best for her, but she has to be allowed to figure it out for herself.*

Jen had bunched her hands into little fists. "I get so *mad* to think that someone got hurt," she said. "Why is this happening, Mom?"

"Because there are people who carry around a sickness in their heads. Sometimes they get so sick that they do really bad things. But there aren't many people like that in the world. We just got very, very unlucky."

"What about the little girl? The little girl with her poor hand?"

Little girl? She's probably the same age as you. "Well, they're gonna find her now because there are going to be clues, you know? She got even more unlucky than us, but those people with the sickness in their heads, they aren't so very careful about not getting caught."

"Do you think she's dead?"

The hoot of an owl, somewhere far behind them. It was just another gentle contribution to the night chorus, but Karen couldn't disguise her shiver.

Did you say dead? No, no, no. We never talk about dead in this family, babe. Didn't you get the memo? I had a sister once, your beautiful Aunt Sammie, only you never got to meet her. She was so pretty, she looked just like you. But there was this one time . . .

"I don't think she's dead," Karen said eventually. "I think the police are gonna find her."

"Well, can I meet her when they do? I'd like to meet her."

Karen ventured an arm around the shoulder of the little ghost.

Jen rocked back into Karen's body, allowed herself to be hugged, legs dangling off the bench, but she still stiffened a little when Mom planted a big kiss on the top of her head. Karen prolonged it anyway.

You see, Mommy has to be tough on us both now. She has to make sure she's doing the right thing. We both know how capable you are of making choices, little one. You tell me so yourself all the time . . .

Karen released, cleared her throat. "Jen, I need to ask you something. Something about how you really feel."

Jen opened her eyes wide, demonstrated that she was listening.

"There's been a lot of talk about your dad recently," said Karen. "About how he's going away any day now, and how you want to go and stay with him."

Jen seemed embarrassed. "Mom, that was just for vacations, I said."

"Yeah, but I wasn't keen on you going at all, even for a vacation, and I knew you were angry. I think that your dad is a good dad, and the kind of dad he is never had anything to do with why me and him got a divorce, you know all that. I guess what I'm trying to say is that, well, if you want to go away with him *now*, you should probably be allowed. I'm thinking that his world is probably more stable for you, with all that's going on."

"*Mom* . . . I was only playing."

"Yeah, but you experienced something that a little girl should never have to deal with, no matter how smart and grown-up she is. Dad could take you, and you could come back once everything gets back to normal."

Jen blinked. "Are you . . . do you *want* me to go?"

"Oh baby, that's the *last* thing I want." Karen had never meant anything more in her life.

Come through for us now, babe. For the team.

"I don't know," said Jen, finally. "Dad's great, and Ash too, but . . . they don't seem like two people I could really *live* with. Not *really*."

"Oh?"

"I mean, there was this one time, like, Ash borrowed my hairbrush, the bristles came back all gummed up with spray. And they never watch *The Daily Show*, I don't think they understand it." Jen grinned, blue eyes twinkling with mischief. "Besides, can you imagine what kind of shit they'll be in trying to build their own house in Hawaii? I love Dad, but he'll nail his sleeve to the wall, you know? Maybe I'll visit next year, thanks all the same."

Karen couldn't help laughing, despite her thumping pulse, her fear and exhaustion. Right then she could have danced her daughter around the garden.

Jen was in the process of dislodging herself from the bench, gathered up the quilt like a complicated robe of state. "Mom, I think I'm tired. Will you come to bed? Grandma said I didn't have to meet with Dad tomorrow, but I kind of think I wanna."

The owl hooted again. It *was* late, and getting cold, too.

"Sure," said Karen, still smiling.

Will I come up to bed? Which one of us is the child here?

They walked back towards the warmth of the house, hand in hand.

Thirteen

The Cessna 206 taxied away from its spot near Concourse S of Salt Lake City International Airport and was soon waiting in a short line for take-off, dwarfed between a couple of Delta's Boeings. Afternoon sunlight washed into the small cabin as it made the turn, and two miles or more of shimmering runway beckoned.

Karen Wiley saw, rather than heard, the pilot communicate with the tower, and the little bush plane jerked forward, accelerating towards lift-off, needing only a fraction of the available airstrip to achieve flight. The pilot climbed rapidly through some turbulent wobbles, and the land dropped away to reveal a golf course, a reclamation ditch, the grid of the city to the east. The aircraft banked to fasten on to her southward course, and Karen watched as they leveled with the thin veins of snow atop the Wasatch Mountains. Then she looked west, towards the green, light-filled mirror of the Great Salt Lake.

Half an eye on the vista, Karen also took an opportunity to glance at the hard-edged profile of Egan Blake. With the exception of the warmth in his smile when he met her off the flight from SFO, there had been little of the eccentric, shrewd old man she'd first gotten to know back in his cozy basement; he'd spiked his thinning gray hair with gel, and the face above the well-worn hunting vest had become lean, focused, wolfish.

Because Karen's connection had been delayed, there had been no time to talk as they rushed through the terminal, and no opportunity to speak in the moments spent in a dark, ground-floor departure lounge, the solitary check-in girl tapping her fake Gucci and cradling a telephone to her ear without speaking.

The plane leveled at 9,000 feet, the engine settling into a peaceable drone. To the west was the Point of the Valley, where the Wasatch and Oquirrh Mountains meet in a congested pass. Beyond Blake, Karen saw tiny SUVs overtaking tiny semis on I-15.

He felt the ghost of her scrutiny. "You know," he said, turning, "I'll say again, I'm glad you've come along. If I were you, I'd be going mad in the city."

Karen glanced towards the front of the plane. They didn't need to moderate their voices for privacy because they were the only two passengers on the flight, the second of CanyonAir's twice-daily SLC–Canaan service, and the pilot was keeping his headphones on.

"Okay," said Karen, cautiously. "You didn't need to make the round-trip though."

"This morning we caught a real break. At least, I think we did. The flight gives us time to talk."

"What kind of a break?"

"The postmark."

"The postmark?"

"I thought it might lead to something," said Blake. "We got a postmark off letters one through five. That's how we first knew it was Canaan, it was written on the envelopes in black ink, but I got specific with the numbers and it was far easier than I thought."

"What do you mean?"

"Okay," he said, and because they were too close to maintain comfortable eye contact, he used his hands for emphasis. "This kidnapper, he might know how to wipe clean his own crime scenes, but he's going to make other mistakes, perhaps rudimentary ones, it's inevitable. He might be borderline idiot savant about one thing, but inexplicably careless about another. Well, I think he got careless about *how* he mailed his letters, at least the first ones."

"The postmark," Karen said again.

"This morning, I stopped by the central post office in Canaan, was wondering if our boy had mailed his stuff to you from there, wanted to confirm the code with a clerk. I was surprised just how much information my little question yielded. Do you know what an MPP is?"

"An MPP?"

"A Mailer's Postmark Permit."

She shook her head.

"Okay," he said. "If you're tenacious enough, go through the right procedures, you can apply to frank your own mail. Entirely legal. You still have to use your post office to drop it off, but, well, if you choose, you can rubber stamp your own outgoing."

"What's the point?"

"No point. Depends on the individual. Philatelists, interested in the whys and wherefores. Maybe you run a stamp-collecting club, want to make your own mark. Why do people do things? Because they can be done, because they're allowed."

"And my letters were stamped with a, what was it?"

"A Mailer's Postmark Permit. As a result, the clerk in the office could identify the genesis of your mail immediately, because it took the guy who made those markings six months to get approval to do so, and he was memorably antisocial in the process."

"You mean . . ."

"Right. A good citizen of Canaan has been rubber-stamping his own mail for going on four years. And he stamped the kidnap letters sent to you."

"What, you got a name?"

"Name, address, everything. They know him in the post office. They know him roundabouts. Canaan isn't a big town."

"Then what? This is the guy?"

"His name is Howard Freed."

"Howard Freed."

"That name mean anything to you?"

"Freed. I don't think so."

"Me neither. He owns a store specializing in security equipment and consultation, a single-story fortified-looking pile off of Main, but when I cruised past and pushed the buzzer it didn't look open for business. Metal bars behind filthy windows, a sign so faded you can barely read it, security camera. Suspicious type, obviously. Thing is, Mr. Freed and his business have a website, and whilst he *is* selling security equipment, he also allows himself to be personally forthcoming in his online incarnation, not that it's been updated in a while."

"How so?"

"Freed's site is essentially a big how to regarding extremist survival skills and weapon maintenance. Stockpile is another big message. He's a right-wing radical with a warning for the government. Some links lead to instructions on how to manufacture basic explosives, *Anarchist's Cookbook* type of thing. I suspect the desire for a personal postmark might be an extension of his paranoia, or at least it was initially."

"This is the guy who sent the letters? Did you tell the cops? You could have saved me the trip out here."

"A reasonable-sounding candidate, no?" Blake's smile was wry.

"He's not? Isn't the profile convincing enough?"

"Whichever way Howard Freed voices his political anxieties, the man is a decorated army reservist who spent the last three months as an artillery mechanic in the Middle East. He's out of the country with an alibi as solid as morning roll call."

"But surely," she said, "the *date* on the postmarks—"

"Of course, he was out of the country when your mail was sent. But on the website, one of the so-called security services that he claims to provide is that of a remailer."

"What, people send their mail to him and he forwards it using his personal postmark?"

"Anonymity for the original sender. At a price, no doubt."

"But if he's out of the country . . ."

"Yeah," said Blake. "He makes like a loner, but Freed has a wife and two children. I don't know if he trusts them around the high-nitrate fertilizer and underground bunkers he seems so fond of, but it's easy money for Mrs. Colleen Freed to open up the office while hubby's away and forward the mail using his mailer's mark. I don't know if Mrs. Freed knows what she's sending, but I doubt very much that she cares."

"So it's *not* Howard Freed or his family. It's someone else, someone hiding behind Freed's remailing service, which is perfectly legal."

"That's the theory."

"So then," said Karen, and her frustration was starting to show, "where's the carelessness?"

"What do you mean?" said Blake, bouncing with the slight turbulence.

"The mistake," said Karen. "You said the perp wasn't careful about how he mailed the letters. Sounds pretty careful, taking advantage of an absent and paranoid middleman."

"But it *is* a mistake. It's a mistake because he's tied to something. Why not drive to opposite ends of the country to send different letters, guarantee there'd be no scent? Something might be in Freed's office, an invoice, receipt, the original envelopes—if we're extremely lucky, a name and address. If Freed is as obsessive as I think he is, he's maintaining files on everyone he comes into contact with."

"And you're just going to walk into that office and ask for this information? You might as well ask for the combination to his safe."

"Asking politely wasn't what I had in mind."

"Local police? The FBI?"

"I'd considered that," said Blake. "But they'll need a warrant to search Freed's office, which they won't get immediately because they'll have to make the links that we've made, and then present those links convincingly to a judge—remember that your original letters are locked in an evidence room in San Francisco. Then there's the complication of Freed as a hard-working patriot serving abroad with no priors, when we can't tie his business to anything but harassment letters—Katy Trueblood's hand came through a package delivery company. *Then* there's the possibility that his wife will dump anything incriminating the minute she gets a whiff of an oncoming siege that Howard Freed has prepared his family for since before the perceived Y2K threat. And Katy loses the rest of that limb."

Blake seemed breathless, like he was building up to something. Karen turned away, stared out of the window. Far below them, occasional settlements were giving way to a reddish-brown wasteland through which snakes of river winded, any water hidden in the depths of shadow.

"This isn't a lead at all," said Karen, unable to keep the bitterness out of her voice. "How is any of this a lead?"

"Because," said Blake, "tonight I'm going to break into Howard Freed's office and have a very thorough look around. And I'm gonna need your help to do it."

Ella slid back the plexiglass door that covered the broad bulletin board in the deserted lobby of Canaan's police station and hunted around and between the wanted posters and community info flyers for a spare pin. Though it was a stretch for her to reach, she settled on downgrading the DON KEYNES: MISSING WANTED FOR QUESTIONING poster from four pins to two. Behind her, the creak of the floorboards announced the arrival of Deputy Ernie 'Slim' Johnson, who wouldn't have dared lend an inch of his bulky six-foot three-inch frame to reach over her head and help without being asked.

"Mm-huh?" she mumbled, not bothering to turn around, pins in her mouth while she rearranged items.

"Salt Lake Bureau called again," he said, careful with news she wouldn't want to hear; Chief McCullers had been in a terrible mood for days now.

"Mm-huh?"

"Well, they *are* going to put in an appearance, but it might be late," he said. "Want me to hang around?"

"Damn straight." Ella finished clearing a space, turned and marched past her loyal Deputy like he was an oak tree growing in the middle of the floor. "What, you don't like administrative procedure?"

Johnson said nothing, watched as Ella collected a scroll of paper from behind the tall processing desk. She strode back around him and busied herself trying to pin it to the board, which was no easy task, given its size and tendency to roll back up.

"Shit," she said, finally, dropping her head. "You wanna help me out here?"

Slim reached over, stuck two pins in the top corners of the paper while she held it at arm's length. It looked to him like a picture drawn by a child, and he stepped back, confused. The paper took up a big quotient of the board; in fact, it seemed to be overlapping some *real* bulletins.

Then he realized she was staring him in the eyes.

"Well," said Ella, face stern, "what do you think?"

"I . . . I don't know," he said, lost. "If I were you, I wouldn't quit the day job."

She didn't smile. "That picture look like anything to you?"

"Honestly?"

She nodded, once.

"Honestly, I think it looks like we're opening an elementary school. You think this is a lead? You think we'll get results putting it where everyone can see it? The boys are gonna get disheartened if they think we're working off something a kiddie drew."

"Yeah, well, we probably should open an elementary school, the rate we've learned anything in this case. You gonna tell me what you see here or not?"

"A freak, I guess. Doesn't look like much of anything to me."

They were interrupted by the clatter of double doors, the arrival of Jeb Kyle and Jerry Unwin back from patrol. They were laughing together, Unwin looking far too dapper for Ella's liking in his immaculately pressed uniform. As usual, he didn't hesitate, made a beeline for the focus of the two senior cops.

"What," he said, after half a moment scrutinizing Holly's drawing, "we're allowed to display our kids' pictures here? My Robbie paints a mean damn tractor, think that deserves an airing."

Ella glowered, and Slim Johnson awaited the roasting.

"Pretty creepy," said Kyle, the younger cop. "There a reward for Freddy Krueger now?"

Unwin snorted. "Freddy? You forget to put your contacts in?"

"Halloween a ways off yet," said Kyle to Johnson, confidentially.

"What?" said Ella suddenly, in a tone that made them all blink. "Jerry, you *don't* see a boogeyman here?"

Unwin became self-conscious. "Well . . . maybe," he said, not knowing the right answer.

"No . . ." said Ella, with finite patience. "What *were* you going to say?"

Unwin glanced at Johnson, no help there. "Yeah," he said. "Well, I can see, big square eyes, the hair's all wrong. Kyle could be right. I thought a kid had drawn someone's grand-maw."

They all studied the picture, Unwin taking the silence as a cue to narrate.

"My son Robbie, he draws tractors, but he draws people too. Funny how kids of a certain age focus on certain features. I got a big nose, see, so what's the first thing he draws? My wife's old ma, she's got lines on her face like a shriveled prune, so there's all crow's feet in his picture. Looks like an Indian in war-paint by the time he's finished with the crayons. It's cute now, but he'll have to grow out of putting down people's bad points else grow some tact."

"What," said Johnson, "just like his old man has?"

Ella had stopped listening, reabsorbed herself in the drawing.

A grandma? It was just possible. Perhaps she'd been looking for too much significance when she shouldn't have been looking for any significance at all. She had seen slashes across the face. Were they just wrinkles?

Of course I saw a monster. My head is full of blood and knives and fear. Unwin's head is full of windmills.

But *what* grandma, if that was the subject of the picture? Holly had no living grandparents. An old woman, then? Holly doesn't know any old women.

Gladys Walson. Gladys, of Mountain Pastures Mobile Home Park. The woman with the dead cat.

It came in an instant. Holly had even gotten the curlers in the hair and the bobbles on the old-fashioned gown that Ella had been mistaking for dragon's scales, or something.

She's dressed Gladys like she was dressed on the morning of the kidnap.

Let's take Holly to see Gladys, maybe that'll trigger a memory, a reaction, something.

Well aware that she was clutching at straws, Ella pushed through her officers, tearing at the nub of her thumbnail like she never wanted it to grow back.

"No," Unwin was telling the others. "Robbie shows talent with people. But his real gift lies with the tractors."

*

Quantico, Virginia.

Janel Grant, an FBI lab supervisor on her fourth espresso, decided to miss a lunchtime racquetball date in anticipation of her man in latent prints finishing with the cardboard box that had arrived that morning from San Francisco with an all-too-familiar expeditious examination request. The box—and the dismembered hand and ear—had inspired the kind of hushed animation amongst the team that always accompanied a case of this nature, but Grant, an old pro who'd worked on the Unabomber from well before the brand-new facility, privately rated the buzz a middling 7 out of 10. Nonetheless, with the human tissue securely repackaged in fresh ice and placed in the short backlog for DNA analysis, there was still something about the box that had stood out to her as unusual. Unfortunately, it required the other technicians to finish documenting before she could satisfy her hunch.

Janel had been watching Ed Barry through the glass for about twenty minutes, though she could have gone in if she'd chosen to. He hadn't even seen her when he walked over to switch off the overheads and use the blacklight, such was his concentration.

When Barry eventually emerged from the room, he was blinking and running his hands through his hair, with a fading ninhydrin headache from time in the humidified chamber.

"It was a long shot," he said as a greeting. "You know, if they processed it good in the field, and they did DFO it."

She knew this. "The adhesive tape?"

"Liqui-Drox, the usual." He pursed his lips. "Nada. The little girl recipient, delivery guy, no one else. I thought it was our best chance, but. They find anything else?"

"He was careful," said Janel. "Gloves all the way, not a damn hair that doesn't match someone we already know about. But there'll be something."

Barry shrugged. "The scene is where it's at, if anywhere. I heard they thought the perp went in the building a few days before the delivery."

Janel had heard this also, and it was neither of their concern. Barry was fishing for info, but it'd pass—he was new, it was an imaginative case. But he was also very thorough, which was why she'd given it to him. This particular evidence hadn't only arrived with a thick plot and a degree of media interest; someone in Justice had asked her to shepherd it personally, and she was supposed to forward the findings to a person she'd never heard of, a man named Arnold Lau, who came with all kinds of clearance. Maybe there was scandal here, a senior politico involved somewhere.

Janel, a veteran observer of in-house gossip, licked her lips.

Ed Barry was waiting, and she gave him the curt little nod that meant she was satisfied, watched him head around the corner to help the poor bastard who had been assigned the packing peanuts. Then she canned her takeout coffee, pushed open the solid safety door to the examining room.

The box and the coil of adhesive tape were still up on the bench, but Janel washed her hands and then went over the photographs first, confirming that if she took the box apart piece by piece they still had it documented in minute detail. It was exhausted for surface evidence, more or less; they knew the brand of cardboard, could tell at a glance it came from a ubiquitous source, what little blood that had seeped into the box was swabbed and in analysis, and the bloody plastic baggie that was used as packaging had been Barry's first job. Precisely how and with what the appendages were removed was becoming a source of debate in a different suite of rooms.

The most persistent titbit of information had been given to Janel that morning from her adhesives, calks and sealants guy. Fritz had immediately confirmed more than one kind of glue when she showed him the tiny blobs of amber on two of the opened corners. In other words, aside from the recyclable starch that usually cemented cardboard of this kind, someone had gone at the box with a small amount of polyvinyl acetate.

"Wood glue," Fritz had said. "Looks like Titebond, want me to type it for sure?"

Which suggested to Janel Grant that the corrugate on one of the cardboard flaps itself had been loosened and then glued back down by hand. But why?

She switched on a constant-tension desk lamp, pulled the light over by its neck, noted the rose-petal smudges on the box from Barry's ninhydrin reactions. Holding the glued flap with her largest pair of tweezers, Janel gently worked a scalpel between the cardboard sandwich like a woman opening a letter very carefully, aiming to work through the glue and recreate the activity of the person who had prised apart the sections on the first occasion. If anything, a little too much product had been used in sticking it back together, causing her to wonder if this wasn't something that she was supposed to be doing, wasn't something she was supposed to find, especially given the obvious care that had gone into wiping clean the rest of the evidence.

Once she was an inch or so in, a little less than the length of the blade, she prised apart the sections, used the light to peer into the small papery purse, but there was nothing there to see.

Undaunted, Janel moved the scalpel around, lightly sawing at the sides of the material, separating the liner from the wavy corrugated filler until she had a separate flap she could actually lift. She was hoping for a hair, an imprint, something she could use to justify another round of examinations, but what she found were two tiny lines of handwritten message.

She was so surprised, she dropped the liner off the blunt shelf of her scalpel. Taking the tweezers this time, she ignored the high tone that sounded in her head when uncovering a piece of evidence that could be crucial—a sensation worth waiting all day for, that was certain.

Someone had loosened the material of the box, written a message in the corrugated grooves, and then glued the cardboard back together. This had been done painstakingly, not least with the writing itself, which was almost microscopic.

Look what Mommy has done the first sentence read.

Beneath, in capitals:

THIS IS WHAT SHE MADE ME DO

Egan and Karen reached the city limits, then passed right on through.

Abraham Smith & Son, Monumental Masons (est. 1959), was one of Canaan's oldest and most successful businesses, but what had once been a location on the outskirts of town had now become a thick artery of parking lots and crosswalks, off which straggled a host of fast-food joints and gas stations, built to welcome and encourage the boom of adventure travel that was now the region's lifeblood. Blake, pushing the Land Rover a little too hard to avoid catching a red light, initially missed the small, handcrafted sign that couldn't compete with the bright corporate logos, and Karen was surprised to see how rapidly the shiny new buildings reverted first to cheap clapboard housing, then to the occasional trailer, then back to the beautiful scrub and rock primitiveness that had been the scenery for most of the journey from the single-strip airport.

Blake's second pass was more successful, and he made the turn on to a small, empty lot, his target a narrow alley that squeezed between an Arby's and the low-slung mock-temple frontage of Zions Bank. Behind the structures, Blake made an expansive turn across a dusty yard, and the mountainous vista was with them once more, out past a solitary service road and framed by a series of crooked chain-link fences. The impression was that the whole of Canaan was only a slightly more substantial version of a film-studio backlot; shells of buildings masking a blank canvas out back, upon which to construct the latest Hollywood dreamscapes.

Nightmares, more like, thought Karen.

Blake had told her about the tombstone that he'd found with her name on it, and the story was hardly something Karen could believe, let alone process. But Blake, as ever, had reported his experience at the abandoned church in an unfazed and pragmatic way; another strong lead, he had said, another piece of the puzzle. And, not for the first time, Karen Wiley got the impression that Blake was somehow liking it all a bit too much.

The red ball of the sun was beginning its descent through a green-tinged mackerel sky, and Karen shivered in the warm desert breeze that embraced her as she stepped down from the LR3. Blake was already over by the tall fence that bordered the western edge of the plot, happily tormenting the largest dog that she'd ever seen. Tacked to the fence was another Smith & Son sign, and behind it was any amount of heavy-looking debris, along with some beautiful and highly polished funereal masonry. There was also a large workshop of some kind, and through two raised garage doors she could see rows of trestle tables, above which hung large pieces of unfamiliar machinery painted in striking primary colors, presumably equipment for cutting stone.

The whole place looked deserted, but after a few more sentinel barks from the wolfhound, an old man in denim overalls emerged from a side door, wiping his hands on a rag.

"Duke!" he said to the dog, which quieted at once, tail wagging. "Gets frisky when the weather's on the turn," he said to them. "Can I help you folks? We gotta gate here in the side."

"My name is Egan Blake, this is Karen Wiley."

"That so?" said the man to Karen, and raised two of the bristliest eyebrows she had ever seen. "I do believe I heard one of those names at some stage, and names has been my business for going on forty years. You recently lose a relative, miss?"

"No," said Karen, quietly.

"Ah," said the man, and he narrowed his eyes.

"I think," said Blake, "that Smith & Son recently put that name on a tombstone for somebody, and that somebody is using it to play tricks on my friend here. Can we trouble you with a few questions?"

"There've been stranger things," said the man, touching a finger to his cap. "My name is Abe Smith. We gotta gate in the side."

"Ayuh, we put a maker's mark on every one," said Smith, having led them into the office behind the workshop. "I got my initial on the back of stones from here to Timbuktu, and proud of it. You talk to my son about how all that came about; we did pretty good mail-order in the day, news about craftsmanship gets around, I guess, but my grandson, he got his diploma in computer sciences, boom, Internet. Now I employ six people, on and off. I don't know how it works, Mister Blake, and though I'm grateful for the business it brought me, I don't much care to know." He rocked back on a swivel chair that was losing its stuffing, tapped his chest with a strong, tan finger. "Seventy-two years old, still hard a' work, and you know what they say: simple men don't die of complications."

Karen and Blake were across from him, perched on a battered couch. Blake resisted the urge to glance at his watch. "What about the man?" he said. "The man who bought Karen's stone?"

"Ayuh," said Abe. "We're going back six weeks or so, this fella comes in, requests the stone you're speaking of. Tells me it's a replacement stone for a long-passed relative, do I make replacements? Well, no problem I say, but why don't you contract me to restore the original one?"

"You do restorations?"

"Not often, but when we do, they usually work out a whole lot cheaper for the customer, certainly if it's local. No new material to buy, see? Course, I couldn't know the condition of his old stone, but I've seen pretty bad. Lead infill, the kind that drops out, was the last thing my daddy learned and the first thing he forgot."

"Did this man have any specific requests?"

"Mostly the name," said Abe. "He was big on the name. Karen Wiley. Kept repeating it when he thought I wasn't listening. Though now I think on, he *was* pretty specific about the stone itself, you know, size, finish and so on, but that don't stand out too much in my memory."

"Oh?"

"Well, I guess because it was nothing fancy or unusual, and I've made some specialty pieces, believe you me. Anyway, I agree to make him a new one, and that's when he comes out and tells me the name to put on it."

"Karen Wiley," said Karen.

"Right," said Abe. "No dates, I ask? No born/died? No epitaph? Nothing else? And then he looks at me in this strange way, tells me I can write R.I.P. Now, I'm thinking he's a bit of a kook, but his money was green and it's a free country, so fair enough. I tell him, do you want delivery or do you wanna collect? He says collect, in two weeks. But that in itself was unusual, because if the job is local, me and a few boys from the town usually do the site ourselves. Still, there you are. It wasn't a big headstone, but heavy enough for one man to have to carry hisself."

"You have any contact details?" said Blake.

"Can't rightly remember. But there was cash up front, that much I recall, then he was gone. Came back when he said he would, mind, polite, aside from the strange way about him."

"Can you give us a physical description?"

"Ayuh. He was a big man, broad across the shoulders, fit-looking. Had a four-wheel drive, like everyone else around here." Abe reached for a pouch of tobacco on the desk, found he already had one rolled.

"Anything else? Distinguishing features?"

"I'm not good with faces. Downright poor, I've been told."

Karen heard Blake expel air through clenched teeth.

"But there was another thing made him memorable, though you folks might think it daft."

Blake and Karen leant forward.

"This fella. When he first come in, Duke, he near-on turned tail and ran."

"Your dog?"

"Ayuh. And Duke's a big ol' mutt, never much seen him scared of anyone before. Leader of the pack around here, 'cept for me. Wouldn't hurt a soul, though. Still, I keep him away from kiddies and the like."

"What happened?"

"I just said it. Whimpers, growls, acting like a puppy who peed the carpet. I remember the man tryin' to pet him, but I think that was mostly for my benefit; he didn't seem the type to wanna pet a dog. You know, that pooch got a jones for gettin' his ears scratched, but Duke just slunk off under the table. Took a bone from the Irish butcher to bring him round. Don't suppose that helps you much."

"Will you tell us if this man comes back?" said Blake. "Or if you remember anything else about his appearance? I have a number you can call."

"That I will," said Abe, putting fire to his roll-up. "No one likes a prankster, especially when there's a lady involved." He twinkled at Karen for so long that she had to look away.

"How about a name?"

"Oh, they all got to leave at least a name. I don't recall it from the top of my head, but we got records here startin' when my pappy moved the business from back east: who's buried where and under what, local-wise, at least. I'm *son* y'know, of Smith & Son, but I kept the sign the way it was. Abe Junior, that's me. Now hold on, you got me kind of curious misself."

Smith kept his set of keys on the end of a chain that was attached to a belt loop. He swung out of his chair with a grunt, unlocked one of several filing cabinets, busied himself searching through the bottom drawer and sending up clouds of sweet-smelling smoke. After a moment he had levered out a vertical file, thick with documentation. Blake and Karen waited patiently while Abe selected a spreadsheet covered in the scrawl of many different colored inks.

"Here we are: August 27, paid in full. The address is 3, 1907 Leavenfield Street, San Francisco. Knew he was from outta town." Abe flipped a stapled receipt. "And he gave the name of Sam Wiley, guess that's why I thought it was a relative." Abe looked up, cigarette clenched between his teeth. "Suppose this means something to you?"

"A little," said Karen. "Sam Wiley is the name of my sister. And the address that he's given you there is mine."

Abe may have been long on pleasantries, but he let Blake and Karen show themselves out.

"You didn't tell me you had a sister," said Egan Blake, as they walked back to the truck.

"I don't," said Karen. She was lost in thought, measuring the length of her shadow along the ground.

"Karen?"

"I mean, I don't anymore. At least, she's not living." Karen's voice threatened to catch in her throat. "She died when we were children."

"Ah," said Blake, and they leant against the fender, watched the sky.

She felt him laboring over the requisite pause ahead of a sensitive question, a pause designed to tell her that he didn't *want* to ask the question, not really, and she should save him the trouble by just coming right out with the answer. It was irksome to her, a clumsy man-move.

"I'm sorry to have to pry," he said eventually. "But is there anything I should know about this?"

"No," said Karen.

"Because if there is, if there's something to do with your sister that means that we can find this guy any faster, then you're better off telling me now."

His tone, parental. His face, aged and austere: *You're better off telling me now.*

"I don't think so," she said. "At least, I don't think there is. No one could know."

It was NEVER my fault about Sammie, about what happened.

"Okay," said Blake, looking at her.

It was an ACCIDENT. She DROWNED. What the hell was I supposed to . . .

I was NINE YEARS OLD.

"Huh?" he said.

"I didn't say anything."

"Okay then," said Blake, still looking quizzical. "But if you can remember something . . ."

She rounded on him. "What do you think I have to *gain*?"

And then somewhere, distantly, a phone was ringing.

Blake snapped his head up like a gundog. "That's Lilly's cellphone," he said.

"What? Why do you have Lilly's cellphone?"

"I found it at the church."

"The church?"

But Karen wasn't getting anymore information. Blake strode around the truck, he hadn't locked it, reached into the glove compartment on the passenger side, the latch of which seemed to stick, wasting precious seconds. It was on top of a pile of folded maps, the battery still good. Blake took another moment to identify the correct button, not wanting to lose the call. He pushed it with a forefinger, like someone unused to the device, put the phone to his ear.

"Hello?"

Karen watched him from across the hood, he was staring right at her as he spoke, eyes wide, face gaunt.

"Hello?" he said again.

"I . . . *Lilly*." Blake nodded. "Can you . . . yes. Yes, she's here with me." He raised his finger, pointed at Karen with a couple of stabs, was telling her something.

His voice into the phone became calm. "It's okay now. I'm going to . . . *okay*, Lilly."

Blake put his hand over the mouthpiece, walked around the car. "It's Lilly. She says she has to talk to you. But I'm not sure she's necessarily in a *position* to talk. Do you understand me?"

Karen nodded.

"Just listen if you have to," he said.

Karen accepted the phone from his dry hand, brought it to her ear as though something in there with teeth might bite her. She didn't speak at first, but listened to the dry hiss of the line, remained calm by focusing her visual attention on tumbleweeds moving across the dusty lot.

"Hello?" she said, half-expecting Lilly's usual rush of talk. "*Hello?*"

"He wants you . . . to come and get me," said a voice that sounded like Lilly's.

"What?"

"He wants you to come and get me because *I'm* not the one he wants."

"Lilly? Are you all right? You sound . . . different."

"He wants *you*. Because *I'm* not the one he wants."

Karen looked at Blake, his eyes wide in that haunted way of his. *Blake doesn't know what to do.*

"Who is *he*, Lilly?" said Karen, and she took some gulps of air, tried to inject normalcy into her voice. "You know, you had a bunch of people worried since you disappeared yesterday. You're supposed to let someone know before you head out into the desert."

Silence. That stretched.

Blake made a hand over hand tumbling gesture. *Karen, keep talking.*

"Who is *he*?" said Karen, again.

The hiss of the open line.

"Is . . . *he* there now?" said Karen.

"Yes."

"Can I speak to him?"

"Just listen, you fucking *bitch*," said Lilly, in the same moderated, slightly cracked voice.

"I . . ."

"You *didn't* come to the church. You *didn't* follow the letter. You *could* have saved lives."

"Lilly . . ."

"You will meet . . ."

The voice tailed off into more silence, not before Karen heard what might have been a sob.

"You will meet him and I will live . . ."

"What about the girl? Lilly? What about the *girl*?"

"This . . . is where you will go." Lilly was crying. Karen had never heard her friend cry before. "This is what . . . this is what you will *do* . . ."

"Lilly . . . *Lilly*?"

There was a rush of static followed by a distorted clatter, so loud and sudden that Karen jerked her head from the phone. Just as quickly, she pressed her ear back to the device.

"Lilly?"

Sounds, movement, heaviness. Maybe the phone was on the floor. Then there was an almighty crash, and Lilly was shouting from a distance, like someone trapped in a cave. She now sounded like herself, but she sounded scared, terrified, her voice hoarse with urgency. Karen couldn't make it all out.

"Thirty minutes ride! Basement . . . very quiet . . . and he's *here* . . ."

"*Lilly* . . ." said Karen, knowing she wasn't being heard.

"I found Katy . . ." yelled Lilly, perhaps she was on the floor as well. "Got no time . . . the books are all covered in blood . . ."

There was a short scream, followed by a strange and hideous *meat* noise that could have been almost anything, and the line went dead.

"Hello dearie . . . is this for me?"

"I think it *is* you, Gladys," said Ella, as the old woman took the large drawing from Holly with two shaky hands. "Do you remember Mrs. Walson, Holly?"

Holly blinked and turned away to stare at the wall of the trailer, where a child's prayer had been framed in cautious needlepoint. She was still lost in her own world, but it was, and had been since the encounter with Jon Peterson, a new world of peace; one where fathers couldn't punish and scar by leaving you to the mercy of boogeymen with sharp teeth and wild eyes just because you were bad, because you dropped a dish, because you cried when you fell during recess and made a fuss but really you had fractured your little finger and yet still no one cared to know . . .

"Don't be rude, Holly," said Taslima, closing the door behind them. "Aren't you going to say hello to Gladys?"

Holly blinked again; after many days of practice, she could now silence, or at least dull, the adult voices around her with a minimum of effort. But there was something else in this place, some new vexation, and because her subconscious couldn't figure out what it was, it couldn't shut the negative feeling out straightaway.

Gentle Jesus, meek and mild . . .

Ella watched Gladys peering at Holly around the sketch, her wrinkly smile of welcome turning into a concerned frown. "You weren't always this quiet, little one," said the old woman. "I remember, one time, your big sister rolled you up in my good clean washing."

Holly said nothing.

"Is this drawing for me to keep?"

Holly said nothing.

"This is Taslima," said Ella to Gladys. "She's a nurse at Mercy, we owe her a lot."

"There's a tired little girl today," said Taslima. "She didn't sleep so well."

"Oh, she'll talk when she's good and ready," said Gladys, with a wink. "Most folks, they got far too much to say, so much that when you do get a person with some real hush, other folks look for a solution like there's a problem." She turned to Holly again. "My good washing, you little runabouts."

Taslima looked over at Ella, who was well practiced in ignoring skeptical glances.

"Please, be comfortable," said Gladys, ushering them onto the three-sided couch filling the bow of her home. Taslima let go of Holly's hand with reluctance, and both grown-ups had to scootch to squeeze their generous frames behind the table, the pressure releasing a cloud of lavender that was almost thick enough to see.

"If I'd known you were calling I would have cleaned up. Do you girls want some tea?"

"Thank you," said Taslima, watching Holly continue to stare blankly at the prayer. This behavior was unusual; Holly typically found herself a tight corner or comfortable place to sit before vanishing into personal oblivion.

"That'd be great," said Ella, who loathed tea because it reminded her of detox.

"How about you, my dear," said Gladys to Holly, selecting three cups from a row of neat hooks. "You want some Tang? My daughter used to love the taste."

Holly said nothing.

"You like my needlepoint? They don't much do it anymore." Kettle on the stove, the old woman's reedy voice sailed around a worn but spotless kitchen unit. "See that cushion there, Ella? Berlin work, my own granmaw taught me to embroider. And now I'm a granmaw of my own, that's his picture on the wall."

"A good-looking boy," said Ella, and Taslima nodded.

"How's Mandy bearing up with it all?"

"You can imagine how it is," said Ella.

"And that Milton Trueblood, I wouldn't wish this on anyone, yet the company that he kept . . . Poor fool, in my prayers despite himself, though rumor has it he's learning the error."

"I haven't heard from him in a while."

"If you like, Holly can take back that old bit of needlework," said Gladys. "Poor dear probably recognizes it from when it hung in her own home, God bless her soul."

"Take it back?" said Ella. "I thought you said that *you* made it."

"Oh, I did, a long time ago. That needlepoint was my gift to Mandy Trueblood on the day of the wedding. Hung it up on her wall, pride of place, just like I said she should. Religious girl, used to read the Bible out loud, till the devil got a hold of that man of hers, turned him into a good-for-nothing husk." Gladys busied herself with the tea. "Mandy gave it back to me when they moved out, said they were short of space for things."

"That's right," said Ella, realizing it. "I *knew* I'd seen that picture before. It was on the . . ."

The words caught in her throat. Holly had stopped looking at Gladys's needlepoint prayer, was now looking at her.

. . . on the crime scene photos of your trailer, Holly.

Ella didn't flinch, held the child's gaze. It was the first time she remembered Holly looking at her directly.

Are you ready yet? Ready to help me find your sister?

Ella swallowed. ". . . on the wall of Holly's mobile home. That's where I'd seen it."

"Right," said Gladys, screwing scalding hot cups onto the doilies in front of them. "There's milk, sugar. Oh, perhaps I should have brewed it in a pot . . ."

"You wanna sit down, child?" said Taslima to Holly, whose activity rarely escaped her attention.

Slowly, Holly turned her back on them, returned her gaze to the prayer.

"Prayer of peace, that's what it means to me, though the lord God himself has meant a few different things to a few different people in this town," said Gladys, pulling up a spare chair. "I would say those words over and over to the ones who returned to us. Gentle Jesus, meek and mild. Gave them hope. Preacher LaGrande's God was of vengeance and fire and foolish blasphemy."

"James LaGrande?" said Ella. "The Church of the Final Days?"

"Oh, I don't remember what he called it. I just got hold of the ones that got away at the end of things, tried to give them some comfort. But you didn't come here to talk to me about the past, I'm guessing, though I dare say if you didn't, you're out of luck—it's what I have."

Ella smiled, but the old woman wasn't joking.

"I see you around sometimes, Chief McCullers, but you never chose to speak to me until the devil got a hold of Katy Trueblood." Gladys took a sip of tea. "Well, I seen him *before* he came for Katy, I could have told it you then. Given you a warning, sort of."

"Oh?"

"He's been in town a while," Gladys said to Taslima. "Though few care to notice."

"The devil?" said Ella. "You've *seen* him?"

"What did I just say?"

"Do you . . . can you give me a description?"

"Don't be foolish, girl. I'm not senile. Don't say you haven't felt it, the fear in the community. Best place for me now, alone on this rock, though I wouldn't have known it when we last met—I had the sense scared out of me, or rather, back into me. Confusion, bafflement, the lies they print in the paper. History has a way of repeating, don't you think?"

Beside her, Ella felt Taslima fidget, shifting weight from one thigh to the other.

The nurse hadn't been keen on the idea of taking Holly to see Gladys, couldn't even make out the likeness of an old woman in the picture that Holly had created. Ella also knew that Taslima was bothered by the legality; they'd taken a long detour from the hospital, and with no authorizing signature. Ella herself had to admit that returning the girl to what was more or less the scene of the crime might have a detrimental effect, changed beyond recognition though the trailer park was, but so far Holly had seemed fine. Still, the passage of time was clearly of less importance to Mrs. Walson than it was to anyone else, and pretty soon Ella would have to get to the point.

Unfortunately, she had no idea what that point was supposed to be.

"So," said Gladys. "What is it that I *can* do for you?"

Ella dumped another two sugars into her tea, said: "Perhaps you could tell me more about your relationship with the Trueblood family? With Katy? Like I said on the phone, this isn't a formal interview, or . . ."

. . . look upon a little child

pity my simplicity . . .

Holly's attention gave a dull spike at the policewoman's mention of Katy, but then, like a sleek dolphin, it dived back under the surface of her consciousness where all was warm and clear and sparkly blue. She had always had an active fantasy life, so it was very easy for Jon Peterson to eradicate one of her dual worlds—the painful, unpredictable one—and tip her permanently into a mixture of fantasy and memory, just as he was capable of doing with his own consciousness. Today, Holly had chosen to screen happy memories and make them real to her again: the play area in Daddy's favourite casino with the fast slide into the ball pool, the first time she watched snow fall, her painting, she loved to paint, and the time that her sister, usually so aloof at school, had strode into a group of bullies who were pulling her hair and sent them packing.

Katy.

. . . pity my simplicity, suffer me . . .

Milton Trueblood's boogeyman stories were always directed at

Katy, her big sister. He'd back her into a corner just before one of his trips out of state, tell her *all* about the boogeyman. Sometimes Holly could hear the conversations, sometimes she couldn't.

Katy was scared at first, before Holly was really old enough to talk about it, but eventually she adapted, got herself into a place where she could almost be optimistic once Milt and Mandy had gone. Katy certainly didn't *feel* brave, left alone with a little sister and a baby, but she could pretend to be, which is sometimes a more impressive thing.

He won't get us. I know that big ol' boogeyman.

Holly wasn't as strong. She'd quiver, she'd cry, she hated her father but hated being alone even more. It was the not knowing, and Milton was clever. He'd claim ignorance of the boogeyman's ways, claimed not to know what the monster was capable of, claimed not even to know what he looked like, beyond sharp features and meanness and far worse things, designed to scare young minds. Holly would beg her mother not to leave them to the boogeyman, but Mom seemed just as scared as she was, so Holly turned to Katy, who always had an answer.

We've nothing to be scared of. Not really.

You don't know that, Katy.

Yes I do. The boogeyman is fat and slow and we're quick and clever.

Although Katy couldn't know for sure that her father was lying, she could recognize that the parameters of Milton's stories were liquid, changeable, like the behavior of Santa Claus on any given Christmas. If the beast was real, it was still of the imagination. So Katy manipulated it, made it fat, stupid, slow, almost comic. The laughter would be hollow, but it let Holly come out from the bunk where she'd hide, and they'd watch TV and even, once Katy gained confidence, they made flapjacks one time and cleaned up the mess.

But it got worse at night, as these things often do.

I think I heard a noise, Katy.

Go to sleep.

I think I heard a noise.

Just the wind, the creaky trees.

But that's not what I heard . . .

And Katy would have to get angry sometimes, not because she wanted to, but because it was the right thing to do. Fear is a virus, it catches on, it breeds and feasts on the turmoil of the mind. Katy knew this, had to stamp on the fear like the first runaway sparks of a forest fire.

You wanna get up, Holly? Is that what you think we should do? You wanna get the flashlight, take a look outside?

No . . .

Why don't I go outside on my own, make sure everything's okay?

Don't leave me . . .

Don't be a stupid baby. Look, I got it all charged and ready.

And they'd switch all the lights on and Katy would sit Holly in the living room, go outside with a flashlight so heavy it required both hands. Holly would have to wait, not sure if she'd ever see her sister again, but somehow knowing that she would, of course she would, because the boogeyman is fat and slow, and we're quick and clever . . .

Gentle Jesus meek and mild, look upon a little child . . .

The prayer on the wall that she read over and over on those occasions; her mother's prayer. Holly had no developed ideas about God, the randomness of her life up until that point hardly suggesting any existing force that could be representative of goodness, but Jesus, the baby Jesus, who was talked about in Sunday school, *there* was a tangible, loving image, something to hold on to while your sister is out hunting monsters, and . . .

Bang!

A bang on the wall of the trailer, right behind her, not all *that* loud, but Holly, who was already tightly wound, would jump up like there was a firecracker under her. Then there would be this strange *dragging* noise . . .

The front door of the trailer swung open, Holly jumped again, and there was Katy in the warm night, tired and messy like she'd been in a fight.

Where have you been . . .

And Katy would smile, pretend that she'd found the boogeyman, he'd been lurking outside. She'd bashed him on the head with her flashlight and he'd turned tail and slinked away like a scalded cat.

They'd laugh, a lie within the lie, but just as valid. And on that occasion, the boogeyman wouldn't come back.

But one time he did. And he wasn't fat, he wasn't slow. He didn't come at night.

And he was very, very real.

Gentle Jesus . . .

On the day Jon Peterson came, she remembered the prayer in its frame from her vantage point on the floor, on the day when Peterson came and she felt the air rushing into her brain where he'd broken into her skull, and the words were the last thing she saw before the blood ran into her eyes and she was hit again, but this time so *hard . . .*

I saw the boogeyman, he was real. He took Katy. She ran for help and never came back.

And Mrs. Walson was there too. But AFTER he took Katy. And Mrs. Walson saw me on the floor, and then she was falling, I thought she was dead, dead like me . . .

In present time, the words of the prayer swam in front of Holly's face.

Suffer me to come to thee . . .

She was conscious of having gasped, of having made a sound. Everything started to move quickly. The adults stopped talking, looked at her. Taslima was saying something.

Holly, disoriented, cast around for the electronic game that she used to distract herself from the bad thoughts. It was nowhere to be seen, left in the car. She wavered, began to fall.

Taslima was moving, strong fingers digging into her ribs, holding her up.

Holly draws and paints because she can, because she likes to, but since Peterson she's only felt the need to paint when agitated, as a release, to share the locked horror. She drew Gladys because she was frustrated, because it was the most angry thing she could think of at the time, but the drawing of Gladys was only skirting around the association with the crime scene, not like that first picture of the boogeyman, the one she drew with Dr. Lau, the one she had to fill in with black paint because it was looking at her, because it reminded her, because . . .

"Is she all right?" Ella's voice.

"Holly?" said Taslima. "*Holly?*"

"Should I get some water?"

"Let her sit, make a space."

Holly was bundled onto the built-in seating, cups of tea were cleared, and she began tracing shapes on the table with her finger, rapid loops and frustrated, stabby dots.

"Gladys," said Ella. "Do you have a pencil? A pen?"

"I have some . . . oh dear."

Gladys spent a long time retrieving a leather-bound pad and a pen from beside the telephone, by which point Holly had already sat back, apparently exhausted. But it took no time once the materials had been put in front of her to start making familiar shapes, shapes that Ella had seen before, a gross human figure with sharp teeth in a sickly grinning mouth and hands that were huge and frightening and grasping.

Peterson.

It took a while, it was in more detail than before, and the adults looked on in silence as though a miracle was occurring. When it was done, Holly threw down the pen and turned to Taslima, buried herself in the arms of the nurse, released big, shuddering, silent sobs.

*

Ella ducked outside to give Holly and Taslima some space.

Gladys had a semi-tumbledown porch bolted to the front of her home, and once Ella had established that the swing-seat would hold her weight without the entire structure crumbling like a pratfall in a silent movie, it turned out to be a pretty comfortable place to sit and think. The wrecker's yard across the way was still an eyesore, three columns of car shells reaching above the perimeter wall, skeletal shapes silhouetted by a vanishing sun, but with the other trailers removed, Ella had a view for several miles up the deserted road. That and the orphic silence made her feel a little like the proprietress of the world's last truck-stop.

Gladys emerged, closed the door. She stood there for a second, like a person winding up to make a speech.

"You're walking around like an empty vessel, Ella McCullers," she said. "Sometimes not thinking of yourself is the worst arrogance of all."

"I came out here to think. I can think in the car."

"You come back in your uniform, I'll treat you like an officer of the law. I've been meaning to get you on your own."

Ella said nothing, but made no effort to move.

"Ah, forget it," said Gladys, lowering herself onto the seat. "The more experience you got, the less people want to listen, and I've been an old woman for a long time. Bein' old is gettin' old, to quote my mother, before she gave it up. I don't complain. You wait in your car, if you like."

"What, I'm *not* thinking of myself? You barely know me."

"I know what it's like to doubt. You think finding this little girl is going to make it better? Make everything shiny and new? You got a fever the way you carry on, the way you stomp around on the news. And people gossip, my great-nephew at your station, folks at the church. When are you gonna stop running?"

"I don't listen to gossip."

"You're very wise."

"I have no time, Gladys."

"No, that's *all* you've got. You find Katy Trueblood, maybe God exists, am I right?"

"I don't . . ."

"And then, well, maybe you can't find her and you gotta carry on wondering. Or maybe you believe a little bit less, in God, in the goodness of things. Well, let me tell you, Chief, God exists whether you find that girl or not."

Ella studied her feet. Flat, square feet.

"We're in a battle here," said Gladys. "It lasts our whole life, but the way you carry on you'll run out of energy after this one damn war."

On the other side of the clearing, wind stirred the spindly branches of the willow tree.

"Holly drew the picture of you because she saw you at the crime scene," Ella said. "She drew the exact clothes you were wearing."

Gladys sighed. "I got nothing else for you, I wish I did. I blacked out at all the blood, at the girl on the floor. Don't think I'm not ashamed enough to weep."

"It's fine."

"It isn't, I pray for vision. What did Milton's friend say when you asked him?"

"Which one?"

"The one in the picture. You know, the one with the face."

Ella was confused. "What, in the paper?"

"Where've you been, girl? The one Holly just drew in my address book. Milton's friend. And friend of that mechanic he used to hang around with also."

"Don Keynes?"

"That's him. Awful close, they seemed to be."

"What . . . when was this?"

"Night of the whenever it was. The following day, Katy was taken."

"You saw someone else? With Milt and Don?"

"Yes."

"A third person?"

"Sure, though it must've been well past midnight. I was out looking for Edgar with his box of food. He never came back at his usual time but sometimes he doesn't, and on that occasion I found him, God rest his soul. Anyways, I was wide awake—I don't sleep so well when I nap in the afternoon—and this tow-truck pulls up, I'd seen it around before. Milton was a passenger, but he damn-near needed hauling out by his ankles."

"He was drunk, it's on the report."

"Oh, he was more than that. He was sick, pig-sick, and I'd seen the fool drunk before, but this time he was up-chucking before he got to his front door. Not of this earth. And his two friends were helpin' him. Fat, gray-looking guy, Donald Keynes, I'd seen him around, and the other one. A name doesn't come to mind."

"Someone you knew from elsewhere?"

"I'm pretty sure not. But he's the person that little Holly just drew, I'll bet my life. Same face, different clothes. A lot of talent, that girl, for likenesses."

"Did they see you?"

"I kept hidden, not my affair. Bright moon though, and my eyes are good."

"Will you come back with me, make the statement official? That there was a third person?"

"Sure. You think this helps any?"

"I think . . . I don't know. That there was another person? I hope so."

Ella gave a brief smile, then a cat appeared from nowhere, sleek and black with a white muzzle and green eyes. It did that tense pause that cats sometimes do where they're judging the distance of a jump, and then it landed squarely in Ella's lap, where it did two loops before dropping onto her legs like a warm hug.

"You done it now," said Gladys. "This is Cornelius, I think he wants you to stay."

"Huh," said Ella, stroking the cat and thinking about what Milton might say about the character in his daughter's picture, someone he was with on the night before the kidnap.

A new suspect.

From inside the trailer, she could hear Taslima moving about; it was time to get Holly back to the hospital.

"Weather's turning," said Gladys. "Big storm coming, look of the sky."

"I saw the forecast," said Ella.

"Probably not get here tonight," said Gladys. "Forecast says it'll hit sometime tomorrow."

"I know," said Ella.

Fourteen

San Francisco.

"The best part is the part where the streets cross over, right babe?"

"Dad, don't be so lame."

David John Wiley might as well have spent his last full day as a resident of California talking into the breeze. Contrarily, the words of his daughter were falling around his ears like hot rocks; each reply a challenge, every response a rebuttal. Was she joking with him? He couldn't tell anymore.

"Man," he said, trying again, "it'd be like Magic Mountain if it went any . . ."

"Dad, isn't this our stop now? I think I'm getting a migraine."

Migraine? That's a new word. A mommy word?

It was one of those days when the city was not living up to the brochure. There was rain, that could be expected, but there was also a clammy, seaweed-scented tinge to the damp that snuck up sleeves and clung between body and cloth like a layer of cold wet cotton. Cotton, too, masked the bridges, but Dave, who'd lost love in overwrought, merchandized San Francisco but reclaimed it amongst the prosaic, hardworking clatter of Oakland, was in no mood for romantic notion.

He hopped off the cable car before it came to a complete standstill and crossed the road, stepping over strips of track that were shiny in the wet.

Dave knew how easy it was for him to drop into character when talking to his daughter; intelligent, perceptive, sardonic Jen, who, whether she knew it or not, had the power to crumble his fragile confidence. The personality of the sad clown came most naturally to him, the willing entertainer who could never quite win over the crowd, but some days she saw through that, wouldn't let him get away with the bad jokes, worse, wouldn't let him get away with slipping into his version of inconsequential teen-speak.

Dave felt that the time was right to glance back at Jen crossing the road behind him, one of her eyes closed to the bland, inadequate sun, features screwed into an amused expression of demurral. She turned, and together they watched the crowded streetcar drop out of sight amid its rumble and chime of Victoriana, onward to Chinatown and the Financial District.

"You know, you're supposed to wait," she said. "Walk the lady across the road."

"You're no lady."

"Damn right, mister."

"And less of the cuss-words. You never know when Mom might be listening."

Jen rolled her eyes, but there was still the smile playing across her lips. She took her turn to seize the initiative, strode past him in the direction of the manicured square that served to draw the customer into the luxury of the hotel, and Dave felt pleased with his partial recovery.

It had been Ashley's idea to spend their last night at The Fairmont, one of the city's most prestigious addresses, though Dave, being wary of the expense and having a genuine resistance to hauteur, was far less certain. But those household items most comforting and familiar to them were long in storage, packed, ready to ship, and Ash felt they deserved a treat.

Dave caught Jen up, but was thrown into fresh confusion by the look on her face. She'd stopped dead, was staring across the elaborate shrubbery at the hotel's gray empire frontage and limp flags of nations.

"Dad," she said, with horror in her voice to match the expression. "He's here again."

"Who?"

"Over there. Don't look so hard. From the candy store."

Dave bristled a little, stared anyway. Sure enough, there was the guy whom they had first seen on Fisherman's Wharf where Dave had taken Jen to buy Red Hots after lunch.

A tall man, slim, but solid through the shoulders. In designer glasses and a gray raincoat.

Really, the whole thing was Dave's fault, it had come from nothing, a side trip for some candy. The guy looked so little like a tourist—and so unlikely to be interested in fifty different flavors of jellybean—that Dave had caught himself in a blank stare, wondering in a vague, day-dreamy way if this person actually knew he resembled a character from a bad spy novel, or a private investigator, or a . . .

Yet there *was* something strange about him. Nothing overly sinister, just a weird artifice.

Jen's attention, so acute, had noticed her dad's interest and followed his gaze over a row of blood-red lollipops. When Dave, in turn, noticed her noticing, Jen immediately directed his attention to something else, reaching for a lightness of tone that had been lacking from the day. There was a note of hollowness to whatever it was she had said, but Dave was delighted to be shown a way in, any chink in the armor, and the man in the raincoat was forgotten.

But then he was on the cable car.

Not the California Street line, but Powell–Mason, and Jen had frozen up when she saw him. That time the man in the raincoat actually smiled, he smiled at Dave; they were clinging to the running boards on opposite sides of the car. It wasn't a big smile, rather a tight-lipped gesture of familiarity; nothing too inappropriate or untoward, probably he recognized them from the candy store, was acknowledging the coincidence.

Before he knew what was happening, Dave was nodding back at the man. Then he felt a little hand tugging the front of his sweater.

"Dad? Do you know that man?"

"Yeah, he was in the candy store."

"But do you *know* him?"

"No." Something occurred. "Do you?"

"No. Is he following us?"

So it was all to do with the shadow of events surrounding Jen and Karen. Dave had reflected that this was probably inevitable: Jen needed to occupy a cool, adult place when thinking about what had happened to her recently. *How is Mommy coping*, Dave had said when they first met up. Has there been anymore letters, any news from the FBI? Have you heard again from the Internet stalker—*that bad guy*, Dave had called him, uselessly—and he'd asked her these questions so early in the day, ostensibly—*selfishly*—to get that subject—that contrived, impossible, *all-absorbing* subject—out of the way, so they could *really* be on their own.

It had been a mistake.

Sure, Dave was involved in Karen's problem, as involved as any estranged husband had any right to be, and that was before taking into account his own inconvenience; the seizing of his computer equipment, the extensive, repetitious interviews that he'd had to give to cops, to feds. He'd even had to come up with alibis for the first time in his life.

Perhaps his new future in Hawaii was the source of the bad current. Dave was pulling in a different direction, there was no use denying it. But these events, this godawful ongoing *thing* with Karen, seemed to have pushed Jen closer to her mom, when only a month ago they were verging on years of typical teenage combat. And the real outcome seemed to be a lack of closeness towards *him*.

"Remember how you used to see boogeymen all the time, boo-boo?" he had said to Jen on the cable car, careful to keep his tone light, one eye on the man in the gray raincoat. "Remember the boat to Alcatraz? And the hobo on the bench when we last rode these cars? He scared us a bit, you remember?"

"No." The controlled voice had sailed up, a few cute freckles on a smooth forehead, freckles on the tip of a button nose. There was a finality in the tone that belied the cuteness, and Dave kept his mouth shut.

That was the end of the worry for the time being. Dave was careful not to look in the direction of the man again, and when, finally, he did care to glance, the man had gone.

But there was no denying it: here he was yet again, the man from the candy store, striding along the sidewalk towards the outstretched portico of the hotel.

Had he heard them discussing The Fairmont and then followed them? Should Dave use his cellphone, call the police? No, no. It was coincidence, a business traveler far from home, unexpectedly cut loose for the afternoon, takes in the sights. What could be more normal than that?

Almost on cue, they watched through the mists as the man in the raincoat pulled out a wad of change, peeled off bills, handed them to a doorman. The move was so natural, so ordinary, it couldn't be mistaken. In seconds, he had gone from psycho-stalker to mundane hotel guest.

Dave gave a sigh of relief for the benefit of Jen, and the man in the raincoat disappeared into the shadow of the hotel, another car, more guests, already pulling up. Beside him, he saw Jen's shoulders unclench. Even in her heightened state she could surely recognize a coincidence.

Idly, Dave began to wonder what grade of smile he'd get

from the man when they ran into one another at the breakfast buffet.

"Well," said Jen, "I guess this is just about it."

Neither of them needed to reference the black, highly polished Mercedes holding down the closest parking spot to the entrance; Dave and Jen were already an hour late for the rendezvous with Karen's mom.

"We could go inside," said Jen. "I could buy you a drink. You wanna beer?"

"Yeah, Grandma would love that."

"Think they'd card me?"

"What, you wanna be playful?" said Dave. "Now? I had, like, a whole farewell speech ready. Where was this Jen three hours ago?"

Jen sighed, and Dave saw a maturity in her face he'd never been aware of before. Lines and shadows, lines and shadows. She was squinting at him. "I'm sorry, Dad. I don't know how many big goodbyes I have in me right now."

He looked heavenward.

"What," said Jen, smiling. "You want my permission? Permission to go live abroad? You had it weeks ago."

"I don't need permission."

"Sure you do. Just like I needed you to ask me, I needed that *so* badly. I'm jealous, is all, totally jealous." She hesitated. "I love you very much, Dad."

"I love you," said Dave.

They stood there, huge buildings all around. Rain fell.

"What," said Dave, never feeling more awkward. "I mean, you wanna hug now? It's been a while, and I know how you don't like . . ."

He was rocked back on his feet by a tackle that squeezed the air from his lungs, Jen's long, slim arms reaching right around him, under his jacket, head burrowing into his chest. Dave could only move at the neck, so he did that, pressed his face and his nose into her hair, breathing her in.

"I love you," he said, tears in his eyes, marveling at the power those words have when you rarely have permission to say them. He wasn't sure that she heard him, but he got an extra squeeze. Then she was gone, walking away, the memory of her body, her scent, her delicate animal warmth.

He watched her go. Anyway, it would have been awkward walking over and speaking to Angie; Dave had always been on pretty good terms with his mother-in-law, even during the separation, but they'd said their final goodbyes when Karen's mom dropped Jen off that morning at the place they'd agreed to meet: Karen's apartment building.

His daughter turned back once, just after she'd opened the car door; gave him a big smile, waved like they were the best of friends despite it all, and Dave's heart was full.

The Merc took a long time reversing out and pulling away, but he waited anyway, watched it until the last, out into Mason and left on to Sacramento, the tail lights a wet red haze.

It took the harsh clang of another cable car to shake him from his reverie. Dave shrugged his shoulders, tried to focus on the supper he'd promised himself, the minibar he would raid, the beautiful, voluptuous, fragrant woman who was, that minute, waiting for him on the fifth floor, plump breasts swaddled in a hotel robe.

Dave Wiley even managed a whistle as he walked towards the hotel doors.

At the end of the lobby, Dave had a choice of open elevators, so it was surprising when a strong, tan hand reached in after he'd pushed his button, halted the doors mid-closure.

Dave's irritation was compounded when a familiar face followed the hand, a face floating above broad shoulders in a gray raincoat.

Having rushed to halt the elevator, the man from the candy store was now taking things slowly. He seemed far bigger close up than from a distance, a few inches over the six-foot mark, and Dave, politely but wearily, had to step back to make room.

The man, in turn, registered a surprise upon seeing Dave that was mildly exaggerated, took a while choosing which button to push.

"Looks like we're headed for the same floor," he said, eventually.

"Yeah," said Dave.

The doors closed.

"Good day?" said the man.

"You know," said Dave. "The weather."

"Ah, yes. Checking out tomorrow?"

"Right," said Dave, thinking about Hawaii, about Ashley.

The man nodded. "Leaving San Francisco is like saying goodbye to an old sweetheart: you want to linger as long as possible. Cronkite said that, I read it in a airline magazine."

"You in town for long?" said Dave, because he felt he had to.

"Just the one night this time," said the man, and he seemed to be thoroughly enjoying himself. "I've just started renting an apartment in the city, not that I'm going to use it. Little scheme I've got going, you understand."

Dave smiled.

"I also had a therapy appointment I felt I had to honor, but she cancelled on me last minute. Illness, out of town, I don't know. Very disappointing, but she always seems to know best."

"Ah," said Dave.

An empty corridor. Low lighting. Hotel opulence.

Above the elevator doors, electronic numbers slip by. A soft twang of cables, mechanisms.

It is coming.

The doors open. Two men.

Dave Wiley doesn't look so well right now. His face has paled. He's spinning the key-card that opens the door to his room like it might somehow magic him away. His malaise stems from an instinct telling him there is something sickly and unwholesome about the person he has been forced into proximity with. He wants to get away, but can't break the social taboo.

He doesn't know how much danger he is in.

The other man, Jon Peterson, looks as clear-eyed and confident as we've ever seen him.

"Sprung for a suite, eh?" Peterson says, as they step out together.

"How would you know?" Dave says. He's not feeling as polite as he once was.

Peterson chuckles, gestures. "The floor you're on. You get the best views."

"Ah." Dave nods a little, as if in farewell, but Peterson follows him down the corridor.

"Well," says Peterson. "That and I've *seen* your room."

"What?"

"I said, I've seen your room," says Peterson, with jovial patience. "That's also how I know it's a suite. I've been in."

"You've been in?"

"When I knocked, that slut of yours just pulled the door right open."

Dave spins around, more angry than afraid: "Look *mister*, I don't know what . . ."

Peterson moves fast, slams Dave against the wall, hard enough to dislodge generic art, several feet away. There is a bloody smear where the head connects.

"That's right," says Peterson, breathing hard. "I invited myself in and took a blowtorch to her face, her lips, her eyes. Her name was Ashley, now she smells like bad barbecue. *Great* view of the city though. Coit Tower, Transamerica Building. Are you awake? Dave?"

Dave's head hangs, drools a little bloody spittle. Peterson shifts, props him behind a powerful forearm.

"You know, I was never coming back to Frisco. But then I

thought, well, I'll stop by Karen's apartment while I'm here, old times. A risky thing to do, but I am a psychopath, right?"

Dave's eyes refocus. He can't struggle because he can see a knife now; a short one, flexible, serrated and thin, something to worm between ribs. He tries to speak, garbles unintelligibly.

Ashley

The man in the raincoat seems to be growing taller, his body blocking out the light.

"Incredible how fast they got the police tape down," says Peterson. "Anyway, *you* show up, and then Jennifer. I can tell she's Karen's, she has to be, she's so beautiful. Jeez, your last day together, and this awful weather." He looks sympathetic, twirls the knife around in his hand like an expert.

"Please don't . . . *kill* me . . ."

"*Shhhh*, Dave. Lucky for you I don't stick my cock into little girls, and Jen's a peach. Guess I got a full slate of problems as it is, don't need to add pedophilia to the list." A frown darkens his face. "Should I try fucking her anyway? Should I *fuck* your daughter for you, Dave?"

Dave tries to move a little, but his limbs have turned to water. Casually, affectionately, Peterson presses a massive hand across his face, like a vet forcing an animal to take a pill.

"So I lost my advantage, I lost my way. But who's taking the initiative now? Aw, Jesus *Christ*, Dave, are you pissing yourself?"

Peterson leans in, the knife flashing. His smile is horrific, possessed.

"You don't know how much I wanna tell you my *name*."

Oh please GOD

not like this

In the dark, impenetrable pit of the car, Blake handed Karen a black ski mask.

"Put this on."

"But I've never . . ."

"There could be cameras inside, I know there's one on the corner. You can tie your hair back?"

"It's okay."

Karen had been waiting for this moment since parking up. She took a gulp of air and slid the mask over her face. It was like forcing herself into a big sock, static electricity crackling across her head. There were more anxious moments while she identified the holes for her eyes and mouth, and then a trial breath delivered the scent of lemony fabric conditioner and she had to stifle the urge to laugh, to ask Blake if he'd laundered them prior to the caper.

"You ready?" said Blake.

Karen glanced across the street at a boxy, floodlit building where a crappy plastic banner moved a little in the breeze, black printed words on faded blue: Howard Freed, Security and Security Solutions. Then she turned to Blake, his own mask making him look like an evil, badly stuffed scarecrow.

Haunted eyes were imploring her, asking the question.

"Right," she said, looking again to the building, this time imagining she was able to see through the walls, to the information being protected, information that might save Katy Trueblood's life, maybe even Lilly's too.

Karen felt the tight cloth of the mask making her feel more awake, more alert. It seemed to be fusing there, becoming a second skin, giving her permission to move outside herself, to become another person.

"Right," she said again, this time meaning it.

Blake twisted the ignition key, and, without using his beams, drove smoothly across the street and into a dimly lit service road at the side of the building. Seconds later, the engine was off and they were stepping out of the car into a silence so absolute that the sound of the doors closing seemed to ricochet off the walls like gunshots.

Every moment prior to leaving the motel, Karen hadn't quite

accepted that Blake's plan to break into the remailing service was real. She knew he *meant* to do it, understood when he *said* he'd do it, but it took her to leave the warmth of her room to really *know* it. There, past the darkly curtained windows of the other occupants and around the corner of the motel's external walkway, had been Blake's ashen face in the diffused light of a disguised moon. He'd parked the SUV at the bottom of the steps and was looking up at her, leaning on the hood like he'd been waiting forever, the eternally employed boatman for the river Styx.

There was no question then that Karen wouldn't help him do it, it had all gone too far; perhaps breaking the law in this case was the right thing to do, would be the only way to get the answers they needed in time. But Blake, strangely, hadn't been much use in calming her nerves. In fact, he hadn't said much of anything since receiving the phone call from Lilly.

They were both in the car before Karen was told the plan.

"Freed's got a camera on the front door, but that wouldn't be our point of entry anyway," Blake had said. "We have three deadbolts there, reinforced glass, high-pressure sodium vapor lamp like a sunbeam, though I suspect the camera is for the benefit of business hours, checking who's calling before opening the door. If it wasn't, there'd probably be cameras elsewhere, and there aren't. Regardless, the thing is on, you can see the blinking light, so we won't even bother."

"What, a back door?"

"Better. Freed rents the property on the corner, there's the tall department store to the left. Their fire escape leads out onto Freed's roof and down a ladder at the back. It was all mapped out on a nice clear laminate when I browsed the sporting goods: *in case of fire*. I also had a good look out the store window, and there's a skylight on Freed's roof, two of them. There'll probably still be an alarm, but I have a plan for that."

"You want us to climb onto the roof?"

"There's a ladder to pull down, then getting onto the roof should be as strenuous as climbing the stairs to your apartment. I go through the skylight, you stay up there in case I need help getting back out—and that's the extent of your involvement."

And here they were, walking towards a smaller, darker alley off of the main artery, crowded with garbage cans and boxes. Even before Karen spotted the fire escape suspended above them, Blake was moving the cans, thankfully empty, he needed to make room for the horizontal ladder to pull down properly. Wordlessly, she reached to help, conscious of the noise, though they hadn't seen or heard anyone since parking up across the street, not even the ubiquitous drunks.

She was sweating a little once they were through, the mask a hot glow around her face.

Blake gestured for her to climb onto his shoulders. She hesitated, was going to say something, but he was already down on one knee. The foot-space either side of his head was disturbingly narrow.

Karen put down one rubber-soled shoe and Blake bore up immediately, boosting her against the wall, Karen scraping her gloved hands in the process. The wall was a godsend, Blake rose so fast, but then Karen was up, she wasn't going to fall.

She could see deep shadows in the alley from this position, dark pools of open bins. She looked to the left and saw she was almost level with the roof of the building across the way, and it reminded her of the purpose. Their balance was too precarious for Karen to look up much, but she knew where the fire escape was, so one hand groped, found a solid metal bar. She adjusted her grip, made it secure, felt reassured.

Then something occurred, a blade of panic, something they hadn't discussed. She was remembering the fire escape on her building at home.

"Blake!" Her whisper sounded strange, was hardly her own. "Blake!"

"What!" He sounded annoyed, maybe it was the exertion. They weren't supposed to be speaking now.

"What if the escape is alarmed?"

"No circuit, I checked before!"

"What?"

"We're not in the city now! There's no crime here! Do you have both hands on it?" Far below, she could feel the tremor, his waning tolerance.

"It won't budge . . ."

"Do you have both hands on it?" It wasn't a question, it was a demand.

"I . . ."

"*Both* hands?"

Karen grabbed upwards with her other hand.

"I got it," she whispered, sweat running down her spine.

"Hold on," said Blake, and he walked away, left her hanging there.

He walked away.

"*Wha . . .*"

FUCK

The urge to kick was greatest, so she did that, legs cycling in the air, but it only lasted a second because her dead weight was pulling down the ladder in short jerks, a hellish scraping noise on each bounce. Before she knew it, her feet were back on the trash-strewn ground, her legs like failing rubber, the fire escape suspended in mid-descent a few feet from the dirt.

"Good job," whispered Blake, but before Karen could regain presence of mind to slap him, he was scrambling up the corrugated-iron stairs, his own weight causing them to judder all the way down.

She stood there alone for a second, feeling foolish.

Up on the roof, it took further moments to identify Blake amongst the other shadows.

"This isn't alarmed," he said, when she got over to him. He was on his knees, looking intently at the larger of the two skylights. The glass was filthy.

"How do you know?"

"There's no magnetic contact switch, there's no foil." Through the mask she saw him pull a lunatic grin. "Guess I overestimated Mr. Freed's paranoia."

Karen sat back while Blake rummaged in his backpack, got to work with pencil flashlight, duct tape and a small circular glass cutter. He seemed to take an agonizingly long time, and as the minutes ticked by, Karen couldn't help scanning the blank eyes of the other buildings, straining her ears for noises that didn't exist. Eventually, Blake pulled out what looked like a sheet of newspaper, tapped on a circle he'd made in the glass. It was a small, neat hole, and probably wouldn't be noticed for days, or at least until the next rainfall.

He reached in with a bony hand, found the latch by feel, and, after some exertion, the whole skylight swung around on a central hinge. It was rusty, gummed up with God knows what. Then Blake sat back, nodded at Karen.

"There's an alarm, but it isn't on."

"You don't know," said Karen.

"Watch this." Blake grinned, dropped his backpack through the skylight as if to put paid to further debate. It thumped into an office chair, skidded along the ground. Karen winced at the sound, waited for sirens, bells, whistles.

Nothing. A stone into a moonlit lake, circles spreading back out to stillness.

"You could wait in the car," whispered Blake. "I'll call you when I'm done."

"Christ. Just get on with it, will you?"

"Okay, I'm gonna drop a rope, you put it over that unit there. There still might be a security system I can trigger, in a safe, in another room—I'm not ruling out the need for a quick getaway. He's supposed to sell these systems for a living, so God knows why we've got it so easy."

Blake slid a slim, coiled rope out of his backpack, strategic hitches along its length to ease climbing. The end was looped with an adjustable knot, all Karen had to do was slip it over a nearby AC duct, pull it tight. The unit wobbled, but it would hold.

Blake was already halfway through the hole, legs dangling, the flashlight between his teeth.

"Happy landings," he mumbled. Then he lowered himself down to his fingertips, held for a second, dropped.

The ceiling was low slung, so Blake only had a short fall, and he landed like a cat. His first sensation was the smell, which was pretty bad; a mustiness, but something else also.

Vaguely, Blake wandered over to the control panel for the deactivated alarm, pushing back boxes as he did so, boxes of electrical components, as well as TVs, DVDs, nothing particularly to do with security or security solutions. Sure enough, it was state of the art. Why wasn't it on? Perhaps something to do with the person who was forwarding the mail, possibly the wife. Maybe they couldn't work it?

Dissatisfied with this theory, Blake moved on.

His first instinct was to look for a computer, but it'd have to be pretty foolproof: if someone else was doing the forwarding and they couldn't be trusted to set the alarm, then they likely couldn't negotiate Microsoft Office either. There were three computers against a far wall, set up in a sales display, but they were ancient, each coated in a thick layer of dust. Blake turned around, focused elsewhere.

What is that smell . . .

There was an organic quality to it somehow. Blake arced his flashlight around, dust particles suspended in the beam like undersea silt. Yeah, this could just about pass for a shop, or at least a commercial property; there *was* some logic to the mess, a route through the junk to an old-fashioned steel desk piled high with papers, empty CD cases, a cash register.

Blake picked his way back over to the door, the outside security light peeking through thin bars where the chipboard and mesh window coverings had been inexpertly nailed. There were letters on the mat, an accumulation of probably four or five days. Blake flipped through them, veering from optimism to a nagging suspicion that the trail here was very, very cold.

"*Egan!*" Karen's voice from above, he'd almost forgotten about her.

Nothing on the mat looked appropriate. Flyers, statements with return addresses. He didn't want to start wading through Freed's final demands from the bank.

"Blake!"

"What?"

"There's a police car!"

Blake froze, killed his flashlight beam. He couldn't hear anything. "Where?"

"It just cruised by, a block away. I think it's gone."

"Probably routine patrol."

"How do you know for sure?"

Blake ignored her, they were wasting time. He twisted the flashlight back on, moved between furniture. The desk was in front of an open door that led to what looked like a storeroom. In the moonlight from a narrow, barred window, Blake could make out a dirty sink, metal shelves with more equipment.

Nothing obvious on his first sweep of the desk's surface, though there was plenty he could come back to. The drawers were similarly crammed with junk, and at one point Blake was rewarded with a dead mouse in a trap, the head half taken off. But it was fresh, and not the source of the bad smell, which seemed to be emanating from the storeroom behind him.

Blake didn't turn around, didn't get distracted, continued with the sweep.

The drop-down filing drawer was locked.

Bingo.

Blake knew all about how to get into desk drawers. It only took a moment to spring the lock. It slid on heavy castors, made a lot of noise. He took more care with the files inside than he had elsewhere. There were names, addresses, billing invoices, but nothing and no one that he recognized. There were also opened, stamped envelopes, addressed to Howard Freed, empty of their contents. At the back, tucked in behind the stuffed accordion files, were five rubber stamps that existed to apply Freed's vanity postmarks, and a thick ink pallet in different colors.

This is it.

The information was all there, in the files. Freed's admin center.

Blake stood up, shrugged his shoulders. There was too much to sift through right now, and he was beginning to lose his nerve for fumbling about in the dark.

He opened his backpack, there was just enough room to lever in the two heavy files. Then Blake closed the desk drawer, carried the heavy, misshapen bag over to the thin rope dangling from the skylight like a bead of spit.

"I can't climb with this," he said up to Karen. "And I can't throw it. I'm going to tie it, and you're going to have to pull it up."

"Okay," said Karen. Blake fastened the loops of his backpack to the rope with a knot that he hoped she'd be able to undo. "Go," he said. He couldn't see her anymore, but the slack began to take, the bag floating up in front of him with irregular heaves.

Blake moved back to the desk, inspecting his handiwork. It was impossible to disguise he'd been in there, though the mess thrown up by his rifling hardly looked any worse than before. He massaged his hands through his gloves; at least there'd be no fingerprints.

And that smell?

The bag was nearing the top of the shaft of moonlight, in a

moment Karen would have it. Blake decided to nudge open the door to the storeroom, give it a proper look.

The smell was stronger here. Rotting food, rotting animal, rotting . . .

corpses?

No.

If anything, it was a little tidier than the main store. But in the middle of the room was what looked like a square trapdoor, and he padded over to take a look.

Unlocked. In fact, just a wooden panel placed over struts. But when he prised it up, the stench made him recoil.

It was pitch dark below, maybe a cellar, but this was a strange place for cellar access. Heart pounding, he swung down the flashlight beam. There was another door beneath the trapdoor, a more solid one with a proper lock on the inside, though this was wide open now.

It was a fallout shelter.

Blake was looking down into a 1950s-style radiation refuge, but the room itself was as big as the rest of the store combined. Shelves groaned under the weight of canned goods, but there were also fresh goods, or goods that had once been fresh; boxes of cereal, corners gnawed off by rodents, a loaf of bread covered by a layer of blue fur. There was the same kind of ubiquitous junk as upstairs, but it was as though a tramp lived in the place. There were dirty sheets strewn about, a stained mattress, empty liquor bottles. In one corner was what looked like a fully stocked medical station, a couple of archaic diagrams on the wall, a stretcher with a dirty sheet thrown over it, and under the sheet a human body.

My God, I'm looking into a MORGUE.

Blake looked back over his shoulder, ran a dry tongue over dry lips.

"I've found her," he whispered. "She's here, this was where he held her, but is he still around? Is he . . ."

Blake shook his head, steadied himself, pointed the flashlight back towards the corner of the shelter, to the body under the sheet.

Too big for Katy Trueblood.

Lilly?

A ladder led from the trapdoor to the basement floor. Blake reached for his gun.

"Blake! *Blake!*" Karen's voice from the other room. She sounded distant to him, harsh from whispering. But his decision was made. Blake swung his legs over and was climbing down, boots clanging dully on hollow bars.

The shelter felt even larger once down on the ground. To Blake it appeared that someone had prepared sufficiently to spend months in the shelter, maybe years—or to keep someone there.

He didn't like to move his flashlight off the body under the sheet, but he needed to check his route across the floor. It was the perfect location to keep a hostage; already self-sufficient, air, water, probably soundproof. Blake had his hand over his mouth to tide the stench, but he forced himself to move it. At least the smell of decay likely wasn't human; it predominantly came from a large bowl of fruit that had gone to slush, and there was more of the same rotting material in an open, inactive refrigerator, maybe fish or meat or worse.

He found a light switch, wasted a moment debating, flipped it on.

Nothing.

No power. Maybe the master switch for the electricity was upstairs.

What the hell is this place . . .

Blake approached the body under the sheet. It was on a stretcher, a raised hospital bed. There was no blood, the stains were more like grease. He found a first-aid kit, an old one, next to the headboard.

Blake cleared his throat, as though giving the disguised body opportunity to respond.

Then he pulled away the sheet.

His first thought: A *naked woman.*

A naked woman in mid-scream.

She's no eyes, she's got no eyes

But it was a dummy, just a medical dummy, the type first-aiders practice on. It was considerably worse for wear; torn, bruised. But a medical dummy nonetheless.

What the hell is this doing here? A sick joke?

Blake had been holding his breath. He released it with self-disgust, disgust with this place, with the smell of rotting food, with the . . .

Then all the lights went on.

He heard before he saw, it sounded like a big spring switch, like someone turning on stage lights all at once, *whumpph*, and Blake was too surprised to do anything but blink. Then he had his hands on his gun.

Doors were banging, a professional search of the premises.

From above, a man's voice, then a woman's: "Clear! Clear!"

There was nowhere to hide.

Footsteps. Hasty, authoritative footsteps. Blake thought of Karen on the roof.

"Drop it."

The command came from the trapdoor. A young man, confident, assured.

"Drop it or I'll shoot."

Still squinting from many hours in darkness, Blake slid the Glock onto the trolley with the medical dummy, but close enough so he could still reach it. He was looking at steady hands on a law-enforcement issue gun.

He was a fish in a barrel. The game was over.

"FBI. Move away from the weapon."

Blake tried to smile, but the adrenalin was beating the heart right out of his chest. He pulled off his mask, tried to play for time.

"Wondered when you guys would show," he said. "You sure as hell pick your moments."

"Sir, you're under arrest. Move away from the weapon, do it *now*."

*

". . . if you keep your seatbelts fastened, even when the sign is off, we won't have to disturb you."

Dave Wiley wasn't the greatest of passengers, particularly at take-off. He didn't like to talk about it, but Ashley knew, and she placed her hand over his, was surprised to find barely a tremor of tension.

"Baby," she whispered. "We're going to Hawaii."

Dave turned to face her, the greasy, battered magazine from the seat pocket unopened on his lap. "I know," he said, but his smile was lifeless. He was pale and sick, the pain of the last few days like a shroud over his face.

Yet he was lucky, he'd been told it by so many people. By his doctor, by the detectives.

How the fuck am I lucky?

Because you're alive, Davey-boy. And your wife-to-be is alive. That knife was never stuck in you. It was all a bluff, that fucking psychopath.

She smells like bad barbecue.

"I mean, I know they're not *my* family," Ashley was saying, pressing his hand. It was the continuation of an exchange that had started in the terminal, another version of the conversation they'd been having ever since Dave's encounter.

". . . I know they'll always be yours. You have every right to worry, but my worry is you."

But no one ever did use a blowtorch on you, Ashley. And you never even had to lay eyes on the man who claimed to have killed you—a man with a smile that will haunt me forever . . .

"Thank you," Dave said, because a response was necessary.

Jen is alive, and Karen. There's been no real victim yet, at least, no one personal to me.

But is that it? I'm lucky because I'm ALIVE?

"We're lucky people," said Ashley. "You're a good man, and I'm proud."

I was left there, sobbing in a hotel corridor, hot piss all down my trouser leg. That was lucky? I gotta carry on being a man now?

"I love you very much," she said.

Dave wasn't listening, but if Ashley felt a snub she didn't show it. He looked past her, through the cabin window at damp, scrolling tarmac, listened to the bump and rattle and whine, items shifting in overhead lockers.

"Cabin crew, seats for take-off."

None of it ever happened, Dave. None of it was ever real.

You tell yourself.

Dave, stricken, looked once more at his wife-to-be. She'd taken his magazine; there were pictures there, bright, swirling colors. She was reading something about infinity pools.

Fifteen

The sky is bright and blue, a startling aquamarine that force-floods through little Karen's contracted pupils and crams her mind with color. She breathes, takes her first breath sharply, as though this was something she'd forgotten how to do. The air is so salt-sweet it stings the inside of her nostrils, the back of her throat. If she were sleeping, she would probably kick out right now.

"Sammie?" Karen's voice, strange, tight; her own, but somehow not.

She sits up, blinks. Her legs stretch out in the yellow-white sand. Beyond them, a vast expanse of beach. Beyond that, in the distance, the ocean; walls of waves powerful enough to upend giants. Beyond again, the azure heavens, a sun without warmth, a three-tone wilderness.

The Big Sur coast. It must have been, what . . . years?

Karen shifts her bare feet in the coolness, imagines she can feel the sift of each individual grain. Fine sand sticks to small, white, unpainted toes.

The rocks where Sammie went are a solid mass, away to the right. Karen can't look in that direction just yet.

She reaches out a hand, there is a soft old backpack, a faded green backpack. If Karen were to hold it to her face she'd get the smell of her mother's perfume, the metal and fur trunk of the Lincoln that Dad used to drive, a whiff of stale sunscreen, of damp towels.

Inside the backpack is a Tupperware box. Karen draws it out, holds it in young, capable hands. There are crumbs, crusts, gelatinous tomato seeds clinging to the inside of the plastic.

You remember making these, Karen? Far too much food for two little girls.

Where is she? Do you know where she is?

Karen drops the box. Finally, she turns her head to face the rocks. They look like a melting gothic edifice, half-submerged in the sea.

Footprints guide the way over. Footprints made by small feet.

You want to follow the footprints? Who made those footprints?

"Sammie."

Karen runs well, keeps her head down, has only a vague sense of distance. You get good at what you practice.

The rocks arrive faster than she expects, and she knows where to climb. They are impossibly smooth where the tide comes in, but up towards the trees, at the edge of the beach, there is a place to scramble.

On top of the rocks now. Sammie is nowhere to be seen.

"Sammie?"

You're wasting time.

Karen ignores. She uses her hands to magnify her voice: "Sammie . . ."

Lost in the greedy thunder of the sea.

Watch your step now. We didn't come this far to lose you.

Karen, knowing what she has to do, walks out onto the rocky promontory, dress fluttering and blown against her legs, the sea surrounding her on three sides. She doesn't look in the rock pools, or even at her own bare feet, which are stained from the grit and the sand. She won't lose her balance, but when she approaches the far edge and the line of the ocean constitutes her entire horizon, Karen goes down to a kneeling position, gently, because the last vestiges of a bloodless scrape from some forgotten childish tussle is working its way out on her left knee.

For some reason, Karen feels the only way to see into the cauldron, to properly see over to where the water thrashes and churns, is to slide forward on her belly.

What do you see?

Nothing.

Look again, Karen. Are you so sure?

Nothing. There's nothing there.

Just the water slapping against the rock, the spume and stench of the brine.

No body, no whites of eyes, no flooded dolly sister.

And Karen is no longer scared.

She's *terrified*.

"Kar?"

A voice from behind. An ageless voice, yet more childish than her own.

"Kar, what are you doing?"

Karen can't look straightaway, she has to get up again, at least to her hands, and the rock is so slippery. She scootches back a few inches from the edge, her dress riding up. She turns now and sits in the grime, clothes filthy, face shiny from the spray and the sweat.

Sammie.

Sammie is here.

Her little sister, in the flesh.

Jeans shorts, pink backpack, bare feet, similarly muddied. And beautiful, more beautiful than Karen could ever be, because Samantha Wiley only ever looked like a child and her appearance is wholly shaped by memory.

"What the hell is wrong with you?" Karen shouts. She has to shout because of the noise, but she's angry and afraid, she'd probably be shouting anyway.

Sammie pauses for a moment and then laughs, the irregular breezes delivering the sound. It is lyrical, playful, innocent, and Karen's terror subsides a little.

"Here," Sammie yells. "I'll sit with you!"

Sammie announces this in a way that tells Karen she wasn't laughing *at* her, that she understands the responsibility a big sister has to be serious. Before Karen can respond, they are side by side at the edge of a rock pool, bare arm pressing bare arm.

"I checked," says Sammie, slightly breathless. "There's nothing to see around the other side. Our beach is the best one."

"I thought you were . . . I thought . . ." Karen trails off. The notion that Sammie could have fallen into the water and actually *died* sounds stupid now, and to mention it out loud might be to breathe fresh life into the fear.

Karen, caught between past and present, badly wants to lean over, to press her face into Sammie's hair, to confirm that she's *real*, but she can't, because . . .

"Hey, look at this . . ." says Sammie, who has spotted something in the rock pool, something Karen can't quite see. Fearless, Sammie thrusts in a hand, and there is a foamy convulsion while she grabs a hold of a small blue-black crab, only it isn't that small, the thing is as big as her hand, and the claws jitter and flex, very, very alive. It seems to whirl around with primitive vengeance, and Sammie loses her nerve, drops it half-in and half-out of the water. The crab makes a dash down the side of the rock at an impossible angle, apparently unhurt.

Sammie looks to Karen for approval, or perhaps disapproval.

"Let's get out of here," says Karen. "We're gonna catch hell from Mom when we get back."

So nothing really happened on the beach?

"What?"

I said: nothing happened on the beach? Nothing happened on the rocks?

I didn't say that. It was a big deal to me. I thought I'd lost her. I *did* lose her that day.

But how would it have been different if she had died in the water? Wouldn't that have made you MORE responsible, and not less?

Karen finds herself whirling through time and space.

She has one eye on Sammie, as her little sister stands up with grudging obedience and brushes at her clothes. Karen's other eye begins to focus on a stained patch of wallpaper in the crappy motel room where she spent the previous night.

The previous night.

Canaan, Utah.

Or did you forget, Karen?

She was sitting up on a cheap bedroom unit, her body wrapped in a threadbare toweled robe, naked feet wearing four-day-old nail polish. She doesn't have to look in the mirror to confirm she is a child no longer.

She blinked again, reintegrated herself into the present with reluctance. It was frightening to evoke that day, but it was a place where Sammie was still with her, was *alive*, albeit for only a short time longer; a clear view into a portion of memory that had long been walled off.

"Karen?" The familiar voice in her ear, sympathetic but concerned, and Karen tuned it back to a discernible frequency. She pulled away the receiver of the telephone, stared as though the thing was completely alien to her.

"I don't understand," said Karen, perhaps to herself. She was hundreds of miles from the coast, but could still smell the sea.

"You've been talking to me, though you trailed off," said Mary Huntingdon. "Why don't you take a minute?"

"No, no. It's fine. I didn't mean to worry you."

The hallucination had been so vivid, like an extension of her dreams the night before. She should have given herself time before calling Mary, at least had a cup of coffee. But she was ready, that much was clear. She needed to talk.

"Take the minute." Mary's voice was as smooth and controlled as always, and it imparted an essential adult authority. "This isn't an ideal session of therapy to be having over the phone. I mean, I know you're away and you still wanted to do this, but it isn't something I would typically agree to."

Karen breathed, placed the receiver on the desk.

Am I really ready to talk about this? About Sammie?

No, never.

Do I need to talk about it?

Yes.

Will I ever give myself permission to talk about it?

No, but . . .

Would I ever previously have given myself permission to break into private property, to steal information, as I did last night?

Would I ever previously have given myself permission to abandon Jen and disappear into the desert to track down a madman?

Have I ever in my life previously felt so powerful and yet so vulnerable at the same time—powerful enough to stand up and protect myself, my family, the things I hold important to me, yet vulnerable enough to acknowledge that I'm probably being driven by fear alone?

Karen glanced at the thick file of information by the side of the unmade bed, the file she had winched up from the remailing service shortly before Egan Blake was arrested and she forced herself to flee the scene. She hadn't looked in there yet, hadn't searched out the fateful name connected to her own address, but she sure as hell intended to, just as soon as . . . as soon as she finished the hour with Mary that she'd paid for in advance, as soon as she finished talking about . . .

this.

Now or never, Karen. Pick up the phone.

"I lied to you before," Karen said to Mary. "Like my parents lied to me and I lied to them. Of course Sammie didn't drown. It was just . . . easier for us that way."

"How was it easier?"

"Maybe easier for everyone but me."

"How was convincing yourselves that Sammie drowned supposed to make it any easier?"

"There are worse things than drowning," said Karen.

The therapist remained silent.

"My parents knew it, *I* know it. Sammie drowning became the big communal lie—unofficial, of course. It was initiated not long after the reality had been dealt with in physical terms; you know, after the police report, that initial *howling* grief—my mother was inconsolable. Sammie drowning was easier than the reality; it was tangible, unlike the reality. I even had *dreams* where she drowned, because the dream provided a kind of finality, closure."

"So what really happened?"

Carefully, Karen allowed her conscious mind to prod back into the tender memory, like pulling apart stitches to access a wound.

Sammie and Karen are holding hands.

They did this occasionally when they were younger, sometimes they were *made* to do it by Mom, but it was an affectation that faded with age. For some reason they're doing it now and Karen doesn't know why, it was another portion of the memory she'd forgotten.

They've just emerged from the shelter of the trees and are strolling back along the empty highway, Karen trying to remember which side of the road she should have them walk on so they face into traffic, like she's been told to do.

There are places on the walk where the road bends, not quite a switchback, but sharp enough to need to drive carefully because of the obstructed vision. Where the Pacific Coast Highway intersects Big Sur it ducks a little away from the ocean, dips into scented redwood copses and hops over small bridges crossing steep streams lost in depths of foliage.

Karen had a thing, or maybe it was Sammie who came up with it, where they'd assign personalities to cars or trucks based on their faces; you know—headlights for eyes, grill for mouth, bumper for a jaw. So it is that neither girl feels particularly worried when they round a corner and find themselves face to face with the huge, bookishly inquisitive face of a Mack Midliner parked by the side of the road, no cargo trailer attached to the back.

There is a man behind the wheel, name of Bertram Reid, and when he spots the two little girls rounding the corner, he looks far more surprised than they do. He hasn't seen another vehicle in almost an hour, let alone two children out walking on their own.

Since we're doing this, some information about Bertram Reid:

Bertram is twenty-four, native of Portland, Oregon, and a construction worker, although he lived until that morning with his girlfriend and children in San José. He is of moderate build, chews looseleaf tobacco when he's nervous, and has an obsession with guns, particularly lever-action shotguns. Following months of practice, he can now reload with staggering speed.

A little over three hours ago he walked into a coffee shop in downtown Santa Cruz, ordered, paid for, and drank a large glass of milk. Then he shot four people dead with two sawn-off Model 1901 Winchesters that he had in his sports bag.

Blood ran down the windows.

Yet that was his second massacre of the day, following the destruction of his family in their beds while they slept, though they won't be discovered for a little while yet, because Bertram murdered them with one of his favorite antiques: a De Lisle carbine, which a dealer had him believe was ex-British SAS. It has a very effective suppressor, and no neighbor was woken.

All of these guns—and more—are with him now.

Bertram's getaway was spontaneous, but pretty good. He doesn't own a car, but his wife had one she wouldn't be needing, so he fled both scenes in that, made for a truck-stop a little out of town. There, he dumped the car and convinced a trucker heading south to give him a ride.

The trucker, initially, was glad of the company.

They got as far as Big Sur before Bertram feigned stomach cramps. When the trucker pulled over, Reid slit his throat with a Bowie knife and let him bleed out into the dirt on the side of the road. Although guns are Bertram's thing, it was the most satisfying kill so far.

Now the trucker's body—and some blood-sodden furnishings from the cab—have been discarded in the trees, just a few feet from where Karen and Sammie are standing. There is also a little blood dripping down the side of the dirty paintwork of the truck, and blood on the road, even some blood on the soles of Bertram's boots, but not that you'd notice unless you were looking.

Karen and Sammie are a little intrigued to see this lone driver; there has been plenty of action for them already this morning, but they haven't laid eyes on another human being today. But then they carry on walking. There is no other way back to camp, except to pass right on by.

"Morning," says Bertram, from the open cab window.

"Hello," says Karen, who doesn't talk to strangers.

"What are you two doing out on your own?"

"Nothing," says Karen, still walking. She doesn't like this man. His mouth is black with tobacco, and he seems to be drooling.

"Stop right there, will you?"

Karen and Sammie are well behaved and polite, and he seizes on their hesitation.

"You wanna see what it looks like inside a truck?"

"No, thank you."

"What about you?" Bertram says to Sammie. "*You* wanna see inside the truck? You wanna hold the wheel?"

"Uh-uh," says Sammie, shaking her head.

Neither Karen nor Sammie can see below the cab window to where Bertram Reid is holding one of the sawn-off Winchesters with which he killed four people, but both are prepared to run if necessary. Something here feels very, very wrong: Reid is wearing his newly acquired evil like a talisman.

"It's okay," he says, sensing the fear. Bertram has become quite the expert in fear since that morning; he watched a pregnant woman scream for the life of her unborn child. "I just ran out of gas. Can you believe that? You girls know if there's a gas station around here?"

Both girls shake their heads, are backing up.

Bertram opens the door, reveals both the gun and his blood-splattered torso.

"Maybe there's one further up the road," says Bertram, in the same measured tone of voice. He addresses Karen. "What do *you* think?"

A *gun*.

Blood.

Say something, Karen.

"I don't know," she says, staring at the weapon.

"See, I need one of you to show me," says Reid. "I don't know these roads, and I'm new to driving a truck. I need to *concentrate*. Which one of you wants to come with me?"

Karen and Sammie look at one another.

"We don't know the road either," says Karen. "We're on vacation."

Reid's eyes glaze over. The gun swings unevenly, standstills in the space between them.

"No," says Sammie, with no fear in her voice. "I'll go. I know the road."

"We'll both go," Karen says quickly, and Bertram is *so* pleased with himself.

"No . . ." he says, in the patient tone he likes to use with children. "I only need *one* of you." The gun trains on Karen again. "You. Why don't *you* choose who comes with me?"

And then Karen figures it out. Really figures it out. She looks at Sammie.

He means to kill us both.

What?

He says he only wants one of us. He's going to shoot the other.

How do you know?

I just know. Look there, he's covered in blood, it's running down the side of the cab. I think he wants one of us to beat or to touch or something. But this man is a killer. He's going to kill the one he leaves behind.

But how do you know?

Because look at him . . .

"Choose now," Bertram says to Karen, and his face over the sawn-off barrel is grimy and mad and the brain controlling it is capable of anything.

The one who goes with him might have a chance to escape.

"Should we run?" says Sammie to Karen, and Bertram Reid laughs.

Anyone who says no to this man is dead.

"Time's up," says Reid, spitting out blackness. "Who's coming with Uncle Bertie?"

"You show him where there's a gas station," Karen says to Sammie.

"But I don't know . . ."

"Five miles south. You know the road . . ."

Karen eyes Reid, believing she has only moments to live.

". . . and I'll tell Dad where you've gotten to." Karen says this last part as if conveying some kind of meaning, though neither girl knows what that meaning might be. Whatever it is, she isn't showing the man she's scared, won't give him the satisfaction.

How bad can dying be, anyway?

Sammie walks forward, and Bertram cocks his head to one side, eyes Karen differently now; maybe even with simple-minded respect. Karen shudders.

"Wait," he says, getting out so Sammie can climb in ahead of him. He knows the smaller girl won't do anything her big sister won't do first, so he keeps the gun on Karen.

"What's your name?" he says to Karen, once Sammie is in the cab.

Karen shakes her head. She's not meaning to defy him, she just has nothing left.

Let's get this over with.

Bertram raises the gun.

Death is there.

Karen ignores, stares past it, stares him straight in his hateful eyes.

Reid wilts a little under her gaze, and the gun quivers, but he doesn't turn his back. Instead, he swings up to the cab with the barrel still trained. Only when seated does he lower the weapon, and then, when he closes the door, Karen loses sight of Sammie forever.

Still Karen stares.

She stares as he starts up the engine, continues to stare as he sets off in a series of unsteady lurches, unused to driving the big vehicle.

Once the truck has vanished and the sound of the engine has faded, she stares at the bend in the road where it disappeared from her sight, stares through the silvery dust that hangs in the air. There is a light breeze, and trees stir.

Then, for the second time that day, Karen runs as though her life depended on it.

"That's all I have," said Karen to Mary, feeling as empty as she'd ever been. Karen had carried the phone to the bed during her recounting of the tale, and she sank back among the sheets.

"I think you should probably rest for today," said Mary.

"Not possible," said Karen, becoming aware of Blake's file again, of her current responsibilities.

"Did they catch the man?"

Karen stared at the ceiling, and the remainder of the scene played out in her mind.

"State Troopers set up a roadblock outside San Simeon," she said. "Bertram Reid pulled over, then climbed from the truck and ran at them, guns blazing. He didn't manage to kill anyone else that day—outside of the movies you can't discharge those guns one-handed with any accuracy. But the cops dropped him, obviously. There was an ambulance, but he was dead on the scene."

"And . . . Sammie?"

"That's the thing," said Karen. "And this is it, this is really *it*."

"What is?"

"We don't know. She wasn't in the cab when the cops got Reid, which suggested that he must have dumped her off the highway somewhere between Big Sur and the roadblock. That's a maybe fifty-mile stretch, with few places to turn off; Santa Lucia Range on one side, Pacific Ocean on the other. And given the slapdash way he dumped the driver of the truck, you wouldn't think he'd have done much to hide the body. This wasn't an escape route, it was a random killing spree."

"But . . ."

"But Sammie was never found. To this day, Sammie was never found." Karen sat up on the bed. "Months they searched; police dogs, coastguard, local residents. Nothing. I'd like to think she somehow got away from him, that she escaped, that right now she's living a life somewhere, the reason she never turned up again was because she was angry at us, at me, because *I* made her go in my place, but . . ."

"But what, Karen?"

"Who knows if Reid meant to kill us both? He didn't kill me. I believed he would and I was wrong. I was the only person he met that day who he *didn't* try to murder. And now I'm here, and Sammie is gone."

Just then, Karen had an acute and unsettling sense of déjà vu. She rubbed her head with her hand, rubbed her face. It wasn't talking about Sammie in this way or describing the encounter with Bertram

Reid. Perhaps it was something about revealing herself to a person that might not have her best interests at heart, not really—not that Mary was bad, but she wasn't invested personally in Karen, that was the nature of therapy.

Karen, a therapist herself, suddenly felt sick to her stomach. Why should the whole thing suddenly feel so false? Karen knew what therapy entailed.

Can we really tell these things to strangers and expect to stay safe?

Or maybe it was just Mary's voice, so familiar, so synonymous with difficult questions and secrets revealed. But still . . .

"Christ," said Karen. "I have to take a shower. I have a long day in front of me."

"You've done a brave thing here," said Mary, who knew that words couldn't be enough right now, especially delivered down a telephone. "Did you ever hear me say a thing like that? I only wish you could have been here. I need you to be careful. Can you do that for me?"

Mary's concern was palpable, but she still sounded so cool, so detached. Karen knew that those were the rules of engagement, but that knowledge wasn't helping right now.

Whose walls are you trying to break down, Karen? You think if you reveal enough stuff to your therapist then she's going to open up as well? Become your friend?

"I mean, why the *fuck* didn't he take us both?" said Karen, startling herself. "Reid didn't even know what he was doing. He could have killed us *both* on the side of the road. You know what I pray for sometimes? In my next life, I pray to God that he kills *me*."

Mary said nothing.

Egan Blake, in his clothes, napped fitfully on a board-like mattress in the first of a short row of cells at the back of Canaan's police station. He was the only prisoner that night.

By seven-thirty in the morning, the concentrated shaft of light through the single narrow window was striking the floor like a laser, and the odor of bleach mixed with the slightly exotic smell of hot, hollow stone buildings became masked by the tang of bad coffee and toasted cheese. Blake was hungry, and he nodded thanks when the young deputy unlocked his cell and handed him breakfast.

At eight sharp, Federal Agents Ronnie Vasco and Regina Stowe strode into the corridor, both glossy-looking, young, and dressed in dark suits. Blake stood up straight, knowing how wild he appeared; his hair, his rumpled cat-burglar outfit, his gaunt and mostly sleepless face, and he bristled at the memory of how he'd been handcuffed and maneuvered into the back of a blue-and-white, a local cop he didn't recognize looking on. He particularly remembered Stowe's small, strong hand on his skull, the unnecessary way she pushed him down before the car door slammed.

Beyond reading the charge and barking instruction, the agents hadn't said much then, but Blake knew the silhouettes through the mesh in front had listened while he ran through the case details in short order. Blake was on the way to jail, about that he was under no illusion, but it was crucial the Bureau took over where he left off.

"Did you find Karen Wiley?" he said, immediately.

The agents looked at one another.

"Did you find Karen Wiley?" he said again, resisting an urge to grab hold of the bars.

"Why did you break into Howard Freed's property?" said Agent Vasco.

"I told you last night."

"And I said we'd talk in the morning."

"What got me in the end?"

"Silent alarm," said Agent Stowe, removing stylish sunglasses from her forehead and sliding them neatly into a breast pocket. "Three miles away, you got Colleen Freed out of bed, scared her half to death, it had never gone off before. She called it in, guess who was around?"

"Bullshit," said Blake. "Whatever intrusion detectors Freed has in there weren't active."

"On the desk drawer," said Vasco. "The drawer was wired."

"Ah."

"Tiny, remote, slots in just below the lip. And you took so much care, that cute little hole you cut in the skylight. You'd better bet she'll press charges."

"Why alarm the desk and not the property?"

"Colleen's younger brother is in town," said Stowe. "Maybe *was* in town—he keeps strange hours. He'd been having family problems, needed a place to hole up. She let him stay in the furnished basement, you know, the bomb shelter they have there. You saw evidence of that, though they're not on great terms. Still, live-in guard beats electronic alarm system."

"Until he skips out without telling anyone."

"And switches off the generator, defrosting eight months of emergency supplies, designed for consumption after the A-bomb drops."

"The Freed family seemed well prepared for the apocalypse," added Vasco, with a smirk.

"But they've been forwarding mail recently," said Blake. "No one who went in there noticed the smell of rotting food?"

"So maybe they're also slobs," said Vasco. "That isn't against the law."

Blake let out a laugh that sounded more like a cough, he couldn't help himself; he was recalling his fear of the night before, the CPR dummy under the sheet.

"Something funny, Mr. Blake?"

"Not at all." He addressed Stowe, she seemed to be in charge. "You find anything else? In the refrigerators? And did you see all those electrical goods? Really, something's going on there."

"You're not on this case, Blake," said Vasco.

"Why *were* you answering the 911?" said Blake. "Why not the local cops? Where's the Chief?"

"We know about the postmarks on the letters to Karen Wiley, same as you; we know Mr. Freed runs a remailing service. Why didn't you share the information? Why are you operating on your own?"

"Takes too long to get a warrant. A little girl is dying."

"And yet," said Stowe, "Colleen Freed would have been amenable to us taking a look around without a warrant. She's as horrified as the rest of the town about the Trueblood brutality."

"Then why hadn't you done it yet?"

"Don't lecture me," she said. "You want to find Katy?"

"Let me out of here, I can help."

"I don't think so," said Vasco. "What's your relationship to Lillian Hersh?"

Blake felt a pang of horror. "You found Lilly?"

"No, but we found on your person a cellphone that evidently belongs to Ms. Hersh. Can you explain that?"

"Lilly Hersh is a San Francisco journalist. I told the Chief I thought she'd been taken."

"You saw it happen?"

"No."

"Then how would you know?"

"She called her own cell from somewhere, the number wasn't logged. I believe she was being made to speak under duress."

"Ms. Hersh was helping you? How many women are you going to tie up in this?"

"She was following leads independently of me."

"Who do you think took her?" said Stowe.

"I don't know."

"Doesn't look good, Mr. Blake. Why do you have her cellphone? Why are there pictures on it, pictures of a tombstone that reads *Karen Wiley*?"

"Listen to me," said Blake. "Just find Karen. She's in serious danger."

"You said that last night."

"And . . .?"

"And she wasn't at the motel you gave us," said Vasco. "We don't know where she's gone. We need the information she helped you to steal."

"What, she checked out?"

"No, she'd upped and left. Put the money for the room on top of the TV."

"Then, *Christ*, find my car, she must have taken it. It's a silver LR3, there aren't that many around. The registration is . . ."

"You gave us this last night."

"And?"

Vasco and Stowe looked at one another.

"Your gun carries an FBI serial number," said Stowe. "We'd rather you explained *that*."

Blake sighed, hung his head. "Not right now."

"We have time." Stowe folded her arms, flicked back her hair.

"I just took the *frame*," said Blake, wearily. "It's a composite of two guns. I had written permission."

"And you have that permission here today?"

"You know damn well that I do not. I also told you to contact Dr. Arnold Lau in DC. Did you?"

They were staring at him through the bars. Flat, dry stares. No, then.

"Sleep well last night?" said Blake, beginning to lose his temper. "Did you both sleep *soundly*?"

"Mr. Blake . . ."

"Call your office. Don't hesitate. Get Salt Lake to talk to Washington. Get your SAC."

"You don't tell us what to do."

He was losing them. "No, Agent Stowe, you listen. Keep me in here, someone will post bail eventually. But don't waste time asking me useless questions. I'll say it again—you're looking for a white adult male, physically strong. Despite this, he might have some kind of disability. He might be missing a limb, or an ear, or a hand, or maybe have a prosthetic. It's his MO, there's some link there; he took the girl's hand, he took a part of her ear, he removed the legs of the cat in the trailer park. I think he killed Don Keynes and stashed the body, but at some stage he took one of *his* hands as well, slapped the dead man's prints on the mobile home to throw a false trail. He probably has a basement within a half-hour radius of the turning to The Church of the Final Days. That doesn't even quite cover Canaan, so get people out there."

"I'd like to ask you about this church," said Vasco.

"What, is this your first day? Just find Karen Wiley."

"She's in danger?" Stowe was listening to him now.

"Without protection, she's going to die."

"How do you know?"

"Don't you get it, Agent Stowe? Did you read the letters? Karen Wiley was what he wanted all along, and now she's out there unprotected. Finding her is the way to catch this man before he butchers Katy Trueblood to death."

"Sir," said Vasco, "step back from the bars."

"And Karen is in harm's way because, in the best interest of that child, I put her there."

It was a little past eight-fifteen in the morning when Ella pulled into the quiet parking lot of a white, neatly maintained chapel, a little to the north and the east of town: the First and Second Wards of the Church of Jesus Christ of Latter Day Saints.

Ella's local church. And, three weeks earlier, the place of her baptism.

However else Milton was improving himself, he hadn't yet learned to park his car like a Christian; the fat tires of his orange Camaro were straddled well over two spaces. Ella remembered Milt's ride well, a real beaut: an RS/SS 396 with a powerglide and

10-bolt single drive, a burnt-out Indy 500 pace car that Milton had crossed half a dozen states to pick up.

Not that I'd be impressed by such a thing now, Ella thought, pushing down the lock of her rusting '98 coupe with her thumb because the remote keyless system was temperamental.

The doors of the chapel were open but the lights were off; Ella could see the glow of a small window of stained glass at the far end. It was barely any cooler inside the church, and Ella's sweater was sticking to the back of her neck before she even made it across the threshold.

She spotted his skinny shadow immediately; Milt had positioned himself on the front pew. Ella didn't hesitate, strode down the aisle, and her eyes on the altar were wary. She paused a little where his peripheral vision would pick her up, bowed her head respectfully.

"Ella McCullers," said Milton Trueblood. "Who says you don't get what you pray for?"

"Watch yourself, mister," she said. "Don't you dare blaspheme in this building."

"But you're here, aren't you? And I've been asking for you. I mean, really asking."

Ella looked around, squinted into the dark corners of the chapel. "Who let you in?"

"Man named Harris," said Milton. "Lives across the road. Man, does everyone regular to this church talk so damn much?"

"He was helpful, huh?"

"He can't help me like you can."

"And how's that, Milton?"

"I've been thinking, Ella. About all the things you been tellin' me. You wanna sit down?"

Ella positioned herself next to him, the pew creaking, and she took the opportunity to size him up. Yup, Milt had moved on again, even from the day when he'd appeared outside the health clinic; he'd ditched the curious suit, was back to a more suitable jeans and

T-shirt combo, all clean on. He'd even remembered how to shave, and his eyes were clearer than Ella had ever seen them.

"I'm sorry . . ." he began to say.

"And you're forgiven," she said, cutting him off.

"I didn't say nothin' yet."

"Well, whichever part you were about to apologize to me for, whichever step of the program you're on now, you're forgiven. I've been there myself, Milt. Let's see what you do next, that's what you'll be judged on; by me, God, everyone else. I don't need a laundry list of your screw-ups right now, not with your daughter missing."

Milt sighed, took this in. "You always say the right things," he said. "How do you always know what to say?" She wasn't sure that she'd ever seen him smile before, and Ella found herself staring into the eyes of a whole new person. His face was so cheeky and his features so small, it was hard not to smile back.

"Lord, you're still so beautiful," he said, and suddenly reached out with a steady finger, dared to move one of her bangs back from her forehead. "I really cared for you, you know. I treated you so badly, but we shared something that I'll never forget."

"Milton," she said, cringing. "I don't wear make-up and I smell like the dachshund who shares my bed."

"Is there anything I can do for you, Ella? Anything? I mean it. No side, no angle. I could volunteer at the station, I could . . . "

"Just tell me something. Mandy says you still have trouble sleeping."

Milt seemed surprised at the question. "I . . . I hardly sleep," he said. "I can't let myself."

"Because of the dreams?"

"The nightmares. I get scared."

"Scared to go to sleep?"

He nodded.

"Do you still see . . . you know . . ."

"The devil?"

"Right."

"He's everywhere," said Milt, whispering now. "And, you know, I don't even *have* to be asleep anymore. I swear, I see him when I close my eyes. He's after me because I abandoned God when I let Katy go."

Ella's eyes circled the chapel. "And you think you'll find the answers in here?"

"Yes," he said. "I mean, where else would I find salvation? What else can I *do*?"

She reached into the shallow pocket of her sweatpants and pulled out Holly's folded drawing, Milt watching carefully. When she'd finished opening it out, he stared for a long time at the picture his daughter had drawn.

"Is this him?" said Ella. "Is this the devil you see every night?"

Milton nodded, jaw slack. "But how did you . . . *how* do you . . ."

"Because, Milt, this isn't the devil. This is a man, and that's all he is. And I think that you—of all people—might hold the key to catching him."

This is it.

This is where the letters come from.

Karen Wiley sat behind the wheel of Blake's Land Rover and eyed the small, ranch-style home. It was remote, like most places out here, but surprisingly well kept and tidy; unexpected azaleas thriving in kitsch swan-shaped plant pots on the front lawn. There were a couple of cars on the driveway, and perhaps, at the back, a fire was lit; some smoke was rising.

The address had been no trouble to find—the only thing Karen couldn't get from the stolen file was a name—and when she stopped off at the post office in tiny La Sal for directions and soda, the information was just to "keep on driving, you can't miss it."

So Karen found herself approximately fifty miles south-east of Canaan, on Route 46 towards Colorado, and even Blake would have struggled to sneak up on this property; there were views in all directions, spectacular ones at that.

Let's finish this now.

Not thirty seconds after she'd pulled up, she stepped down from the Land Rover. The dull, oppressive heat that signaled the approaching storm had caused Karen to ditch her jacket, and the tank-top and jeans combo she wore somehow complemented the invulnerable, mercenary feeling she'd had since that morning. It wasn't supposed to be vigilantism; she simply believed the police probably wanted to arrest her as they had Egan, while Lilly and Katy would be left to die, or worse.

It was a little past noon, but a standard lamp was on in the front room. Karen stepped up onto the porch and banged on the screen door with one flat hand.

The other hand was in her bag, on the 9mm P11 she'd found in the glove compartment; another cannon in Blake's arsenal, albeit a small one.

Karen banged again, the screen door rattling in its frame.

"Hold *on*," said a heavily accented female voice from within, and Karen was left to wonder for a little while longer.

When the mesh curtain behind the door was finally pulled, Karen was surprised to find herself face to face with a short Hispanic woman in her late fifties. She was wearing an apron and wiping her hands on a dishcloth.

"Yes?" she said.

"I'm sorry," said Karen, further confused by the smell of fried peppers wafting out to her. "Do you live here? I mean, is this your house?"

"Of course," said the woman, eyeing Karen's bare shoulders.

Karen hadn't come this far to be deterred. "Have you recently used a remailing service in Canaan?"

The woman didn't look surprised. "Are you the police?"

Karen shook her head.

"Then who wants to know?"

"My name is Karen Wiley. The remailing service belongs to a man named Howard Freed. I believe someone at this address asked him to forward letters to me. Letters of a disturbing nature."

The woman glanced up the road. "That remailing service was broken into last night."

"How do you know?"

"They informed the customers." The woman spent a long moment scrutinizing Karen's face. Satisfied, her attitude lightened. "My name is Pilar," she said. "I'm glad you're here, Karen Wiley. I'd invite you in, but I have my sons for lunch and we're sitting down. Besides, this won't take long."

"Excuse me?"

"This won't take long. Then you'll want to be on your way, I'm sure."

"What won't take long?"

"What I have to tell you. You're expected, Karen Wiley."

"Expected? I don't understand."

"I sent the letters, but I didn't write them," said Pilar. "I don't know what they said, I'm sorry if they were disturbing. I don't even know if Zhenya wrote them, but she wanted me to send them to you."

"Zhenya?"

The woman shrugged. "She could have sent them direct from the hospital, but you don't argue with Zhenya. I wasn't to know if you'd even show up, if there even *was* a Karen Wiley. That poor woman is crazy in the head."

Karen was totally bewildered. She had been primed for a struggle, for a showdown, not for a chatty and impatient Mexican lady who spoke in riddles. "Who's Zhenya?" she said.

"No, you listen," said Pilar, amenably. "I'm telling you all I know, because that's what I promised to Zhenya. Then, off you go, and good luck to you. I'm a cleaner, I work the laundry at the Mount Peale Sanatorium."

"A private hospital?"

"Mount Peale. You know it?"

"No," said Karen.

"If you came from the La Sal junction then you passed the hospital turning, there's a sign to look for." She gestured at the Land Rover. "Big car like yours, you'll have no trouble with the road; two miles, all uphill. There's a patient there, name of Zhenya."

Karen played along; she had no choice. "Does Zhenya have a last name?"

Pilar shrugged. "Of course. But the long-term patients, the last names drop away. Anyway, everyone knows Zhenya. Probably two months ago, she ask me would I mail some letters for her? I say sure. It isn't my job, but I'll drop them in the mail. She says *no*. It was the most excited I ever saw her. She says I have to do it a certain way. I have to send them through Canaan, and on certain dates. It all gets spelled out real clear. I have to send them to Karen Wiley in San Francisco."

"To me."

"Well, I'm not sure about sending out mail for a patient, but I want to help her out. I did ask who is this person I'm sending letters to, but Zhenya says she won't tell me. And then I said *why* won't you tell me, but Zhenya, you don't ask her too many questions. There's a lot of money paid for her to stay there, so I did as I was told. They're only letters."

They're only letters.

"You have anymore?" said Karen.

"No," said Pilar. "I sent the last one a while ago, there are no more. She even made me write instructions down so I wouldn't forget: where to send them, how to send them."

"You had instructions?"

"I threw them out. My job is done, except for one thing."

"What's that?"

"Well," said Pilar, her eyes bright. "Zhenya said that someday soon, you, or someone else, might turn up at my door. Someone asking about the letters, perhaps the police. She said they might not, but then they might. I thought she was joking, or was taking a bad turn like she sometimes does. But I always take the patients seriously, someone has to. The nurses, they can be cold. But this was the bit I was least happy about, because no one likes strangers at their door." Pilar folded her arms, as though the conversation was over. "You're to go up there, and to see Zhenya. That's what I was told to say and I've said it, done my part."

"If she wanted to see me, why didn't she just ask?" said Karen. She had so many questions, she didn't know where to start.

Pilar seemed impatient, as though it all made perfect sense. "What did I say? That's all the facts I have. Just do that poor woman a favor, go see her. She obviously wants company."

"What kind of hospital is it?"

Pilar sighed at this continued display of ignorance. "Psychiatric," she said. "A secure facility. But they'll let you in to see Zhenya, they're probably expecting you. She never usually talks, and she couldn't possibly be a threat to anyone."

"Why not?"

"It's impossible. I've been talking to her for years."

"But why?" said Karen, and this seemed critical. "Why is it impossible for Zhenya to be a threat? Why is she in a secure facility?"

Before the woman could answer, a small boy with long hair appeared from the shadows and hugged Pilar around the waist. He looked up at Karen with brown eyes and stuck a thumb into his mouth.

"Siéntese, Antonio," said Pilar, patting his behind and pushing him away. "My grandson," she said, a trace of apology in her eyes. "Excuse me, Karen Wiley, I guess he wants his food."

Blake, having convinced Vasco and Stowe and the officers on duty that he was neither insane nor a threat, was permitted special dispensation with the telephone when Arnold Lau finally called the station long-distance. He was shown into a storage space that probably doubled as an interrogation room, and it had less natural light than his cell, though it was private and he wasn't handcuffed. Even so, Officer Kyle locked the door, nodding apologetically as he left.

The phone was old-fashioned, the receiver chunky green plastic, and it was perched on the edge of the desk. Blake followed the extension cord with his eyes, it ran out under the door to a port in the corridor; there wasn't alot of slack there.

"Lau," said Blake, sitting on the folding chair.

"You don't think I have enough to contend with?" Lau sounded hassled; wherever he was, there was alot of background noise. "Now I'm answering questions about you."

"Just like old times."

"Hold on, I have to sign something."

Blake waited, studying fingertips still stained with ink from his processing after the arrest the night before. He pictured Lau somewhere in the Hoover Building, maybe taking receipt of a document from an eager young intern.

"I asked you to consult if you were interested," said Lau's voice, eventually. "That's all we're supposed to do. I asked you to bring your experience to the girl."

"Holly."

"Right, the one who wouldn't talk. You caught Ernst Richter based on testimony from his preschool daughter."

"Eighty-seven."

"This isn't a trip down memory lane. Did you even bother to meet with Holly?"

"It isn't the strongest lead."

"You're a hell of an investigator, Egan, but I have to distance myself from this. Stop mentioning my name to people."

"I work for you."

"It was never like that," said Lau. It sounded as though he'd moved into a quieter space. "Even if I knew the new Attorney General, you think I'd be putting in a request for some kind of favor for you? Over this tawdry, useless mess? We don't have the clout we once had. People didn't want you in The Group for this exact reason, your goddamn ego."

"*The Group*. There's a concept I haven't heard in an age."

"You won't be hearing it again. You're terminated."

"I got results. I always get results."

"You're impetuous and you're forever trying to use us to get back on the map. I thought you'd mellow in your old age."

"Officially, I *am* retired."

"There's an Agent DeMedici in San Francisco," said Lau. "Karen Wiley skipped her appointment with him yesterday morning. Now I hear she's out there with you, but you don't know where she is. You withheld evidence, the cellphone belonging to the journalist. You broke into private property. And because of your bungles, now the crucial information is missing."

"What about the Freed family? Do they know their client?"

"A cash account, no name, only—maybe—an address. Which an agent there tells me the Freed family can't remember, nor should they be expected to. That's why people keep information in files. Files you lost." Lau sounded angry as Blake had ever heard him.

"Can I speak?" said Blake.

"Goddamn it, Egan. You're a dinosaur. Cloak and dagger is over. You promised me transparency. You're like *The Lone Ranger* out there."

"No," said Blake, talking quickly. "This is not a case best handled by the Bureau, your instinct to call me was right. They've sent two kids down here to investigate, Vasco and Stowe, they're recruiting twelve-year-olds in Salt Lake City. Talk about transparency—I've given them everything I have, and they're still looking for Don Keynes."

"They follow orders. The real investigation is in San Francisco."

"I don't think so," said Blake, deepening his voice for emphasis. "He's *here*, Lau, I can smell it. You trample over these small towns with inexperienced agents flashing badges, he'll slide right under the surface and he'll take that child with him. You've got all the facts, but you're not on the ground here. You'd know it if you were, your instinct is as good as mine. He's close."

"Was it Karen Wiley, Egan? Was that it? Is that who you're trying to impress? She's a real looker, I've heard. Should I remind you why you don't teach at Quantico anymore?"

"Don't be ridiculous."

"Personal glory, Egan, your priorities have always been skewed. You wanted to make the catch on your own. Now you'll have some time in a cell to reflect."

Lau sounded tired, and Blake, in dirty clothes and badly needing a shower, permitted himself a grim smile. He'd made mistakes, he knew it, borne of the old arrogance, and now there was a nagging, crawling fear in his belly that this one last case had been too much, had run away from him, that complacency and old age had finally let him down. But he was never far wrong when it came to the profiling, and, based on past results, he was aware his superiors couldn't refuse to hear his opinions. Blake knew he was a rogue, just as he knew he had a problem with authority, evidenced by the murky circumstances that screwed up part of his adolescence and, far later, saw him expelled from law-enforcement proper in the first place.

Despite this patchy record, when Dr. Lau, a highly decorated and well-connected consultant, was asked to "retire" from his official duties at the FBI and set up a covert countrywide network of similarly marginalized experts with varying but unquestioned talents, Egan Blake had been at the top of his list. Blake had been flattered, but it turned out he only received a half-dozen calls during his tenure, never enough to disrupt his private agency business, and he'd only met one other member of the cell that Lau had dubbed

The Group. Tweeny McDonald may have been a blasted, mad-eyed old woman who claimed to work as a psychic-to-the-stars in the San Fernando Valley, but she had managed to extract a full confession—in English—from an inscrutable Eastern European serial rapist, a language that the suspect allegedly couldn't speak.

It was cases like this that fascinated Blake, seemingly unsolvable murders, patchy, incomplete forensics that defied logic, bizarre ritualistic killings that were the perfect foil for his arcane knowledge and analytical style. But this time he hadn't been granted any temporary credentials, hadn't been told to liaise with a field agent, had, in fact, received specific instruction *not* to wade into the vagaries of the case, especially given his secondary, personal connection to Karen Wiley. But that was sometimes how it went; an initial meeting, the emergence of unlikely leads, any amount of contrivance, and besides, Blake demanded a degree of autonomy in his work, it was practically expected of him. This was only the second time his actions had got him arrested, though . . .

"Why San Francisco?" said Blake. "You're looking into the clients from Karen's private practice? I tried that, there's nothing there."

"You only have one half of this case," said Lau, with another big sigh. "If you'd bothered to check in, you wouldn't still be skulking around in the middle of nowhere."

Blake felt his flesh creep. "Another hand in the mail?"

"No. He attacked Dave Wiley."

"The husband?"

"In a downtown hotel."

"And he let him go?"

"He'll live, but he got pretty shaken. Now there are agents on the residence of the parents—that's where the daughter is holing up. Karen would be protected too, but for this."

"You get a description?"

"Artist's sketch," said Lau. "Nothing very distinctive. But that isn't the most mind-boggling thing."

"Oh?"

"The lab has all the evidence in one place now; Karen's letters, the hand in the box. They typed the blood—you know, procedure. But the blood smeared on the bottom of letter four, one of the early ones that presumably came through the remailing service, didn't match the hand."

"There was blood on letter four? And it *isn't* Katy's?"

"Right. It belongs to someone else. And it can't belong to the journalist because the letter was sent before she was taken."

"Ten days before she was taken," said Blake.

"Wrong," said Lau. "You ready for this? *Thirty years* before she was taken."

"What?"

"I didn't believe it either," said Lau. "But the test results are unequivocal. Letters one through six were all written thirty years ago, or thereabouts."

Blake was astounded. "That's impossible."

"We got it from the dried blood on letter four, we got it from the ink used, the paper . . ."

"Which means . . ."

"Right. Every letter sent to Karen Wiley is practically an antique."

"I don't understand," said Blake. "I saw the second letter with my own eyes. I touched it."

"They look almost new because they must have been handled with kid gloves for all this time. Someone took extreme care. Only the envelopes were manufactured this century. I mean, we got a slew of partial prints, but nothing that matches up on the database."

Blake was silent.

"Egan? You have any idea what this means?"

"Perhaps," said Blake, and the whites of his eyes seemed to glow in the darkness. He was thinking of James Earl LaGrande and The Church of the Final Days.

*

"Hello Lillian," said Jon Peterson, into the darkness.

Lilly came to, found her face stuck to the concrete floor by strands of snot and blood. Since he had taken the pliers to her face, her mouth and nose wouldn't stop leaking.

Got your nose! Where is it now? Can you see it?

She couldn't see much of anything, but she didn't feel too much pain either, probably due to the cocktail of drugs he'd been forcing into her, just an interminable itching where Peterson was gradually taking apart her features. Jon knew he didn't have the length of time he'd had with Katy, so he had played with her almost constantly in the first few hours since she'd woken up in the basement, half a broken needle in her arm the evidence of how he got her there without a fight. Asides from his insanity, he was angry, Lilly knew.

Angry because she wasn't Karen, for some reason.

I'd like to speak with you, Chip . . .

Yet Lilly knew some things based on instinct. She thought she was still in the desert. She was pretty sure she hadn't been transported very far. And she'd experienced her attacker growing less coherent and more violent with each hour, particularly when he made her speak into the phone, to Blake, to Karen, and later again, when she couldn't see who she was talking to. He sounded calm now, though. It must have been at least twelve hours since she'd last heard those measured tones, the longest time she'd been left on her own, and a plan was forming.

"They have your *cellphone*," said Peterson, as though it was a dirty word. "That was how I was planning to bring Karen to us, since you fucked up my other plan. That won't happen now."

"Gnnn," said Lilly, shifting position to test the strength in her battered muscles. She exaggerated the extent of her injuries, in case he could see in the pitch black.

"So I was wondering. Did you have any other suggestion? For how I can get Karen Wiley?"

Lilly reserved her strength.

"I thought not," said Peterson. "Guess that means you've reached the end of your usefulness. Sometimes it feels more fun to let people go, it fucks with their heads. You should have seen Dave Wiley—he peed like an incontinent puppy. Not so much with you, I'm guessing. You want to *live*."

He flipped on the lights.

Lilly was naked, spread-eagled in the center of the floor. Her small white body was covered in bruises, but was basically unharmed. Her face, however, looked like a jammy mask that was slipping.

"All these books," said Peterson, looking around.

Lilly knew all about the phone books; the walls were lined with them, there were even more in freestanding cases. She'd had glimpses into other basement rooms that were equally crammed. Earlier on, when she was still chained to the chair, he'd ranted insensibly about the phone books, about how much time they'd caused him to waste, then he tore pages out and tried to feed them to her until she sicked up mush that made her throat bleed and she passed out again.

"And to think," he said, "I could have put a pool table down here."

Somehow, Lilly still had vision in one eye. Her feet and hands were chained to rings that were bolted into the floor, but the one on her right hand had some slippage, made greasy with blood and sweat. With one hand free, she was pretty sure she could remove the pins that held the other old-fashioned cuff.

Peterson jerked his thumb in the direction of the corner. "Has *she* said much while I've been away? She seems very quiet."

Katy Trueblood, equally naked bar a sheet covering her from the knees down, was prone on what looked like an embalming table. Where he'd removed her hand, the bloody stump was elevated by more chains. There were bandages and a tourniquet, but the side of her body had been stained an ungodly yellow from the iodine he'd thrown about, was criss-crossed with green-blue veins. There were tubes and devices, including an oxygen tank and a plasma bag filled with Lilly's own extracted blood. It looked as though Katy was caught in the cradle of an infernal machine.

The girl was silent, motionless, had been since Lilly arrived, though there'd been times when he hadn't kept them in the same room.

"Well?" said Peterson to Lilly.

"She's *dead*," said Lilly, spitting out a little more blood. He wasn't looking in Lilly's direction, so she yanked down on her hand, ignoring the pain. The chain was already tight, it didn't make much noise.

A little more . . .

"Do you know what a hemicorporectomy is?" said Peterson. Lilly couldn't see him now, he'd moved into another room, the room that passed for his workshop. With a final effort, she heaved at the chain, not caring how much noise it made.

"I had to look it up on Wikipedia," he said, calling through. "Can you imagine that? Translumbar amputation, where you amputate a person at the waist. I used to love the magic trick where the woman got sawed in half. We take away legs, genitalia, urinary system, pelvis, anus and rectum. If you want to try and keep a person alive then you have to do it in two stages, and it'll take a hellish long time. You can understand how I'll be glad of the company."

One of the leg shackles was sticky, Lilly's fingers quivering, but it came good in the end. She glanced up; he was still in the other room.

Lilly stood as rapidly as her shaking legs would allow, had to fight dizziness, nausea. Then she was moving.

Peterson's voice, "Regrettable, I know, and invariably terminal, though I'll try my best. But there's a sickness here that needs cutting out, and I can always find other little girls to mail to Karen Wiley."

Lilly walked forward, each step agony, like running in a bad dream. There were stairs, wooden stairs.

RUN . . .

Peterson appeared in the doorway behind her wearing surgical greens with a white mask across his mouth. He looked like someone going to a costume party as an insane dentist. There was a large curved blade in his right hand, and he was pushing a rattling trolley full of vials and syringes and home-made medical tools.

"What's wrong?" he said to Lilly's naked back as she dragged herself up the basement stairs. "It wasn't like I was going to operate on *you*."

Sixteen

The Mount Peale Sanatorium was not hard to find.

Just as Pilar had said, there was an exit on the road back to the 192, freshly painted gold lettering on an arrow-shaped sign. But the track was not well maintained, and as it pushed higher, the trees began to drop away, and the great shadowy hump of Mount Peale itself rose through the windshield to dominate the vista.

In winter they must be all but cut-off, thought Karen, relishing the protection of her vehicle. It took ten minutes to cover the three or more miles, though it felt far farther, and Karen felt a genuine sense of relief as the building neared.

The sanatorium and surrounding outbuildings were fairly small, certainly smaller close up than they had seemed from a distance, probably because they were the only structures for miles around. It had a tidy, alpine quality, two wings stretching out behind an attractive facade. The track switched to the smooth blacktop of what felt like a freshly laid parking lot, and Karen pulled in behind a row of neatly planted aspens, foliage turning yellow in the season.

It was quiet, but still hot, despite the increase in altitude. There was no one around, only a couple of other cars to indicate any life was present. When Karen got to the entrance, she identified no bell or buzzer, just a neat plaque, but the double doors were unlocked.

Karen took a deep breath, pushed through.

She found herself in a large and empty hallway that presumably passed for a reception. The juxtaposition was startling; the gravel under her boots was replaced by spotless black and white tiles, and the oppressive, storm-threatening atmosphere outside was vanquished by silent air-conditioning, powerful enough to make Karen shiver and rub her bare arms. Most striking of all was the opulence of the interior. Although there was a stark, faux-Victorian quality to the whitewashed walls and exposed pipes, there was an expensive finish, from the teak counter over which she could see into a richly furnished office, to the huge, framed Rorschach ink-blots that lined the corridors leading to the left and right.

Certainly a private hospital, thought Karen, studying Plate IV behind a single, well-polished pane of glass, almost as tall as she was.

"Can I help you?"

Karen spun around. There was a small man in a spotless white coat, maybe four or five inches shorter than she was, with a head of thick silver-gray hair. He'd been in the office all along. Karen was surprised; the whole building had given the illusion of being deserted.

"I'm Karen Wiley," said Karen, feeling rather like Alice in Wonderland.

"Dr. Anton Gillespie," he said, staring in a way that made her feel both self-conscious and severely underdressed. "Are you looking for the trail?"

"Excuse me?"

"The old mining road. You *are* a hiker, no?"

"I'm here to speak with Zhenya," said Karen, pronouncing it exactly as Pilar had done. "Is she a resident here?"

Dr. Gillespie chuckled at his error. It was a low, gracious sound. "Forgive me," he said, and emerged from the office through a door that Karen hadn't spotted. "We share the trail with the hikers. I don't know if they think we're a motel, a ranger-station or what, but anyone who works here becomes adept at giving directions. Second nature, in fact." He gestured at the framed ink-blot test. "I see Plate IV caught your eye."

What is this, a test now? Karen was primed for anything. "I'm sure the APA would be delighted to see you're respecting the ethics of assessment security."

Dr. Gillespie laughed again. "Rorschach was a fool, of course. One might as well perform projective tests using oil stains on the highway."

"Could be a little more dangerous that way," said Karen.

"Zhenya may be sleeping," said Dr. Gillespie. "Shall I wake her?"

"Forgive me, Doctor. Do you know what this is about? Why I'm here?"

Gillespie shook his head.

"But you'll just let me in to see her? Without question?"

It was his turn to look surprised. "Is there some reason why I shouldn't?"

"Isn't she in a secure ward?"

"All of our wards are secure," he said. "We have CCTV, you'll be under remote supervision, and despite appearances, we are very well staffed. *Ms. Wiley*, was it?"

"Yes."

"I don't know what you know, Ms. Wiley, but we don't prescribe a cure at Mount Peale. Few here have been involuntarily committed. I'm charged with maintaining quality of life for individuals who require specialist care in a protected environment, and I take my job very seriously. I'm happy to ask Zhenya if she would like to speak to you. If she refuses, I'll have to ask you to leave. But I'm very happy to ask."

"Thank you," said Karen, even more bewildered.

"Are you expected?" he said.

"Yes," said Karen, because it was the only answer she could think of. Dr. Gillespie nodded, started to walk away.

"Wait," said Karen, feeling rising pangs of desperation, or maybe fear. Her voice seemed loud in the collegiate stillness, and, to her own ears, almost unhinged.

Gillespie turned, raised his eyebrows politely.

"Zhenya," she said. "Can I ask you some questions first, Doctor? You see, I'm not . . ."

She fell quiet when the psychiatrist raised a finger to his lips; he looked disappointed in her. "Discretion," he said. "Discretion, Ms. Wiley, one of our other watchwords. That's why the hikers can get so infuriating. Could you wait here please?"

With that, he turned and disappeared down one of the empty checkerboard corridors, and the stacked heels on his wing-tips clickety-clacked all the way.

The door closed behind her with the quiet sound of a latch slipping back into place.

"Hello?" said Karen, into the silence. The figure on the bed was in shadow.

"*Karen Wiley.*" A thin voice, but commanding.

"Zhenya?" said Karen.

"You're very pretty," said the voice. "If you want, you can let in some light."

This felt like an instruction. Karen picked her way through the room to a big window, pulled the cord to raise some Venetian blinds. Zhenya's room was a corner suite, up a flight of stairs, and the prospect over the forests and La Sal range was breathtaking. Karen gazed at her Land Rover in the parking lot with a vague sense of unease, wondered if the figure on the bed had watched her arrival.

"Now," said Zhenya. "Where to begin?"

Karen turned back around, and time seemed to stop.

Particles of energy flowed towards the figure on the bed like light through a spinning crystal, but slowly, as though Karen could almost distinguish individual atoms. It wasn't just that Zhenya had no arms or legs, though the oddity of her appearance might have had something to do with the effect. No, it was the powerful presence of this person, and of what she might mean, of the knowledge she held.

Journey's end, thought Karen. *The source of the letters.*

The face was remarkable, alabaster white and completely unlined, with huge ice-blue eyes that swiveled in a small, perfectly structured skull. Her hair was blonde, thick and shiny, and framed the face on the pillow. Paralysis was not one of Zhenya's conditions, but she certainly gave the impression, because her stillness was so complete. It was as if she'd lain there forever, a face floating above a torso.

Time means nothing to me, the eyes seemed to say to Karen. *Until now, maybe.*

Yet there was a coiled energy as well, as though she might be capable of devastating movement, irrespective of such severe disability. Karen couldn't help but stare at the stumps protruding from the short trunk of body, at the criss-crosses of pale pink, almost translucent scars that congregated in a lumpy tangle of long-healed tissue, just below the shoulders. There was a fat indent there, like a swelling around a dimple, as though her body had sucked in the arm rather than had it amputated. Karen didn't feel horror or displeasure, just ignorant wonder, and above all, fascination.

She couldn't see the remains of Zhenya's legs, the woman was clad in a sleeveless kimono of red silk that served to enhance the paleness of her skin. This garment tapered down to the spotless white sheets like splattered blood.

She looks like a ghost, the way that red silk trails. As if she could rise up off this bed and haunt these corridors, the dress flowing behind her. And not as some ethereal, see-through entity, but a spirit made of flesh and blood and bone.

What would you do if you had a power like that? Would you use it for good, or for . . .

"Please, stare as long as you want," said Zhenya. "I have more time than you do."

"I'm . . . I'm sorry," said Karen.

"I have prosthetics, I simply choose not to use them. I can walk, I choose not to. I know who I am and what I am. Can you say the same for yourself?"

Zhenya's lips were painted as red as her dress, and they barely moved as she spoke. Perhaps she was a few years older than Karen, but it was hard to tell, there was something almost artificial about her remarkable, devastating beauty. Irrationally, Karen thought of a ventriloquist's dummy, or something from science fiction; synthetic flesh stretched over cogs and springs and metal.

"I'm learning," said Karen, hating her own imagination, her need to filter Zhenya's appearance through layers of cultural reference as though she represented something unacceptable.

"I neither speak for nor represent the legions of people similarly afflicted," said Zhenya. "And there *are* legions. Many lead full, happy lives. I read on the net of a climber who was caught in a snowstorm, lost his four limbs from frostbite. Only a few years later, with willpower and the wonders of medical science, he ran the Boston marathon. Does that inspire you?"

"I think so," said Karen.

"I'm pleased for him, but I wouldn't trade places. He makes my condition acceptable. No disrespect to the man, just disrespect to the appetite of a public demanding to be fed such things a certain way. Meningitis can take arms and legs; flesh-eating bacteria. War, of course. Whole countries full of limbless people. We're so flooded in America with the imaginary horrors, far beyond *this*, of course. Books, movies, TV. We're confused by reports of reality rather than reality itself, of that which gets warped according to the whim of this bizarre media. Then we wonder why we get confused upon finding that real horror disgusts rather than stimulates. Are you disgusted by me?"

"A little bit," said Karen, believing total honesty was the way forward. "I mean, not by *you*, but . . . I don't know. There are worse things." She tailed off, feeling pathetic.

"Quite right," said Zhenya. "And besides, I chose to present this way. When Dr. Gillespie told me you were here, I wanted to be gawped at. With my prosthetics, with crutches, perhaps I could have walked to the door and opened it. But what I am will press home the message to you, as if you didn't know how serious this was already." The eyes opened wide at Karen, who got the glimpse of a soul driven cold. "But perhaps you know it too, I can see something in your face."

"I've known trouble," said Karen, thinking of Sammie, and of memories so long suppressed that they seemed new, recharged, with fresh power to harm. "Haven't we all?"

"Yes," said Zhenya. "And now that you're here, the extent of my ambition exists within these four walls."

"Your ambition was to bring me here? To talk to me?"

"No. Before you walked through the door, I had no ambition. I'm waiting to die, though I wait it out in comfort, as you see. Some would call that mental illness. I don't care."

"If you wanted to meet me, why not contact me direct? Why use the remailing service? Why send cryptic letters? Why did you not just tell me who you are? Where you are?"

"You're not listening, Karen Wiley. I didn't want to see you. But you're here now, and it means I can talk to you. And now that I see your face, I'm glad of the opportunity to help, to enlighten. You seem like a good person. Perhaps I can clear a few things up. It all must have been very confusing, the letters on the mat."

"That's putting it mildly."

"Do you have things in your life to live for?"

"Yes."

"Then listen to what I have to say and listen carefully. I can't save myself, but I can save you. Outside of my darkest moments, I wouldn't wish my condition on anyone else."

"What do you mean? Someone wants to do this to me? To remove my arms and legs? Is that what all this is about?"

"I don't know for sure," said Zhenya, her eyes flashing. "He's capable of anything. Has he done it to the little girl yet? He'll probably start with the hands. After that, I can't tell you."

"Who? Has *who* done it?"

"Jonny."

"Jonny?"

"My brother."

"Our earliest childhood was relatively normal," said Zhenya, once Karen was sitting. "I had my legs and arms until I was ten, and, up until then, I knew little but contentment. Our father was a doctor of medicine, and we came to Canaan in about 1967. There wasn't much there then, less than there is now, though there was a pretty rich seam of potash nearby, not to mention the uranium, and the Canyonlands have always had some draw for tourists. Our family was from Fayette, New York, and Father was a devout Mormon, though I knew he had his doubts about the politics of the mainstream faith. But that wasn't why we moved."

Karen shifted a little in the high-backed chair. Zhenya had resisted any urge to speak quickly, to get the information out in a hurry, about Katy, about Lilly, and Karen realized if she was to learn anything at all, she was going to have to be patient. "No?" she said.

"Father thought he had found a way to reconcile his science and his religion, and he could achieve it by emigrating west. Not in a tripped-out 'at-peace-with-yourself' kind of way, but with a real bricks-and-mortar idea, a way of helping people. He bought a plot of land in an area outside of Canaan called The Heights, laid the foundations for a residential center of religious advancement. Kind of a back-to-basics retreat for the soul, where he could also flex his muscles as a practitioner. I think he saw himself as a leader, but he was always too weak-willed, too suggestible.

"His heart was pure, but they were beset by difficulty. There wasn't the infrastructure there is now, and after a couple of years there was just a ragtag collection of wooden cabins; nothing remains today. We almost lost everyone one winter, and lines of supply were terrible. I understand The Heights has become a wealthy mini-suburb now—at least wealthy for the town. But Father was devout, he persevered, and he began to make a real go of things.

"My family has money, Karen. Not old money, but good money, grafted from a desire to help people and to contribute to a community. More successful than his religious enterprise was the house he built back in Canaan, one of the first real mansions there, though it'll probably look small by today's standards. Big old wraparound porch, like a replica of our house back east. Those were good memories; I must have been nine, Jonny was ten, and Mother's sickness wasn't too bad yet. We were easily the smartest kids in the local school, and when we weren't studying we were out in the wilderness, camping, building fires, chasing down the wildlife. Don't you think Canaan is beautiful?"

Zhenya wasn't looking at Karen, she'd been staring at the ceiling for the last five minutes.

How many years must she have spent staring at this ceiling?

Karen took the opportunity to scan the room, found herself gazing into a small closed-circuit television camera, mounted unobtrusively in the corner. This was presumably the surveillance that Dr. Gillespie had mentioned earlier.

Karen wondered if it had the facility to record sound.

"I've never been to Utah before," said Karen, carefully. "My parents would call it flyover country. But it *is* beautiful, I've never seen anything like it."

"You should have met my brother then," said Zhenya. "I can't excuse what he's doing now, but people are not born evil, I truly believe that. Jonny was such a happy boy; creative, disciplined, gifted with his hands."

"They let you explore the desert on your own? At that age?"

"Father was busy, preoccupied. He didn't care what we did. Mother had other problems."

"Did you say she was sick?"

"Increasingly so. Manic depression, they'd call it today."

"Bipolar disorder."

"Not so bad as you think," said Zhenya. "She'd deliberately smash a vase, then spend hours crying about it. When Father failed to chastise her, she'd take a week fixing it, painstakingly gluing shards of china back together. She'd show it to him, but he still wouldn't take the bait. Then she'd smash it again, hurl it at the floor. Mood swings, but she was never violent to us, or to herself. At worse, cyclothymia, I think. There's a computer over there, my window to the world. I've had a lot of time to think about these things, to study the past."

"Mood disorders were hardly understood back then."

"In a very religious family they could be seriously misunderstood, if you were so inclined."

"What do you mean?"

"Later, Mother claimed to have visions."

"Visions?"

"Right. Jonny and I would be there, and we'd be scared, it was like a fit of hysteria. But the strange thing was, she always saw good things, you know, like graphic depictions of a loving heaven I could have aspired to myself. Her visions were more like stories, bedtime stories, at least the way she'd describe them to us. But Father seized on it. He may have had elements of mental illness as well, though I never saw him enough to form a proper opinion."

"He thought she was possessed?"

"Worse. He thought the visions were real. And Mother compounded it, played up to his latent religious mania. It was always hard to get Father's attention, he was so committed to his work as a missionary. I often wonder if this was the cause of her madness, because she lived her life as such a lonely, dominated woman. Father was so active in promoting moral fiber to complete strangers, yet so distant and cold in the family home. But Mother's visions finally got his attention, so she began to have more of them. She loved him so much, it was her way of making contact."

"The madness wasn't real?"

"It was real to us. It was real to my father. And it was outside anything in his experience, scientific *or* theological. He decided he needed help from somewhere else, and whatever else the town was lacking, there were no shortage of preachers to call on for counsel. But the mainstream churches, the LDS, they would listen and sympathize and offer support, but they couldn't interpret. I suppose they didn't much want a disruptive influence like my mother in the congregation, not with her outpourings; people were so easily led in those days. But there was one preacher nearby who had the answer. One preacher who could tap into her divinity in a way that finally made sense to my father."

"Who?"

"James Earl LaGrande," said Zhenya. "The Church of the Final Days."

Midnight, or thereabouts.

The moon was full, thin clouds skidding across a starlit sky.

Only a few of the tents that filled the valley surrounding the church had yet to extinguish their lanterns. Somewhere, a baby was crying, the sound echoing around the shadowy hills. Most of the faithful were sleeping; in their cars, in donated silver Airstream trailers, in those few ghost-town shell-buildings that remained, anywhere else they could find. They have flocked to this place because they believe the end of the world is coming.

In days maybe. Possibly weeks, but very soon. And they are glad.

Dr. Christopher Peterson needed no lamp; even in slumber, the encampment seemed to glow with a religious fervor bright enough to see. It filled his heart with joy; these were the chosen ones, the few who would survive the floods and fires that were shortly to descend and blast away the sins of the world. Christopher himself, as one of the founder converts, had been allowed to assign his own family one of the caves in the hillside, the old mine-shaft a suitably biblical house of earth and rock from which to press home the teachings of the leader to the junior boys. Despite his skills as an orator, men and boys were the only ones Christopher was permitted to minister to.

LaGrande had chosen to educate the women himself.

In contrast to the makeshift shantytown surrounding it, the church was resplendent. Christopher could see the interior blazing with candlelight through the high windows; LaGrande had taken to sleeping during the day. Those devout locals with the skills necessary had worked tirelessly to replace windows, patch up plastering, even install a stand-pipe for fresh water, and the church had become the focal point for this small new community in more ways than one; all deliveries of food and other essentials were administrated by LaGrande himself, along with a couple of thick-necked local boys he claimed were his sons. Besides, the church was built on this most sacrosanct of ground, it had been foretold by Christopher's wife in one of her many visions, the most recent of which had become remarkably specific. And, appropriately, LaGrande had made the church his home as well as his ministry. Originally, any of the faithful could have entered and consulted with him, but as the number of converts had grown, so had the requirements of the leader and his wives.

Now the church was only opened for the weekly service, but tonight was different. Tonight, he, Christopher, had been sent for. He had fallen somewhat out of favor since his re-baptism, and he hoped his star was back in the ascent.

The large wooden doors were closed. Typically, they were locked. Christopher took a deep breath of warm, scented desert air to steady his nerves. Then he knocked three times, and the sound boomed.

There was no reply. After a moment's hesitation, he pulled them open.

Despite the high-ceilinged airiness that had characterized the interior of the church when Christopher had last been allowed access, it was now a grotesque mess, and it stank of rotting food, perhaps even human waste. LaGrande had first come up here on his own, and, used to living like a cussed-out dog, he had not seen fit to change his habits. However, due to the row upon row of candles and lamps that were strewn so abundantly as to cover half of the floor space—a recent donation from one of the smaller churches that had elected to merge—it was extremely bright, especially when compared to the oyster glow of the moon. And it was hot, feverishly so. Christopher looked past boxes of food, crates of beer, stacks of paper, guns, kneelers, Bibles, and some preposterous biblical tapestries hanging heavily from the walls; all donations to the cause.

LaGrande himself was naked, his back to the door. A hefty, unwashed figure, covered head to toe in wiry black hair, he was up at the head of the church, fucking Christopher's wife across the altar. Abigail was on her back, feet dangling down, and Christopher couldn't see her face. She was lying on the sheet that the leader used with all his chosen women; it was stained with the blood of girls far, far younger.

They grunted like pigs. Because of the excessive film-set illumination, Christopher had a perfect view of the penetration, LaGrande clumsy and thrusting with his dark stubby penis. The doctor averted his eyes, turned back to close the doors as quietly as he could.

Finished, the preacher stepped down from the raised platform, unconcerned about his sweaty nakedness, his body shining in the candlelight.

"God be with you," said James Earl LaGrande, thickly.

"And also with you," said Christopher.

"*He* is here," said LaGrande, a little out of breath. He popped the top on a warm beer and drank deeply. "Do you feel Him? Are you strong enough?"

"I am," said Christopher, eyeing his wife, her vagina glistening.

LaGrande hurled the beer at the wall, and it burst, painting the plaster with a foamy arc. Christopher had no time to take this in before he was slapped, hard, with LaGrande's open palm. It hurt like hell, but he didn't recoil.

LaGrande leaned right in, as was his way, eyes fizzing with the glory and the power and charisma of true righteousness. He had four or five inches on Christopher, and his neck and arms were thick with muscle and fat.

"She lacked willingness tonight," he said. "You wish this woman to be a wife of mine?"

"With all my heart."

"Do *you* tithe to me willingly?"

"With all my heart."

"Blood atonement, Christopher. I order the slaying of my own brother so I may lead the faithful to heaven, and this woman you brought fails to give herself *willingly*?"

"What did she say?"

"You wish to join God, his angels, in heaven? I doubt it. You curse your family to *hell*."

Christopher was crying. "What did she say?"

"She lies. Her visions are false testimony."

"She doesn't know what she says, she doesn't know . . ."

"How old is your daughter?"

"What?"

"The Virgin Mary was a girl of eleven."

"My . . . my daughter?"

"Purity. The purity you would hide from me. The purity you would hide from God." LaGrande belched, wiped his mouth with the back of his hand. "Bring her to me now."

"*No* . . ." It was Abigail Peterson. She'd struggled up to her elbows, her face black and blue from the beatings—LaGrande had to stop the women from taking pleasure while he spread his love. "You will not take our daughter . . ."

LaGrande ignored her. His response was framed as a punch to Christopher Peterson's jaw. It was signaled in advance, but the disciple made no move to block it, and sagged, seeing stars.

"Weak *apostate*," spat out the preacher, the vision of his fat naked body flooding Christopher's mind. "The sword of vengeance will hang over the heads of those who should fail to hear the *word of the Lord*. Today, your wife commits the crime of rebellion against God." He was shouting, filled from top to toe with the spirit.

"No," wept Christopher. "She doesn't know what she says."

"She knows. She is a whore. Her visions, the ones you claim are glorious. They are a *fiction*, sold wholesale by Satan. Would you have me commune with Satan?"

"But . . . but you believed before."

"The Old Serpent is convincing. I am only a mortal vessel."

"Then take her again. Make her clean."

"Silence," said LaGrande, suddenly calm. "Your words are as sin and should not be uttered in this holy place. Get to your knees." He shot a glance at the corner of the church, raised his voice once more. "Malchus?" he called. "*Malchus?*"

LaGrande renamed his flock as he saw fit; it was usually considered an honor. Christopher, bleary eyed and defeated, turned his head to where LaGrande was speaking, witnessed his young son Jonathon—now Malchus—emerge from the shadows. His son's feet were bare and grubby, but he was wearing shorts and a torn T-shirt with a cartoon character on it.

"Malchus," said LaGrande to Jon Peterson, gesturing at Abigail, who was scrabbling for garments to hide her shame. "Remove your mother, this *whore*, from my presence. Your father will stay here with me. We will pray for her soul."

"Yes," said Jon. His face was twitching, but his shoulders were thrust back. He would not cry for this man.

"Bring me your sister," said LaGrande. "The one with the heretical name. Bring her now, so we all can save ourselves from the damnation your father would curse us to."

The boy would not cry for God, or for anyone.

"Return with your virgin sister so that you may all yet live. Do it *now*."

And his name was not Malchus. It was Jon.

"What happened?" said Karen, aghast.

"They ran," said Zhenya. "My mother and my brother."

"They got away?"

"Well, they got out of that church, got away from those madmen, and they ran. I think there was still the family car somewhere, so they piled in, escaped the encampment, drove back to the house in Canaan. It was Jon of course, my mother was brainwashed. He told her where to drive, probably even propped her up at the wheel. He saved her life, and she followed him because she'd always followed someone. The physical act of leaving turned out to be as simple as walking away."

"And Jon took her back to the house in Canaan? LaGrande, your father, they must have known where to find them?"

"He was eleven years old. Where else would he go?"

"And your mother played no part in the escape?"

"I don't think she knew where she was by that point. But even if she *did* have presence of mind, she had nowhere else to go, no one else to turn to. She'd disowned her own parents when she swore allegiance to the church; rejection of the non-faithful was part of it. Of *course* LaGrande knew where to find them. It was what he chose to do with that knowledge."

"And what was that?"

"We'd lived up at The Church of the Final Days for maybe six weeks at this point, though we'd been members of LaGrande's congregation for far longer. But these really were the final days; it was already fragmenting, falling apart. And LaGrande had begun to cull some of the dissenters, even some of the faithful; in secret of course, but with a small number of adherents, perhaps including my father. Publicly too, LaGrande was getting more erratic. God had been telling that man to murder from a very young age, to cleanse and sacrifice, and he'd finally worked himself into a position where he could fulfill his life's work, could even command others to do it for him. But people will only tolerate so much, even the truly faith-blind, those terrified of eternal damnation. I don't know how many he got in the end, how many were buried in the canyons. A dozen perhaps? No one knows exactly."

"But where were you in all of this?"

Zhenya didn't reply. She just stared at the ceiling.

"Zhenya?" said Karen, a little concerned. This was a patient in a hospital, and she wasn't incarcerated because of her physical condition. "Zhenya?"

"They didn't take me with them," said Zhenya, finally, meeting Karen's eyes.

"They didn't . . ."

Zhenya chose to smile, she had long white teeth. "That's right. I was left behind. When they ran away from the encampment, they left me behind."

"Why?"

"Because Jonny couldn't find me," she said, voice brittle. "I was sleeping elsewhere. There wasn't much room for us all in the cave, so a friend of mine let me sleep in her family's campervan from time to time. Talk about misfortune. Jon searched and searched, but it was dark, they'd been with LaGrande all afternoon, neither he nor my mother knew where to look. And Jon knew they'd soon be missed, both him and Mother, he had no time."

"How did that make you feel?" The tired old therapist's question.

"How do you think it made me feel?" said Zhenya. "But I don't blame Jonny, he did all he could. I'd have done the same thing, given what he faced. My mother is the one I can't forgive; incapable of saving her own daughter yet capable of leaving me to *him*."

"I don't understand," said Karen. "Your mother ran away because of the threat of violence to you, the threat of your rape, and then she *left* you?"

"My mother ran away because Jonny made her run away. Perhaps he thought they'd be able to come back, stage a rescue. Or perhaps Mother thought it was a small price to pay, given the circumstances; at least she had one of her children with her. Or perhaps she was just sick."

"And then LaGrande did this to you? He removed your arms and your legs?"

"Not at first," said Zhenya. "At first, I was made to write the letters."

The family saloon, dust-streaked and running on empty, pulled up outside the dark-windowed house under the bone-white glare of the moon. A woman, bruised and battered and limping badly, was helped down from the driver's seat by a shoeless boy. Leaning against one another for strength, they struggled up the short, steep path. In the distance, blue mesas reared, and pinnacles of rock clawed at the stars.

The front door had been left unlocked, as, weeks ago, James Earl LaGrande had instructed all of his converts to do with their property. Most items of worth inside had been sold, pawned or donated for the cause. Worldly possessions were not required where he intended to take them.

He may have been exhausted, but the boy, Jon Peterson, shoved his mother over the threshold with enough force to make her stumble. Afraid to switch on the lights, they slept that night with their backs to the front door, trembling when they heard a distant car, the creaking of the porch, or the howling of a stray dog.

But, perhaps surprisingly, no one came for them.

The Petersons didn't own a gun. Tomorrow, Jon would try and find one.

The following day, there was still no retribution from James Earl LaGrande, though Abigail had not the presence of mind to leave the property. They sat up to the greasy kitchen table, eating canned meat and staring at the road through smeary windows, waiting for someone to come.

The house was full of dead flies.

Days passed, and no car pulled up, no man with a gun, knife or Bible. Jon borrowed a shotgun and any amount of ammo from a sympathetic neighbor, and he spent hours practicing out back, on birds, on tufts of grass, on cans that he lined up on the fence. On the second day, the recoil blacked his eye and knocked him silly.

Yet still no one came for them.

And, haltingly, life began again, as it invariably must. It was a draining, haunted existence, and both mother and son were reluctant participants. They walked as spirits in purgatory, ghosts in an empty house, waiting for the madness they knew was growing in the desert to spill out and engulf them once more.

It was Jon who rallied first.

A local support group had been set up in Canaan; Methodists and Episcopalians who would defy LaGrande, made up of some of those who had run him out of town in the first place. It was the sympathetic neighbor, the one who would give a shotgun to a child, who suggested to Jon that he take his mother along. But Abigail chose to shun the offer of friendship, of emotional support.

She was advised to move away, to take her son out of town, but she had nowhere to go. She was advised to find a lawyer, one with the mettle to get her daughter back, but Abigail had no money, and probably would have refused anyway. Whatever it was inside of herself that Abigail had said goodbye to on that long evening with James Earl LaGrande, the same goodbye could now extend to her own daughter. And Jon couldn't look his mother in the eye, not after what he'd seen, after what she'd done to them, how she was hanging on in her empty shell of a house like anything meant a damn anymore.

Jon decided that his mother was a weak, *weak* woman, and when she called him Malchus, as she still occasionally did on those rare moments when they spoke to one another, he knew that she was still under the sway of the Church.

But at least the support group provided food and clothing. Jon even decided to return to school, though he would not speak to those who had previously been his friends. At night, he came home to a house where his mother shrieked and sobbed, the sound painting his dreams in various shades of horror.

Zhenya was soon to come back to them.

Jon was out on the day the first letter arrived. He had been learning about slavery, about how it was abolished. He could smell burned food before he had pushed through the front door.

Inside the house, choking black smoke. Jon ran to the kitchen, shut off the oven, threw the blackened lump of whatever-it-was into the garden. He opened all the doors and windows, even though he had forbidden his mother to leave anything unlocked.

He found Abigail in her bedroom, curled up on the floor. She was shaking, wouldn't speak. In her hand was a note, hand-delivered. More would come, pushed under the door by persons unseen, usually in the middle of the night.

> Help me o god help me hes going to hurt me if you dont do what he says jentle jesus meek and mild look upon a little child save me jesus save me

Just like that, meaning all running together in a flood of concentrated panic.

Jon recognized his sister's handwriting. He recognized the *jentle jesus*, a prayer that had been repeated to them during the limited number of deprogramming sessions they had attended. It was the favorite prayer of a kindly woman with sharp eyes: Gladys.

He was being mocked.

That night, Jon Peterson, freshly turned eleven years old, did not sleep. His bedroom had a view of the road. He sat with his shotgun resting on his forearm, and he watched.

Later, when he was drowsy, Jon began to hear voices in his head; jubilant chatter that lifted him above the fog of fear, and he was grateful of the opportunity to listen.

It was the first time he heard the demons.

The second letter was pushed under the back door. Jon found it himself, the following morning:

> Okay listen he knows where you are now I had to give it to him and im so sorry so sorry but id be dead if I didnt and now hes coming hes coming for you now and I cant stop him
> If he knows I told you id be dead so dont show anyone this note just dont trust me

Jon knew precisely what it was that Zhenya must have *given*. True to his sister's request, he folded the note carefully, placed it in an empty drawer with the first one. They wouldn't be touched again for thirty years or more, except to add to their number.

He was in no doubt as to what this really meant, and it wasn't Zhenya sneaking notes to him. She was being made to write the letters. They existed to put the fear of God into both Jon and his mother, and they worked far more effectively than any physical threat.

Jon cocked his head to one side, was pleased to find that he could summon the voices he had heard the night before, sought comfort there. But this time, the voices introduced some ideas as to what Jon Peterson might like to do with his day.

Years ago, an outdoorsy uncle had given him a rabbit snare, and, sure enough, Jon found it in the garage under some old newspapers. He skipped the wait for the school bus, instead took a long walk into the desert.

Shortly afterwards, a letter arrived with a different tack. It even had punctuation:

> Daddy says all is well. Come and see me. Bring Jonny, he is not what you'd call a well boy, but he can yet be saved.
> Mother, there was a mistake. It was not you, you are an angel made flesh, as am I. Bring Jonny, that he may be made as pure as we. Do it or I will give my body.
> Know that the seventh trumpet has sounded.

Jon didn't even know how this letter got into the house, his mother wasn't speaking to him, she was lost in a world of her own.

She didn't even want to be rescued. She wishes she was back at the church.

It wasn't important. Jon folded the note carefully, hid it in his bedroom. Then he took his gun, which was almost as big as he was.

He marched into the kitchen, tore open his mother's purse. He was looking for the keys to the car. She didn't try to stop him, just stared into the middle distance, silent tears coursing down her face.

Jon couldn't drive, yet despite running every stoplight, he made it through town without incident. He was heading for The Church of the Final Days.

He meant to kill his father, and he meant to kill James Earl LaGrande.

He meant to avenge his sister. He meant to save her.

When the car finally ran out of gas, halfway down the 192, Jon Peterson pulled the stalled vehicle over to the side of the road with care. Then he pressed his face into the steering wheel and sobbed with fury, hard enough so the horn echoed in one long, continuous howl.

He was twenty miles from town, twenty miles from the church.

They found him walking the road, a solitary child in an endless wasteland. The church was too far, the desert too hot. But he'd have crawled on hands and knees if he had to.

At the behest of his mother, Jon Peterson spent that night alone in a police cell, ostensibly to teach him a lesson. There was a fat, jovial police chief, and he meant well, even asked the deputy on night shift to sit with the boy, make sure he was all right. The deputy was instructed to release Jon and take him home at any sign of remorse or discomfort.

The following day, the deputy looked far more spooked than the boy.

"He didn't speak a word to me all night," the officer confided to a colleague. "But he sure was speaking to someone, and I didn't much like the things they discussed."

A police cruiser dropped Jonny at the house. His mother was gone, as was the car, and the front door was wide open.

On the kitchen table, Jon Peterson found another letter in his sister's handwriting:

> **now i bleed, you never came to me, come soon. Church of the Final Days, 2pm Monday.**

Unnecessarily, there was fresh blood splashed across the bottom corner.

It was dark when Abigail Peterson returned home; she'd been

gone for eleven hours. From his bedroom window, Jon trained her in the sights of his shotgun. He had no intention of shooting her, it was just a nicer way of looking at the world.

She was weaving, staggering, like a drunk; LaGrande had raped her again.

In her hand was another note. Jon turned to face his bedroom door, waited for footfalls on the stairs.

"Malchus," Abigail said to Jon, when she was standing in the open doorway. It was as though a drowned person had somehow found voice. "Malchus, the seventh trumpet has sounded."

Jon Peterson sat on his bed, hugging his knees. He said nothing.

"I cannot be saved, even God himself could not save me, and how they have tried. I accept this. Zhenya has written, now she writes to you."

Abigail dropped the fifth and sixth letters onto the floor, limped away.

I am the serpent. I will be destroyed or destroy you all. I would deny my own mother the kingdom of heaven

Go to church
Daddy says Go to the church of the final days
2pm Tuesday

Jon could hear his mother, sobbing in the bedroom.

It was important now that he save his shotgun ammo, so he went downstairs and took a knife from the kitchen drawer. He didn't bother to lock the door behind himself.

Jon headed out into the nearby canyons, to where he'd laid his jackrabbit traps. The moon was obscured, just a bright fingernail, but there was light from the stars. It didn't take him long, he practically ran all the way.

Jon had covered the jaws of the trap with split garden hose, to restrict the impact on whatever animal he caught. He wanted something living, if possible.

Sure enough, a rabbit, pinioned across its belly. The creature's eyes were frozen in terror at the extreme periphery of its vision.

Jon's knife wasn't really sharp enough. He had to sweat with the exertion of sawing the rabbit's head from its body, and it died before he could draw blood from the neck.

He reset the trap. Tomorrow, he'd spend hours with stone and oil, grinding his blade to a razor's edge. He was learning about the value of tireless preparation.

Nonetheless, the relief permitted to him by the kill allowed Jon to sleep well that night, more soundly than he had done in months.

He slept in the cradle of the demons.

"There's a bottle of spring water over there," said Zhenya. "Could you pour me a glass? This is the most talking I've done in years."

"Sure," said Karen, standing up.

"Normally the nurse is regular as clockwork." Zhenya nodded at the CCTV. "They probably don't want to disturb us."

Karen walked over to the sideboard. "So what were they playing at?" she said, filling the beaker. "What was the preacher up to? Your father? What did they think they were going to achieve with this campaign?"

"I suspect that LaGrande had never been defied before," said Zhenya. "And never by a child, of all people. I think he saw potential in Jon, recognized his ability, his inner strength. But LaGrande wanted Jon to come back willingly. I think the prospect amused him."

Karen brought the glass to Zhenya's lips and she drank. It was a strangely intimate process for Karen.

"And this was his big idea?" said Karen. "Terrorizing Jon by destroying you? Making you write these letters?"

"Remember, it was an age of madness for the whole town. To this day, Canaan lives in fear and uncertainty. You only have to scratch the surface."

"But . . . cutting you into pieces?"

"I'm just fortunate to not remember any of it," said Zhenya, in a way that communicated to Karen that she likely remembered every horrific moment, perhaps relived it each day. "At least, I don't remember any of the operations. My father was a doctor, he could spare me the pain."

"At the church? They did this to you in the church?"

"No, no. In his tiny clinic, back in town. That's how I'm alive today, he took every care. Tourniquets, sterilization, transfusions, I don't need to draw you a picture. I was my father's masterpiece. You see, LaGrande wanted to turn me into a serpent."

"A *serpent*?"

"Like in the Garden of Eden." Zhenya smiled. "Don't you think I'm beautiful?"

Karen nodded, her throat tight.

"The afternoon of that Tuesday, Jonny never came to the church," said Zhenya. "He didn't do as my letter instructed. Again, he dared to defy. But this time, there was a greater price to pay."

Wake up.

I am awake.

Wake up, Jonny.

"Who's there . . ."

Don't try to speak. What's that noise?

Scrape, scrape.

Eleven-year-old Jon Peterson sat up in bed, startled out of sleep. The first thing he saw was the moonlight glinting off the shotgun he'd propped against the bedpost.

What's that noise? The demons sounded alarmed.

Scrape, scrape. Very faint, but it was there.

"Zhenya?" he said. "Is that you?" The words sounded strange in the empty house.

But why is the house empty?

Scrape, scrape.

It wasn't a sound from inside the house, it was outside. Jon hopped out of bed, padded over to the window. The yard was empty, the road was clear. Beyond, the Canyonlands.

Nothing here, Jonny. Out back.

The noise was like someone shoveling, a regular series of blunt thuds and drags.

You know what? Perhaps Zhenya has returned to us.

The night was hot, Jon didn't even pull on a sweater in his eagerness. Naked except for his shorts, he ran downstairs, ran through the dark house, ran out the back door.

Zhenya wasn't there. Instead, there was the vision of his mother, using a spade to dig a hole in the dry earth. She wasn't getting anywhere, she was barely even trying.

Scrape, scrape.

Abigail Peterson was in nightgown and slippers, and she looked up when Jon charged out, slamming the screen door against the wall. Her face was white and ghostly, as though there was no comprehension behind the eyes, no recognizable consciousness. Jon had suspected as much, but it was never made more evident to him than in that one look: his mother's madness was complete.

"*Jonny*," she said, in a strange, sing-song voice. She hadn't used his real name in weeks, and, surprisingly, he didn't like the sound of it. "Jonny, don't just stand there. Help your mother."

"Mom . . .?"

"Didn't you hear her arrive? You're such a sleepyhead. A man dropped her off not ten minutes ago, on the porch out front."

Jon walked forward, fear in his belly a cauldron of boiling maggots.

Why didn't I do as I was asked? Why didn't I go to the church?

There was a box at his mother's feet, an apple crate. The box was lined with tarp. Jon didn't want to look in there.

The demons: *Don't worry, Jonny, we're here now. We can help you do anything.*

Jon peered in, saw his sister's hands and forearms, neatly amputated at the elbows.

Later, as his murderous tendencies developed, the memory of that vision would give him ideas; creative inspiration for killing the animals.

We can help you do anything.

"But now you're here, you should grab a spade," said Abigail, bending down to dig again. "The hole needs to be deep. Too deep for the dogs."

If you asked Jon Peterson what he thought he was doing, he'd have told you it was the demons controlling his actions, and he might even have said it with a hint of pride, not an emotion he was usually prone to. Though, of course, it was him all along.

The car had sufficient fuel this time, and, it being the dead of night, there was no one around to stop him. He almost lost control of the wheel a couple of times on the tortuous track from the 192 to Crescent Canyon, but he had some distinctly *unnatural* inspiration to keep his direction true and his grip on the wheel iron-clad. In the past, due to LaGrande's paranoia, there was frequently a guard posted on the road to the encampment, but Jon didn't see anyone; that was what the shotgun in the seat well would have been for.

Two hours after burying those parts of his sister and leaving his mother babbling to herself, Jon Peterson was able to round the corner to the place where it all began: The Church of the Final Days.

As usual, the church was aglow, and he killed his beams, so as not to attract attention. Beyond the structure there were a few lamps alight in the ghost town, spread out around the valley like glowing algae. The encampment seemed smaller than Jon remembered it; perhaps people had figured out the insanity, had seen LaGrande's charisma for what it was.

In fact, the flock was already beginning to disperse.

Jon left the motor running, stepped out of the car. He crept around the side of the church, looking for something to boost himself up, to peer through a window. He found a ladder, a leftover from reconstructive work that had been done to the roof.

Moments later he was staring in at his father, kneeling at prayer. The usual carpet of candles was spread out across the floor. LaGrande couldn't be seen, but Jon knew he'd be in there; the preacher barely ever left, especially at night.

Satisfied, Jon slid down the ladder, sprinted over to the car. Inside the trunk were three portable canisters of gasoline, used to power the generator at home when the electricity cut out. He lifted them carefully, small muscles straining. Then he got back into the car.

This was the most delicate part of the operation. Jon released the handbrake, let the car roll forward. He executed a passable three-point-turn in the clearing, wincing at the grind of the transmission as it slid into reverse. Then, with extreme care, he backed up so the car was pressing against the doors of the church, blocking it, barring the single exit; the doors only opened outwards.

He was building a giant oven.

Had someone inside heard him? The doors were stout, and Jon had been very careful. Could they raise the alarm if they had? Jon didn't know.

Climbing out of the car again, the night was as still as ever, though Jon imagined he could feel the air charged with a new tension, a new sense of promise. This wasn't just about retribution; he had to destroy the church once and for all.

He had some empty cartons of orange juice on the backseat, some empty cartons of milk. He moved back into the shadows, filled them with the gas from the canisters, fumes making him dizzy. There were so many naked flames in the church itself, he assumed he wouldn't need a fuse. Job done, Jon realized he had some spare fuel. After a second's thought, he poured it direct from the canisters around the exterior of the building in a broken loop.

It should have been a challenge to climb the ladder with the cartons of fuel, but Jon managed the steps two at a time, barely wavering. He lined up his makeshift Molotov cocktails on the sill of the window, then braced himself with the shotgun like a club.

Smash!

His father spun around, and Jon got a brief glimpse of a shocked face, but he didn't hesitate. No sooner was the window broken, he was hurling his bombs. The result was spectacular, far more spectacular than he expected. The first carton was aimed at the largest clump of candles, and a sheet of flame ran along the ground and up one of the heavy tapestries like it had a mind, made a delighted roar he could actually hear. Jon only had the opportunity to hurl two more—one towards the door, one at his horrified father—before the heat at the window became too much, and he had to jump to the ground, rolling as he did so.

Moments later, there was an explosion above his head, a dangerously close firework display where his unused cartons had incinerated in the heat. Lit gasoline ran down the walls like radioactive tears and set off the ring of fire around the church.

Jon was running. He'd given no thought to his escape.

Windows exploded, showering hot glass down around his ears. Smoke poured, and Jon felt his skin tighten with proximity to the flame.

Bolting out from his cover at the side of the building, he saw the car where he'd left it, driver's side door open. He needn't have used the vehicle to block the exit; there was no way anyone inside could have made it through the wall of flame.

The church doors had yet to buckle, but fire was trickling out, licking at the rear tires. Above and around, the world was heat and light and fury.

Decide.

Do it.

Jon ran and jumped, slid in feet first, knowing he was seconds away from the ignition of his own gas tank.

The air turned orange. Sparks, branches of flame, reached around the car in hellish embrace. Jon twisted the key, stamped on the pedal. The car kicked forward like a bullet, and it was all he could do to rock the wheel towards the dark pass to the desert, driver's side door swinging drunkenly from the chassis.

Away to the left, pilgrims and disciples were running towards the inferno.

Jon allowed himself just one glance in his rear-view mirror, and only when he was back out on the dirt track, carefully negotiating the dips and ruts. The landscape had closed in around the town, obscuring his view, but it looked as though a volcano was erupting in the valley, and the glow of the burning church accompanied him all the way back to the main road.

We've got you, Jonny. We'll keep you safe, we said we would.

Jon grimaced, his thoughts turning to his mother.

"But she was already dead," said Zhenya.

"Excuse me?" said Karen.

"When he got back to the house, Mother had taken her own life. It was a tawdry, pathetic thing. She'd filled the bathtub with water and dropped in a portable electric heater. It would be pitiable, if I could ever feel pity for that woman."

"What was Jon planning to do to her?"

"I don't know," said Zhenya. "But I know he needed retribution, and she denied him it. That was her final act of being alive. And now, this is who he is today."

"What happened to James Earl LaGrande? Was he in the church?"

"No. The abuse he ordered on me may have been his worst atrocity, but at least I lived, there were those who did not. He was already running when the church burned down, running from any number of parallel investigations: fraud, adultery, incest, murder."

"He escaped?"

"Hardly. He was extradited from Mexico, and he died in prison, a pathetic, wasted man, stripped of power and glory. Justice found him. I *know* LaGrande. It would have been a fate worse than death."

"What about the aftermath of the fire?" said Karen.

"Of course, there had been witnesses to the arson. They hadn't made out a person, but they recognized the car as it sped away. Official verdict: my mother was responsible, then came home and committed suicide. It made sense to the law after learning what had happened to her; the rapes, my ruined body, and Jon didn't deny it. Six months later, he was in a foster home. A pretty good one, I believe."

"Where were you?"

"I was at the clinic all this time, close to death. I should never have lived, but when no one could account for my father immediately, they searched all the premises where he could have been holed up. Again, I have no memory of it, but some cop must have gotten quite a shock; they also found my legs, packaged up and ready to be delivered. Of course, it was all too late, the hospital at Salt Lake City had to cut my limbs back if I was to ever stand a chance of survival."

"I can't imagine possessing your strength," said Karen, and she really couldn't.

"You could say the rest of my childhood was pretty unique. I was given days to live, then weeks, then years. Doctors have been forever predicting my demise."

"But you must have wanted to live. You must have had that desire."

"Anger is a powerful motivator," said Zhenya, looking directly at Karen. "Defiance, probably the one thing I have in common with my brother. You can understand now, how he and I have little use for morality in the typical sense of the word. We were forsaken by God, we were forsaken by justice. I often wonder: if I had his mobility, would I be capable of doing the things he does now? Truthfully, I don't know. I prefer not to think about it. Yet that same defiance allowed Jon to suppress his memories, to build a career for himself, despite his psychotic tendencies. At any rate, he's never wanted for money, honestly earned, hence this gilded prison you see around me. Paying for my care assuages some of his guilt about failing to rescue me. I've told him, he was eleven, it couldn't have been his responsibility. But he won't hear that."

"What does Jon do for a living?"

"I'm not going to tell you. And I'm not going to tell you where he lives. You have a name, Jonathon Peterson. You can get the rest, or the police can."

"Why not? Why not tell me?" said Karen. "There's a girl, Katy. He took an innocent girl, he cut off her hand, and Lilly, my friend . . ."

"*No*," said Zhenya. "He's my brother, and I love him. I *know* what he is. I know he's a monster. But, surely you can see, I am the one person on the planet permitted to be able to reconcile that."

"Perhaps," said Karen, uncertain.

"He's talked about doing something like this for a long time, yet he's never acted. He's been talking about revenge for near on thirty years. And Jonny is a procrastinator, his fantasy life was usually enough. It was only when you walked through this door that I became aware that it had started for real. But if the girl, Katy, has survived this long, then he might let her live. He respects endurance; his own, mine, anyone's. He used to construct games, based on it; he bought pet animals to exercise that purpose. Or so he told me."

"You mean he tortures things," said Karen.

Zhenya ignored this. "I can't be directly responsible for his capture," she said. "He's my brother, my only living family."

"He needs to be stopped. You must be able to see that."

"And you'll stop him with what I've given you," said Zhenya. "Ask me about the past, ask me anything, but don't make me be the one to give him up."

Karen wasn't going to be put off. "So why me?" she said.

Zhenya blinked. "What?"

"Why *me*?" said Karen, with heat. "It might not seem important to you. Hell, it might not even *be* important given the extent of this thing, but since it began, since the first letter, I've wanted to know. I've searched my mind for any connection that I could have, to you, to your brother. And I can't find any."

"I don't know the answer to that," said Zhenya.

"You don't . . ."

"I *have* wondered it myself, you have to believe me. Look, I see Jonny maybe once every two months; his job takes him to different cities, but he always visits. He gave me your name, gave me those old letters, gave me instruction to get them out to you, told me how to do it, the remailing service, the intermediary. I asked him why, he said it would be therapeutic for us both; but I'll tell you, when he brought those letters like he'd kept them pristine, my heart was in my mouth. I didn't get it, he doesn't always make sense. But you don't say no to Jonny."

"I think he has a personal association with me," said Karen. "Did he ever mention a Sammie? A Samantha Wiley?"

"No," said Zhenya.

"Sammie is my sister," said Karen. "She died in unusual circumstances when we were young. I wouldn't have thought there could have been a connection, but when Jon bought a gravestone with my name on it, he put the account in the name of my sister."

"I don't know what you're talking about," said Zhenya. "A gravestone? He asked me to send these letters to you, that was it.

And once again: you *don't deny Jon*. Do I look capable of refusing him?"

"I can grasp the idea of him wanting to relive the events surrounding your past," said Karen. "Perhaps you've explained his delusions, his psychopathic tendencies. But why did he target my daughter? Symbolically, metaphorically, what has she to do with the story you just told me?"

"And I didn't know you had a daughter," said Zhenya. "I promise, it was never mentioned."

"I think he targeted her through the Internet somehow. He addressed a package to her. Jennifer Wiley. Can you explain that?"

"This is the first I've heard," said Zhenya. "I think you're looking for connections where they may not exist. Jonny is not a well boy, how much more do I have to spell it out? You might as well ask why Katy Trueblood, why San Francisco, why anything. Bad luck, Karen, I'm sorry you were targeted. Perhaps I know a little something about bad luck."

Karen looked away from the figure on the bed, stared out of the window.

Much time had passed. The sky had closed in further, and darkness was encroaching on the room. It felt to Karen like she'd been in this hospital for an eternity. The darkness heralded the coming of the storm, and it was a long way back to civilization.

"I should go," said Karen, rising to her feet.

"Will you come back?"

"What?"

"Will you visit me?" Zhenya smiled, smiled warmly. "Usually I don't speak to anyone. I'm alone. I mean, I always wanted to be, I told you, I made decisions. But I like you, Karen. I've never spoken to anyone who understood. People love tragic stories, they listen, tears well up in their eyes. But I get no sympathy from you, I get steely determination, and I can see, you've been living with pain as well, it's real to you."

"What do you mean?"

Zhenya suddenly reared up off the bed, she had tremendous abdominal muscles. It terrified Karen, who wasn't expecting it.

"Don't let him get you, Karen," she said. "He wants to kill you, and he always gets everything he wants. It's part of his plan."

Zhenya lowered herself back down, looked up at the CCTV camera, moderated her voice. "They'll be coming in soon. If they're watching, they'll be disturbed by that little display." She smiled again. "Besides, don't you have a little girl to save?"

"Right," said Karen, confused.

Zhenya closed her eyes, and then the nurse opened the door.

"Tori?" said Zhenya to the nurse fluffing her pillow, once Karen had gone. "Tori, can you do something for me?"

"Yes?" said Tori, mildly surprised. The unusual quadruple amputee in Room 22 was a patient whom she had quietly diagnosed as *difficult*, not least because Zhenya had never deemed to speak to her before, and reports from the other staff were far from complimentary.

"Tori, go over to the window there. The person who just left me is called Karen Wiley. Can you see her?"

Tori, intrigued, moved over to the window. Sure enough, there was the tall woman; elegant, despite her casual attire. Tori, several pounds overweight, envied the body, the long limbs. God knows what Zhenya must have thought of her.

Karen was jogging towards her vehicle like the sky might be about to fall, and given the portent in the ominous black clouds, this didn't seem beyond the bounds of possibility.

"Can you see her?" Zhenya's voice was impatient.

"Yes," said Tori. There were a couple of tame deer at the extremity of the silent parking lot, and they ran from the hastening woman like vagrant dogs.

"She'll have a car," said Zhenya.

"A Land Rover," said Tori. "It looks newish."

"What color?"

"Silver."

"Can you catch the license plate?"

"Not until she backs up, she's side on."

"Okay," said Zhenya. "Don't make a mistake now, Tori. Read it when you can."

"Why would you want . . ."

Now there was danger in the voice, a lyrical threat. "Can you think of a reason why not?"

Tori couldn't, but was saved from reply by the distant sound of Karen's engine starting up.

Zhenya stared at the ceiling again, and in her mind's eye she could see Karen Wiley, beautiful Karen Wiley, hands on the wheel.

Tori, confused but obedient, read out the numbers and letters, and Zhenya listened as though experiencing some kind of transcendental music.

The nurse watched the Land Rover drive away, watched it for a little while, until it was a speck on the landscape. When she turned back around, Zhenya was grinning with her mouth wide open, rocking her limbless torso on the bed.

It was another first for Tori, and very disconcerting to witness.

"She'll be taking the 192 back to Canaan," said Zhenya. "Get me the telephone."

Seventeen

"This area?" said Adwick, gesturing around the brightly lit cafeteria of the sorting facility. "The Islais Creek Channel? It might look like an unassuming San Francisco warehouse district, but, pre-1950, it was home to the world's largest sardine canning industry."

Impress your friends, thought Celso, his long-suffering colleague. Celso was suffering a hangover, which had teeth, and, after some initial uncertainty, had decided to build an extravagant nest in his top three cervical vertebrae. *If this college noob doesn't hold off on the fascinating trivia, I'm gonna have to transfer myself into the bay.*

"I was thinking," said Adwick, popping the top on a 7-Up and drawing back a chair with an intolerable scrape. "How did the creek get its name? *Islais*. That sound Spanish to you?"

"I wouldn't know," growled Celso. "I'm from Campinas." *Some fucking coffee break.*

"Ah," said Adwick, swigging.

Celso felt the keen blue eyes on him. *Man, you'd think we were related, the way he hangs around me. Look at his stupid bald head, I hope it explodes.*

The older man eyed the door to the small dining hall, prayed for the curvy silhouette of Clara from Shipping and Receiving, or even Clara's friend Amy, who had a laugh like a freefalling hyena. In the background, through the thickness of one wall, the two courier company employees listened to the whirr and clank of the huge distribution and sorting facility, the endless processing of hundreds and thousands of packages from all over the country, most of which were shortly to be farmed out to San Francisco's central business district.

"Tough night last night?" said Adwick, realizing.

"I gave my brother his send-off." Celso managed a smile. "He got what he deserved."

"Are you married, boss? Bet you thought I was too young to find a wife." Adwick ran a hand over his smooth skull. "Important institution, marriage. Been around since ancient Egypt. Course, back then, you could marry your sister. Bet you didn't know that."

"Nuh-uh," said Celso. "You swallow an encyclopaedia?"

Adwick laughed, he'd heard this before. "I should go on *Millionaire*, huh?"

Damn, thought Celso. *And the kid's so keen. Probably be the boss of me soon.*

Celso himself was a model employee, but he had a strange inferiority complex when it came to the new college kids; the ones who knew how a spreadsheet worked before you showed them, and who remembered just how you liked your beverage.

Just then, Celso's prayers were answered, and Clara pushed through the swing door, pants snug as ever around cute little hips. He kind of figured she'd just get coffee, they hardly ever spoke, but she seemed to be looking for someone. It took Celso a moment to realize that person was him.

"You wanna come down to the floor?" she said. "Materials support?"

"Something wrong?" Adwick said, but Clara was already walking away. Celso dragged himself back to his feet.

The enormous warehouse was roughly the size of a football field, and it carried the faint smell of damp concrete and gasoline from the clean white trucks lined up outside the grade-level loading doors. Celso watched Adwick to make sure his eyes weren't on Clara's butt as the three of them threaded through the facility, and they weren't. *Impressive discipline*, he thought, and was rewarded with another dull throb of headache.

There was a box standing alone on a trestle table, it had been separated from those on the conveyor. It was a 10kg package, emblazoned with the company logo. Clara was standing over it.

"What's the problem?" said Celso, and then he saw.

The FBI hadn't wasted time. Following the delivery of Katy Trueblood's hand and ear to Karen Wiley's address, they had sent a bulletin to every courier, ground and freight company in the city, UPS, the company that Peterson had first used, but also DHL, USPS, FedEx. The directive was in a hard font, pinned to enough notice boards to be difficult to forget. And Celso had seen the local news, he knew what this address might mean, and this name: Jennifer Wiley.

No one wanted to handle another piece of kidnapped girl.

The box looked hastily packaged, clearly a re-use; it was dog-eared and leeching electrical tape. There were also SameDay markings, the company's fastest option.

"Look at this," said Adwick, horror in his voice; clearly he knew as well. Two hands on either side, he slid the box a little bit, it was light. Where the cardboard had been resting, there was a small smear, wet and bloody, already turning the same color as the table.

It jolted Celso back to life. "Don't you touch that again," he barked, causing heads to turn. "Clara, no one else comes near. *No one.*"

He jogged towards the telephone, oblivious to the stares of those around him.

"No," said Kathleen R. Jackson, trying to keep the concern out of her voice. "I don't want you to focus on his face anymore. Relax again, think about your breathing. Feel the air going in, count each time you breathe out. One, two, three . . ."

At Ella's abrupt mention of the devil, Milton Trueblood, prostrate on the therapist's couch with his eyes closed, had begun to sweat and whimper.

"Remember," said Kath, with a glance at the policewoman who had made the offending remark. "You're back in the tow truck."

Milton quieted at the sound of her voice, but Kath could see his eyes darting beneath pale, red-rimmed eyelids. Ella was over in the corner chair, slumped mannishly. *Get a fucking move on*, seemed to be the message radiating from that direction, but Kath couldn't have rushed if she'd wanted to. Chief McCullers was already in luck; Milton had proved to be a subject who relaxed into hypnosis readily, though it had to be said, Ella's chunky, awkward presence was what had seemed to reassure him the most.

Earlier, on the phone, Kath had been skeptical. "You want me to try forensic hypnosis?"

"Well," Ella had said. "You can tape it if you want, have Milton sign any consent form you might need. But this isn't something I'm using to build a prosecutable case. I just want information leading to Katy Trueblood."

"Something specific?"

"Can you . . . I don't know what you call it. *Regress* him?"

"Memory recall."

"Yes." Ella sounded excited at the prospect. "I mean, Milt can always be hypnotized *again*, right? If we need his testimony for legal purposes?"

"I don't think it would be admissible in a Utah court," Kath had said. "But I don't know that for certain."

"I think you're right," said Ella. "So there is no legal issue, provided the subject is willing."

"Still pretty irregular," said Kath, knowing it wouldn't do the slightest bit of good. Ella had made up her mind, and that was that;

Kath Jackson was going to try and hypnotize Milton Trueblood, no matter how long the odds. She had tried to tell Ella early on that she only used hypnosis very occasionally; to calm clients, to help them with issues of self-esteem, to give them a temporary boost. Yet the session so far had gone well, remarkably well; Milton had been very responsive. Once up on the couch, he had waggled his toes, nervous. Then he had been asked to close his eyes, to engage in a series of progressive relaxation exercises.

"Beauty pageants?" Milton's lip curled in scorn. "You some kind of *fag*?"

Over in the corner, Kath saw Ella sit up a little straighter.

Kath's voice, like warm honey: "Are you still in the recovery truck, Milton? Are you still with Don?"

Milt sobbed a little. "I got a little girl. She's a beauty, better than any of those assholes."

"You have two girls, Milton. Holly and Katy."

"Yeah!" The skinny frame on the couch gave a little lurch. His head turned towards her, the eyes still closed. "You wanna meet them?"

"I'd like that," said Kath.

"Can I have another pill? I got an empty bottle here." He was slurring his words.

"A pill, Milton?"

He pouted. "Like before. I'll have Don's, he's square as shit, don't know what he has to get up for tomorrow."

"Milton," said Kath. "In your mind's eye. Remember we talked about that before? In your mind's eye. Describe what you see right now."

"Okay," said Milton, settling again.

"What do the pills look like?"

He thought for a moment. "Plastic bottle."

Kath glanced at Ella. "Anything else?"

"Too dark to see. We're in the back where Don can't watch."

"In the back of the truck?"

"Another pill. I want another pill."

"Is there a taste?"

"No . . . wait. Salty."

"Could be anything," said Ella to Kath, in a bad stage whisper. "But he was more than just drunk. No wonder he couldn't remember anything."

"I'm not drunk," said Milton, producing a little spit with the plosive *d*. "I can *drive* this crate, if you want. What did Don ever know about fixin' cars before I showed him? You want me to do the alphabet backwards, officer? Zee, wye, ecks. Wait . . . *dubble-you* . . ."

"That's all right, Milt," said Kath. "So he gave you a pill?"

"Shhhh," said Milton. "Don't tell Don. Don hates drugs. Am I gonna get in trouble?"

"No, Milt. But I want you to think back a little bit now. To before, when you first met the man who gave you the pill."

"The devil."

"He's not the devil. He's just a man."

"You never saw his face," said Milt, shivering. "I'm cold. Is it cold in here?"

"Did he tell you his name?"

"No. But he sure liked names. 'Katy Trueblood', he kept saying it. I miss my girl."

"You said his jeep had broken down. Now, I want you to think. Can you remember the plate? The letters and numbers? Think very carefully, this would really help."

Milt squinted. "I . . . I never saw them."

"Are you sure?"

"I never got out the truck. Don doesn't want me to get out of the truck. He thinks I'll show him up." Milt raised his voice. "Let him report us. Dead-end shift anyway."

Kath glanced over at Ella. She wasn't watching anymore, she'd started tearing at her thumbnail. *Wrong answer, Milton. We really could have used a plate to run.*

"Then can you tell me," said Kath, "where it was that you met him? Which road?"

"Canyonlands," said Milt, shuddering.

Salt Lake City.

Lilly's cellphone, the one confiscated from Egan Blake, had started to ring. Special Agents Vasco and Stowe, after a hurried phone call with their SAC, decided it would be best to get the device back to their Home Office, so Ron Vasco had found himself strapped gingerly into the little bush plane that plied the route from Canaan twice daily, tie slack at his neck, clutching the briefcase containing the cellphone like a life preserver. Stowe remained on the ground to review the case as they'd found it, but there didn't seem to be much to go on.

Vasco was granted an immediate audience with Special Agent in Charge Gerald "Grimmie" Borman. There were a couple of other agents around the conference table, one of whom Vasco didn't know, and together they listened to the traffic on South Street.

"What does Lillian Hersh actually say when she calls?" said Grimmie, pushing through the door connecting the conference room with his office. As was his way, there were no formalities.

"There are two messages," said Vasco, folding his hands. "The first one is a prayer. The second one is a message to Karen Wiley; cries for help, and it sounds like she's being tortured. They're both recordings."

"You can be sure?"

"They're repeated, and they're identical. The phone has been switched off to conserve the battery, but we're turning up a compatible charger, shouldn't be hard."

"Can you be sure the voice belongs to Lillian Hersh?"

"We think so. I had the man we arrested, Egan Blake, verify the voice. The call is placed to the cellphone roughly every fifteen minutes, and it started about three hours ago. Both messages last around two minutes, I've made a transcript."

"Did you find Karen Wiley?"

"Not yet. Agent Stowe is on it. Mr. Blake is cooperating, but he can't predict Ms. Wiley's movements." Vasco tugged at his collar a little. "Sir, Blake talks like a cop and has an FBI serial number on his gun. Was he assigned to this case?"

"I've never heard of him," said Grimmie. "And I'm still waiting to hear from DC."

SAC Borman, red-faced and choleric, was particularly displeased with this strange Egan Blake angle. When, as Agent Stowe had suggested over the phone, he made inquiries into the man they had in a Canaan holding cell, the initial response hadn't, as he had hoped, come back entirely negative. But neither was the Justice Department telling him in what official capacity, if any, Mr. Egan Blake was doing breaking into buildings in an area that fell under *his* territory. Grimmie smelt the prospect of intra-departmental error and a soon-to-be fluttering ticker-tape parade of miscommunication. In his mind, the best solution was to close this case before the whole thing got bogged down, and this cellphone was the key.

"Sir . . ." Grimmie's secretary poked her head around the door. "I have the *San Francisco Chronicle*. They're getting reports that a freelance journalist has been kidnapped in Grand County. They're worried about her, will talk to you off the record."

"Ten minutes," said Grimmie, which meant twenty at least. He gestured at the man with the prematurely gray hair, the person in the room whom Vasco hadn't recognized. "Agent Vasco, Agent Stoller. Stoller, you can trace the signal of the repeated calls to this cellphone? Find out where they're coming from?"

"Of course," said Stoller.

San Francisco Field Office.

Agent DeMedici cradled the phone. "The court order came

through," he said. "Record time, seems like. Salt Lake City just got the carrier to unblock the repeated blocked calls to the cellphone belonging to Lillian Hersh."

"Well?" said Agent Rice. "Spit it out."

DeMedici smiled. "An apartment in San Francisco."

"We're sure?"

"Every single call today, at least. And he's gonna be *our* collar."

"There's an address?"

"Treasure Island."

"I knew it," said Rice, resisting the urge to bring his fist down on the desk. He wasn't a man who spent much time regretting his actions, but he'd been badly wrong about Karen Wiley and her poison-pen letters. It made his thick neck tighten with shame to remember how he'd accused her that day on the roof. Of course, that was before the case had become tied to the girl in Utah, before the hand and the ear in the box, before . . .

Agent Menzies swung the office door open, didn't bother to knock. Rice might have been pissed off but for the look on his face, and Rice imagined that he knew what the man was going to say before he said it. It was the last news any agent in the building wanted to hear, short of some kind of multiple-fatality terrorist attack on the Golden Gate Bridge.

"FedEx just turned up another body part," said Menzies.

Rice looked at DeMedici.

"A package addressed to Jennifer Wiley," said Menzies. "A foot, initial reports have it taken off nice and neat."

"A *foot*?"

"Forensics have scrambled, but that'll be some damn coincidence if it isn't Katy's."

"Fuck," said Rice.

Agent Menzies was pulling on his coat. "You wanna ride out with me?"

"Treasure Island," said Rice to DeMedici, through gritted teeth. "Call Brookes, we don't know what kind of monster. Suggest we coordinate with SWAT."

"Okay," said Ella to herself, easing up on the gas. The scrolling desert scenery began to slow.

Based on the revelations from Milton, she could now narrow down the point in the desert where he must have met the man

The devil

in Holly's picture to a three- or four-mile stretch of highway. She knew the call—or at least *a* call—had come in to Sal's Garage from the payphone at the Salt River lookout, and that must have been the one Don and Milt had answered. Combining this information with what had been revealed when Kath Jackson painstakingly walked Milton back from the point when he had woken up the following morning led Ella to believe she was pretty sure she could identify the rough location of the fatal meeting, even if she couldn't pinpoint it exactly on a map. Milton's subconscious memory had been far stronger earlier in that evening, before, she assumed, the effects of the drug had kicked in.

And what exactly did you hope to do with this information? Perhaps your perp dropped his goddamn driving license out here for you to find?

The fact was, Ella couldn't sit in Kath Jackson's well-appointed living room and listen to the burbling of Milton Trueblood any longer. Every dead end in this case—and this appeared to be another one—she'd advanced beyond because she'd butted her head against it; repeatedly, stubbornly, senselessly. But, sure enough, Ella had discovered little more than mile after mile of desolate beauty, thick storm clouds swirling overhead. She'd driven this stretch back and forth maybe five times now, just waiting for inspiration, a sign. It had reached the point where she could predict the passing of individual aspects of terrain: pastel-colored rock formations, sculpted sandstone walls, dry desert grasses, the dips in the heaped-earth shoulder where recreational 4x4s had headed out into the canyons on a makeshift, unmarked trail . . .

A *trail?*

Ella slammed on the brakes, and her car screeched to a halt. She spun it around, throwing up a curved cloud of dust, then pulled over, reached across for her map. It was a ranger issue, one of the most comprehensive.

Yes, the trail was there. It was one of those that led into the heart of nowhere, with a couple of tributaries leading off. She was miles away from Crescent Canyon—the ghost town and the church were at the other end of the park—but something made her think of Egan Blake; of how he had been fatigued, yet still prepared to travel all the way out from Canaan in the middle of the night because he thought there was the slim possibility it might have led to something.

It wasn't as though Ella needed precedent.

But no one even knows you're out here . . .

No. Have faith.

All of the makeshift desert roads were pretty bad, this she knew; but Ella couldn't tell from the map just *how* bad. She'd just have to turn back if necessary.

If you can turn back.

With no fresh water, and only a little more than half a tank of gas, Ella McCullers knocked the car into drive and shot across the road, nose bouncing as it left the blacktop and chewed the dust, grit spitting out from the rear wheels in twin fountains of scorched earth.

Detective John Gardner had popped the two aspirins into his mouth before realizing his water bottle was empty. Rather than stick his head above the flimsy walls of the cubicle, he crunched them like candy, taking grim pleasure from the harsh taste.

He'd been feeling pretty sick for the last few days. He knew Lilly had somehow gotten the better of him, had made him reveal information he shouldn't have. It was that impish, forthright way about her, and now, perhaps as a result of his mistake, she was missing.

Gardner didn't particularly care about the dark bureaucratic hole he'd likely soon find himself in—he was under no illusion, the responsibility was his own—even Karen Wiley had figured out that Lilly must have gotten the information from him. None of that mattered anymore. Hell, he'd *welcome* a disciplinary if it meant Lilly would turn up safe.

Gardner was sick with fear.

He'd seen some bad things in his time on the force, had heard even worse, but as a committed father, he couldn't imagine the madness that would cause a person to methodically cut a child into pieces and then put those pieces in the mail.

The office was empty, so when the voice called from the door, he knew it was for him. "You want on this jump-out squad or not?" said Penarski, a younger officer. "Because you're gonna miss the briefing; after that, adios."

Penarski was keen, it was his first. "Hold the elevator," said Gardner, standing and tugging at his vest. Beneath the trench coat, the Kevlar made his upper-body seem bulkier than ever.

John Gardner felt some sadness at the prospect of being back-up; he'd like to have taken this suspect personally. The main strike force would be drawn from the SFPD Tactical Unit, but on some level he supposed it was still his case, Karen Wiley's letters having been brought to him in the first place, way back when.

If Ella's entire career as a policewoman could be summed up in one moment, it would be a moment that combined bone-crushing disappointment with the slender affirmation that maybe, just maybe, there might be light at the end of the tunnel.

She'd exhausted the primary route. It had led to a deserted

campsite, nothing more. Now she was exhausting the tributaries, of which this was the last.

Maybe it wasn't as bad as Flint Hill, but Ella had negotiated the police car down 1,500 feet of descent in a little under seven miles, and some of the hairpin switchbacks had her heart threatening to pump out of her chest. Once, two tires had lodged in a pothole and had spun there, useless. Realizing it could be life or death, Ella had gingerly reversed back, then praised God when the rubber finally stuck to the road. She hadn't been able to turn around, so she drove right around the hole, well up a sandstone camber, chassis tilting to a point where she feared the car might overturn.

Recognizing the point at which the trail stopped even being a trail took a level of judgment that she wasn't sure she was capable of anymore; this was the point where she was no longer following markings on a map, she was just desert driving. If she carried on now, she could expect to count the minutes until certain disaster.

What? You gonna cover the ENTIRE park? Don't be ridiculous.

If that's what it takes . . .

Ella emerged from the tight pass onto a deeply cratered clearing. A laccolithic range, she supposed the Abajo Mountains, reared up many miles away to the left. Storm clouds were building upon storm clouds, swirling around peaks like primitive gods of war.

There's nothing here, Ella.

No, maybe there is . . .

THERE'S NOTHING HERE, ELLA.

She killed the engine, fought for air. It would be easier if she stepped outside the car, so she did that.

It was hot. Tears mixed with the sweat on her face. With little sense of direction, she began to walk.

Where are you going, Ella? You can't drive anymore so you're gonna walk? You want this case to claim another life? You wanna be picked apart by buzzards?

"No, I . . ."

Her boot kicked a stone, heavy for its small size, and it went scooting a short distance. It was a strange color, different from all the others. Ella's breath caught in her throat.

Don't be stupid. Lots of stones in the desert, Ella.

"Not like this," she murmured, looking.

There were more, in a small pile, like a cairn. Pieces of faded dark granite.

A *burial marker?*

Someone came out here and smashed up a gravestone?

Ella sank to her knees, picked up a couple of pieces; some had impossibly straight sides, others were irregular, knobbly. There could be no mistake, this *was* a gravestone, a fairly typical one, perhaps broken into a dozen pieces. She scrabbled around, held more of the large fragments in her hands, turning them over, weighing them.

Am I kneeling on a grave here?

She scrabbled around, behind, in front, like a person who had lost a contact lens.

No, there's no grave here. The ground is too hard.

Just the stone. Why?

But it wasn't Karen Wiley's stone, the one Blake had described seeing at The Church of the Final Days. This was an *old* stone. She couldn't tell how old, but it was very weathered. Ella traced her fingers over indents where she presumed, once, there must have been writing.

She raised her eyes to the heavens.

"But I can't *read it*," she said. "If there was supposed to be a name here for me to find, *I can't read it*. What good is it if I can't *read it* . . ."

In the distance, dancing around the mountaintops, the first spiderwebs of lightning.

The two black SWAT vans rolled out of the underground parking garage like dark destroyers, were clocked immediately by the SFPD helicopter circling above.

Their destination was an address on Treasure Island, a man-made atoll residing in the middle of San Francisco Bay. It is connected via an isthmus and a smaller, natural island to both San Francisco and Oakland by the Bay Bridge.

Despite the remarkable and highly scenic location, it is a place scarcely visited by the area's upwardly mobile city dwellers, and the low cost of housing and lack of amenities mean that many of the new tenants are Section 8 migrants. There are some problems, social and otherwise, though the whole area is slated for imminent redevelopment.

A six-man tac-squad was going out in full fatigues, touting AR-15 assault rifles and the usual flashbangs. There were also two feds, and Gardner and Penarski. There was easily enough room, but it still seemed snug in the back of the vans, that intimate throb of adrenalin.

The latest news from Salt Lake City was encouraging. Lilly's phone hadn't stopped ringing, the same recorded messages. Perhaps the kidnapper was still in his place of residence.

"The bastard's going to torment us with those recordings until we bring him down," Agent Rice had said at the briefing, which was swift.

"Ayuh," said Abe Smith of Smith & Son, Monumental Masons, eyeing Ella carefully. "We put a maker's mark on every one."

Ella knew how she must have looked to the old man; windswept and dumpy, feathery fans of clean skin around the corners of her eyes where she'd been squinting against the dust. They were looking into the trunk of the car, a huge wolfhound bouncing gleefully roundabouts. Ella had laid out as much of the smashed tombstone as she could find, had tried to put the pieces together like a heavy jigsaw.

"What can you tell me about this?" she said.

"Ayuh," said Abe. "Well, it *is* one of ours. See on the back of this section here? A.S. The mark sometimes lasts longer than the inscription on accounts of being less open to the elements."

"You made this stone?"

"Coulda been my pappy, maybe one of mine. I got my initial on stones from here to Timbuktu, and proud of it."

"Yes, yes," said Ella. She hadn't begun by making a good impression on Abe Smith, wasn't about to start now. "Can you tell me anything else?"

"Ayuh," said Abe, putting fire to a roll-up, his default rejoinder when he encountered impatience or rudeness or both. "It looks like someone done taken a sandblaster to it."

"I found it in the desert," said Ella. "On an exposed ridge."

"Well, that don't make a lick of sense," said Abe, expelling blue smoke. "You can't get permission to bury like that, and we'd never meaningfully supply product to lawbreakers."

"I didn't find an actual grave. Someone must've just moved the stone out there."

"Looks like more than just canyon winds took that name off," said Abe. "But I can still read the dates on the born/died."

"You can?" said Ella, looking again.

"Well, not the whole of the *born*. But the died, that there's a 69, and the date there is May 12. I've done enough restorations to know. Put your fingers on it, have a feel at the grooves. That should be enough to get you a name, Chief."

"It should?" said Ella.

"Ayuh," said Abe Smith, shooting her a curious glance. "And an address, if that's any use."

"I don't understand," said Ella, knowing how hope was a dangerous thing. "How can you get a name and address off of this?"

Abe gestured towards his office. "Well, we got records here startin' when my pappy moved the business from back east; who got buried where and under what, local-wise, at least. I'm son, y'know, of Smith & Son, but I kept the sign the way it was. Abe Junior, that's me."

The two vans maneuvered out of the busy bridge traffic and headed down the access route, speeding through a set of intimidating brick gates, waved on by a bewildered security guard.

To descend on to Treasure Island is to step back in time; to the right of the wide public road, a flight control tower atop an administrative building just one of many reminders of the island's previous incarnation as a naval station. The quiet streets are characterized by art-deco military structures and Cold War era buildings.

It may have been inhabited, but the whole place felt like a ghost town. The vans chose to ignore the 15 mph limit.

The apartment in question was inside an aluminum-sided building, perhaps old dormitories of some kind; there were some arbitrary numbers stenciled, barracks style. Feral cats looked on as the vehicles pulled up and the men piled out, and no children played in the streets.

Fortunately, the building was fairly easy to move on unnoticed. Agent Menzies had secured a blurry facsimile of the specs, and the apartment windows faced seaward.

Jon Peterson was a lot of things, but he wasn't stupid. He did not allow Dave Wiley to carry on living out of the goodness of his heart, he left him alive to maintain the primary focus of the investigation in San Francisco; a straight kill might have led to the assumption that Jon would flee California. Judging from the small tactical unit that now lined up in the corridor outside his short-lease apartment, at least one more element of Peterson's scheme was going according to plan.

They intended to go in dynamic, blow the apartment door off its hinges with shock-lock rounds. The unit believed they had some idea of what kind of person they were dealing with, and were concerned, should Katy or Lilly still be alive, that the suspect might finish the job if they tried to enter announced—not that a gentle tap on the door was typical for SWAT teams worldwide. Neither did they want a hostage situation on their hands.

The head of this hand-picked element was called Munro, a veteran of ATF. He held up three fingers to the man who would take the door, dropped one, dropped two, dropped three.

The door was flimsy, flew out of the frame, they could have used a ram.

The five-man clearance of the apartment took seconds, the sound of the shotgun still ringing off the walls.

There was no one inside. Neither was there any furniture, just the developer's fresh paint and the outstanding sweep of the city skyline across the white-crested waves of the bay.

There was nothing there.

Five minutes later, and Agent Rice and Detective Gardner are standing in the empty bedroom. They've already decided they don't care for one another.

"What do you think?" says Rice.

Gardner puts a finger to his lips. "*Shhhh.*"

They've been listening to the team investigating the other apartments, a little heavy-handed; the warrant covers the whole building. Some lodgings are occupied, some are not.

But now there is something else.

A voice. Distant, but there.

Lilly's voice?

"In the wall," says Gardner, incredulous, moving in the general direction.

A section of the recently erected plasterboard is, subtly, a different shade of white. Rice presses his ear to it.

"Gentle Jesus meek and mild," Lilly is saying. "Look upon a little child . . ."

Rice looks up, yes, Gardner can make out the words as well. The soulless and disembodied voice of his friend is chilling the big detective to his very core.

"It's the telephone recording," whispers Rice. "How did he get it in there?"

Lilly's voice carries on for a short while, and then there is a subtle click, maybe a receiver.

"It must be some kind of auto-dialer," says Gardner, who also finds himself whispering.

There is a space inside the wall, a space between rooms, and there is nothing on this side to indicate how Peterson's automatic telephone system connects up. Gardner moves into the living area to look, and it is this that saves his life, confines his stay in hospital to a mere three months.

One of the facets that makes Jon Peterson such a fearsome opponent is that he can—through patience and commitment—become extremely proficient at whatever he puts his mind to. He had never constructed a bomb before, though the prospect amused him; the hardest part, as it often is for would-be bombers, was acquiring the nitric acid. But even this had barely posed a problem for Peterson's resource; there was a plentiful supply in the labs at Reno High School.

In his final experiment, Peterson had filtered off the distilled water for the last time and placed the manufactured RDX into a plastic bag inside another plastic bag and mixed it with TNT in a roughly 50/50 ratio. This was necessary to stabilize the crystals. Then, following some Internet-based information that may or may not have been accurate, he stirred ammonium nitrate into the mixture for the sheer joy of trying to increase the explosive power.

If this actually does make a difference, it hardly matters: Jon Peterson has already manufactured enough cyclonite to reduce most of the building to rubble.

His switch constitutes a length of extremely thin copper wire that criss-crosses the inside of the makeshift apartment wall, held in place by ordinary office staples. Once the electrical current that passes through the wire is broken, the bomb will detonate.

Rice should have known better, but he is highly frustrated, can see the wall is flimsy, and Lilly's voice on tape is an attractive lure; perhaps the only bit of solid evidence they're going to turn up today.

Peterson, naturally, has constructed it this way.

Rice could have smashed through the thin drywall with his fist, but he chooses to use the butt of his gun.

Miraculously, he misses the criss-cross of wire with his first blow.

Gardner hears the blow, his voice from the other room: "What the hell are you *doing*?"

Rice ignores, brings down the gun again.

The entire room blasts outwards and upwards, throwing him sideways in a white-hot ball of flame, the sound of the expanding air bursting his eardrums. At least Gardner has time to think of his loved ones, a luxury not afforded to Agent Rice.

It is a fatal, annihilative explosion, and can be seen and heard as far away as Alameda.

There wasn't another car on the road, and within half an hour of leaving the sanatorium, Karen Wiley was making the right turn onto the long road back to town. The junction was deserted, the red stop sign shaking a little in the rising wind, craggy wilderness all around.

What was it about junctions like this, Karen? Crossroads in the middle of nowhere? Blues songs, hoodoo, the place between the worlds. It doesn't take a genius to figure out what's happening here . . .

"No," said Karen, surprising herself. She caught the reflection of one eye in the rear-view mirror, that morning's mascara so hastily applied. It took a moment to realize she was the one shaking, not the car. She took some deep breaths, feeling hollow.

Her cellphone wasn't working. It could have been the coverage, it could have been the atmospherics, it could have been the battery, but now she'd have to wait to contact anyone, probably Canaan city limits at the earliest. Karen had gotten halfway back down the track from the hospital before she realized she should have used the phone there, should have contacted the police with the name of Zhenya's brother; then the investigation would have been kick-started again. But she wasn't thinking straight at the time, and she hadn't wanted to turn back.

Always moving forward, always . . . what? Running away?

"No," said Karen, the needle on the dial pushing eighty. "That's not it."

There was at least one other reason for her haste: the storm. The idea of not getting back to town before it hit was frightening; there was something about being exposed on this long, lonely road.

Although, of course, she was heading right towards it.

The scrubland rushed past.

She was about to reach over to switch on the radio, maybe catch a weather report, or at least listen to some music—anything to calm the voices in her head—when she saw a vehicle, a biggish one, but not quite as big as her own, heading from the other direction. If she was doing eighty, the oncoming jeep must have been doing the same, because they were staring down one another in seconds. Karen got a flash of a serious face, a wide-brimmed hat, two eyes that seemed to stare right into hers, and then they were passed.

The police? Was that the police?

Instinctively, Karen eased her foot off the pedal a little, and in the mirror she watched the flare of the jeep's red tail lights.

The other vehicle was stopping. In moments, it had turned around in a wide sweep, was pointing in her direction, and Karen could see a tow dolly attached to the back.

He was gaining, began to flash his lights. The intention of the man was clear; he was following her, he wanted to pull her over, something. *Livestock Officer* was printed on the hood of his jeep in large white letters. A cop then, or county official.

No lightbar though, no siren. A Livestock Officer? What's a Livestock Officer?

Karen was still some thirty or forty miles from Canaan. She didn't want to waste time.

But he'll have a radio. Maybe I can use his radio?

The man in the jeep had rolled down his window, was motioning for her to pull over. She couldn't make out the face, but she remembered her glimpse as the jeep flashed by; an intense, studious countenance. Very possibly a cop face.

It was time to get the cops involved.

He was pulling level, the hand waving more urgently.

Then, without warning, Lilly's voice in her mind:

He wants YOU. I'M not the one he wants.

It was as if the man in the jeep had heard it too. Before Karen could hit the gas, the parallel car swung in towards her, metal rasping against metal. Control of the car spun through her cold, wet palms, and there was no time to scream.

Ella was no lone wolf.

While there were avenues of investigation she would surely pursue alone, Ella knew that she worked better in a team, leading a team. It was where she felt most comfortable, which was why the Trueblood case had proved such an emotional stretch—the Chief had feared that if she'd taken some of her less likely-sounding leads to the boys, they might have talked her out of pursuing them, and then the investigation wouldn't be in the position it was now. There was also her messy but unforgettable history with Milton, who had wielded the potential to embarrass her out of authority.

And so, much as Ella McCullers would have curled up into a ball at the thought of anyone seeing the only female Chief of Police in the town's history reduced to her knees in the desert, clutching bits of tombstone, the idea of striding unaccompanied to the residence that had formerly belonged to Dr. Christopher Peterson—and now his son Jonathon—was unthinkable.

The broken tombstone on the ridge belonged to a woman named Abigail Peterson. Why it had been recently smashed, defaced, dragged all that way out of town, Ella didn't know. Neither did she particularly care, although Abe Smith had been able to tell her it had been reported missing from a local cemetery for twelve years or more. The important thing was that the next-of-kin had been registered at this address, and it felt like enough evidence to take back to the station, reassert her command, even if the reasoning was too complicated to explain to the slower members of the class right now. Besides, it would be good for morale if they all made an arrest together, could save Katy Trueblood like conquering heroes.

But this is still a tenuous lead.

No, we're onto something here, I can feel it.

The men were eager, had jumped at the prospect of rolling out, and Ella's other fear—that the FBI would be running the place—had proved to be unfounded. There was just one agent on the ground, who was apparently out re-interviewing Jeanette Keynes—*good luck with that,* thought Ella. And behind bars, she'd found Egan Blake, fast asleep on his cot, emitting old-man snores. Judging from the fluttering eyelids, he was lost in nightmares of one kind or another.

It was getting late in the day. Two squad cars pulled up outside the large house with the wraparound porch.

Ella, now in uniform and with hair neatly brushed, led the way up the path. Deputy Slim Johnson was hot on her heels. Three more officers were primed and ready in the back of the cars, the first spots of rain from the thunderstorm spitting at the windshields.

The area of Canaan known as The Heights had expanded since the late sixties, but the overlook was still spectacular. They'd arrived without lights or sirens, but in houses across the way—newer houses than the Peterson residence—faces still appeared at windows, called behind into shadowy rooms for more faces to *come see*. In yet another house, an old man appeared at his door, then, after a moment's hesitation, came out to sit on a rocker, perhaps anticipating a show.

Ella was oblivious to it all. She banged on the frame of the screen door with her nightstick.

Then they waited.

Ella looked over at big Slim Johnson. He swallowed, Adam's apple bobbing.

She was about to bang again, but a woman appeared from the gloom, thin and pale, but immaculately dressed, like some kind of Stepford wife.

"Is Jon Peterson here?" said Ella. "We'd like to ask him a few questions."

The woman shook her head.

"Can I ask your name, ma'am?" said Ella.

"Teresa," said the woman, lip trembling.

"Teresa?"

"Teresa Peterson. I'm his wife."

Now Ella could smell fear, or possibly madness, perhaps worse. She cleared her throat.

"Can we come in, take a quick look around?"

The woman's mouth began to twitch, and tears sprang up in her eyes. She dropped her head onto her chest, said: "Thank God you're here . . . thank *God* . . ."

"Ma'am?" Ella was already pulling open the door.

"I think . . ." said the woman, "I think he still has the girl. In the basement."

Ella left the woman with Slim, she was hysterical, wasn't making sense. They'd already signaled for back-up and an ambulance, and Ella pushed through the kitchen door to where the woman had indicated.

The whole house was spotless, polished up like a new pin, as though everything had just been removed from the wrapping. There was a strong, almost overpowering smell of bleach.

The basement door was bolted in three places, but there was no lock. Ella had the door open in seconds, drew her gun.

The stairs were dark.

"Hello?" she called down.

No reply.

Ella found a switch, a trail of wires leading to bulbs with powerful wattage. Satisfied that she probably had better visual than anyone hiding below, she descended.

The basement was enormous, must have spread out farther than the boundary of the house, but it only constituted four large rooms. The first was a scene from a nightmare, ancient-seeming medical equipment, curved blades, Victorian-style phials, charts of human anatomy. Books lined the walls; chemistry, munitions, psychology.

The basement wasn't as tidy as the rest of the house. In fact, it was positively chaotic. And there was another smell down here, a stronger, more ominous one.

Ella found more switches to illuminate the space, followed her gun through a door.

She didn't let her surprise compromise her caution, but what she saw made her take a step back nonetheless.

Telephone directories.

Hundreds of telephone directories. They were arranged like a funeral pyre in the huge, high-roofed space, and Ella didn't have to look beyond to know what the smell was, there were empty red cans thrown about the place, peeling flammable stickers.

Gasoline. These books are drenched in gasoline.

Lying atop the potential bonfire, a small body under a bloodied sheet.

Ella holstered her weapon, began to scramble, resisting the urge to cough and sputter in a room lacking air.

She pulled off the sheet.

Katy . . .

Katy was dead.

Ella, in shock herself, took in the bloody stumps of the hand and foot, some kind of plastic flexi-cuff stemming a bleeding that had clotted. There were intubation tubes snaking out of her in various places.

How long ago did he take these out? Some kind of life support?

The thought was barely through her mind, when the small body moved, seemed to cough, though there was no sound.

She's alive . . .

Ella couldn't comprehend this, waited for more. The girl's face was bloodied, but there was a twitch behind closed eyes.

She's ALIVE.

Ella was going to turn, scramble for the stairs, for the medics, but men were already streaming into the room, two men with a stretcher, a couple of her officers standing and gawping, guns drawn. Above, in the main house, the stomping of feet, hastily shouted instructions.

Extreme trauma, don't touch, thought Ella McCullers. She'd liked to have grabbed the little wounded girl, hugged her as though both their salvation depended on it.

Eighteen

Now she will know horror.

Drip, drip.

Karen Wiley is sleeping. There may be no glassy-eyed toys or shiny boy-posters to stand sentry for her, but when the diffused light catches the curves and hollows of Karen's face as it does now, she could be more than simply mistaken for her beautiful daughter, she could actually *be* her.

Or anyone else, for that matter. Take your pick.

Drip, drip.

Wake up, Karen.

I am awake. I was always awake.

Drip, drip.

You remember that old urban legend? Jon Peterson certainly does. Something about a girl who finds herself house-sitting overnight in a crusty mansion block, all alone but for a friendly sheepdog. "Don't worry," she is told by the owners. "If you get lonely, or afraid, the dog will protect you. He sleeps under the bed. Just put your hand down, and he'll give it a friendly lick, remind you everything is as it should be."

However, not everything *was* as it should be. Late at night, there was this strange dripping sound; consistent, ongoing. It was a big house, but even so, a noise like that can carry. It disconcerted the girl, but she was mostly fine, because she could always reach out and the dog would be there, licking her hand.

The sound still played on her mind and she couldn't sleep. She was spooked, it was dark, but she went all over the upstairs of that house, checking the faucets, making sure there were no leaky pipes. And there were not. So she went back to bed.

Drip, drip.

Pretty damn restless night the girl had. You know how a single, repetitive noise can keep you awake? Thank goodness for the friendly sheepdog under the bed, licking her hand once in a while, letting her know everything was fine.

The following morning, down in the kitchen, the girl found the friendly sheepdog hanging from the door of the fridge. It had been garrotted with steel wire, and its guts were hanging out. *Drip, drip, drip* went the blood. It had been dead for hours.

Smeared in stinky doggy gore on the white tiled floor: *humans can lick too.*

Lillian Hersh had become a plaything, almost a confidant, and Jon Peterson had enjoyed sharing that story with her. *Oh, these things from our childhood,* he had said.

Now Karen opens her eyes, lets out a short scream.

It is dark. Not pitch, but dark. She turns her head towards the gentle drip, temples throbbing with narcosis. The floor is textured beneath her back, holds the coolness of earth.

Am I outside?

Drip, drip.

She can see the liquid making the noise, it splashes into a small pool in the uneven ground only a few inches away. It is thick and dark and glossy, not like water.

Strange that it should be an unrelated dripping sound to cause the realization, or perhaps Karen knew it all along and her brain was just waiting for her drugged body to catch up. Either way, it seems to occur in a series of instances; tumbling, *horrible* knowledge.

He's got me.

Karen scrambles up to a sitting position, and all of her senses fight for attention at once. She's not outside, she's inside, but there are holes in the roof, no stars visible. There are long gray rectangles of windows and the fatter gray rectangle of an open doorway. It has the feel, the look, of a firebombed, post-apocalyptic barn

a church?

She is lying where the altar must have been.

The Church of the Final Days.

Outside, the rumble of thunder. It is night-time.

She reaches to her wrists, expecting shackles. There are none. Standing too fast, Karen almost keels over as the blood struggles to feed her brain. Then she is fine, and the throb of bruises on her upper arm and shoulder inflicted when the car ran off the road are almost too trivial to mention. There is another ache as well, a more acute one, where he put in the sedating needle.

Karen steps forward, lurches for the exit.

Drip, drip.

She remembers the sound that woke her, the vision of the dark droplet creating ripples across the tiny lake. Karen turns and sees the mutilated and suspended corpse of Lillian Hersh, she'd been sleeping beneath it all along.

The job is so ugly because he didn't have time. Jon has fired his nail gun gratuitously, but it didn't occur to him until afterwards that Lilly looked like a crucifixion, *was* a crucifixion, but then he rather enjoyed the symbolism, although when James Earl LaGrande had preached in this very church he hadn't been all that big on iconography.

Still, interesting how these things come together sometimes.

Lilly's arms and legs had been pegged to a makeshift, irregular cross with so many nails that it looked as though she'd been sewn into it. But then, when he attempted to raise her via cables looped over a beam, her head wouldn't stay up, it slumped onto her chest, no matter how many nails he pumped into the face. There just wasn't enough skull tissue left to hold her up, each nail making it worse, a dark and twisted knot of metal. But then he had the great idea of crucifying her upside down, where the head could swing freely. Surely that was even *better* symbolism, because the little whore journalist wasn't worthy of Christ, or even of St. Peter.

Lilly doesn't look like a body anymore, she looks like a gigantic, dissected albino bat. Blood drips from the legs, the arms, runs down to the scooped-out grapefruit half where her face used to be, congregates until gravity can hold the liquid no longer, quivers there for a second, and . . .

Drip, drip.

Karen takes in the remains of her friend with a kind of strange serenity, though her gut is churning in a way that threatens to make her vomit. Frankly, it would have been worse if there was a face, eyes to accuse.

Karen turns, walks towards the exit.

Outside.

No discernible moon, just a kind of *haze*, where the storm clouds diffuse the light. Karen has never personally visited Crescent Canyon, although she has seen it in a photograph, and the place seems all too familiar from the story told by Zhenya.

A pole has been hammered into the ground in the church clearing. At the top is speared a human hand, a finger pointing towards the churchyard. The hand is dirty, decomposing, and, as Peterson is no longer making any effort to preserve it, by tomorrow will be seething with maggots.

The hand belonged to the mechanic, Don Keynes, though Karen doesn't know this.

Dutifully, she looks in the direction indicated by the outstretched finger. There is something there that she can't quite see, so she walks over.

The graveyard is also dark, but not so dark as to render Karen incapable of making out the tombstone with her own name on it: Karen Wiley – R.I.P.

After the visceral nightmare of awakening beneath the body of her best friend—and even compared to the hand on the pole—the tombstone seems tawdry, pathetic, a bit of a let-down. Karen never lost respect for her opponent before, the man who has painstakingly arranged to draw her into his world, but this stage-prop isn't doing anything for her.

"Hello," says Jon Peterson, appearing from somewhere.

"This isn't doing anything for me," says Karen, gesturing at the stone.

"C'mon," says Jon. "I want to show you something. Something over there."

In his hand there is a sword.

"Okay," says Karen.

"I thought I'd missed the storm," says Karen. "I thought I'd slept through it."

Jon Peterson smiles at her, shakes his head.

Together, in silence, they have climbed up the side of the wide, shallow valley, and are now standing on the spot where Egan Blake had previously hidden himself. But Karen and Jon do not look inward, towards the church. Together, they are looking in the *other* direction, away from the church, in a kind of shared wonderment.

They look to where the storm rages.

It could be ten miles away, maybe more, a mass of moving cloud that cuts the horizon in half; an ash-black hull, alive with a fire of white flame. Beneath the repeated, oft-simultaneous lashings of lightning, the astonishing geography appears to move, to writhe and thrash, rock formations rearing up and crashing down like dinosaurs in final throes of death. The mercury forks keep on coming, one atop the next, scorching their image into the air with the piercing memory of light, and the distant thunder is one long continuous growl of fury. It looks like the coming of Armageddon. It looks like earth and heaven are at war.

Jon and Karen look on, gifted, celestial tourists.

"Better it heads in the other direction," says Jon. "We wouldn't want to be caught in that."

"We were fortunate," says Karen.

"We were," says Jon. "You can't predict a storm."

"Perhaps you can," says Karen, turning to face him. "Killing me isn't going to change anything. Do you know that?"

"Excuse me?"

"I talked to Zhenya."

"That's good. She doesn't get many visitors."

"Whatever it is, I can help you." Karen doesn't plead, she just tells.

"You already are," he says.

"I know about the past. I live in the past. We both do. We all do. I know about what happened, Jon. I know all about your mother."

"You don't even look like her, you know that?"

"Zhenya told me about the demons. Trust me, you don't need them anymore."

"You're right," Jon says, truthfully. "And you know something? They've gone."

"They have?"

"As of today, I think." He uses his sword to gesture at the storm, two or three jabs. "For all I know, they're over there. I'd like to think that they caused it, my romantic notion. But yes, this is just you and me now."

"I'm glad of that," says Karen.

"How about Sammie?" he says. "Do you still see Sammie? Does she still walk the earth with you?" Jon looks serious, concerned for her. Karen considers asking him how he ever knew about Sammie, decides the time might not be appropriate. Instead, she shakes her head, no.

"In your dreams?"

"Dreams are just that," says Karen. "Dreams."

"Then this really *is* just you and me," says Jon. "I'm glad it happened this way."

"Perhaps we can help each other."

"Yes," says Jon, drawing back his blade.

Karen Wiley, running, falling, rolling back towards the church. Blood streams from her left arm where he opened her up, and she can't move those fingers now. Are tendons cut? She's in pain, but adrenalin is a wonderful thing; Karen doesn't know how bad it is.

Behind, Jon strides, fast but steady, more careful with his footing. He thinks Karen has nowhere to go, and he really wants to relish the hunt.

Karen catches her head on a rock, it knocks her silly, then she's up on her feet again, running, running, running, breasts aching as she moves.

No help from the church, so she runs away from it, runs towards the pass, slick fingers pressed against the rawness of the wound. The face of Blake's Land Rover surprises her. Peterson's jeep is here as well, he used one to tow the other. Neither appear much compromised by the altercation on the road.

The gun in her handbag. The handbag in the car.

Karen wrenches open the door, screams as she does so. Her bag is in the well of the seat. How slowly can you pull open a zipper?

She can't afford to waste time, but looks towards the pass anyway. Why? Because when Karen Wiley dies, she wants to *know* she's dying. She doesn't want the power to just cut out, like some pulled plug, an electrical cable getting severed in her neck.

She's going down with a fight.

Peterson is here, of course he is. Jon rounds the rock with his enthusiastic stride, grinning, sword held in an iron grip. There's little more than the length of a room between them now. Karen turns back to the bag, the gun is waiting.

A little gun. A pop gun.

Karen grabs the weapon, her stance is adequate. She cocks and squeezes.

Click.

No ammo. It isn't loaded.

It was never loaded.

Blake had it in the glove compartment and he never loaded it. She squeezes again anyway.

Peterson brings in the sword. He uses barely half the power he has at his disposal. Karen's thigh slices like warm ham.

Karen screams again, and, running on instinct, brings up a fist. It catches Peterson hard in the face, but he isn't even defending himself. It seems to travel through the hateful, lunatic grin, but the blow only puts him on his back heel.

Also in the bag, Karen's can of mace . . .

It looks like a relic from another era, from her old life, an era of imagined muggers and rapists and walking home late at night and . . .

She knocks off the cap with one hand, presses down like she could discharge the whole goddamn chemical at once and maybe there's a look of uncertainty in Peterson's face but it doesn't last because she's got him with it good, she's got him in the whites of his fucking eyes.

Jon drops the sword behind him, goes down to his knees, cradling his head in his hands, but he makes no sound and

It burns

She kicks out with her uninjured leg, her left, not her best, but this one really does connect, and hard enough to make him keel over, the sound is satisfying. But look, he's already sliding his hands from his face, a little fucking air-freshener isn't going to stop him for long, so now

Stop and think

Blake must have ammo for this weapon. For the little Kel-Tec. His vehicle is loaded, the Land Rover is Blake's field unit, so get in the glove compartment because there might be bullets.

Yes, a couple of clips, beneath maps and Tic-Tacs: 9mm Luger Parabellum pistol cartridges. Christ, get them out already, you know how to load a gun . . .

Peterson is on the ground, writhing like a snake, almost like he's faking it.

Sure enough, he gets up, spitting out dust. Karen pumps one clip out, it drops with a short clatter, slides one clip in.

She cocks and aims and fires and, somehow, misses.

He's walking. But at least he hasn't picked up the sword.

Karen fires again, aiming at his heart, his head, she doesn't know. She gets his shoulder, maybe, but with his right arm he manages to hit her across the face, hard, an open palm. The gun slips from her hand, and Karen sees stars.

Peterson falls with the impact of the bullet he's absorbed, but he falls forward, a tactical fall, like he's still following.

Get away, Karen.

Get away, because he won't stop.

Peterson has fallen on the gun. But Karen knows he won't be interested in shooting her.

Just GET AWAY.

The keys are in the ignition of the Land Rover. She slams the door, twists the ignition. She can't reverse, his jeep is behind, and the tow dolly. But are they uncoupled?

Karen stamps, the LR3 lurching forward unhindered; if only there was room to run him over. In the rear-view mirror, Peterson is back to his feet, arm across his chest, pressing his wound.

But Karen has never been out here before. She doesn't know the way back to the highway. She races back through the pass, races past The Church of the Final Days, races towards the canyons, is driving at a dangerous speed in the wrong direction, blood flowing down her arm and *my God it hurts.*

Thunder. Miles away, the storm still raging.

Peterson strides towards his jeep.

The track runs out beyond the shafts of the old mines, and Karen suddenly finds herself bouncing over lunar terrain with no markings to follow, cairns of dark rock on either side. Behind, the twin beams of Peterson's jeep; an experienced desert driver, he's gaining on her. In the distance, on the plateaus, the dance and the crackle of the lightning, although there is no rain here.

There's nowhere to turn around.

Should she pull over, try and finish it?

He has all the weapons, the sword, even the gun.

Just drive. Just concentrate.

The Land Rover hits an unexpected bump, and Karen's breath catches in her throat as the vehicle leaves the ground momentarily. There is the brief experience of flight, engine roaring as the wheels spin in the air. Then the car hits the ground hard enough to clatter her teeth in her head, and it is all she can do not to lose control completely.

But this is more or less still the even ground. This isn't going to last forever.

Karen slips on her seatbelt, wrestles with the wheel, is vaguely aware of descent. Having left the basin, the land slopes downwards, but the surrounding geography has been reduced to dark, hulking shapes by the enclosing clouds, and she can't read the distance, can't read *any* distance, can't even make out a spot on the horizon to head for.

Stop!

She stamps on the brakes, swings the wheel, and the Land Rover skids to a halt just short of the edge of a canyon. She can't see into it, can't see how deep.

Then, the whole right side of the car floods with light.

Peterson.

Karen attacks the ignition, too hard, the engine chokes, was already turning over. Peterson's jeep, bouncing towards her like a giant, overeager puppy; she can't see his face behind the glare of the headlights.

She's stamping on the accelerator, she's sure she is, but nothing is moving and then his jeep is on top of her, and ramming her, trying to push her over the edge, into the canyon.

Peterson doesn't impact hard, but he comes in with more than a nudge, and Karen's car rocks up on two wheels. She can hear the shriek of his engine as it bears the load, or maybe she hears the scream of her own engine, or maybe she's screaming herself, but it doesn't matter because the world tilts and now she's going over the edge, falling into the blackness, all is blackness, a blackness she can lose herself in.

Strangely, there seems to be more light at the bottom of the deep, narrow canyon, where the Land Rover now rests on one side. The chassis is dented, ruined from the roll, but is strong, has just about protected the occupant.

Karen's face is pressing into the dirt. The driver's side window has smashed, she has glass in her hair. One shaky hand reaches for the seatbelt release, and she does a kind of awkward back somersault, is now ass-down to the ground. She struggles, manages to stand, gets a glimpse of her bloodied face in the mirror as she does so, mascara running like gothic tears.

Above her, the door. Gravity makes it unusually heavy, it won't stay open unless she holds it, and she isn't quite tall enough. Karen scrambles up onto the handbrake, the seat, raises it with her back and her neck, teeth gritted, muscles straining.

Free.

Sounds are different in the canyon. There is a kind of hollow, rumbling echo, not the thunder. It is getting louder. Careful of her injuries, Karen lowers herself down to the earth.

No . . .

Peterson is here already, thirty or forty paces away. He knew a safe place to climb.

They face each other, weary gunslingers. He grins like the madman he is.

The rumble is growing. It seems to be coming from *behind* Peterson. Now Karen can feel something at her feet that she never, *ever* would have expected.

Coldness.

Wetness.

Water.

Already ankle deep, and rising.

A flash flood?

The water is flowing, fast. Even at this shallow depth, Karen can feel the insistent, irresistible tug of current on her legs. Next to her, she sees the Land Rover beginning to shift. It settles, creaks, shifts again.

Peterson hasn't noticed the rising tide, or is choosing to ignore it. He steps forward, sword in one hand, gun in the other.

The earth shakes.

A six-foot wall of water, a tidal wave of run-off from the distant storm, throws itself around the corner of the canyon, buffeting the walls with any amount of large and lethal debris. Peterson turns into it, and his scream of rage is lost in the all-encompassing *sound* of the thing, this most unlikely force of nature. Karen watches as he is flattened, can't even see his body as it sweeps towards her.

MOVE . . .

Karen is already leaping back up onto the vehicle, is knocked over again as the water hits it and launches the mighty car forward like so much driftwood, but still she clings, filthy water smacking her in the face, in her nose, her mouth, and it's all she can do to *hang on and hang on* and maybe, someone somewhere will have her live through this yet.

Hours later.

A golden eagle cocks a bright eye at two shapes resting at the bottom of the valley; uncertain, she takes another pass.

Both look like muddy carrion, are displaying wet red flesh, but the eagle is disconcerted by the looming presence of the SUV, which is displaying a muscular underbelly.

Hungry, and with chicks to feed, she must investigate further.

Down on the earth, which is already drying out, Karen Wiley opens her eyes to the bird. Then she closes them again, gratefully, because the morning brightness is so piercing.

Karen turns her head to take in what remains of Jon Peterson; she's been doing this sporadically since she regained consciousness, wanting to make sure he can't hurt her anymore, can't hurt *anyone* anymore. Quite dead, Jon's face is at an impossible angle to his neck where it was bashed repeatedly against the rocks, and it leeches thin redness from every orifice.

His eyes are open, though the pupils seem to be missing, and his mouth is gaping in a way that suggests his jaw was dislocated. The head is half buried, mouth shoveled full of dirt.

Karen closes her eyes again, straightens her aching neck, forces herself to look up at the magnificent, circling eagle, at a sky of impossible blue, framed by the opposing edges of the valley.

It is going to be a beautiful day.

Nineteen

Between medications and between dreams.

Snippets of surreal, otherworldly conversations.

"Flash floods," Egan Blake said, squeezing the hand attached to her good arm. "You know, they kill more people annually than tornadoes and hurricanes put together? You were very lucky."

Karen Wiley, full of painkillers and lying on a hospital bed, found herself wanting to redefine the word *lucky*.

A rescue helicopter had been scrambled, but it was a team of cops, including Chief McCullers, who had found Karen back up at the church. She'd been wandering, delirious, caked in any amount of dried mud, but the mud, while contributing to an astonishing appearance, had probably stopped her two most serious wounds from bleeding out too much. Ribs were also bruised, and there was a concussion.

But hell, you'll live, were the first words she remembered hearing, as she watched under local anesthetic as the young-looking doctor sewed up disturbingly loose flaps of her own skin.

Lilly didn't live, though.

"That's a tough one to think about," Karen mumbled to Blake, and drifted off again while he ran to fetch a nurse.

*

Later.

"Teresa Peterson chirped like a canary," Blake said, and this time there was light through the blinds behind him. "After Jon got the call from his sister that tipped him off as to where he could intercept you, Mrs. Peterson knew exactly where he'd be."

"The Church of the Final Days," said Karen. She was sitting up, arm numb and bandaged. She took a sip of juice.

"But it took time," said Blake. "That woman's been enslaved most of her adult life, we couldn't get the information until the following morning, she had a hell of a lot of hysteria to cry out. That's why it took so long."

"Did she . . . know? About what her husband was doing?"

Blake nodded. "We think so. But I'm inclined to believe she was powerless. Peterson had the whole house ready to burn to the ground, we'll probably never know why he didn't go through with it. His wife believes it was because he got the phone call from his sister and he had to drop everything to catch you, because *you* were the priority. But Teresa Peterson's fate is far from secure; the DA will have to consider whether to press charges, aiding and abetting."

"It sounds like she saved my life," said Karen.

"You could see it like that. And she cooperated as capably as she could when the police showed up, these things might go some way to saving her from severe sentencing. And there'll be psych analysis, you know how these things go on."

"But how could she do it?" said Karen, mostly to herself, because she was beginning to feel drowsy again. "How could she live with him? What kind of life must she have led?"

"You've seen yourself, what some people subject themselves to," said Blake. "The easy answer? I don't know. What happened to Teresa Peterson is a whole other story."

Karen took another sip of juice.

The Freed family eventually decided not to press charges for the break-in on the remailing service, and so Egan Blake had found himself released from jail without ceremony. Ella McCullers, after a series of hasty telephone conversations with Arnold Lau in DC, had decided to take advantage of his expertise on what was left of the case and his involvement with Karen, now a prime witness in a delicate situation. So it came to be that Blake rarely found himself far from Karen's bedside, had put himself in charge of her debrief.

"I'll never understand this town," he said, bringing in the morning newspapers. "We found Lilly's rental in a garage at the back of the Peterson residence, but no one on the street will testify to having seen it, on the tow dolly or otherwise. And, like we suspected, he probably murdered Don Keynes—we know the hand at the church was his, but we're damned if we can find a body—yet no one living locally to Peterson can testify to anything. How likely does that sound to you?"

"He was careful," said Karen. She was itchy, awaiting a change of bandages.

"He *was* careful," said Blake. "And he had the perfect cover, a nice house, upstanding wife. But Canaan is a damaged town, I guarantee. Can you imagine, a place as small as this, harboring so many disturbed people over the years?"

"You're talking about The Final Days cult now? That's ancient history."

"I suppose," said Blake, sitting.

"Jon Peterson must have had money," said Karen. "Beyond what he inherited from his parents. What did he do for a living?"

"He was a freelance structural engineer," said Blake. "Consulted around the country. He helped to build and maintain bridges."

Karen spoke to Jen on the telephone as soon as she felt able to do so without worrying her. Jennifer, still with Karen's parents, sounded happy, but was wondering in a persistent way about when Mom might be coming home. Karen was delighted at this, said not to worry, and soon.

Jen didn't know anything about what had happened, but when the time came, Karen wasn't going to hide it. There would be plenty of opportunity to talk, to explain.

The rest of their lives, in fact.

It was no coincidence that this was also the day when Karen asked to go and visit Katy Trueblood, who was recovering in a ward on a different floor.

The girl was sleeping, surrounded by machinery, but finally free from strife; an unlined, angelic face on a clean white pillow.

"She'll be fine," said the doctor who received Karen at the elevator. "At least, as fine as we can hope. There'll be prostheses, transtibial and transradial. And there's the emotional cost."

"Is she talking?" said Karen.

"Yes," said the doctor. "Katy is very aware, and that can only be a good thing. But we won't wake her now."

"No," said Karen. "Let her sleep. She deserves some peace."

The doctor sighed. "She *does*, but . . . do you have any idea why she would blame herself?"

"Excuse me?" said Karen. "For what?"

He seemed surprised at Karen's reaction. "Well," he said, retreating behind his clinical facade. "She seems convinced that she ran away."

"What do you think she means?"

"I'm sorry, I thought you knew. Apparently, when the man who did this came for her, she ran. There was a chase through a junkyard. But she feels terrible for leaving her brother and sister behind in the trailer. We're telling her—sometimes it can be a fine thing to run away."

"Yes," said Karen, not taking her eyes off the girl. "You know, Egan Blake told me the reason Peterson probably took Katy instead of Holly was because she *did* run away. Teresa Peterson told the police that Jon always respected vitality, initiative."

"I don't know anything about that," said the doctor, worried he might have said too much.

Karen Wiley, now fast asleep herself.

She wanted the blinds open, and vivid moon-shadows are moving across the floor of the hospital room with the slow smooth swing of many different Daliesque clock hands, sometimes growing shorter, sometimes growing longer to the point where they probe the dark wells beneath the furniture and slide out onto the corridor.

Wake up, says Sammie. *Are you awake?*

I was never asleep.

Karen opens her eyes. Yes, her sister is here; jeans shorts, pink backpack, bare feet swinging beneath the chair because the hospital furniture is too large for her.

"Are you mad with me?" says Karen. "Are you mad because I ran away?"

You didn't run away. You had to make a choice.

"You know what I mean."

I'm gone, Karen. You'll have to answer that for yourself. What do you think?

"I think we're fine." Karen is surprising herself. "I never let myself think that before."

So I guess that leaves one more thing, Kar. Just one more thing.

"Don't go, Sammie. Don't leave me yet."

One more thing about Jonny.

"Peterson's gone. He can't hurt us anymore."

We need to know how he knew so much. How did he know so much about us?

"Zhenya Peterson is dead," said Egan Blake. "They found her this morning."

Karen explored her senses for surprise, for shock, for grief, detected very little. But his eyes were on her, like *she* was supposed to have some answers.

"How did she die?" said Karen.

"She swallowed her own tongue."

"What? Is that even possible?"

"She managed to bite it, then drowned in her own blood. They're calling it an accident, or an accidental suicide, something, but there'll be some serious questions asked about Mount Peale hospital. And *I'll* do the asking, if necessary."

Blake was pacing back and forth, very angry. Karen was tempted to wave him away, knew his irritation stemmed from not having the opportunity to analyze Peterson's sister himself.

No limbs on that woman, but two remarkable faces.

"Is something funny?" said Blake. He wasn't angry now, he looked concerned.

"Life on her own terms and death on her own terms," said Karen, as if to close the conversation. "I hope Zhenya didn't have the satisfaction of too much pain."

The answers were coming slowly, far too slowly for Karen's liking; even more slowly, it seemed, than it was taking for her broken body to heal.

One of the ugliest revelations was that Dave, her ex-husband, had been attacked by Jon Peterson in San Francisco. Although he'd survived to tell the tale, it created fresh panic in Karen. She could ... reconcile the issue once she'd spoken to him, knew for certain ... really *had* lived through his encounter.

... was long-distance, from Hawaii. Dave spoke from a ... new home, and in the background, Karen could ... waves.

... son let me live because he likely wanted ..." said Dave, voice tinny over the speakerphone. "I was never targeted for anything more serious, neither was Jen. Did they tell you about the explosion? The bomb near the Bay Bridge?"

"Yeah," said Karen. "I heard."

"They think that was designed to be more of the same. Misdirection."

"Right," said Blake. "That's why he left Lilly's phone at the church for someone to find. We know from the records that Lilly made calls after I saw her leave. Misdirection."

Karen looked over to where Blake was sitting. He was in shadow, fingers tented, a ubiquitous, almost *irritating* presence now.

"Peterson put plenty of people in hospital," said Karen to Dave.

Karen had already taken a call from the wife of Detective John Gardner, ostensibly to offer her condolences about both Karen and Lilly, but mainly, Karen suspected, because the poor woman wanted to make contact with someone who had been similarly afflicted by the madness.

Gardner himself was going to be fine, Karen was assured. There'd be months of physical therapy, burns treatment, but he was going to be fine. Eventually.

"So what," said Dave. "You gonna come out and visit?" His voice sounded hopeful. "You gonna come to Hawaii, bring Jen?"

"That might be a little weird," said Karen.

"You come out here," said Dave. "We'll put a cocktail in your hand, you'll watch a couple of sunsets. Anything sound too weird about that?"

"Never underestimate the healing power of a sunset," said Karen.

"I hear you, babe." There was a pause. "Listen, can I ask you something else?"

Karen sat up a little straighter, there was a new tone in Dave's voice. "Shoot," she said.

"He *said* things to me," said Dave. "Jon Peterson. He said thir about Ashley. But he couldn't have possibly known her name. Where did he get that information?"

Karen said nothing. Dave carried on, his words echoing out of the speaker.

"The FBI conducted interviews in the hotel, talked to staff, they couldn't tell me how he knew."

"Peterson knew things about me as well, Dave," said Karen, and Blake was looking at her again. "Important things, about the past. And I'm afraid it doesn't make sense yet."

The shock came on the day Karen was due to be discharged, a full eight days after the death of Jon Peterson.

"I've officially decided," said Egan Blake, sliding a steaming cardboard cup onto her bedside cabinet, "that this is the best coffee in town."

"Victims in Southern California?" said Karen, catching the headline on the local paper that Blake had brought in.

The *Canaan Daily News* had practically tripled in circulation since the Peterson event, and Karen had to admit, Earl Michelson spun some mighty interesting prose. He had, however, stopped shy of a full-blown reinvestigation into James Earl LaGrande—this despite the town legend being inadvertently revealed as one of the murderer's primary motivations.

Obviously, Canaan wasn't ready to be reminded of The Final Days just yet.

"Just a theory," said Blake, gesturing at the headline. "The *Daily*

is speculating. We're all speculating."

t understand."

d Blake. "There are unsolved murders across the

they can't *all* be pinned on Jon Peterson, but

between the events of his being orphaned

ent. We know from his wife that he

reation and as part of his job, and

we also know he never brought victims home before now—or so she claims."

"So what, there could be others? Other victims?"

"Could be," said Blake.

"In Southern California?"

"Peterson took inspiration from the desert," said Blake. "And he had a strange habit of always signing his own name—remember how he signed my clipboard in San Francisco? Damn, we were never closer to catching him then. I can't even remember his face, and I'm good with faces."

"He was very big on his own name," said Karen, trying to bring Blake back to the point. "Probably because he was renamed as a child, was denied his own name. Identity is crucial to him. Identity is crucial to us all."

"Yes," said Blake. "And, for whatever reason, he left a little paper trail in the Mojave. We're looking into it, but the case is very cold, a couple of hotel bookings, a car rental receipt. It goes back ten years or more. Like most modern lives, Peterson's can be measured in documents, but it'll take an age to trace him everywhere."

"Just like those ancient letters he sent to me."

"Perhaps," said Blake. "But all I would say is: take it easy now. Earl hasn't got a whole lot today, and I suggest you flip that paper over to the funny page."

"Right," said Karen.

But, try as she might, there was a little flicker of inspiration there, something indistinct in her peripheral vision. Karen turned towards the idea, tried to see the full picture, but the harder she looked, the farther it seemed to dance away.

"*That's* why," said Karen, having read half the newspaper without digesting any of it.

"Why what?" said Blake. He looked bored now, was picking at his thumbnail.

Come on, Blake, you're supposed to be good at this.

"That's why the phone books, the names on the tombstones," she said. "Maybe Peterson was going to burn the books because he didn't need them anymore. He smashed his own mother's gravestone—the one the Chief found in the desert—because he couldn't draw inspiration from it anymore. Jon Peterson obviously started out with a very clear vision. It was a mad, illogical vision, but he had personal clarity, a *goal*."

"His wife said he spent weeks, months, poring over the phone books to find a name at random," said Blake. "That sounds pretty focused to me."

"But it *wasn't* random, was it?"

"I don't know," said Blake.

"Or at some point it *stopped* being random. And why was he so inconsistent later on? Why did he procrastinate at some times but not at others? He murdered his father, but then we're presented with nothing significant until these current events."

Blake gestured again at the headline on the paper. "As far as we know."

Karen used her good hand, waved this comment away. "Yes, as far as we know," she said. "But surely we'd have heard of some vast, vicarious revenge fantasy towards a mother-figure before now? Or at least of failed attempts at such?"

"Maybe," said Blake, but he wasn't committing.

"So then, and this is the crux: why now? Something here, in the *present*, must have sparked it. Or he would have done it before, no? ...ast is misdirecting us. Jon drew from it, certainly, it made him ...s. But maybe we should be looking to the present for

... this," said Blake, sipping coffee. "You told me

...uld function in society. He did it for ... to do that. You said yourself, the imaginary voices in his head enhanced rather than diminished his psychopathic tendencies."

"His wife?" said Blake.

"No. You think Teresa had control over him? Even if she wasn't weak, it surely takes an outsider."

"Okay," said Blake, patiently. He'd spent enough time with Karen Wiley to know this obsession wouldn't go away any time soon, and she really needed to rest.

Karen was at reception when Egan Blake called on the phone, was preparing to say farewell to Canaan for good. The doctors had been impressed with the speed of her recovery—especially given the shock and the psychological trauma—though she had been informed in an extravagantly grim tone that there would be some scar tissue.

Karen laughed. *There are worse things*, she had said.

Yes. Yes there are.

Her old suitcase had been swamped in the flood, the contents ruined, and the new case she dragged behind her was practically empty, just a few essentials.

New life, new possessions, new everything.

On her way down, having managed to talk them out of putting her in the hateful wheelchair, she'd bumped the suitcase to a private room on the children's ward, had found another victim demonstrating a remarkable recovery; although Katy's stay would, inevitably, be far longer. And this time, Karen was also granted the opportunity to say hello and goodbye to little Holly, visiting with her parents. Holly had not said anything to Karen, but had been far from shy, had held Karen's hand in a grasp that suggested they might be doing some kind of business in the future. Karen had been amused.

Blake wanted to drive her to the airport himself, but Karen had said no, perhaps they would catch up in San Francisco? If Blake's feelings had been hurt by Karen's repeated and obvious rejection of him as anything other than a friend, then he'd hidden it well.

Now Karen could see a taxicab through the tall glass of the sliding doors. In the brightness of the sun, it looked like some kind of otherworldly vessel, a vessel charged with the power to transport her home.

"Karen Wiley?" A receptionist was calling. "Karen?"

Karen turned, a little irritated. *Another form for me to sign?* Her arm still hurt, more than she wanted to let on.

The receptionist was waving a telephone receiver. "Egan Blake. He says to say urgent."

Karen walked over, limping a little, leaving behind the handsome orderly who had walked her downstairs. He loitered at a distance, not wanting to miss Karen's departure.

"Thanks," said Karen to the receptionist. "Hello?"

"Karen," Blake said, in his familiar gravel monotone.

"Can't this wait, Egan? I have a cab outside."

"Can it wait?" he said. "Well . . . maybe it can."

Cunning bastard.

Karen leaned against the fitted desk. "Go on, Egan, I'm listening."

"I heard what you were telling me before," he said. "About Jon Peterson needing someone else to help him to function. And I put your question to his wife."

"Which question was that?"

"Look, it doesn't matter. But I'm calling to say that you don't need to think about it anymore. Teresa Peterson can't say for certain if this is what caused Jon to implement his plan exactly when he did, but he certainly wasn't functioning without help."

"An accomplice?"

"No, no," said Blake. "I mean, he wasn't functioning without *mental* help. You know, like you said—to be able to operate rationally in society for so long. To stabilize him. An outsider."

"I'm not following."

"Peterson had a therapist. He was talking to a therapist in San Francisco."

"A therapist?"

"For eight or nine years."

"Did you get a name?"

"Could you hold on for a second?"

Karen held on.

"Mary Huntingdon," said Blake. "Does that mean anything to you?"

"Yes," said Karen. "Mary Huntingdon is *my* therapist."

Twenty

Two years previous, Jon Peterson was referred to Mary Huntingdon because he came on a little strong during a standard one-on-one with a pregnant HR consultant. The interview was a formality, he'd already secured the contract—one of the freelance engineering jobs that was his staple employment—but for some reason, his offer to personally terminate her fetus (should she decide that selecting a boy's name might cause too much tension between her and her fiancé) hadn't gone down very well. Jon apologized immediately, made up lies, difficulties at home affecting his judgment.

The consultant made a note.

Jon could have kicked himself for the lapse. It was a bad joke. He didn't do jokes.

As usual, through research and practice, he'd already aced the personality test. But in this day and age, companies have to be careful, have to cover themselves for any eventuality. The form letter accompanying his contract had a handwritten addendum recommending that he might like to consider some counseling.

Therapy.

Jon did consider, decided it'd be a wheeze.

Just to be sure, he murdered a random hitch-hiker before his first session with Mary Huntingdon, wanting to make sure that the demons were satiated, wouldn't make him reveal too much. In fact, there wasn't much likelihood of Jon being able to connect in any rational way with his impossible legacy in any number of hours, let alone in an introductory session, but it was still difficult not to bring in the severed hands of Todd from Cedar Rapids, sealed up in plastic baggies with twisty ties.

He settled instead for the middle finger of the right hand, tucked into the breast pocket of his shirt.

Mary didn't even notice the small blood spot, gradually spreading into the denim. Emboldened by this success, he returned two weeks later for a little more chat, and that was how it started. In July, when a new bridge collapsed in Idaho, killing seven, he talked about how he'd previously considered sending an email to the Department of Transport, criticizing the continued use of compromised gusset plates in truss structures. If only he'd done that, at least his conscience would be clear. When a truck spun into a minivan one New Year's Eve on a frozen Wisconsin overpass, he could talk of irrational guilt, knowing all too well how the black ice could build up, especially near to waterfalls.

It was fun to play at being normal!

But back home, things were starting to happen. Other things. Things outside of his control.

Jon Peterson didn't care to analyze things too much. He had voices in his head to do that, voices that were managing quite nicely, thank you. But, now, with the therapy, there was a new voice; Mary's voice. She was very good at her job. A little *too* good.

Hardly conscious of it, Jon was carrying her voice away with him. She seemed to be asking him questions. Questions about the past, clever questions, questions that demanded answers. Even the questions that weren't about the past, about Zhenya, were actually about

Mother

And isn't that what it was about all along?

So he accumulated directories. For the names, of course. Directories of names.

Jon never suspected therapy would be so good for him. But the best was yet to come.

They never found Mary Huntingdon, the slim, elegant, middle-aged woman of whom everyone thought highly, and many had trusted with their most intimate secrets.

Detectives raided her office; found books, belongings, possessions, all was as it should be. The cops went to the apartment she rented; a modest, ground-floor, two-bedroom condo on Nob Hill. All was as expected, but the occupant was gone. A life interrupted, the vanishing lady.

Mary had a handful of other clients, each of whom expressed sadness and regret at her sudden departure, but none had an explanation. It should also be pointed out that every client spoke very well of her, felt better for having allowed Mary Huntingdon into their lives.

Each moved on, found another therapist, but the new therapists never quite measured up.

Later, in evidence processing, a partial thumbprint turned up belonging to Jon Peterson. It was on the exterior of a tape marked *Karen Wiley*, just one of many sessions recorded by Mary with Karen.

The tapes had been stored neatly in sequence on a shelf in Mary's office, according to the dates printed on the spines. This one was out of order, as though hurriedly replaced. On the transcript made by the FBI, it is revealed that Mary and Karen discuss Sammie on this particular tape, though not in much detail. Karen didn't like to discuss Sammie.

Jon might not have entered Karen's apartment, but perhaps he couldn't resist a peek into her life after all.

*

The last recording of therapy that Mary ever made.

Peterson's voice: ". . . even then it went wrong. How do you decide?"

Mary's voice: "Decide what, Jon?"

"Names come easy to some people. Not to me. Not until now. This is where I thank you. Really thank you. It's been a long and winding road, and you've helped me reach the end."

"You shouldn't finish here. You shouldn't quit therapy. The things you've told me . . . we're close to a breakthrough."

"Yes we are. I have a problem, *bam*, you knock it right down. And this was the biggest."

"We knock them down together. *You* knock them down."

"Not this one. You did this one all by yourself, you take all the credit. I was stuck. I couldn't move, couldn't decide, I could have fallen, I dread to think."

"I don't follow."

"Karen Wiley."

"Karen Wiley?"

"Mary, it was right there. Right there on your desk."

"What was?"

"The *name*. Karen Wiley. Right there on a letterhead. Shouldn't you be more cautious with things like that? You leave people's names lying around for others to see?"

"Jon, you should sit back down . . ."

"A letterhead. We found her together, on a letter. Could it be any more perfect? *Karen Wiley*."

A telephone directory, particularly when viewed through the eyes of a lunatic, can be a fascinating thing. Unless, of course, that lunatic is vacillating, and requires a little external stimuli.

No tapes ever turned up of Jon and Mary in session together, but they must be out there; Peterson would never destroy anything with his own name on it.

People are prone to being very careful with their own secrets, as they should be.

Twenty-one

Canaan, Utah, eight months later.

A desert evening in the early summer finds Milton Trueblood throwing a party to celebrate the baptism of his new son, his and Mandy's fourth child, but to an outsider it might have looked like a festival to promote the almighty American beef steer. He had filled his huge five-foot pig-roaster with lump charcoal, and was firing up enormous, fat-rippled wedges of steak, bone in every time because Milt knew it tasted better that way. There was also giant shrimp stuffed with Alaskan crab meat, wrapped in hickory-smoked bacon and marinated in his secret BBQ sauce. Oh, and potato salad, corn-on-the-cob with sweet-chilli butter, frozen peanut-butter cheese-cake, generic but perfectly drinkable red wine, and beer so damn frosty it could give your brain a hurty.

Milt wouldn't be touching the beer or the wine. He was still clean and sober, but he wouldn't be going back to church again anytime soon; he'd tried it for a while, but he just wasn't wired up that way, at least outside of the emergencies.

"I'll take some shrimp," said Karen Wiley, back in town for two days because she had received an invite from Mandy and for some reason believed revisiting the canyons might do her some good.

"Coming right up," said Milt, who didn't recognize her, but on that day was feeling mighty hospitable to all.

"How are the girls holding up?" said Karen.

Milt was busy, clad in a comedy apron, and he pressed a steak against the bars with a satisfying sizzle. "You kidding?" he said. "We got little Holly talkin', and we got Katy scootin' around like that was her *own* damn hand and foot they pinned on to her."

"And you?"

"Well," he said, with a wry grin. "I guess the loan is paid off, and there'll always be cars to fix." The grin erupted into a toothy smile. "Next please . . ."

Karen nodded politely, gripped her plate, walked over to the salad table.

Milt *was* doing well for himself. New house, his own auto-repair shop, even Mandy was losing some weight. Karen herself was not working. She had wanted to throw herself back into private practice, but the clients had evaporated, and she just wasn't sure she *believed* anymore. Instead, she volunteered, found herself drifting into social work, even law-enforcement support. Mostly, she watched the news with her knees tucked up to her chin, and slept through a series of inchoate nightmares.

But she'd steer the ship around again eventually. She'd do it for Jen, not that Jen much seemed to need her anymore, grown-up young woman that she was becoming.

"You not eat meat?" It was the Chief, Ella McCullers. The godmother to the new baby was twirling a bloody lump of flesh on a very sharp fork. Karen grabbed a beer and looked her over, a bizarre sight in a shapeless floral dress and giant, wide-brimmed hat.

"I'm pacing myself," said Karen, and she turned to watch fireflies dancing in the field across the way.

"Well, don't pace yourself too much, or you'll find yourself out of the damn race. C'mon, I've got someone who wants to meet you."

Karen liked the Chief, but she had the impression that the sentiment wasn't entirely reciprocated; either that or Ella didn't take to newcomers particularly easily. Still, they'd stuck together closely through the Episcopalian service of baptism, trying to outdo one another with volume when it came to the loudness of the hymns.

Karen followed the squat, flower-beset shape, and she waved over at Keith as she did so. Keith Bass was the new man with whom Karen had been in a two-month-old relationship, but she already knew in her heart of hearts that it wasn't going to work. He was a successful landscape designer with a perfect smile, but they just couldn't talk. Not really. And now the poor man had found himself out in Utah on his weekend off, supporting his girlfriend through troubles he couldn't be expected to comprehend. To top it off, he was now tied up in an interminable conversation about cats with a very, very old woman and a geriatric chiseler of tombstones.

Ella and Karen threaded over to a newly sprouting willow tree, where an immaculately dressed Asian-American man was standing and enjoying a glass of iced lime cordial with a great deal of satisfied ceremony.

"Karen Wiley," said Ella. "This is Arnold Lau."

"I'm pleased to meet you," said Karen, extending a hand.

Ella turned her back and dissolved into the milling crowd.

"Karen Wiley," said Lau, and his hand was warm and dry. "I'm a colleague of Egan Blake's. He'd like to have made it here today, but he had to go to Florida."

"That's fine," said Karen, although she had wondered if she'd see Blake in Canaan; they certainly hadn't got around to meeting up in San Francisco.

"He asks after you," said Lau, peering over his drink. To his carefully attuned eye, Karen Wiley looked wan, pale, too skinny. Perhaps it was to be expected.

"Oh?" said Karen. "He did?"

Lau chuckled. "No, no," he said. "Not in that way. Egan Blake has gotten married again. Fourth time, I think. He's asking after you because of the plane crash. You know, the one in the swamp?"

Karen had seen it on the news before she left. A passenger jet from Miami to Lima had downed in the Everglades. There were survivors, but just as many fatalities, and there were an awful lot of unanswered questions.

"I thought Blake was on some kind of probation?" said Karen.

"Ancient history," said Lau. "Sure, he got his knuckles rapped. But it turns out he's too important an investigator to lose, though I've tried to suggest retirement to him from time to time."

"And he's asking after *me*?"

"Are you surprised? You're a very smart lady, Karen. You have considerable insight. Would it be too forward to ask if you've found another job yet?"

"Yes, I think that would be pretty forward," said Karen, but she wasn't upset. She took a deep breath, and the air was warm and dusky and strangely familiar.

"How is the shrimp?" said Lau. "I don't eat shellfish, as a rule."

"Arnold Lau," said Karen, musing over his name. "Don't you work for the FBI?"

"Not exactly," said Lau. "I'd like to tell you about that, if you have time."

"Man," said Jen. "You never owned a computer before now?"

Katy Trueblood looked a little ashamed at this, and Jen tried to take it back a little.

"I mean, it's okay, but you're missing a whole world. Here, let me show you."

"We have them at school," said Katy, and she smiled. "Did you meet my dad? If it don't run on four or two wheels, he don't know where it's at."

"My mom is the same," said Jen, though this was a well-meant lie.

The kids had gotten bored, as kids will. They were too old to be charging around the yard, and too young to indulge in lengthy conversations about the usual bullshit. So when Katy happened to mention to Jen Wiley that Dad had recently bought a computer, Jen had spotted a real opening, an opportunity to connect on a personal level. She sincerely wanted to get to know Katy, despite the opposing side of the cultural valley they'd found themselves on.

Once upon a time, Jen had opened a package with Katy's hand in it, and Jen never forgets.

It was just the two of them now, in the freshly painted spare room; Holly was off somewhere tormenting the new baby. Outside, through the open window, they could hear the hubbub of the cook-out, watch the pinkness of the sunset over the Canyonlands.

"I mean, God, there's so much *crap* on the net," said Jen, working the keyboard with ten dextrous digits in a way that made Katy goggle. "Who do you like?"

"What?"

"Like, music. Or it doesn't have to be music. If you like sports, or news, you gotta get the news. Or there's some funny stuff too."

"Mom says Dad probably got it for the porn."

"She's joking. But the porn there, it doesn't take much to find, and it's disgusting. Don't ever show your sister, she'd freak out."

"Yeah!" said Katy.

"You have an adult filter here, I can show you how to turn that off. But worse is, like, the freaks you always find."

"Freaks?"

Jen gave her a look. "Like, sex perverts."

Katy's eyes were wide.

"Aw, they can't *hurt* you," said Jen. "This is only the Internet. But they're there. And all kinds of other people too."

"You *talk* to them? To perverts?"

"God no. But sometimes, you're chatting with your friends, and . . . well, watch." Jen manipulated the mouse, pages flashed up. "There's this guy here, well, he's probably a guy, he sometimes trolls.

We get him banned, but he comes back a week later, different name. Total loser."

"Some bad people in the world," said Katy, gripping her prosthetic hand.

"Total *loser*," said Jen. "Look. I like the chatrooms as much as instant messenger. That way you usually get at least a topic."

TODAY 16:33
TASMANIA 666: I have cofee and something blak and shiny.
QUOTE / IGNORE

TODAY 16:35
SWEETTHANG: nice spelling, dork.
QUOTE / IGNORE

"We flame them when the spelling is bad," said Jen. "Just something we do. We're such snobs. And we don't do leetspeak or indulge the emo vibe."

"Can I have a go?" said Katy.

"Sure, but it looks slow right now. You can see here, who's online."

"No *perverts*?" Katy had learnt a new word.

"I don't think so," said Jen, blinking at the screen.

"What's that?"

"That's an avatar," said Jen. "I'll show you mine. We're gonna create you one and everything."

"Cool."

Jen was pleased, they were finally getting along. "You're never gonna be off this thing," she said. "I guarantee it. Just remember to get your daily dose of fresh air."

Mandy appeared. "Katy, get out here, your dad's about to make a toast."

"I'll hear him, Mom. Through the window."

"No," said Jen, smiling. "We should go. You have forever to do this."

*

CHILLLERKID: That you, Jen? Sometimes u ignore me, sometimes u chat. What gives?

Words, popped up on the screen, with no one in the room to read them.

Jen has left her web messenger account open. Outside, Milton Trueblood is addressing the gathering. He's nervous, a lousy public speaker, but the listeners are sympathetic, well aware it is his food they are digesting.

CHILLLERKID: u got lonely again? I knw how u feel. Know why? u+I r just the same.

Jen has been keen to re-establish her online networking, to get back to normal. Chilllerkid disappeared when the horror ended and hasn't been in touch since.

CHILLLERKID: go back on the board, kid. U should see what theyre saying to that Tas guy.

But Chilllerkid goes by many names, because on the Internet, anybody can be anybody.

Lately, Jen has been speaking to Chilllerkid while Chilllerkid has been using a different handle. Chilllerkid, who knows nothing of Jen's recent history, believes that his original name might have freaked her out, that maybe she had gotten scared off.

But he's better experienced. He's also getting hungrier.

CHILLLERKID: U ignoring me, Still in Utah? How is it?

Chilllerkid feels the time is right to reintroduce himself as he wants to be known.

CHILLLERKID: U know how I hate to be ignored. Let me tell you what it might make me do

The screensaver kicks in then, and tiny stars tumble through infinity.